TROLL

D. B. Thorne is a digital entrepreneur and founding member of a highly successful tech start-up in the UK. Thorne has long been fascinated by the intersection between the digital and real worlds, inspiring him to write the acclaimed thriller *Troll* and the brilliant follow-up, *Perfect Match*.

TROLL

D. B. THORNE

CORVUS

Published in trade paperback and e-book in Great Britain in 2017
by Corvus, an imprint of Atlantic Books Ltd.
This edition published in paperback in 2018.

10 9 8 7 6 5 4 3 2

A CIP catalogue record for this book is available from the British Library.

Paperback ISBN: 978 1 78239 596 6
E-book ISBN: 978 1 78239 595 9

Printed in Great Britain by CPI Group (UK) Ltd, Croydon CR0 4YY

Corvus
An imprint of Atlantic Books Ltd
Ormond House
26–27 Boswell Street
London
WC1N 3JZ

www.corvus-books.co.uk

TROLL

one

FORTUNE LOOKED AT THE MAN IN CHARGE OF FINDING HIS missing daughter with the kind of dismay he generally reserved for the most dismally incompetent interview candidates. This was the man responsible for piecing together her final movements? Chasing down leads and taking names? Overweight, crumpled, he had the look of somebody who'd suddenly found himself in charge of his own washing and ironing. In his recent past, Fortune guessed, was a failed marriage and a whole lot of takeaways.

Looking at him over the interview room table, Fortune had a feeling close to panic. He blinked and said, 'I'm sorry?'

'Scaled it back,' said Marsh. He had little eyes and they weren't looking at Fortune; were looking anywhere but. 'No choice.'

'But she's still missing,' said Fortune.

Marsh nodded. 'I know. I'm sorry. But it's been weeks, and there's still no ...' He stopped. Body, thought Fortune. You mean body, but you haven't got the guts to say it. Marsh coughed. 'We're not closing the investigation. Just ... reclassifying it.'

'Reclassifying it,' repeated Fortune. 'What does that even mean?' It sounded to him like the kind of empty phrase his younger staff used: moving the needle, taking it offline, reaching out. Air, nothing more. It didn't make sense.

'Mr Fortune,' Marsh said. 'You're upset. It's understandable.'

'Of course it's understandable,' said Fortune. 'She's my daughter. She's disappeared off the face of the earth. And you've got no leads, no ideas, no nothing. And now you're giving up?' He tried, but he couldn't quite keep the desperation out of his voice.

'Not giving up. Re—'

'Reclassifying. I heard. I still don't know what it means.'

'It means …' Marsh sighed. 'Mr Fortune, we're trying to find your daughter.'

'Not very hard.'

'As hard as resources will allow.'

'How many resources does a missing girl merit?' said Fortune. 'How important is her life? Ten policemen? Four? One?'

Marsh sat back in his chair, massaged the bridge of his nose. He had thin hair, grey. He couldn't be in charge, running the show, thought Fortune. His daughter deserved better.

'Mr Fortune, we've done what we can. Thrown bodies at the investigation, set up an incident room, knocked on doors, interviewed friends, ex-boyfriends, colleagues. We've spoken to the press, put out an appeal. CCTV, the lot.' He lifted his shoulders. 'Nothing. At this point, there's just not much more we can do. Without …' Again he didn't say the word. Body. Without the body of my only child, my daughter. Sophie.

'You can't give up on her,' said Fortune.

'We're not giving up. We're scaling back. No choice.'

'How many people have you got on it? Right now?'

Marsh picked up a pen, something to look at rather than Fortune. 'Right now, Mr Fortune, we have one officer continuing with enquiries. The investigation isn't closed. But, like I say, it's been scaled back.'

'One. One officer.' Fortune closed his eyes for several seconds. He had come a long way. Taken time off. 'What can one officer do? She's out there somewhere, and she needs help.' He could hear a pleading tone in his voice, imploring. God, but he sounded desperate.

'Mr Fortune,' said Marsh, 'what do you think happened to your daughter?'

'That's why I'm here,' said Fortune. 'To find out.'

'No. I mean, when you heard that she had gone missing, what was your immediate thought?'

Fortune shook his head. 'I don't know. That she'd ... I don't know.'

'That she'd what?' said Marsh.

Fortune shrugged, trying to keep calm. 'Gone on holiday. Run off with a new boyfriend. I don't know. Could've been anything.'

Marsh nodded, leant back in his chair. They sat facing each other and Fortune could hear the hum of the air conditioner, hum and rattle, a world away from the sleek, smooth hiss of his Dubai office.

There was a knock on the door and a young woman came in with two coffees, put them on the table. Marsh nodded to her and she left, closed the door with a gentle click. He lifted one of the Styrofoam cups, took a drink, made a face. He put the cup down carefully, slowly.

'How many times did your daughter attempt suicide?'

There it was. The question Fortune had been expecting, waiting for. The question he didn't want to face. He remembered hospital corridors, hard seats, his wife next to him, the click of heels on linoleum. The slow tick of a wall clock, more than one clock, more than one hospital.

9

'No,' he said. 'No.'

'We're not ruling anything out,' said Marsh. 'But given her history ...'

Fortune wished Marsh had the courage to finish his sentences. To tell it like it was. That his daughter had had a troubled adolescence, all the way through her late teens and early twenties; that she had been moody, anxious, depressed, angry. Lost.

'She'd been better,' he said. 'Much better. A different person.'

No more suicide attempts. No more pills, flatmates finding her after coming back from a late bar shift. No more ambulances, vigils, apologies, tears. She had been better, making a life for herself, or at least that was what he'd been told.

Marsh sighed and opened a file that he had brought with him, placed it on the table between them. It was beige and thin. If this was it, Fortune thought, the sum total of the investigation, then a lot of midnight oil had gone unburned. Marsh took out a clear plastic wallet with a piece of paper inside, using two fingers to slide it into place between the pair of them.

'We found this,' he said, turning it so that Fortune could read. An A4 sheet of paper, covered in scribbles. Fragments of phrases in black pen, haphazardly placed. *This needs to end*, underlined many times. *This ends today*, the words gone over again and again so that the ink shone and the paper was indented, almost worn through. *Can't go on. Can't go on. Can't go on.* In block capitals, at the bottom of the paper, this time carefully printed: *WHY SHOULD I TAKE ANY MORE?*

Fortune looked at the writing, the flourishes on the tails of the gs and ys, the to-hell-with-you freedom of it. It was Sophie's writing, no mistaking it.

'What is this?' he said.

'We found it on your daughter's desk,' said Marsh. 'I'm sorry.'

Fortune looked at it again. It wasn't conclusive, it couldn't be. 'This doesn't mean anything,' he said.

'Maybe not,' said Marsh. 'But given her history ...' Again, *again*, he left the sentence hanging, reached forward and took a drink of his coffee, eyes anywhere but on Fortune.

'This isn't a suicide note,' said Fortune.

'Mr Fortune, your daughter had a history of suicide attempts. She disappeared and nobody knows where she went. There is no body. She had no enemies. Her lifestyle was ... unconventional. I've read her blog. This is London. It gets to people, particularly young people. Big cities can feel very lonely.'

There was another knock on the door and a young policeman pushed it open a fraction, put his head into the room and lifted his chin to summon Marsh. Marsh pushed his chair back, said, 'Excuse me,' and left, pulling the door closed behind him.

Fortune looked down at his daughter's handwriting, tried to picture her face. How long since he had seen her? Months. He could barely remember her, could better remember her as a child. She had been beautiful, that he could recall. He could remember her weight as he tossed her into the air and caught her, delighted eyes sparkling in the sun. Laughter. His daughter, before he lost her, before her happiness was replaced by something dark and alien that Fortune could not understand or connect with. Before she had given up on him. Or he had given up on her.

He closed his eyes, tried to sit comfortably. It felt as if he had spent the last day being passed from one air-conditioned environment to another, a dreamlike journey completely unrelated to the real, living world outside. Watching the desert sands of Dubai's outskirts unreel past him from the cool interior of the company's Mercedes. Reading the paper in the perfect ambient temperature of the airport lounge. Onto the plane, back out at Heathrow and into another Mercedes, an older model than the company's but air-conditioned nonetheless. Dropped at the hotel, then here, an off-green interview room in a dilapidated suburb of London, blighted by cardboard and polystyrene tossed in the wind. He was tired and he did not want this to be happening, none of it. Did not want this to be real.

Marsh came back into the room, apologized and sat down again. Fortune watched him impassively. Marsh took a deep breath.

'Mr Fortune,' he said. 'I am sorry, I really am. I don't want you to think this case is closed. But if I'm to be honest, I think both you and I know that your daughter was troubled, and that the most plausible explanation for her disappearance is that she took her own life.'

Fortune had to give Marsh credit; he'd managed to get to the end of that sentence, difficult as it must have been to say.

'So that's it?'

'No, Mr Fortune, that's not it. But we've done all we can. If there are any further developments, then of course we'll assign more resources. But for now, we're out of options. And we have other cases. Many other cases.'

Fortune sat in silence until he realized that, as far as Marsh was concerned, this meeting was over. He had travelled two thousand miles, taken days off work, to be told that his trip had been wasted and that his daughter was, in all probability, dead. He stood up.

'Who's your manager?'

Marsh just shook his head. 'It won't help.'

'It can't be … You can't just leave it. One officer? It's not right. She's my daughter.' So empty, his words. So needy. He felt ashamed of himself.

'I'm sorry,' said Marsh.

'I don't think you are,' said Fortune. 'I don't think you care at all.'

Marsh looked at his watch. 'We're going to have to finish here.'

The public sector, thought Fortune. It was everything they said it was. The monkeys put in charge, the blind leading the blind, the lunatics running the asylum. He ran out of metaphors. He shook his head. There was nobody out there looking for his daughter. Nobody.

Marsh picked up the thin file, stood up, walked past Fortune and opened the door. 'I'm sorry,' he said, once again. Again Fortune had a feeling of panic, as if, were he to leave this room, any chance his daughter had of being found would be gone. At last he stood up and walked to the door. He should have looked after her. Been there for her. It wasn't this policeman's fault. It was his, his and his alone.

He walked past Marsh without looking at him, not as a show of contempt, but because he didn't want the policeman to see the shame and guilt in his eyes.

Outside the police station, the weather was cold, even though it was spring, or meant to be. Fortune felt every expat's momentary incredulity that the people of Britain stayed here, here in this country of decaying infrastructure and eroding values and soul-sapping weather. He looked for a cab, but this part of London, way out east, wasn't a black cabbie's turf of choice.

He lit a cigarette, cupping his hand around the flame, took in a lungful with his eyes closed, waiting for the nicotine to do its thing. He coughed, tried to stop, coughed some more. That used to be another thing about Dubai: you could smoke anywhere, not like here. He stood smoking on the pavement, watching immigrants walk past as if it were they, rather than him, who belonged on these streets. A man with a tattooed face and crutches asked him for money to get a hostel for the night. Fortune put his hand in a pocket, remembered he'd spent his last British money on a coffee at the airport.

'Sorry,' he said. 'I've got nothing left.'

He watched a cyclist overtake a minicab and swear at the driver as he passed. He watched a Middle Eastern man step outside his convenience store and stand, arms folded across his chest, facing the world with pride. He watched a young woman push a pram while swearing at somebody down a mobile phone. Eventually a taxi arrived and Fortune gave the driver the name of his hotel, upscale, five star, where people understood the rules, how things worked.

two

SO WHAT I'D LIKE TO KNOW IS, SINCE WHEN HAS IT BEEN OKAY to pay a thousand pounds a month to rent a flat when said flat a) doesn't have heating that actually, you know, heats, and b) has no light on the entrance stairs, so at night I've got a good chance of falling over and breaking something important (like my iPhone).

I called Sam and asked him pretty much this question, and he told me that he'd see to it, that it was on his list. I asked him how long his list was. He replied by saying, 'How long is my *what*?' and laughing. That, I think, pretty much sums him up.

But then he said, and I'm still turning this over in my head, he said that there'd been complaints about me.

'What kind of complaints?' I asked him.

'Noise.'

'What noise?'

Sam sighed, like he'd heard it all before. But I was serious, I haven't made any noise, definitely haven't. Let's be honest, it's not as if I have enough friends to invite over and make noise with

'Music,' Sam said. 'Loud music, on all night. I've had a couple of complaints.'

'I haven't made any noise,' I said.

'Of course you haven't. Still, though, you know … keep it down.'

'I told you. I haven't been making any noise, and certainly not at night. Who complained?'

'Dunno. Got a message, left on my phone.'

'I haven't been making noise,' I said again. What else could I say? There wasn't much point in arguing; Sam had obviously made up his mind. 'Anyway,' I went on, 'it's freezing. Can you please sort the heating out?'

Sam said, 'Tell you what. You keep the noise down, I'll put you at the top of my list. Deal?'

He wasn't even pretending to entertain the slight possibility that I was telling the truth. Even though I was paying him a thousand pounds a month to stay in a cold, dark dump. You know what I said?

'Okay.'

But honestly, right then I didn't have time to argue, because I was standing outside a bar called Mingles and hoping that the young lady I'd arranged to meet there had showed up. Because if she was there, and if what she had to tell me was true, then my career as a journalist would be looking up. And I'd be able to move to another flat, one with heating and working lights and maybe even a new television.

The young lady – no names – had told me what she looked like, and she wasn't hard to spot. She'd told me that she was tall and quite pretty, which was close; she was actually tall and stunning. She was also quite clearly only about fifteen, although that hadn't stopped the barman from selling her a bottle of lager. It was quite likely that he'd fallen in love with her, as she looked, well, awesome. She was perched on a bar stool, and her legs nearly reached the floor.

I asked her if she was who I thought she was, and she said yes, yes she was. So then I said, look, I'm sorry, but I can't talk to you here. You're underage, and you're drinking. We need to keep this legitimate, all above board. She rolled her eyes and sighed, as teenagers do, and I hoped she wasn't going to make this difficult.

Let me cut a long story short: she's fifteen, and a well-known TV celebrity slept with her and offered her drugs, even though he knew how old she was. I'm a journalist. It's a story. And I need to keep her onside, until the story breaks.

'Can I buy you a coffee?' I said.

'I haven't finished this.'

'Come on,' I said. 'Make this easy on me. Please?'

There was more eye-rolling, and an extra-long sigh, and then she said, 'Okay.' I can't help but like teenagers. They'll try to get away with anything, but the good ones don't mind getting busted. She slid off the bar stool like water poured out of a glass and looked down at me, and I'm not short.

'Are you sure you want to do this?' I asked her.

'I'm sure,' she said. 'He deserves it.'

And I had to agree with her there.

three

FORTUNE TOOK A TAXI FROM THE STATION AND PAID IT OFF AT the bottom of his drive. The sun was out and he had forgotten how many trees there were, this place where he had lived for so many years before he replaced the leaves and grass with desert sand and high-rises. He wondered for a brief moment where it was he called home nowadays and came up short with an answer. Not Dubai. And not here either, not any more. It had been too long.

He swung open the rustic five-bar gate, closed it behind him and crunched up the gravelled drive towards the house. Once a dog would have barked in greeting, a springer spaniel that had never been anything other than crazy, called Peter, named by his daughter. Peter. Odd name for a dog, but then the dog had been far from normal. They'd had to put it down and nobody had volunteered, so Fortune had put his hand up. That he remembered.

He rang the doorbell and waited, listening to birdsong and the soft hiss of far-off traffic. Suburban Essex, the dormitory-town idyll. Commuterville. Stepford self-satisfaction for the white-collar winners, safe, green, the high streets lined with boutiques and expensive wine bars. He'd never much liked it, this place, so superficial, so artificial. As unreal in its way as Dubai was.

Sounds came from inside the house, and through the distorted glass he saw a shape approach, turn locks, open the door. And there was Jean.

She looked beautiful blinking into the light and Fortune felt his heart lurch in his chest, a brief chemical explosion of sadness and regret. She regarded him with no expression.

'Hello,' she said.

Fortune had an urge to tell her that she looked wonderful, as beautiful as the day they had met, the kind of statement a man still in love with his wife would make, regardless of how long they had shared their lives. He took a breath, knew as he did so that he lacked the courage.

'Hi,' he said. 'Sorry. Forgot my keys.'

Jean nodded but did not look at him, instead looked past him. 'Come in,' she said as if she was addressing somebody standing behind him, although there was nobody there.

'You look great,' Fortune said quietly, but his wife had already turned and was heading back into the house, down the dark hall. She stopped.

'Sorry?' she asked.

'Nothing,' said Fortune.

'I thought you said something.'

'No.'

He followed her into the kitchen, dropping his suitcase along the way at the bottom of the stairs, as if he was at a guest house rather than in his own home, where, in another lifetime, he had made an attempt to raise a family.

They sat opposite one another at the kitchen table, two cups of tea and the ticking of the wall clock for company. She looked tired and detached, as if half of her psyche was occupying some other, unknowable place. Fortune watched her.

'I went to see the police,' he said, though he had already told her on the phone.

'That man, what's he called? Marsh?'

'He told me they were scaling down the investigation.'

Jean picked up her cup with both hands and nodded at it vaguely. 'They think she killed herself.'

'Do you?'

Jean closed her eyes at this question and there was a long silence. When she opened them, they were wet with tears.

'I wish I could say that I didn't.'

Fortune thought of all the times his wife had been there for Sophie. The times she had withstood her anger, forgiven her insults, remained strong when Sophie had given up. She had believed in her daughter. Believed far more than Fortune had.

'We don't know for sure,' he said. 'She could walk through the door any time.'

Jean sighed, shook her head slowly. She still did not look at Fortune, and when she spoke next, it was more to herself than to him.

'Oh hi, didn't miss me, did you? Went on holiday, forgot to say. Can't believe you were so worried.' Now she did look at Fortune. 'You don't think I've told myself that a hundred times? But she's not here, she's gone, and nothing good has happened to her. Nothing.'

'Jean,' Fortune said. 'It's too early—'

'It's not too early,' she said, clearly and slowly. 'It's too late. It's far too late.'

'You can't give up.'

20

She laughed, a sound without warmth. 'I can't what?'

Fortune knew what was coming. He also knew there was nothing he could do about it. 'You can't give up.'

His wife set her cup down on the table carefully. 'And just what kind of moral right do you have to tell me something like that? Giving up's what you do, isn't it?'

'Jean,' he said again.

'You don't like it, that the police have given up on Sophie? Take a look in the bloody mirror.'

Fortune didn't reply, and they sat in silence for some time. He could feel his heart beating and he wished he knew what he should say, how he could bridge the gap between them. But at the same time he knew that they were separated by too many years, too many years and an ocean of disappointment.

'When did you last speak to her?' Jean asked.

'Sophie? A month ago, something like that?'

It had been longer, much longer, but he did not want his wife to know that. Three, four months, without talking to your own daughter. Was that normal? No. No, it couldn't be.

'How had she been?' he asked.

Jean drank tea, closed her eyes to its steam. 'Not good. Chaotic. Paranoid. I ...' She stopped, pressed the cup to her lips, hard. 'I told her I couldn't cope, told her she had to work it out for herself.' She kept the cup to her lips, as if for comfort. This is when I put my hand out, place it on hers, Fortune thought. Offer some comfort. He didn't do it, didn't even get close.

'She was just starting out. It was bound to be difficult, in a new city.'

'I wasn't there for her.'

'She's not a child.'

'She needed help.'

Fortune didn't answer. He wondered how many times he had told his wife to leave it, to let Sophie make her own mistakes, not get involved. Was that just another way of saying that they should give up on her?

'You mustn't blame yourself,' he said, the words so worn and tired that they did not even register, didn't last the journey across the kitchen table.

A cat mewed at their feet and Fortune looked down and tried to remember its name but could not. Jean got up and walked to the fridge, took out milk. She stood with the bottle in her hand and seemed to forget what she was doing, rendered immobile by an unexpected wave of grief and guilt. Despite everything, Fortune felt his throat harden, at the sight of his wife and at the thought of his daughter who was probably dead, who must be dead; weren't they acting as if she was dead?

He got up from the kitchen table and walked over to his wife, but just as he got to her, she turned and said to him, 'Please don't touch me.'

There were many photos of Jean and Sophie in the house, although few of them included Fortune. They were always smiling, their eyes even more alike from the similarity of their expressions. She had been their only child and into her his wife had poured all her love and devotion, an amount that Fortune had imagined endless. He picked up a photo, the two of them on holiday, a Roman ruin behind them, perhaps Greece. He'd missed that holiday, probably been at work. So many missed holidays, missed dinners, missed opportunities to get closer, bridge gaps, give support, show affection. He wondered why he had found it so hard, so impossible. It had always been easier to stay at the office rather than face the hard work of raising a family. And now it was too late.

Jean was upstairs resting and he went to the garage to see if he could find any evidence that he had ever lived in this house, ever called it home. He had never officially left; had only been in Dubai for a year. He felt a hit of resentment as he looked for the garage key. His home. He had paid for it. Worked for it. Where were those keys?

In the garage, his golf clubs were still in the corner, the black and white leather Titleist bag, the full set of irons and woods and wedges and putters. He'd lied about the price to Jean; no way he was going to tell her how much it'd all cost. He wheeled them out, looked at them. Pulled out a seven iron, felt its weight, the balance of it. Imagined teeing off, creaming a drive down the fairway, the snick of the ball leaving the club, faint touch of fade, ball landing in front of the green, his fellow player grunting, 'Good shot,' reluctantly. Drinks in the clubhouse afterwards. Congratulations. Carded a round of sixty-eight.

'You're not,' his wife said from behind him.

He turned, club still in his hands. 'Not what?'

'Going to play golf.'

'No. No, just wanted to see if they were still here.' Jean, the golf widow. They'd laughed about it once. Not for very long.

'They're still here. But you're going to need to take them.'

Fortune frowned. 'Take them where?'

Jean shook her head. 'I don't know.' She paused, took a step back as if worried he might come at her with the seven iron. 'I want you to leave. For good.'

'What?' said Fortune.

23

'Go,' said Jean. 'Just … go.'

Fortune watched Jean and thought of the times they had shared at the beginning, when it had seemed as if their meeting had been preordained, a perfect case of aligned stars. She was standing almost side-on to him, as if to face him directly disgusted her, sickened her. Like the sight of him was an affront. He took a firmer grip on the golf club, as if to defend himself from her loathing. How had it come to this?

And then he realized with a sudden and unexpected sadness that their daughter's disappearance was not something that would bring them together. It was something that would finally drive them apart. There was nothing left, no glue, no reason to keep up the pretence of marriage. No shared interests. No appearances to maintain. The end.

'Where will I go?' he asked.

'I don't know,' his wife said. 'I don't know what you do. I don't know anything about you. Go anywhere you want. But I don't want you here.'

'Who'll take care of you?'

Again, that laugh, devoid of humour or warmth. 'I'll manage.'

'I want to help.'

'You can't.'

'I can try.'

'Please don't.'

Fortune turned to look at the house that he had worked to pay for. 'I'd like to see her bedroom.'

Jean sighed and turned her back on him, and Fortune walked towards his house to say goodbye.

*

He had spent far too little time in this room, although it had been his daughter's for nearly all of her life. Too late home to read bedtime stories. Banned from when she was, what, ten? Not allowed in. Keep out. Private. The bedspread, the few remaining clothes hanging in her wardrobe, the photos of friends stuck on the wall above her desk, it was all unfamiliar, unknown.

But could he blame himself? She had been so difficult, so angry, so unreasonable. Unknowable. He sat on the bed and felt the silence of the room press down on his shoulders, not letting go of its secrets, its intimate details, the life of his daughter.

After several minutes he went downstairs, picked up his suitcase and walked, wheeling his golf cart, back to the road at the bottom of his drive, where he would call a taxi for the station.

four

High Times and Miss Fortune: Five Things I've Learnt in a Taxi

So I was in a taxi last night (yes it was late, no I wasn't drunk) and I was talking to the driver, as you do. Well, I say you do, but some people don't like to talk to the driver. A friend of mine told me that he always asks them not to speak to him, which I said sounded rude. He said maybe, but who cares? They're only taxi drivers.

He's not my friend any more.

Anyway, so I was in a taxi, chatting away, and I told the driver (whose name was Ted, FYI) that I was just back from Brazil. He told me he'd always wanted to go but hadn't, on account of how he has a morbid fear of flying and last time he went on a plane, back from Alicante, he ended up being strapped to his seat by five air stewards, screaming all the while.

But that's not what I learnt. What I learnt was that Brazil the country is named after Brazil the nut, and not the other way round. So basically the nut came first, and then they named the country. Weird, right?

Anyway, it got me thinking of all the things that I've learnt in a taxi. And it turned out that I've learnt quite a lot. So here is my top Five Things I've Learnt in a Taxi:

5. I learnt that one of my ex-boyfriends had slept with not one, but two of my colleagues. Not only that, but one of those colleagues was a man. Not only that, but he'd slept with them while he was seeing me. I found this out because he was in the taxi with me, and he confessed all in a drunken attack of conscience (and in tears, too). Needless to say, I asked the taxi to stop, kicked him out, ignored his pleas that he had no money and no way to get home, and ignored the gazillion text messages he bombarded me with. And good riddance.

4. I learnt that the world is run by Jews, and that they're in league with the Muslims to destabilize the West. Okay, so when I say learnt, it's not that I actually believed it, but I'd been waiting for a taxi for hours and didn't fancy walking home in the rain, so I just nodded and uh-huh-ed as I listened to the man's drivel. Sheesh.

3. I learnt that one taxi driver's daughter was in hospital, and that he worked during the night so he could be at her side during the day, and that he was tired but he needed the money, even though he'd recently found out that the brain tumour she had was terminal and it was only a matter of time. His voice cracked as he told me this, and I also learnt that some people's lives are so hard it is a miracle they continue.

2. I learnt that T— — W— — had been in the back of the same cab only a couple of nights before me, and at the traffic lights on Piccadilly he had leant forward and offered the driver a toot on his cocaine.

1. I learnt that there is no sight more beautiful than two people kissing on Albert Bridge on a summer's night, with the lights of London reflecting in the Thames and the two figures intertwined, as natural as ivy and as gentle as music.

COMMENTS:

SharnaJ: *LOL on the boyfriend, I remember the same thing coming back from a party! He told me he'd kissed my best friend! I didn't throw him out, though ... I married him!*

LozLoz: *Funny!*

CatLover: *That poor driver and his daughter! Heartbreaking.*

Starry Ubado: *Next time you get in a cab I hope the driver rapes you, you stupid bitch.*

It's just a blog. I mean, seriously, it's just me, writing about my life. Hardly anybody even reads it, although I still harbour this crazy dream of gathering a million followers, turning it into a YouTube channel, serving up adverts and making enough money to buy a chateau in France where I'll grow grapes and fall in love with a local ne'er-do-well.

But really, it's just a blog. So why do people feel the need to leave comments like that? I try to tell myself that it's only a lonely teenager in his bedroom letting off steam because he hasn't got a girlfriend yet, but what if it isn't? What if it's some steroid-addled man-mountain with a wall covered in photos of me, with my face violently scratched out in every one of them?

I read an article the other day that said that trolls have the same personality traits as psychopaths. Apparently they share a lack of remorse and empathy. It suggests that perhaps I should spend less time reading things online, but it didn't do much to reassure me.

Still, the troll's not going to win. I'll keep writing, and keep dreaming of the day I can swap my keyboard for a whirlwind Provençal romance with a roguish Frenchman. Right. Dream on.

I think I made some progress with the young lady I met in the bar, who I'll refer to as Child Z. She's still willing to cooperate. I met with her mother (her father's long gone, barely a memory) and she's keen to move things along too. The truth is, she wants the sleazeball TV celebrity locked up. Well, she wants a lot more doing to him than that, and I have to give her credit for her imagination, but I did point out that this was no longer the Dark Ages and that we didn't really do that kind of thing to people nowadays, for any number of good and enlightened reasons.

So now the whole matter is sitting with the lawyers, who are discussing whether or not, if we do run with the story, we'll be sued back into those selfsame Dark Ages. They want everything so watertight that I worry it will never see the light of day, but I'm doing all I can to make it happen. I kind of feel like Erin Brockovich, only not nearly as glamorous, and without the impeccable moral compass. But a bit like her, even so. Somebody a mother (or father!) could be proud of. It's all rather exciting.

five

'WHAT DO YOU MEAN, GONE?'

'Not gone. Well, we hope not. Just … missing.'

'Missing, gone, what's the difference?' Fortune sat up on his hotel bed, put his feet on the floor. He was gripping his mobile phone, could feel the edges dig into his fingers. His colleague on the other end, Alex, paused and tried to collect himself.

'It's missing.'

'How much?'

Silence again on the other end. A worrying silence.

'Christ's sake, Alex. How much?'

'Just short of ninety million.'

'Dollars?'

'Yeah.'

Fortune put his free hand in his hair and closed his eyes, squeezing them tightly as if to blink away this new reality. This was a catastrophe. 'How …' He stood up and walked to the window. 'How did it happen?'

'Don't know. Maybe when we switched servers. We're on it, Fortune.'

'Ninety million?'

'Yeah. Approximately.'

'And it just disappeared?'

'We're on it,' Alex said again, and Fortune could sense the fear and desperation in his voice. Calm down, Fortune told himself. You're the boss. Set an example.

'Okay,' he said. 'Okay, let's not panic. Who's working on it?'

'Everyone. Nobody's gone home.'

'Good. Who knows?'

'The team. We had to tell Owen.'

Owen, Fortune's superior. His only superior. Fortune was technically responsible for the operations of one of Dubai's biggest private banks, and Owen was the CEO. This wasn't good.

'Shareholders?'

'They don't know. Too early.'

'You need to tell customer relations. Tell them what's going on. Come up with a story.'

'What kind of story?'

'Technical glitch, nothing to worry about. Anything, just keep it vague. I don't want this getting out.'

'On it,' said Alex.

'Have you got an ETA on fixing this?'

'Not yet.'

'Tried calling Sadler?' said Fortune.

'Yeah. He said he could come in …' Alex paused.

'Yes?'

'He said he wanted a thousand dollars a day.'

'That sounds like Sadler.' Fortune sighed. 'Okay, doesn't matter. We need him. Get him in, just make sure he puts in the hours. And keep me posted.'

'Owen's going crazy. He wants you here.'

'Does he know my daughter's missing?' He did know that.

Of course he did. He just didn't believe it took precedence over missing M-O-N-E-Y, which, as far as Fortune could tell, was all that Owen cared about. Alex didn't answer. Fortune felt for him. But he needed to be here.

'Alex, don't make me get on a plane. Please? Do not make me get on a plane.'

'I'll try.'

'Do everything you can.'

'I already am, Fortune.'

'Good. Okay. Keep in touch.'

Fortune hung up, lay back on his bed and looked at the ceiling. Ninety million dollars? That kind of money didn't just disappear. It was probably a technical thing, a line of code, a command wrongly inputted. It would work itself out eventually. This thought lasted a fraction of a second before the magnitude of the sum hit him again. Maybe he *should* be there. It was his job, his responsibility. And he took work seriously, took the responsibility seriously. That was the reason he'd missed the holidays with Sophie, the weekends away, the events at school, the bedtime reading. At least that was what he had always told himself. Not that he simply wasn't cut out for family life, didn't understand it, wasn't interested, couldn't engage. No. Never that.

His daughter had been renting a flat in Hackney, a one-bedroom apartment above a coffee shop run by young men with long beards and tattoos. They looked like pirates who'd just come ashore and developed an immediate interest in roasting and grinding. Fortune did not really know why he was going there. He didn't have a key. There would be nobody home. But still he could not help imagining his daughter opening the door to his knock, a smile, an explanation of where she had been, and why.

Of course there was no answer when he knocked on the door. He knocked again, waited, then pushed open the door of the coffee shop, into a smell of roasting beans, music. There were young people sitting at a long table, working on laptops. He walked to the counter, long and high and topped with zinc, pastries arranged below behind glass. They were big and untidily made, artisan, looked good.

'What can I get you?' asked a young man, ear lobes stretched by circular implants.

'Do you know who lives upstairs?' Fortune asked.

'Nah,' said the man. 'Why?'

'My daughter lived there,' Fortune said, corrected himself. 'Lives there.'

The man frowned. 'So why're you asking me?'

'Have you seen her?' said Fortune. 'Tall, black hair. Pretty.'

The man wiped at the high zinc counter with a cloth as he thought. 'Might have.'

'When?'

'Not for a while.'

'How long?'

The man shook his head. 'I don't know, man. Weeks? She the one who disappeared, right? Had the police in here.'

'Did they speak to you?'

'Yes,' the man said, impatiently, as if to a child. 'What I said, isn't it? You want a coffee?'

'No.'

'It's good. Got a new blend in from Bolivia.'

Fortune shook his head. 'Thanks for your time.'

33

The man shrugged, went back to cleaning his gleaming counter. Fortune stood for a moment, lost, with no plan, nowhere to go, nothing to do, nobody to talk to. It was beginning to rain outside, a nasty, spiteful squall making people run, coats pulled over their heads. A man hurried past the window of the coffee shop and stopped at Sophie's door. Fortune watched him. The man took out a key and let himself in. Into his daughter's flat.

Fortune knocked again at her door, fading black paint and lines of bare wood showing through where the paint had cracked under the rain and sun. He waited, then heard feet on stairs, and the door opened. The man he had seen – young, short dyed black hair; were there any middle-aged people in this part of town? – said, 'Yeah?'

'Who are you?' said Fortune.

'Tom,' he said. 'What do you want?'

'My daughter lives here,' said Fortune.

The man looked confused. 'Don't think so.'

'No, she does,' said Fortune. 'This is her flat.'

The man, Tom, looked at him. 'The girl who disappeared?'

'Yes. My daughter.'

'God.' The man scratched his hair, still wet from the rain. He sighed. 'You want to come in?'

Fortune followed him up a dark staircase, putting a hand on the wall to guide him.

'Watch yourself,' the man said. 'The letting agent's supposed to be fixing the light.' He opened a door at the top of the stairs into a bright living room with exposed brick on the walls and badly varnished floorboards. Fortune looked around, looked at the sofa, imagined his daughter sitting on it, her long legs folded underneath her, writing on a laptop. Peaceful.

The man turned to him. He was short and had a friendly face, open. 'She doesn't live here any more. Your daughter.'

Fortune frowned. 'She did.'

'Yeah. Listen ...'

'Fortune.'

'Fortune. I don't know the details. All I know is there was some problem, problems ...' He rubbed at his hair again, uncomfortable. 'I don't know.'

Fortune looked around again, confused, at the magazines on the low table, the books on the shelves. 'So all this ... this isn't hers?'

'No. That's what I'm saying. It's mine.'

'When did you move in?'

'Couple of weeks ago.'

'Then ... where are my daughter's things?'

'I don't know.'

'How do you mean, you don't know?'

'I don't know. The place was empty when I moved in. She wasn't here.'

Fortune stood silently for a moment, at a loss for what to say, what to think. 'Then where did she live?'

Tom looked uncomfortable, not equal to dealing with a bereaved father's bewilderment. 'I ... I don't know.'

'She—' began Fortune, but stopped at the sound of the front door opening and feet on the stairs. A woman came into the room, thin blonde hair. She smiled uncertainly at the scene, the uncomfortable silence. 'Hello?'

'Harriet, this is ... this is Fortune. He's the father of the woman who disappeared, who lived here.'

Her smile flickered but she put out a hand. 'I'm sorry, it must be terrible for you.'

Fortune felt too disorientated to reply, standing here in what he had thought was his daughter's flat, talking to a young couple who knew nothing of her. He started coughing and bent over, put an arm out into the air in front of him, found nothing to hold onto.

'You okay?' asked Tom.

'Need to sit down.'

'Please,' said Harriet, pointing to the sofa. 'You want something to drink?'

Fortune sat, elbows on knees, and shook his head at the floor. 'No.'

The two young people stood over him and watched him, no idea what to do with this strange man who was sitting in their home.

'Who can I speak to?' said Fortune.

'About …?' said Tom.

'My daughter. What happened … what happened to her things.'

'The letting agent,' said Harriet. 'But I warn you, he's a twat.'

'I've got his card,' said Tom. 'Hold on.'

He poked through drawers. Fortune felt weight on the sofa as Harriet sat down next to him. 'You haven't heard anything? News? About your daughter?'

Fortune shook his head, still looking at the floorboards. 'No.'

'Any leads, any …' She stopped, unsure what to say. 'Anything?'

'No.'

'Here,' said Tom. Fortune looked up. He was holding a card and he handed it to Fortune, who reached up to take it. 'Like Harriet said, he's a bit of a—'

'He's a dick,' said Harriet. 'Wanted three months' deposit. Like, whatever, what, he wanted us to rob a bank? Still haven't got Wi-Fi, either. And the heating's knackered.'

'He should know what happened,' said Tom. 'I'm sorry.'

Fortune pushed himself upright. 'Okay.'

'I'm sorry too,' said Harriet. 'I hope things work out.'

She moved closer to Tom. They seemed a good couple, kind and connected and generous. Fortune nodded, turned, then turned back and said, 'Thank you,' before walking back down the dark stairs.

six

IF THE OFFICES OF ALPHA PRIME LETTINGS REPRESENTED THE kinds of properties they rented out, Fortune thought, then his daughter had got lucky. A young woman in glasses and with dark hair pulled tightly back looked up, then down again. She ignored him for some moments before looking back up and asking, 'Help you?'

'I'm looking for Sam.'

'He's doing a viewing.'

'When will he be back?'

She frowned as if the stupidity of the question was offensive, as if nobody had a right to ask such a thing. 'Could be any time.'

'Today?'

She shrugged. 'Yeah. Sometime.'

Fortune looked at the card in his hand, back at her. 'I'll call him.' He dialled the number, listened to it ring. The woman behind the desk watched him, tapping a pen on the desk. The phone rang through to voicemail and Fortune hung up before leaving a message.

'Never answers,' said the woman. 'Drives me mental.'

'Then you'll have to help, after all. I'm the father of Sophie Fortune.'

'Oh.' She didn't say anything else, didn't want to look at him.

'You know her?'

'No, but …'

'But?'

'She …' the woman started but then looked past Fortune with a relieved look. The door opened and Fortune turned to see a man, maybe thirty, with short blond hair, wearing a well-fitted suit. 'Here he is.'

Fortune stood up. 'Sam?'

'Yep.' He smiled. 'What can I do you for?'

'I'm Sophie Fortune's father.'

The smile disappeared. Sam searched for something to say, came up short, managed, eventually, 'Okay.'

'I went to her flat.'

Sam nodded. 'Yeah.'

'Someone else lives there.'

'New tenants. That's right.'

'You know she's missing?'

'Yes.'

'And?' Fortune took a step closer to him. 'You're going to need to do better than that.'

Sam rubbed his face. 'Look … come and sit down.' He put out a hand, showing Fortune where to go, one of the desks at the back, then passed him and sat down behind the desk. Fortune stood for a moment and tried to summon his hardest managerial don't-mess-with-me stare. Sam certainly looked nervous. Fortune sat down across from him.

'All right. So tell me. What's been going on?'

'We, uh … We had some problems with your daughter.'

'Okay,' said Fortune. 'What kind of problems?'

'Kind of, uh …' Sam rearranged some papers on his desk as he

39

thought. 'Pretty serious problems.' He looked up, met Fortune's eye with difficulty.

'Like?'

'Like,' Sam repeated, buying himself time. He wanted to be anywhere but here, having this conversation, Fortune could tell. He was acting like a doctor delivering bad news, explaining that it was a matter of weeks, not months. 'Like, antisocial behaviour. We had complaints.'

'What kind of complaints?' said Fortune.

'Well, kind of, loud music. Parties. Drug use.'

'Drug use?'

'Yeah, all kinds of drugs ...' He stopped. 'Look, I'm sorry, okay?'

Fortune thought of Sophie. She had always been difficult, but he had never thought of her as bad. Complicated, difficult, challenging. Often infuriating. But not bad, never bad.

'We gave her warnings, but she ... she was unreasonable about it. Wouldn't listen, denied everything. I was getting phone calls, twenty, thirty a day. Letters. All complaining. Recordings of the noise, time-stamped. Three in the morning, four.' He stopped, realized he was laying it on too thick, that he was talking to a man whose daughter had disappeared without trace.

'That doesn't sound like her,' said Fortune. Sam didn't respond. He was only thirty. What did he know about problems with children?

'Had the council around, told us if we didn't do something, they would. That kind of thing can cause problems for ...' Sam waved a hand at the office. 'Businesses like ours.'

'So ...'

'So, uh, we.' He paused, took a breath, drew in some courage. 'We evicted her.'

Fortune blinked. 'You what?'

'Served an eviction notice. Gave her a date.' He picked up a sheet of paper, put it down again without looking at it. 'It's not like she gave us a choice. Dealers going in and out, parties, police showing up ... It was out of control.'

'When?' said Fortune. 'When did you evict her?'

'Three weeks ago, something like that.'

'She's been missing for five.'

Sam nodded. 'I know how it must look.'

'She disappears, and you turn up and ...' Fortune stopped. 'Where are her things?'

'We had to take them.'

'Where are they?'

'At our storage place.'

Fortune shook his head, tried to control his voice, to keep the emotion out. 'She was only twenty-seven.'

Sam lifted his hands. 'I'm sorry. But, Mr Fortune, she ... she was ...' He couldn't say it, didn't have the courage, gave up.

'I want my daughter's possessions.'

Sam nodded quickly. 'I'll have them sent. Least I can do.' Like he was doing Fortune a service, like he wasn't the man who had thrown his daughter out on the street. Or would have done if she hadn't vanished beforehand. 'What's your address?'

'Sorry?' said Fortune.

'Your address. Where do you live?'

Fortune thought about it, but could not come up with an answer. Where did he live? Nowhere. Like his daughter.

'Just tell me where you've put her things.'

*

They were in a damp lock-up garage a couple of streets away. Fortune didn't speak to Sam, smoked a cigarette silently as Sam led the way through the rain, fine now, fine and persistent. He unlocked a padlock and pushed the door up and over. Inside on the concrete floor were cardboard boxes, sagging from where moisture had weakened them.

Fortune looked at the collection of boxes and could not remember ever having seen a sadder sight. 'This is all hers?'

'Not all of it. The ones marked ...' He stopped.

'Marked?'

'PB.'

Fortune frowned. 'Why PB?'

Sam looked uncomfortable, wouldn't meet Fortune's gaze. 'Don't know, have to ask the people who cleared out her flat.'

But Fortune had managed teams for too long not to know when people were lying to him. He knew what dishonesty looked like, what it sounded like.

'Come on. PB. What does it stand for?'

'Mr Fortune ...'

'What does it stand for?'

'Listen, it wasn't me, right? Just the lads, a bit of banter. I'm sorry.'

'I'm waiting,' said Fortune.

Sam sighed, a desperate sound. 'Psycho Bitch, all right? That's what it stands for. Look, I'll leave you to it. Lock up after you're done, drop the key round.'

Sam waited for an answer but Fortune said nothing, and he walked away, leaving Fortune surrounded by his daughter's possessions, wondering what had become of her, what the world had done to her.

seven

EVERYTHING'S BECOMING A BIT STRANGE, A BIT FREAKY-
deaky, and not in a good way. Not in a happy, hippy, to-hell-
with-it party way. More in a what-the-actual-hell-is-going-on?
way. To tell the truth, it's all got me rattled. And I never thought
I was one to rattle easily.

Sam, my neglectful letting agent, has been back in touch. He
gave me a call yesterday and I picked up thinking, stupidly, that
he was going to tell me when the light and heating were going to
be fixed. But no. Far from it.

'Sophie?'

'Speaking.'

'Sophie, I've had more complaints.'

'About what?'

'More noise.'

I didn't answer for a while, trying to think back over the last
few days. Had there been any noise? People around? Spontaneous
partying? No, because, let's be honest, I'm not exactly Ms
Popularity.

'There hasn't been any,' I told him. 'No noise at all.'

'Come on,' he said. 'This has got to stop.'

'What has?'

'The music. Parties. You, telling me they're not happening.'

'But they're not.'

Sam sighed. 'Look, Sophie. You've been a good tenant. You pay on time. But I can't have the council getting involved.'

'The council?'

'Environmental Health. They tell me there's been a complaint made. They've had a letter.'

'Saying what?'

'Saying that, over the last couple of months, at least three times a week, they've been kept awake by music, sounds of partying.'

'Who says? Who's been saying this?'

'It's anonymous. Says they're frightened of what might happen if you know who they are.'

'Frightened? Sam, come on, please, this is crazy. Who'd be frightened of me?'

'Maybe not you. The letter says, I've got a copy, it says that there are drugs, strange men coming in and out. That's what's got them frightened.'

Drugs? Frightened neighbours? I mean, this was beyond belief. 'Sam, listen to me. Please, listen. Whoever's saying this, it's not true. Understand? It's a lie.'

'They included a recording,' said Sam. 'Time-stamped, date-stamped. The council says they can't ignore it, that if there's one more complaint then they'll have to get involved. And that, Sophie, isn't going to look good for me.'

Oh, my poor heart bled. But at the same time, Sam said he had a recording. Where had it come from? Who had made it, and sent it? This was getting very weird.

'Sam, again, it's not true. It's not possible. Seriously, you've got to listen to me. Somebody's doing this to me.'

44

'Who?'

I thought of the story I'm working on, of Mr Almost-A-List Celebrity and his underage activities. It couldn't be him, could it? He didn't even know that I was after him. 'I don't know,' I said.

'One more complaint,' Sam said 'One more, and I'll have to serve you notice.'

'Sam ...'

'Look, I've got to go. Help me out on this one, yes?'

He hung up, leaving me looking at the walls of my flat and wondering what the hell was going on. Like I said, it was all going freaky-deaky, but not in a good way at all.

So I wrote to Josh and told him what was happening. And as usual, Josh made it all feel, if not okay, then a whole lot better. I can't wait for him to come back from New York. Having him here, actually physically here, will make this go away, I'm sure of it. I just need an ally, someone to be there for me. I can't face talking to Mum and telling her what's going on. Even if she believed me, which I doubt, what is she going to do? She'll tell me that's what happens, and that I should never have moved to London, and remind me that she told me it was full of weirdos, so what did I expect? No, I can't talk to Mum.

Here's what Josh said. *If somebody's messing with you, I'll come and mess with them. Trust me. You don't need to be worrying about this. I've got your back.*

And with those few words, I suddenly felt stronger. His filming wraps in a few weeks, so I haven't got long to wait. And in the meantime, there's always work, the life of a celebrity journalist being full of surprises. Yesterday, for example, Jessica came over to my desk and told me about this story she's writing. She had a grin on her face like she just couldn't keep it in and just *had* to tell somebody. It turns out that a footballer who plays for Arsenal, let's call him Jerome, threw a party at his house a couple of nights ago.

'The French guy?'

'Right,' said Jessica. 'He comes from Marseilles. Two of his brothers are in prison. And he's making ... well, guess. Guess how much he's making? A week.'

'A hundred thousand?'

'A hundred and fifty thousand pounds. A week. So anyway, he lives up in Harrow, on this road that's just full of mansions, one after the other. And he throws this party and he's got an entourage, they're all French, all basically criminals from what I can learn, and there are girls and drinking and, naturally, he's got a pole in his living room so the girls can dance.'

'Class.'

'You can't buy it, right? So anyway, somebody has this idea to play, get this ...' Jessica stopped to collect herself. 'Tug of war. They had this idea to play tug of war, only with cars. Car tug of war.'

'Okay,' I said. 'I don't know what that is.'

'Nobody does,' Jessica said. 'But they will tomorrow, when this story comes out. So Jerome's got a ... hang on ...' She looked down at her notepad. 'A Ferrari 350 and an Aston Martin Vantage. Don't ask me what they are, all I know is they're cars, and they're expensive. Anyway, they find some rope, and they attach these cars together, back to back, and Jerome gets in one of them, and a friend gets in the other, and it's like, three, two, one, go!'

'Let me guess,' I said. 'This doesn't end well.'

'At all,' said Jessica. 'They're footballers, not sailors, so not one of them has the first idea how to actually tie a knot. So here's the scene. It's dark, three in the morning. They're on the drive of his mansion, two cretins in supercars and a whole crowd of drunk Frenchmen and half-naked women, and there's wheel-spinning and tyre smoke and noise and then—'

'How do you know all this?' I asked.

'Someone filmed it on their mobile.'

'Nice.'

'Very. So, want to guess what happens?'

'The rope comes undone.'

'And the cars, in gear and revving at nine thousand rpm or something, shoot off in opposite directions. One buries itself in a grass bank. Write-off. The other ends up in the swimming pool.'

'This actually happened?' I said.

'This happened. Lifestyles of the rich and stupid, right?'

'It's what pays our rent.'

And there it is, just like I was saying. I'm kind of like Erin Brockovich, only instead of exposing corporate irresponsibility, I expose the questionable antics of household names. But again, like I said, it pays the rent. Until I get evicted, that is.

Anyway, it's not all bad. Because this story, this mega story I want to break? I've got a plan, and it's a brilliant one, even if I do say so myself.

eight

FORTUNE HAD SPENT A LIFETIME TRAVELLING AND HE COULD still remember the time when security had been a breeze; pre-9/11 days when everybody, from check-in through to boarding, had smiled. Enjoy your trip. Have a great flight. Just head on through, sir. Now, he waited next to the X-ray conveyor while an Arab man in front of him emptied his pockets, removed his belt and walked back through the detector arch again in his socks. He didn't look happy. The guy holding the portable metal detector didn't look happy. The lady stacking the plastic trays, she didn't look happy. Fortune considered smiling at her, but figured it might end in him being strip-searched by a grim-faced customs officer. And why were you smiling, sir? Nobody smiles. Not these days, sir. Not any more.

He'd been called by Owen that morning. Owen the CEO; privately educated, well-connected, master-of-the-universe Owen. He was known, in the bank, as Fucking Owen, for fairly obvious reasons.

'Fortune? Where are you?'

'I'm still in London.'

'Fucking missing in action. You know what's going on back here?'

'I heard.'

'You heard.' Owen stopped. Fortune could hear him breathing. 'So why, Fortune, didn't you get on the next fucking plane back?'

'Because my daughter's still missing.'

'I heard. I'm sorry.' He left the briefest of pauses, to convey some kind of understanding, a modicum of sympathy. 'But I need you here, in Dubai, not in fucking London.'

'I—' Fortune started.

'We've got close to ninety mill missing. Gone. Disappeared into thin fucking internet ether or whatever the fuck you call it. Vanished.'

Fortune closed his eyes, listening to Owen's voice. The voice of a superior officer, ordering him over the top. Nothing to negotiate. I own you.

'I'm looking for my daughter,' he said.

'No,' said Owen. 'The police are looking for your daughter. And they'll keep looking, even when you're not there.'

Fortune thought of the police, the one officer assigned to his daughter's case. He didn't say anything.

'So. You're on your way,' said Owen. It wasn't a question.

Fortune squeezed his eyes closed and looked across the room at his suitcase. He still hadn't unpacked. He hadn't been there long enough. 'I'll get on a plane.'

'Good man.'

'I'll see you. Give me twelve hours.'

Fortune didn't wait for a reply, just hit the screen to hang up. He put his phone down and rubbed his eyes again. The same story, he thought, always the same story. Work comes first.

*

He watched the runway reel past him as the plane readied for take-off. There was the howl of the engines as they loaded up thrust and the feeling of compression into his seat as the plane built up speed, the lift as the front wheel left the ground, the queasy sensation of weightlessness as they hung in the air before the steep ascent. He wondered how many flights he'd taken. He couldn't imagine. Say twice a month, for twenty years? Five hundred flights? It was a lot of air miles.

'Tea? Coffee?' a flight attendant asked him, once the seat-belt signs had pinged off. Fortune shook his head. She passed, and a young man handed him a tray.

'Breakfast.'

'Thanks, but no,' said Fortune. 'I'm going to sleep. If you see me asleep, please don't offer me anything. Tea, coffee, food, nothing. My seat belt's on. My seat's upright. All right?'

'Okay,' the man said. 'You're sure …?'

'Sure,' said Fortune. He had the same conversation every flight. 'Thanks.'

'No problem.'

Eyes closed, he thought back on yesterday, thought about his daughter's possessions. There had been nothing he had recognized, nothing that stirred anything in him. Clothes, heels. Some books, photos of Jean, of Sophie and Jean, of Sophie with girlfriends, on holiday. Plates, cutlery, posters. A folder full of payslips, her tenancy agreement and employment contract. She owned almost as little as Fortune did. Looking through the boxes in the damp garage, he'd felt a sense of desolation at her disappearance. She still had it all to do, still had it all to learn and experience and enjoy. Where was she?

He had also wondered at what was missing. There had been

no phone, no computer. Who didn't have a computer? Sophie was always writing, had a blog, updated every week. Where was it? He'd called the letting agent, Sam.

'I can't find a computer.'

'Everything in the flat, it's all there.'

'It can't be.'

'Maybe she took it with her,' Sam said.

'Took it where?' said Fortune, but he hadn't waited for a reply, didn't want to hear Sam's opinion on what his daughter might have done, where she might have gone. 'You're sure?'

'If it was in the flat, it'll be in the boxes.'

No phone, no computer. Nothing personal: no diary, no letters. But then, who wrote on paper any more? He'd put a call through to Marsh, but the policeman hadn't been available, so he'd left a message for him to call back. He wasn't holding his breath. Maybe it was a good sign, that her computer was missing. She wouldn't have taken it with her if she was going to kill herself. Why would she? It didn't make sense. But then maybe she'd had it in her bag and met somebody, got in their car … Fortune tried to stop thinking, stop speculating, stop obsessively examining the little information he had. His daughter had disappeared. Nobody knew anything. And the missing computer meant nothing. Stop, he told himself. Stop thinking about it. Stop now.

But as the plane took him further and further away from London, he remembered the last time he had felt like this. When Sophie had been, what, six, seven, they had gone to London together, just the two of them. Jean had been ill. That was it. She'd been in hospital, having her appendix taken out. It was Sophie's birthday and they'd booked tickets for some play, a musical. Roald Dahl? He didn't remember. He remembered her small hand in his as they walked down the platform from the train, her talking, excited, looking all around her at the people and the vaulted roof of the train station and the size and scale of the city. Her small hand, soft and warm. Sitting in his plane seat, he felt his heart swell at the thought of that small, warm, trusting hand.

They had walked down to the Tube, had needed the Circle Line. The platform had been busy, a crush of people. A train had arrived but it wasn't their train, it had the wrong destination. She had been standing in front of him, protected by his body. The doors had opened, people had got out, pushed past them. He'd looked down and she wasn't there, he couldn't see her. He'd looked behind him, and she wasn't there either; he couldn't see her anywhere in the crush of people. Then, as the doors to the train closed, he saw her through the glass, her eyes wide and scared. Her hand had pressed at the glass, but they were separated, her on the train, him on the platform. The train had started to move and he'd tried to match it, pushing past people, Sophie watching him in mute panic. Making his way down the platform, all the time shouting, 'Next station, next station! Get out at the next station!' But there had been too many people and the train had picked up speed and his daughter had been sucked away from him into a dark tunnel. Gone so fast, gone in seconds.

He had waited two minutes for the next train. He had thought about the people in the carriage with his tiny daughter, the kind of people they might be, the motives they might have, the desires. He had imagined the city sprawling out around him, bigger and bigger, rings of magnitude, the number of people, buildings, locked rooms, hiding places where a six-year-old girl could disappear into and be lost forever. He stood on the platform and closed his eyes and waited for the next train, as he imagined his tiny daughter pulled screaming and helpless into the heart of a city that could swallow her up and never let her go.

The next train had arrived and he had stepped into the carriage, waited for the doors to close. Into the tunnel, the rattle and jostling of the carriage on the rails, the announcement of the next station. *Get out at the next station. Please, please, Sophie, please get out at the next station.* Back into the light and the slowing of the train, and as it had come to a halt, he had seen his daughter standing on the platform. Calm. So calm and so still. And the doors had opened and he had picked her up and held her tight, her smooth, soft cheek against his, and he had stroked her hair, stroked it and stroked it and rubbed his cheek against hers.

And then later, walking in silence through the streets of London, Sophie had stopped and looked up at Fortune and said, simply, 'I knew you would come and find me.'

He had never told his wife what had happened. He had not thought of it in years. But now, hanging in the air, thinking of the daughter he thought he had lost that day, he felt a strange wave of culpability, a sudden panicked guilt. He had not lost her that day. But in the years that followed, he had not only lost her, he had let it happen.

An image appeared in his mind, of his daughter standing in a small boat. He was on the shore. It was dark and the water was black and she was drifting away, slowly. She watched him as she drifted further and further into the darkness, into an unknown that Fortune could not imagine. And before she was even out of sight, he had turned away, turned his back on her. He thought of her small hand in his, and closed his eyes.

Fortune's mobile rang as he walked away from the luggage carousel, towing his suitcase down a glass-walled corridor that no amount of air-conditioning could keep cool. He could see the buildings of downtown Dubai in the distance, skyscrapers shrouded in smog, distorted by heat shimmer and obscured by dozens of cranes, all trying to keep up with the city's relentless expansion.

He stopped, put his phone to his ear. 'Hello?'

'Mr Fortune? It's Marsh.'

'Hi.' Fortune held his breath, felt his heart quicken, readied himself for news.

'You left a message,' said Marsh. 'Calling you back.'

'Oh,' said Fortune. No news. No end to the waiting. Sophie still missing. 'Yes. I wanted to ask you—'

'Where are you?' said Marsh.

'Getting off the plane,' said Fortune. 'In Dubai.'

'Right,' said Marsh. 'Good.' Fortune could hear the relief in the policeman's voice. 'Best place for you. There's nothing you can do here.'

'I wanted to ask you something,' said Fortune.

'Go on.'

'My daughter, Sophie, her computer. I didn't find it. Among her possessions. Or her phone.'

'No?' said Marsh. He did not sound too interested, or too surprised, by this revelation.

'You don't find that strange?'

'Not really. Maybe she had it with her when ...' Marsh, adept at

54

not finishing difficult sentences. When she disappeared. When she took her own life.

'If she was going to, if she decided to end her life,' said Fortune, 'why do you think she'd take her computer with her? Seems strange.'

Marsh sighed. 'Mr Fortune, by definition, she would not have been in her right mind in such a situation. Who knows what she was thinking?'

Fortune did not answer. People walked around him like he was an inconveniently placed rock, obstructing the flow of a river.

'Mr Fortune. If we find a computer, or a phone, or...' Again he stopped. A body. That's what he wants to say, thought Fortune. 'If we find anything,' Marsh continued, 'we'll let you know. Immediately.'

Fortune put his phone back in his pocket. He was alone in the corridor, left behind by his fellow passengers. He started walking again, wondering if there'd be any taxis left by the time he cleared immigration.

nine

High Times and Miss Fortune: What Not to Say on a First Date

Now, I'm no traditionalist. BUT. If you're going to take somebody out on a date, first impressions kind of count. It's like you're on probation, at least up to the second course. So, best to be on your best behaviour.

I've got a friend, and when she was at university, some guy took her to this uber-swanky restaurant. It was in the West End, though she doesn't remember the name. Anyway, as they walk in, the maître d' comes up to them, and her boyfriend whispers to her, 'Don't give him your coat. We'll be doing a runner.'

Mine wasn't that bad, but still … it was pretty bad. I arranged to go on a date with a friend of a friend. Let's call him Chris, since THAT'S WHAT HIS NAME IS. He's okay-looking, though he didn't know whether to shake my hand or kiss me when we met, which was a bit awkward, and he ended up doing both, which just felt weird. Kind of halfway between a business meeting and a date. Pleased to meet … MWAH. Anyway, that's not the worst of it. Oh no.

Ready? Okay …

We sat down and opened the menus, and he said, as casual as you like, 'If you want a starter, we can't have a dessert.'

Puh-lease.

So anyway, if anybody else out there has anything to share, I want to hear it!

COMMENTS:

LozLoz: *LOL! I once went on a date with a guy, and he was looking at the menu and he said, 'I can't have tomatoes because they give me explosive diarrhoea.' I counted the minutes after that.*

TinaTee: *Went to a posh restaurant with this guy. He was some kind of football hooligan, I think. He spends like ten minutes looking at the menu without saying a word, just looking … angry. Then he calls the waiter over and says, 'Listen, I ain't being funny, but you couldn't ask the chef to make me some chicken and chips or summink, couldja?'*

LozLoz: *TinaTee What a catch!*

ShanraJ: *TinaTee Don't tell me, you married him.*

FridayFeeling: *TinaTee Mmmm. Chicken and chips. A man after my own heart …*

CrossMyHeart: *'At the moment I live with my mum.' Cringe.*

TinaTee: *CrossMyHeart Yeah. 'I live with my parents.' Why even say it?*

CatLover: *CrossMyHeart Instant turn-off.*

Specs And The City: *'I'm married, but definitely going to get a divorce.' He was even wearing his wedding ring. I bet he's still married …*

Starry Ubado: *Makes a change, I'm guessing for a starter you usually eat dick. You dumb bitch. Dumb, dumb, stupid bitch.*

MissFortune: *Starry Ubado What exactly is your problem?*

Starry Ubado: *MissFortune Problem? The problem is whores like you, acting like you're above men, when underneath you're just a slut.*

TinaTee: *Starry Ubado ???*

CatLover: *Starry Ubado Go home, troll.*

LozLoz: *Don't feed the troll!*

Starry Ubado: *Hope your next date gives you AIDS.*

MissFortune: *Starry Ubado Get a life. Loser.*

Starry Ubado: *MissFortune I know where you live. Bitch.*

This is actually beginning to get too much. I know it happens all the time, and that if you put stuff out there in the public domain then you're bound to attract the odd nutcase, but I just don't need the hassle and aggravation. It's a blog about me going to parties and getting in taxis and eating in restaurants. What exactly is the problem with that? And now this guy, Starry Ubado (as if that's his real name), he's saying he knows where I live? I'm a good person. Okay, I'm not perfect, but I don't deserve this. I'm pretty sure of that.

So maybe I should just close the blog. Shut it down. But then why should I? Why should I let somebody like this troll dictate to me? I don't know. This, and all the stuff about the noise and partying, I'm tired of it. I'm counting the days until Josh gets here and makes it all go away. It's only a few weeks now. He's working on an advert for Adidas, and he told me that I wouldn't believe it, the amount of money they've got and that they can afford to waste. He told me that one of the people at Adidas didn't like one of the camera angles, so they've got to call the whole cast of the advert back, just for one shot that lasts all of just under a second.

I can hold on for him. I can do that. And no, actually, I won't turn the blog off. Sorry, Starry, but you don't matter. You don't count. I'm young and I'm pretty and I've got an amazing man and I'm working on a great story, and I'm better than you, a lot better.

So there.

ten

FORTUNE SAT ONE SIDE OF THE BOARDROOM TABLE, FACING Owen and the company lawyer on the other side. They were both younger than him, a good ten years at least, with neat hair, expensive suits, flawless complexions. They gave off a complacent aura of power. No, not power: privilege. Hell, what was the difference? Behind them was a huge glass window giving Fortune a view of downtown Dubai from thirty floors up, the city's skyscrapers looking dirty and hazy through the smog and shimmer.

'You look like hell,' said Owen. 'Jesus.'

'I came straight from the airport,' said Fortune.

'Yes, well, thanks for coming.'

Fortune didn't reply, just nodded.

'This whole thing's turning into a situation,' Owen said. 'Wouldn't you say?'

'I think it's too early to tell,' said Fortune. 'We might find the missing money.'

'Find it? Where? Under the fucking table?' Owen ducked in his chair, had a look under the boardroom table. 'Can't see it.'

'We switched servers,' said Fortune. 'So it might be that.'

'Might be that,' repeated Owen. He looked at the lawyer next to him; Jeremy, that was his name, Fortune remembered. 'What happens if we don't find it?'

Jeremy lifted his eyebrows, like he was surprised at the question. 'Well, obviously, we'd be up before the regulator. Doesn't do to be losing people's money.'

'We're insured,' said Fortune.

'We're not insured against bad fucking publicity,' said Owen. 'Are we?'

Fortune nodded, conceded Owen's point. It was a good one.

'I'm not losing my bonus over this,' said Owen. 'You understand me, Fortune? This is your mess, and you're going to fucking clean it up. Yes?'

'Yes,' said Fortune.

'Can't hear you,' said Owen.

'Yes,' Fortune said again, louder this time. He could feel Jeremy's amused eyes watching him, enjoying his humiliation. These two men, younger than him, treating him like a naughty child. He felt his heart beat faster in anger. This was what he had worked decades for, sacrificed everything, his marriage, his family? For younger men to treat him with contempt?

'Good,' said Owen, settling back in his seat. There was silence around the table for some moments, and then Owen frowned at Fortune and said, 'Well? Off you go.'

The bank Fortune worked for was, he suspected, run the same way as the boarding schools most of its senior management had attended. Fear was the primary motivator. There was a culture of bullying from the top down. Do your job or else. The 'else' being public humiliation, scathing reviews, written warnings, a steady application of pressure. How many employees had he seen in tears? The busiest department in the bank, he imagined, was HR, though in Dubai the labour laws were lax to the point of non-existence. You got sacked for not putting in seventy-hour weeks? Tough. That's life. Man up.

Fortune had been a ball-breaker himself during the time he was climbing the ranks, not that he was proud of it. A taskmaster, a tyrant. But age had changed him, age and other things. Looking at the fifteen scared faces watching him from their seats in the ops department, he reminded himself that most of them hadn't been home in two days.

'Okay,' he said, gently. 'I know you've been working around the clock. I know you're doing your best. Yes? We'll work this out.' He paused. 'Now, can anybody tell me where we are?'

There was silence, then Alex said, 'It's gone. All the money. Just ...' He shrugged. 'Gone.'

'Do we know how?'

'Must have been hacked.' Other people nodded. 'It's the only explanation.'

'How can they have—' began Fortune, but Alex interrupted.

'We don't know. We don't know anything.' He shrugged, tried a tired smile. 'Just managing your expectations.'

Fortune felt a burst of panicked adrenalin. This wasn't good. As he rubbed his hands on his cheeks, he felt his mobile vibrate in his pocket and took it out, looked at it. It was Marsh; he recognized the number. He should take it. He looked at the faces of his team, watching him, hoping that he'd make it all right, tell them what to do. He cancelled Marsh's call, put his phone away.

'Okay. Sadler, what's your take on this?'

Sadler stood up. He was young, hardly more than a boy, but

he knew his stuff. At a thousand dollars a day, Fortune thought, he'd better.

'The thing is,' said Sadler, 'this isn't some random hack. Somebody's doing it for a reason, that's what I think.'

'What kind of reason?' said Fortune.

Sadler shrugged. 'Don't know. You need someone more forensic, someone who can walk it back, find out where the attack came from.'

Fortune looked at Alex. 'What can we do?'

'We've changed encryption, put up another firewall. We should be secure.'

'Should be?'

Alex looked unhappy. 'Shouldn't have been able to do it the first time.'

Fortune nodded. 'All right. Everybody get some sleep, come back here first thing tomorrow. Do we think we can manage that?'

The faces nodded, ambivalent, happy to be going home, knowing they'd be back in less than eight hours. It wasn't long, and what they were coming back to wasn't anything they wanted to deal with. He felt for them, but then, it was their job, how they made their living. And who said life was meant to be easy?

Fortune sat back in the taxi as it swept smoothly past tower block after crane after crane after new tower block, along freshly built four-lane roads and past signs in Arabic and English, pointing travellers to airports and malls and business districts. He had always seen Dubai as a kind of Disneyland for adults, a business theme park where the costumed roles of Mickey and Donald were played by imported immigrant labour, Indian and Pakistani and Chinese, who cleaned and built and cooked and served, keeping the business class pampered and comfortable and entertained. It was a place of almost binary opposites, he thought as the highway's Mercedes and BMWs gunned past workers on bicycles or on foot, carrying loads too heavy for them. The haves and the have-nots. Them and us. They lived behind the scenes, in slums outside the gleaming spires of downtown Dubai, filthy and neglected. He tried not to think about them. This wasn't his country. What could he do?

He called Marsh and listened to the call ring through to voicemail as he watched beggars knock at car windows at a red light. Eventually the taxi stopped outside his apartment building, a fifty-storey tower with a gym in the basement and a restaurant on the top floor, another halfway up. Fortune knew the man on the door by sight but not his name, although the man called him Mr Fortune as he opened the door for him. He took the lift to the seventeenth floor, walked along the tastefully lit corridor. The apartment was provided by the bank, a two-hundred-square-metre palace that made him feel, more than anything, like a lab mouse. The only difference between his apartment and a hotel suite was that here his suits were already hanging in the walk-in closets. No photos of family were on the walls, there was no food in the refrigerator. In the year or so he had lived there he had had no visitors.

He checked his answer machine – no messages – and poured himself a Scotch. Sitting down and looking at his empty apartment, he could not help but think back to his daughter's meagre possessions, her life stacked up in a damp garage. Psycho Bitch. The words came unbidden into his mind, ugly and cruel. His daughter. Could it be true, what Sam had told him about her? He thought back to her moods and unhappiness, her unreasonable behaviour. Maybe.

This train of thought led Fortune to find his laptop, get online and look at his daughter's blog. Perhaps he could gain an insight, find a clue, get a foothold in her psyche. Come to know her better, delve deeper into her life. It might be all that was left of her. He read a blog post about a party Sophie had gone to where the drinks had been served by women in bikinis on roller skates, and her unambiguous opinion of it. It was funny, intelligent and irreverent, and reading it, he could hear her voice, sarcastic and scathing and naturally rebellious. A voice he had never managed to enjoy in real life. He finished the post, read the comments below, the community his daughter had created, agreeing with her how it was demeaning, objectifying, patriarchal. Fortune had to agree. And then, at the bottom, a comment that stood out for its hatred and anger. Starry Ubado: *You're all sluts, so what's the difference? Dumb whores on legs or on wheels, same fucking thing.*

He wondered at what would make somebody write such a thing, take the time to deliver such vitriol. It was just a story. A funny story, with attitude. Was that so bad?

His mobile rang, interrupting his thoughts. He crossed to the kitchen bar and picked it up. Marsh. He closed his eyes and offered up a quick prayer: *Please. Let it be Sophie. Let her be safe.*

'Hello?'

'Mr Fortune. Marsh.'

'Yes?' Keeping his voice steady.

'I need you to come back to the UK.'

'Sophie?'

Marsh paused, and for a moment Fortune thought he had lost the connection. But then: 'We've found a body.'

'Is it Sophie?'

'We don't know.'

'What do you mean, you don't know?' He walked to the window of his apartment, looked out over the lights of Dubai, the sun just set. He was aware that his heart was beating hard. 'It is or it isn't.'

'We need your help. Identification. We can wait on DNA, but it'll take time.'

'Have you spoken to my wife?'

'Not yet.' Marsh hesitated. 'Mr Fortune, I've met your wife, and I've met you. Honestly, I think you're a better person to do this.'

Fortune watched cars queuing at a junction below, street lights reflecting off their dark roofs. 'That bad?'

'I'm sorry. We can wait for the lab, if you'd prefer.'

'No. No, I'll come. Do you think it's her?'

Again, Marsh paused. Fortune waited. He could barely feel his legs, his feet on the thick carpet of his apartment. He had an impression of floating, all these floors up, floating over downtown Dubai. 'Marsh? Do you think it's her?'

'It's possible. It's likely.'

The cars pulled away from the junction; even from up here, Fortune could see the lights change from red to green. He put a hand to the window to steady himself. 'I'll come,' he said again.

'Call me when you land,' Marsh said. 'I'll take you to her.'

Opposite Fortune, a light blinked on top of a crane that had been constructed on the highest floor of a half-built skyscraper, on, off, on, off, to warn planes or helicopters, Fortune didn't know. *Her.* Take you to her. To Sophie, my daughter. What did they do to you?

'Will do.' He hung up and stood at his window, looked out over the buildings of Dubai, their indifference, their haughty arrogance. This wasn't real. This wasn't happening. Slowly, he sat down on the thick carpet of his apartment, still looking out over his incredible view. What did they do to you?

eleven

IF ANYBODY READING THIS EVER DECIDES TO MOUNT A STING operation, believe me, it's no stroll in the park. No, it's a whole ton of work, and a colossal pain in the you-know-what (bum, if you don't).

Firstly, the whole thing needs signing off by editors, lawyers, an independent ethical adviser, and the entire management board of the magazine publishers. This board is made up of risk-averse middle-aged white men who will do anything, and I mean anything, to protect their share value. So not ideal, basically.

Secondly, you need money. And to get the money, you have to go to the finance department and lay out your plan. And explaining your plan, which sounds pretty far-out even to me (and I *thought* of it), is tricky. Because they're bean-counters, and you're an intrepid journalist. All they want to do is spend their money safely, while you want to live on the edge. So they look at you as if you're mad, and it takes hours of wheedling, and pointing out the extra sales the story will generate, and assuring them that you've got it all worked out and signed off by editors, lawyers, board, etc., before they hand over the money. Very, very reluctantly.

Thirdly, you've got to find the femme fatale who's going to be doing the entrapment. Because this, my friends, is the classic honey trap for our underage-girl-loving celebrity, and it needs to run like a military operation. So the femme fatale has to know her story back to front, say the right things, and make all the right moves. And she's got to be gorgeous. And at least eighteen. And look, at most, fifteen.

Last, and definitely not least, is luring said celebrity into the trap. In reality, that's the easiest bit, because we know where he's going to be, so we just need to make sure our gorgeous, pouty, leggy fifteen-going-on-eighteen-year-old will be there. After that, it's finger-crossing time.

So anyway, that's what I've spent the last weeks doing. Larry, the head of the magazine, has been coming by my desk every hour, with this worried look on his face, asking if everything's okay, if I need anything, if I'm sure I want to go through with it. I get the feeling that he'd actually rather I didn't do it at all. And of course nobody else on the magazine knows anything about it, it's all hush-hush, not even Jessica. So everybody's looking at me out of the corner of their eyes, whispering and speculating. Sample conversation:

'Hi,' says Jessica, brightly. 'How's it going?'

'Okay,' I say, cagily. 'Not bad.'

'What are you working on?'

'Oh, you know. A couple of things. Nothing much.'

Jessica sits on the edge of my desk and picks up a magazine, leafing through it in silence. This goes on for thirty seconds, then a minute, until she can contain it no longer and she throws the magazine down and says – no, whispers – furiously:

'Just tell me what it is, for God's sake!'

It's all, if I'm honest, a bit stressful.

D-Day is in six days' time, and I'm not going to be able to sleep until it's done, over, and my name is being talked about by every gutter journalist in the country. Hey, at least it's an ambition.

In other news, Sam hasn't called me again about mystery noises and non-existent parties, which is something of a relief, since it means that I'm probably not going mad (FYI, I have, in the past, occasionally gone a bit mad). And Josh has reshot the scene that needed reshooting, and he says it's just a matter of going through the rushes and re-editing, resubmitting, and his job is done. I have absolutely no issue with saying that I cannot wait.

It's weird, but in a week's time, after I've got my story and Josh is here in my life, all this other stuff might just seem like a distant memory. I've got to hang in there for a few more days. How hard can that be?

twelve

FOR THE FIRST FEW SECONDS FORTUNE WASN'T SURE WHAT HE was looking at, couldn't work it out. It was like a person, but at the same time not; more like a crude reassembling. Blonde hair, like Sophie's. Pale skin, like Sophie's. The mouth was a mess, and the eyes. He looked away, turned physically away and walked to the opposite wall of the morgue, as far from the body as he could get. Marsh covered it back up and watched him, gave him a moment, waited patiently.

'What happened to her?' Fortune said. He didn't look at Marsh, spoke to the floor.

'We don't know,' said Marsh. 'All we know is she was murdered. No hands, the teeth were ... damaged. She'd been underwater for some time.'

'Jesus.' Fortune rubbed his eyes, his face. 'Horrible.'

'Is it your daughter?'

Fortune didn't answer, worked the heel of his hand into his forehead.

'Mr Fortune? I know it's difficult. Is she your daughter?'

Fortune took his hand away from his face. 'I don't know.'

'No tattoos, no birthmarks?'

'You already asked. No. Not as far as I know. My wife, too. No.'

'Okay. I'm going to need you to look again. Look carefully.'

Fortune shook his head. 'No. There's no way.'

Marsh sighed, looked at Fortune and nodded. 'I understand. We'll wait on the lab.'

'Earring.'

'Sorry?'

'At the top of her ear.' Fortune thought. 'Her left ear. In the …'

'Cartilage.'

'Right.' Fortune had lost it, when she'd come home. Had asked her what she thought she was doing, how was she going to get a job looking like that, did she know the impression it gave? He'd asked her if she was doing drugs, the two things, in his outraged father's mind, inextricably linked. She'd looked at him with contempt and hadn't said anything. Not a word; just looked at him. 'There should be a piercing, right?'

'Should be.' Marsh hesitated. 'Left ear?'

Fortune thought again, pictured his daughter, remembered her sullen look. 'Yes. Left.'

'You might want to turn around.'

Marsh walked to the body. It was on a metal table and Fortune turned away from it, closed his eyes, held his breath.

'Nothing,' said Marsh. 'You're sure?'

'Sure.'

A brief silence, then: 'No. Definitely not.'

'Then it's not her.'

'Okay. Okay, that's … Okay. Thank you.'

'Can I go?'

'Yes. I'm sorry. That you had to see this.'

Fortune didn't answer, just pushed the door to the morgue open and walked out, away from the chemical smell and the cold, wishing that he could erase what he had just seen from his mind. Some things you couldn't unsee. Some things would stay with you for ever.

Fortune's wife had come down to London and was waiting in her hotel lobby for him to call. She broke down when he told her that the body wasn't Sophie. Thank God, she said, oh thank God, thank God, while Fortune stayed silent on the other end, listening to her cry in relief. He asked her if she wanted him to come, to be with her, but she said no, there was no need. An hour later, she called him back and told him that, actually, they should speak, that they had arrangements to discuss.

'What kind of arrangements?'

'About us. The house. What we do.'

'It can't wait?'

'Wait for what? You're here, I'm here. Let's be adults about this.'

'Adults.' Fortune didn't like the sound of that. It meant unpleasant conversations and harsh truths. He'd rather do it remotely, by email, through intermediaries, get someone else to deal with his shortcomings as a husband and father, manage the fallout. Wasn't that what lawyers were for, what they were paid to do? But instead he said, 'Okay.'

'I'll book a restaurant. No reason why we can't do this pleasantly.'

'No,' Fortune said, though he didn't believe it. What was pleasant about your wife leaving you? Well, throwing you out. Call it what it was. 'Let's do that.'

Now he was sitting opposite her in an Italian restaurant in Mayfair, wondering what to say. He wasn't sure why she'd chosen the place, somewhere so expensive. The tablecloth was crisp, the glasses fine, brittle, rather like the atmosphere, he thought. The waiter brought a bottle of Chianti and poured some for Fortune to taste. He smelled, swilled, tried it and nodded. 'Fine. Thank you.'

'I want the house,' said his wife. She was wearing a black dress and heels that showed off her calves, which remained shapely after all these years. In fact, she looked wonderful. It occurred to Fortune that she must be having an affair, that she was seeing somebody else, and the instant the thought struck him, he accepted it as a self-evident fact. She wasn't keeping herself attractive for him. They hadn't had sex in a decade, and never would again. He closed his eyes. There was no love, no affection, nothing left for them. He had failed, and now his wife was as lost to him as his daughter was.

'Fortune?' his wife said.

'Where would I live?' said Fortune.

'You don't live there anyway. What difference would it make?'

'When I retire.'

'Retire? You? What would you do without work?'

Fortune didn't answer, hadn't thought about it. He drank wine and waited for his wife to say something. She was dangerous, he thought. Out for all she could get. Good on her. She probably deserved it. No, she definitely did.

'You're not going to make things difficult, are you?' she said.

'No.'

'Because I can tell you, and I've taken advice, you're not in a strong position. After what happened.'

That again, after all these years. Would she ever let him forget it? 'Fine,' he said. 'Whatever.'

'Just like that?'

Fortune sighed. 'Just like that.'

He had imagined that placation was the way to go, that non-resistance would be the easiest course. But it seemed to make his wife angry, infuriate her, though he could not imagine why.

'You really don't care, do you?' she said.

'I care,' said Fortune. 'Of course I do.'

'And never did.'

'Jean,' said Fortune, 'what do you want from me?'

'Only what I always wanted. For you to give a damn. About me and Sophie.'

'I came back from Dubai. I looked at a murdered girl's face.'

'You came back from Dubai. What a sacrifice.' Jean laughed, shook her head. 'Left your precious work.'

'I thought you wanted to do this pleasantly.'

She didn't answer that, instead picked up a menu and opened it. She pretended to read it for a couple of seconds, then put it down again, slowly and purposefully, and looked at Fortune.

'Did you ever wonder what it was like? For me? Dealing with Sophie on my own?'

'Jean ...'

'You knew nothing about her. Nothing. Did you know she was having problems at work? That she thought people were out to get her, causing her trouble?'

'What kind of trouble?'

'I don't know.' She took an angry swig of wine and Fortune wondered if she'd had a couple before she came out. 'I told her I couldn't help. I said she needed to speak to someone. A professional. We argued.' She closed her eyes. 'That was the last time I spoke to her.'

'You think she was right? People were out to get her?'

'Who knows? No, no, I don't. She wasn't making sense. She sounded ... unwell. Unstable.'

Pyscho Bitch. The ugly words came back into Fortune's mind, unwelcome, impossible to erase. 'Problems at work?'

'Yes. I don't know. I don't know what was going on.' She picked up the menu again, again put it back down. 'This was a bad idea.'

'Jean ...'

She swallowed the last of her wine. Definitely, thought Fortune, she's definitely had a few. She'd never been a good drunk; it had always awoken something malicious inside her. She handed her glass to Fortune, who filled it.

'I want the house,' she said.

'You said. And I said, fine.'

'Good.' She nodded. 'Okay.'

'Listen, Jean ... I just want to say ...' Fortune stopped, took a breath, as if he was about to take a leap into the unknown. 'I know I wasn't there for you, or for Sophie. I don't know, I can't tell you why. I was ... I just wasn't good at it.'

Jean laughed, a derisory sound, but said nothing, so Fortune ploughed on, not looking at his wife, instead at a patch of tablecloth just past his plate.

'I want to say sorry. For all of the things I did, or didn't do. For all the things I got wrong.' Now he looked up and saw that Jean was watching him with no emotion, none at all. 'That's all,' he finished, meekly and quietly.

She kept gazing at him for some moments, then said flatly, 'Oh, well that's okay then. That's fine.'

'Jean ...'

'After twenty years of, of what, of *misery* ... you're sorry? Your daughter spends her adolescence trying to kill herself while you hide at work, can't hear any cries for help from there, right? And now she's disappeared and you're *sorry*?' She stood up, pushed her chair back. A couple at the next table were watching, a man at the table behind Jean turning.

'Twenty years,' she said, raising her voice now that she was standing. 'That's how too late this is. Twenty years.'

Fortune put his hands up, showed her his palms. 'All right. All right, Jean, please. Sit down.' The couple exchanged words, the woman's eyes big and round.

'Where were you?' Jean said. 'Every time she needed you, needed a father, where were you?' She ran out of words, stood still for a moment before knocking her glass of wine over, with force, so that the spilt wine reached Fortune, soaked his shirt. He heard the woman at the next table breathe in, a gasp of excitement. Jean turned and walked out, slightly unsteady on her heels, the muscles of her calves visible beneath her nylons.

Fortune mopped at his shirt with his napkin, trying to ignore the looks of the other diners. He couldn't blame her, he couldn't. She was right. And he'd been wrong, done everything wrong, all of their daughter's life.

Back in his hotel room, Fortune lay on his bed and closed his eyes. He was tired, so tired. He let his thoughts drift to the edge of sleep, but was snatched back to reality by his mobile.

'Hello?'

'Mr Fortune? It is, ah, Dr Aziz.'

'Oh. Hello.'

'Yes, ah, you, we, there was an appointment. We had ...' Fortune listened to Dr Aziz clear his throat. 'Ah, you had an appointment.'

Dr Aziz was a man who took his time getting to the end of a sentence. An irony, Fortune thought, given that he was the man who had told Fortune how little time he had left.

'I know,' Fortune said. 'I had to fly back to the UK.'

'You are in the UK?'

'Yes. There's been a ...' What to say? 'My daughter is missing.'

'Oh my, ah, my goodness,' said Dr Aziz. 'I am very sorry.'

'Thank you,' said Fortune.

'You will come, ah, you will return to Dubai, ah, soon?'

'I'm not sure.'

'You are missing your, ah, your treatment.'

More chemotherapy. Like the previous treatments had done anything, had made any difference. 'I don't think I'm going to continue the treatment,' said Fortune.

'But Mr, ah, Mr Fortune, without it ... without it, you, ah ...'

'And with it?' said Fortune. 'It's not as if it's going to cure me.' He thought of the X-ray Aziz had shown him, of his lungs. There had been misty swirls in them, like smoke trapped permanently inside, steadily growing and spreading.

'Of course it might. Of course, we must never rule out, ah ... And certainly, ah, possibly, or even probably, Mr Fortune, it will, ah, prolong your life.'

Fortune thought of his wife. Of his daughter, missing, long abandoned by him. Wondered just what his life was worth. 'I understand,' he said. 'But still.'

'Mr Fortune—' began Dr Aziz, but Fortune interrupted.

'I'm in the UK,' he said. 'I'll call you when I'm back.' He hung up on the doctor's protesting voice, turned his phone off and lay back on his bed. He felt numb, detached from what was happening. From the cancer that was silently killing him, from his daughter's disappearance, the dreadful sight in the morgue. It occurred to him that he might be in shock. He didn't know. Didn't care. He closed his eyes and tried not to picture the girl in the morgue, the face that made no sense. It wasn't Sophie. No, it wasn't Sophie. But he now knew what was possible, what people were capable of. There was horror out there, pure horror.

High Times and Miss Fortune: Last Night a GI Saved My Life

I went out to the magazine's Christmas party last night. Dressed to the, well, sevens at least. Maybe eights. LBD, heels, nails, the lot. I thought I looked pretty good. And I suffer from low self-esteem, among other things (too boring to go into now), so I actually probably looked getting-on-for-amazing.

Anyway, whatever. I was tottering along Great Portland Street in my £500 shoes, feeling like a million dollars, or at least a million roubles, and I passed this homeless person, a young man. And these are the thoughts that went through my mind, in quick succession:

That's so sad I wonder what happened to him to be homeless God he's so young I'm wearing really expensive shoes it's cold tonight shit I can't just walk past but I haven't got any change sod it I've got a job and money and he hasn't I'll give him a tenner.

So I did. And he said thank you, and smiled, and I smiled back. And at that moment, at that precise moment, I felt much better than I looked.

And then I go to the magazine's party and drink shots and dance and giggle and have an awesome time, the kind of awesome time that when you think back on it is just this crazy montage of lights and music and laughing.

So anyway, here's when things go dark. I'm tottering (properly tottering now) back to the Tube, and out of nowhere this guy grabs my arm. He's wearing a mask over his mouth, it looks like some kind of bandanna.

I'm too scared to even react, to even try to get away, it's like I'm just rooted to the spot and my scalp's gone all cold and all down my back, too. I'm in total shutdown panic mode. He looks at me and all I can really see is his eyes, and he says, quite slowly and calmly, 'Ever wondered what it's like to be ugly?' He holds up a bottle with the arm that's not holding me; it looks like a washing-up liquid bottle, something like that, and it's full and I can see the liquid inside it. Still I can't scream but I do start pulling away from him, though not as hard as I should, not as hard as I know I can. What's the matter with me? And I know that it's acid he has in the bottle and that this is really, really bad.

The next thing, the homeless man's there and he's pulled the other guy off me, and pushed him away. No, not pulled him off me, thrown him off me and out into the street. The man with the mask is on his hands and knees, and he turns his head to look at us, slowly, like I'd imagine a wolf would turn to look at possible prey. Then a car approaches and he gets up and walks, then runs, away.

And then the homeless guy asks me if I'm okay, and when I nod and thank him he stops me and says, 'You think I'd forget you?'

It turns out Jake, that's his name, is an ex-soldier who couldn't readjust to life on the outside. I took him for a coffee after the police left, but he wouldn't accept any more money. He was nice, funny, troubled. Okay, so he wasn't exactly a GI. But he was all hero.

COMMENTS:

LozLoz: *Oh my God. Are you okay? Acid? How many sick bastards are out there? Get well, honey!*

TinaTee: *Stay strong!*

CatLover: *Hope the police catch him. Frightening.*

Starry Ubado: *I liked your shoes. Red. Made you look like the whore you are. Next time you won't get off so easy.*

LozLoz: *Tell me they weren't really red.*

LozLoz: *Sophie?*

LozLoz: *Your shoes. Were they red?*

I'm done with this blog. Done, done, over. It's time to pull the plug. Yes, my shoes were red, bright red. The first thing I did after I read the comment was go to the police. And you know what they told me? This desk sergeant and his colleague, a disapproving woman in civilian clothes who looked at me like I smelt bad, told me there was nothing they could do, because a crime hadn't been committed.

'Knowing the colour of somebody's shoes isn't against the law,' the woman said. I had the feeling she was trying not to smile. I could have slapped her, except of course I was in a police station, which is just about the worst place to go around slapping people, regardless of how supercilious they are.

'But how did he know it?' I said. 'That's what worries me.'

I showed them the other comments Starry had left on my blog, and they read them like I was showing them pornography, like what did I mean by showing them such filth?

'No crime has been committed,' the woman said again, this time slowly, as if I was a backward child. 'Nothing we can do.'

'Two nights ago, I was attacked. The police were called. I have a crime number. And now somebody's writing to me, telling me, basically, that they were there. So they probably did it. Are you still telling me that no crime has been committed?'

I looked at the desk sergeant but he just shrugged. 'Stay vigilant,' he said, 'and if anything actually happens, then come back and tell us. Or call 999.' The way he said 'actually happens' made it pretty damn clear that he didn't expect anything at all to happen, on account of the fact that, in his and his colleague's opinion, I was merely a hysterical young woman.

So anyway, I went home, and there were two men in cheap suits standing outside my door. They were both overweight, one *overweight* overweight. Or, as they used to say before it wasn't allowed any more, *fat*.

'Can I help you?' I said.

The fat one, who I shall call Fatso (I don't care any more, okay?), took out a card and gave it to me. I read it. *Environmental Health, Borough of Hackney.* Oh God.

'Yes?' I said.

'We've had complaints,' he told me. 'Noise complaints. We're here to investigate.'

'What kind of complaints?' I said, feeling this sense of déjà vu from having had exactly the same conversation with Sam. I thought it had stopped, all this.

'Music, partying,' said the other man, who I shall call Tubby (I said I didn't care, okay?).

'Not me,' I said.

'Your name is Sophie Fortune,' Tubby said, not even as a question.

'Yes.'

'And you live here,' Fatso said.

'Yes.'

'Then, Miss Fortune, I'm afraid that the complaint has definitely been levelled at you,' he said, not without a certain relish. What is it with me and authority?

'Do you mind if we come in?' Tubby asked, nodding at my front door.

Yes, I thought, I do mind. I mind a lot. So I said:

'Yes, I do mind. I mind a lot.'

This didn't appear to faze either Tubby or Fatso. Fatso just handed me a folder.

'And what's this?'

'This is a dossier,' he said, making it rhyme with 'mossier'. 'In it is a list of all the complaints that have been made regarding this property. And this,' he said, handing me a piece of paper, 'is a formal warning that if the antisocial behaviour continues, you will be taken to court and likely evicted from your property.'

'Oh,' I said. Yes, I know. I need to work on my pithy comebacks. And that was it. Off they went. And I'm now Public Enemy No. 1 in the eyes of the Borough of Hackney, I'm being stalked by a psychopath, and I have absolutely zero idea what is happening, none at all.

I honestly don't think I can take this any more.

fourteen

FORTUNE WAS USED TO OPULENCE IN THE WORKPLACE, PAINT-ings worth millions hanging on lobby walls, lifts lined in marble, a complacent hush in the corridors. The quiet calm and comfort of money. Gym membership, a parking space. Order and privilege, the wonderful world of private banking.

The office where his daughter had worked wasn't like that. On arrival, he'd been greeted at what passed for the front desk by a young woman on her mobile, tattoos up her arm, who'd glanced at him and then continued her conversation while he waited. She'd been pretty, so Fortune hadn't minded too much, had listened to her talk to a friend who, he gathered, had got so drunk that she'd stayed at a boy's flat and couldn't remember if she'd slept with him or not, though from the general drift of the conversation and the receptionist's reaction, if she had slept with him, no good was likely to come of it.

She eventually hung up and said, 'Help you?'

'My name's Fortune,' he said. 'My daughter works here. Sophie.'

'Right,' the receptionist said, slowly, as if she was a doctor and Fortune had just told her he'd found blood in his stool. 'Okay.' She looked around, as if hoping somebody else was there, somebody who could help her out. 'Want to take a seat?'

The reception area was on the sixth floor of a central London office building, just off Oxford Street. Framed front covers of the magazine his daughter had worked for hung on the walls. Bright colours, shots of celebrities, bold headlines about surprise weight loss and relationship splits and late nights, worse-for-wear actresses spilling out of taxis. He sat down on a sofa and flicked through a copy of the magazine that was on the low table, without reading. The receptionist picked up the phone, looked at Fortune, then thought better of it and put it down, and instead went to fetch somebody. Fortune felt a spike of anxiety, again as if he was in a doctor's surgery, awaiting bad news. But of course he'd had enough bad news from doctors recently. The worst kind of news. Try beating that.

He'd waited for some minutes before the receptionist came back with another woman, also young. She approached Fortune, stopped and reached down a hand, which he shook.

'Mr Fortune? My name's Anne. Would you like to follow me?'

Now they were sitting in a meeting room, glass-walled and set in the middle of the open-plan office of his daughter's magazine. Anne had asked him if he wanted anything to drink and he'd said coffee, and she'd left him to find it. He looked out at the people at work, ranks of desks, computers, mostly young people typing, on the phone, talking. At the far end an overweight woman was speaking with a young man and laughing, her head back, letting out a shriek that he could hear from where he was sitting, through the glass walls.

Anne came back in, carrying Fortune's coffee. She set it down and sat opposite him, taking a moment to collect herself before looking at him.

'I'm sorry to hear about your daughter. She's still missing?'

'Yes.'

She shook her head. 'Terrible. You must be so worried.'

Fortune didn't believe that Anne was old enough to understand the pain and worry of a missing daughter, but he only nodded. 'Of course.'

'Have the police made any progress?'

Fortune shook his head. 'Nothing.'

'Terrible,' Anne said again.

'Did you work with Sophie?' Fortune asked.

'No, not directly,' she said. 'I'm from HR.'

'Right,' said Fortune. He paused. 'So, the reason I'm here is, it'd been some time since I spoke with her. But I heard that, I don't know, that maybe she'd been having some trouble at work.'

'What kind of trouble?' asked Anne, attempting to sound innocent and failing, not able to look directly at Fortune.

'I don't know. That's why I'm here.'

'The thing is,' said Anne carefully, 'Sophie, she … well, she doesn't work here any more.'

A young man walked past the glass walls of the meeting room they were in and looked at Fortune, a look of fascination, as if he was an exotic reptile that the young man had only heard of in legend.

'She doesn't?'

'No. She left.'

'I see. My understanding was that she loved the job.'

'Sometimes things don't work out.'

Fortune thought of all the people he'd been asked to fire over the years. How difficult the first had been, how routine and bloodless the whole process had become. Warning one, warning two, and here we are. Sorry. The job's not for everyone. Here's the package. Goodbye.

'She left of her own accord?'

Anne paused. 'I can't really speak about the specifics.'

Fortune frowned. 'Well, did she leave or was she fired? That's all I want to know.'

'I really can't discuss the circumstances,' Anne said. 'I'm sorry.'

Fortune leant back in his chair and looked out of the glass windows. He caught the eye of one, two ... Christ, how many people were looking in? From their desks, glancing away as soon as he caught their eye. Like motorists passing a grisly accident. Fascination. He thought of the receptionist, her gossiping. Word of his arrival had spread quickly.

'Okay,' he said. 'Please. What's going on?'

'Sorry?'

'What's going on? What happened?'

'Like I said—'

'You can't speak about it. Yes, I know, you told me.' He looked at her directly, tried his most intimidating managerial stare. These were kids, he thought. He played with the big boys, had done for years. 'I want to know what happened with my daughter, and I'm not leaving until I do.'

'Mr Fortune, please—'

'Sophie is missing,' said Fortune. 'I've flown over from Dubai. I'm here. And I'm not going anywhere until you tell me something useful.'

'I can't. I really can't.'

Fortune sighed. 'Listen, I understand that there are things you can't talk about. So how about you find somebody who can? Could you at least do that? Please?'

Anne was quiet for a moment, then stood up. 'Wait here.' She walked out of the meeting room and through the open-plan office, and as she passed, every head at every desk looked up and watched her.

He hadn't heard anything from Jean, no call or text, and he imagined that the next he'd hear would be from her lawyer. He couldn't blame her. She could have the house, have whatever she wanted. It wasn't like he was going to be around to spend it, anyway. Sitting in the glass room, it occurred to him that he had nowhere in the world that he could call home. He was fifty-four years old. As far as existential failures went, he thought, that had to score pretty high.

'Mr Fortune?'

A man this time, forties, black-framed glasses, grey hair. Fortune stood, shook the offered hand.

'Yes. You are?'

'Larry. MD of this ...' He flapped a hand at the office outside, the people and near chaos. 'This madhouse.' He had an upper-class accent and he spoke slowly and lazily, as if he was above most of what he witnessed. 'Sit down, please. I understand you've flown in from Dubai. Haven't been there, but heard it's the most ghastly place. What is it you do there?'

'Banking,' Fortune said. 'Looking after people's money.' Or not, he thought.

'Nice,' Larry said. 'You have to love the tax situation over there.'

Fortune nodded, staying aloof, trying not to succumb to the man's easy charm. 'I'm here to find out about my daughter.'

'Sophie,' said Larry, nodding. 'Yes. Wonderful girl, bags of promise. Hungry, which is what you need in a place like this.'

Again he waved a hand at the office outside. 'Animals, some of them. Happily eat their own parents to get a story.'

'Why did she leave?'

Larry pulled a face, a gentle wince. 'Now that, well, that is complicated.'

'I've got time.'

'I'm sure,' said Larry. He was still standing and he pulled a chair out from under the table, sat down. 'The problem is, there are things I really can't say.'

'Come on,' said Fortune. 'Let's stop playing around.'

'No,' said Larry, 'I really can't. It's a legal thing, apparently. Or so the lawyers tell me. I'm simply not allowed to disclose any details.'

'You do know she's missing? I just … Look, I just want to know what happened.'

'And I'd love to tell you, I would, believe me. I can't imagine what you're going through, simply cannot imagine. But I'm not allowed to disclose any details. Sounds like bollocks, I know. But alas, it's the situation.'

Fortune sighed, slumped, his shoulders dropping. He suddenly felt tired and old, surrounded by these young people, full of life and energy. What was he doing? 'Just tell me this. Did she leave, or was she fired?'

Larry gazed at him, nodding, thinking. At last he said, 'Put it this way, Mr Fortune. I don't imagine she wanted to leave. I can't say anything more. I'm sorry, I really am.'

Fortune was silent for some time, looking out at the office where his daughter had worked. 'What was it she did here?'

'Stories,' said Larry. 'Chased down stories. At first we'd give her the story, tell her what to do, who to talk to, where to go.

Before we knew it, she was finding them herself. She went out a lot, to parties, events, spoke to people, made contacts. Oh, believe me, she was good. She was very good.'

'What kind of stories?'

Larry smiled. 'The kind of stories our readers want. Who's shagging who, who's in rehab, who's anorexic, who's let themselves go. Those kinds of stories.'

Fortune nodded. 'Scandal.'

'Scandal sells,' said Larry. 'And Sophie, Sophie could sniff it out.'

He stood up, looked at his watch.

'I am sorry, Mr Fortune, but ...'

Fortune got to his feet. 'There's nothing more you can tell me?'

'I wish I could. I do. I really do.'

Fortune nodded. Larry opened the glass door, held it open, waiting for Fortune to walk past him. 'I'll see you out,' he said.

They walked through the office and Fortune felt the weight of surreptitious glances on his back.

'I hope they find your daughter,' said Larry. The way he said it, it sounded like he hoped they'd find her body, like he didn't expect any other outcome.

They walked through into the reception area and Larry held out a hand, which Fortune did not want to take but did anyway.

'Good luck,' said Larry, and turned away without waiting for a response. He walked through the door to the office, and before it had closed on him Fortune saw a young woman run up to him, for the news, what had that man, what had Sophie's father wanted?

*

Outside on the street, Fortune stood for some minutes, unsure of what to do or where to go. He didn't want to return to the hotel, but it occurred to him that he had absolutely nothing more to do, no other business. Sophie's office had been a dead end. Instead, as ever, he turned back to work, calling Alex's number.

'Hello?'

'Alex? It's Fortune.'

'Oh. Hey.' Alex didn't sound too happy to hear from him.

'What's the latest?'

'The latest?' There was an edge to Alex's voice that normally wasn't there. A man at the end of his patience. He was probably exhausted, Fortune thought. Probably hadn't been home for days. 'The latest is, almost ninety million dollars has gone missing, nobody's got a clue where it is, the CEO's riding me like a horse, the team's close to mutiny ...' He sighed. 'The latest is, there is no latest. Nothing to report.'

He was close to finished, at the very ragged edge. Fortune had worked with Alex for years and he both respected and liked him, would go to great lengths for him. He felt a twang of guilt for being here, not there in Dubai, doing his job.

'Okay,' he said. 'Okay. Take a break. Go home, get some rest. Come back to it fresh.'

'Yeah,' said Alex. 'Yeah, whatever. When ...' He paused, unwilling to ask. 'When are you coming back?'

Fortune thought of his lack of progress, the dead end of Sophie's work, the pointlessness of what he was doing. 'Soon,' he said. 'Very soon.'

He hung up, considered doing something cultural, something Dubai was chronically short on. A gallery, a museum. A show? But instead he turned, headed for the Tube, for his hotel, where there was a bar and films on demand. At the Tube entrance, the top of the stairs, ready to descend into London's bowels, he felt a touch on his shoulder, turned, and saw a young woman.

'Mr Fortune? Sophie's father?'

'Yes.'

'I worked with Sophie. I can tell you what happened to her.'

fifteen

IT WAS DONE. IT WAS DONE AND I HAD HIM, I HAD IT ALL ON film and it was all above board, beyond doubt. After all that work, all those weeks of planning and the guts of the women involved, I had him. The champagne was flowing and Larry made a speech to the whole floor. Jessica cried and pretended that she wasn't jealous. Even the lawyers were smiling. I mean, even the finance department told me I'd done a nice job. I had it *made*. I was the golden child.

And then, guess what? Guess what happened?

The scumbag got away.

How? Good question. And the answer is, I haven't got a clue. Well, okay, that's not quite true. What happened is, the original victim decided, overnight, that it hadn't actually happened, any of it. She said that she'd never met the guy, that she hadn't been there. She said that she'd got confused and that she was very, very sorry for everything. She was only fifteen. She just wanted attention. What fifteen-year-old doesn't?

You know how I felt about that, right?

Right.

So the first thing I did was get on the phone to her mother. Her mother who, let's remind ourselves, wanted our favourite sleazy celeb hung, drawn and quartered, boiled alive, and eaten by dogs for good measure. What is it they say? Get medieval on him.

'It's Sophie,' I said. 'From the magazine.'

'I don't want to talk to you.'

'Please, Mrs ——. Come on. We're a team. Just tell me what's going on.'

'I can't. Please don't call me again.'

'Did somebody say something? Threaten you?'

'If you call me again, I'll go to the police.'

'Please,' I begged. Yes, I did, I begged. 'Help me here. Don't let him get away with it. Whatever he's done, whatever he's said, we can work something out. Keep you safe.'

Honestly? I shouldn't have said that. Because I had no idea if we could keep them safe or not, which I don't feel too great about. But anyway:

'I am going to put down the phone, and I never want to hear from you again. I have nothing more to say.'

And she put down the phone.

So now the question is, who blew the whistle? How did that scumbag find out what was happening, and get to our star witness? Now his lawyers are accusing us of entrapment, harassment, malicious allegations, libel, I forget the rest. A great long list that made *our* lawyers' eyes go all big and worried. Game over. All those weeks of work, wasted. All for nothing.

So who knew? Larry knew. The lawyers knew, the editors, the board. That sanctimonious nodding dog of an ethics consultant. And me. And our femme fatale, and her agent. And that's it. That is it.

So, as the saying goes, *WTF?*

Josh said shit happens. I told him that that wasn't very useful, that clichés weren't what I needed right now. It was the first time we've fallen out, the first time we've not been, what's the word people use nowadays? *Aligned*. God. What a dreadful world we live in, where people use words like that.

And then, a week later, the police came to my door and told me that they'd had complaints, reports of harassment.

'Harassment of who?' I said.

'Charlie Jackson,' they said. They told me that I'd been sending him emails, among other things. They said that it amounted to a campaign of harassment.

'I haven't done anything of the sort,' I said.

They just smiled, like I was a challenging kid. 'You have,' they said, 'and it's going to stop, or you'll be arrested. Understand?'

No. No, I don't understand. Of course I don't understand, none of it. I wish I did, but I don't.

I called Mum, thinking that maybe a friendly, understanding voice might help. Hope springs eternal.

'Sophie, you work on some, some … I don't know what to call it. *Scandal* sheet. And you're living in London, no, in *Hackney*. Darling, I read the papers, I see it on the news. Why don't you just come home? All this, it's not good for you. It *can't* be.'

'So, okay, so what, you're saying all this is my fault? My fault for having a career? For being ambitious?'

'All what?' Mum said. 'Is it even happening? Have you listened to yourself? People out to get you, parties, drugs? Sophie, for God's sake.'

Thanks, Mum. Thanks for everything. First Dad abandons

me, and now you. I'm sorry for existing. Sorry for being born, for being such an intolerable burden.

'I've seen you like this before. You need to come home. You need some distance, some calm. Are you taking your medication?'

'No.'

'Sophie! You know what happens.'

'I don't need it. I'm okay. I'm happy. Was,' I corrected myself. 'Things are good. It's nothing to do with before, what happened. I just need … I just wanted to talk.'

'Come home.'

'No. I've got a job, a career.'

'I can't help you if you won't help yourself.'

Oh Mum, please. Don't guilt-trip me. I'm not the person I was two, three years ago. And you know why? Because I worked on it, tried, did my best, created a new life out of the wreckage of my previous one. But of course, I didn't say that. No, what I said was:

'Okay, Mum. I'll call you later in the week.'

'Do not put the phone down, Sophie.'

'Goodbye, Mum,' I said, and did exactly that. With family like this, I can't help thinking, who needs enemies? A control-freak mother and a dad who could not care less about his only child, who hasn't picked up the phone to speak to her in six months. Josh, please get here soon. Because – and this is the sad and tragic truth of poor Sophie Fortune – she hasn't got anybody else.

sixteen

'SHE WAS REALLY GOOD,' THE YOUNG WOMAN SAID. HER NAME was Jessica and she'd told Fortune that she had worked alongside Sophie, given her advice when she first joined, shown her the ropes. She said that pretty soon Sophie hadn't needed her help, that she had been a natural. They were sitting in a café, her and Fortune. She had short black hair that made her look like a pixie, and big blue eyes. Pretty. Striking, even. She sipped her coffee, a flat white. What was a flat white? Fortune wondered. When you couldn't recognize a country's coffee, he figured, you'd been away too long.

'But she got fired.'

Jessica nodded. She was intense, very intense, a petite bottle of energy. She looked at Fortune with her blue eyes, fixed him with them. Fortune felt an urge to look away, but met her gaze and held it. 'Yeah. And nobody's allowed to talk about it. But, you know ...' She drank from her coffee again. 'Whatever.'

'So what happened?'

'It's a long story,' said Jessica. 'And before I begin, I need to ask. Do you want to know? Really?'

'Of course I do.'

'Because Sophie doesn't come out of it well.' She smiled, not a happy smile. 'Nobody does.'

'I want to know.'

'Okay,' said Jessica. 'So, where I work, what I do, what Sophie did, it's ... well, it's shit, basically.'

'It can't be that bad,' said Fortune with a smile, although from what he had seen in her office, he didn't find it too hard to believe.

'It works, I guess kind of like the police,' said Jessica. 'It's all about investigation. We need informers, people on the inside. And to do that, we need to go to all the parties, all the events. Get to know the right people. You with me?'

Fortune nodded.

'How it works is, we help the C-listers. Feature them in the magazine, help them get to be B-listers. To show their appreciation, they give us stories. Who's taking drugs, who's cheating on their wife, who's into gay sex, sex with prostitutes, who's going to rehab. You understand?'

Fortune nodded again. 'Symbiosis.'

'Right. Right, exactly. We raise your profile; in return, you dish the dirt. That's how it works, generally. Like I said, shit, but it's all part of the celebrity machine.'

'And Sophie did that?'

'Yeah. We all do. We hang out at parties, events. Schmooze. You ever read her blog?'

'Yes.'

'So you know the kind of thing.'

'I suppose.' Fortune paused. 'It's not exactly my world.'

Jessica looked at him, his sensible haircut, his suit, his conservatism, but she didn't comment, just drank more coffee. 'Anyway, what happened with Sophie, this was something else.'

A man passed their table and stopped. He had groomed hair

and was well dressed. His face was skinny and pale, his eyes dark. 'Hey, Jess. What's this? Sugar daddy?'

Jessica didn't smile, barely looked up. 'Frank.'

'You remember my name. Thought you'd forgotten me. What's happening?'

'Not much.'

'Yeah? Maybe I've got something for you.'

'I doubt it,' said Jessica. 'You see I'm busy?'

'Hey,' the man said, feigning hurt. 'You can't be nice?'

'I tried it,' said Jessica. 'Wasn't me.'

'Yeah?' the man said again. He leant in, close to Jessica, to her ear. She didn't turn, didn't look at him. 'Well screw you.'

Jessica nodded slowly but still didn't look at him. 'Uh-huh.'

Fortune started to get up, to do something about this man, but Jessica raised a hand. 'Don't worry about it. Frank's just going.'

'Yeah, I'm going,' said Frank. 'I'll take it somewhere it's wanted.'

'Good luck with that,' said Jessica. Frank stood for a second, tried to think of something to say, gave up. Instead he left, walking jerkily, agitated.

'Who was that?' said Fortune.

'That,' said Jessica, 'is what happens to C-listers who become B-listers, take a whole load of drugs, piss off everybody they meet and find themselves Z-listers with a cocaine problem.'

'Right,' said Fortune, trying to process this story of Frank's rise and meteoric fall in the world of minor celebrity. 'I see.'

Jessica flapped a hand dismissively. 'Just another failed reality star. He'll disappear back to the suburbs soon enough.' She picked up her coffee, looked at it, set it back down. Empty. 'Look, d'you mind if we go for a walk? Feels better to talk out in the open.'

They stood, put on their coats. As they left, Jessica took out cigarettes and a lighter. She saw Fortune watching her and said, 'Yeah, I know. These things'll kill you.'

They walked down Regent Street, took a right and wandered through Mayfair. Along the way Jessica pointed out doorways, entrances to exclusive clubs, celebrity hangouts that looked nondescript and unexceptional in the crisp sunlight. Fortune lit up too, smoked, coughed. Coughed some more.

'You okay?'

He nodded, still coughing. 'I'll be all right.'

'Sounds nasty.'

'It's nothing.'

'Let's go to the park.'

They crossed Piccadilly, into St James's Park. It was early afternoon and there weren't many people. A man in a hi-vis jacket walked past, pushing a rubbish cart. They sat down on a bench.

'I'm not supposed to tell you any of this,' said Jessica.

'I know. Larry said.'

'Larry. Jesus. The walking suit.' Jessica laughed. 'So, all right. Sophie had a source. Not your usual minor celeb looking for a leg up. This was a proper, out-of-the-cold, big-story source with something serious.' She stopped.

'Go on.'

'Hold on.' She took out cigarettes, offered one to Fortune, which he took. She lit his cigarette, lit hers, inhaled, exhaled.

'A girl. Young. Said she'd slept with ...' Jessica looked at Fortune. 'How well do you know British television?'

'Not well.'

'Ever heard of Charlie Jackson?'

'No.'

'So, okay, he's a presenter, kids' TV. Kind of, yeah, you could call him A-list. Started out on the radio, now hosts TV shows, guests on panel shows, presents music awards. He's kind of hot right now.'

'And?'

'And this girl, she tells Sophie that he'd met her in a club, given her drugs, taken her to a hotel and slept with her.'

'How old was she?'

'Fourteen. Maybe fifteen, can't remember. Really young.'

'Oh.'

'Oh indeed. This was big, this was … This was going to make her. Course, none of us knew about it at the time. It was her story, she was keeping it quiet. And she wasn't content with just printing the story. She wanted to catch him at it.'

Jessica explained it all to Fortune, how it had gone down. She told it with admiration and feeling, as if it had been she, and not Sophie, who had put it all together. This was their dream, what journalists like Jessica and Sophie got out of bed for. What made their jobs worthwhile. A kids' TV presenter, exploiting underage girls, giving them drugs, having sex with them. Gold. Pure gold.

Sophie had gone to a casting agency, found an actress who was nineteen but looked fifteen, tops. She'd got budget from the magazine, got the whole thing signed off by Larry. She'd paid the actress five grand to go to a club, get talking to Jackson and see what happened.

'Sophie did this?' Fortune could not help but sound astonished. His Sophie? Lost, confused, directionless Sophie?

'Organized the whole thing. With advice from the magazine's lawyers. A thing like this, well ... you don't want to get it wrong.'

The actress told Jackson that she'd got into the club using fake ID, that she did it all the time. She was miked up, with a pinhole camera in her handbag, which she put on the bar as she spoke to him. According to Jessica, the quality wasn't great but good enough.

'You want to see?' she asked Fortune.

'You've got it?'

Jessica dug in her bag and took out her phone. 'I've got it. Not supposed to, but ... This is in confidence, right? You tell anyone, I've lost my job.'

'In confidence,' said Fortune. 'Absolutely.'

The camera was positioned so that he could see Charlie Jackson but not who he was speaking to, the actress, though he could hear her. It was dark and Jackson's face was in shadow, only partially illuminated, the ridges of his nose, cheeks, chin. The sound was okay, though the club's music and other people's voices made it difficult to hear. Fortune held Jessica's phone close to his face, the better to listen.

'I do it all the time.' The woman's voice. Jackson laughed.

'How old are you, then?'

'Not old enough.' The woman giggled. 'Do you mind?'

'No,' said Jackson. 'Nothing to do with me.'

'I've seen you on TV. Can't believe I'm talking to you.'

'Your parents know where you are?'

'They don't care. Think I'm at a friend's house. Staying over.'

Jackson didn't reply to this, didn't say anything for a few seconds. Then: 'You want a drink?'

'Yes please.' A nice touch, thought Fortune, the 'please'. Sounded like a child.

'What would you like?'

'Dunno. How about vodka and tonic?'

'Coming up.'

Fortune watched Jackson lean in to the bar, note in hand, and wait for the barman's attention. He ordered the drink and paid, then turned back to the actress.

'Here you are. Cheers.'

'Cheers.'

She drank, coughed, laughed. Jackson laughed too.

'Ever tried anything stronger?' he asked.

'Like what?'

'Like, you know. Cocaine.'

'No.'

'You want to?'

Jessica took her mobile from Fortune's hands, stopped the footage and put the phone back into her bag.

'What happens next?' said Fortune.

'Nothing. She's got what she wants. She tells Jackson she needs the loo and leaves, doesn't come back.'

Sophie, thought Fortune. Good on you. 'So, okay. That's all good, right? So what happened? What went wrong?'

Jessica sighed. 'Everything. Jackson found out about the story, don't know how. Lawyers got involved. Next thing, the original source, the girl? She's saying she made it all up, she was paid to say what she said. It never happened.'

'But he was on camera. You had him.'

'Doing what? He bought an underage girl a drink. An underage girl who wasn't really underage. Big deal. His lawyers argued entrapment, said if we did anything with the film, they'd sue. Get the girl, the original source, get her on the stand. That kind of thing, it doesn't do the reputation of a magazine like ours any good.'

'What did Sophie do?'

'She didn't take it well. Don't forget, she'd been working on this for weeks. And Jackson was guilty, no doubt about it. He slept with that girl, then got to her. No doubt in Sophie's mind, no doubt in mine. He's a scumbag.'

'So what happened? She got the sack for this?'

'No,' said Jessica. 'For this, she got everybody's sympathy. Great job, unlucky, shit happens. No, she got the sack because, after he got away with it, she started stalking him.'

seventeen

I CAN'T THINK. I CANNOT THINK STRAIGHT, CANNOT WORK out what is happening to me. I want to hide, to go to bed and wrap myself up and never come out. I want to wake up and realize that this was all my imagination, and that none of this actually happened. I want this to stop. I want this all to stop *now*.

Okay, so this is what's happened, in, I hope, some kind of chronological order.

First, the police came by. Again. How many times now? I've lost count.

'One more incident,' they said. 'One more incident and we'll nick you. This has to stop.'

'What does?' I said. 'I keep telling you. It's not me.'

'One more incident,' they said, and they went. They came and threatened me with things I hadn't done and then they went. It's a pattern. But aren't patterns meant to be easy to understand?

Then, Charlie Jackson sent me an email, asking to talk. That happened, it did, it definitely did. I've got the email. It exists. I have it in my inbox. He said enough is enough, let's get this straightened out, face to face.

So I went to his house. He told me his address, so I went to it. He told me his address in the email, and I'm looking at the email, and it's real.

He opened the door and asked me who I was, and I told him, and he basically just completely lost it, telling me that he'd reported me, that his lawyers were on it, and that if I didn't get off his property immediately he'd call the police. He was screaming and spitting and I was just looking at him in astonishment because *he* asked *me* to come. I have the email.

But anyway, I left, telling myself that it was done, that it was over, and that I wanted nothing more to do with him, with the story, with the whole sorry mess. I went home, ran a bath, poured a massive gin and tonic and thought, to hell with this.

Only there was a knock on the door, and I got out of the bath and put on my bathrobe and opened the door and the police were there, and they told me that they had found a knife outside Charlie Jackson's home, and that they believed it was mine.

'No it isn't,' I said. 'Hold on.' I walked into the kitchen and looked at my rack, my wooden rack where I keep my knives for cooking, and the big one was missing. Gone. My knees trembled and everything went dark for an instant, and the next thing I knew I was lying on the kitchen floor and a policewoman was holding a glass of water next to my lips, and I started to cry and I couldn't stop, and the policewoman just watched me and didn't say anything, and eventually I stopped and they asked me to get dressed. They took me to the police station and it was terrible, horrible, and now I just want to sleep and I don't want to wake up. Ever.

eighteen

FORTUNE WOKE UP AND LAY QUIETLY, SQUEEZING HIS EYES closed against the pain in his chest, wondering where he was. Everything was wrong, he knew that. It had all gone wrong. He didn't want to be awake, didn't want to emerge into reality, because there was something out there, something terrible ...

Work. Christ. The first disaster in his life hit him, a jolt in his heart like it was reacting against some dark injection. Just short of ninety million dollars gone missing. Ninety million dollars, missing on his watch. What the hell was he doing here? Why wasn't he there?

And then, God. His daughter. He let out a sound, involuntary, a small cry, a whimper. The tragedy of his daughter's disappearance washed sickly through his mind, flooded his body with a dreadful rush. His daughter. Sophie. Who had been evicted from her flat, fired from her job. He thought back to his conversation with Jessica, what she had told him about Sophie. He closed his eyes again. There was nothing waiting for him in the waking world that he wanted to face. Nothing he felt equal to.

But with his eyes closed, he imagined himself back on the bench in St James's Park, next to Jessica as she told him about

Sophie, about her descent from investigative journalist to *persona non grata*, and from there to obsessed stalker. Sending emails to this guy, Charlie Jackson, threatening him, insulting him. Telling him she'd tell the world. How, next day, he had the word *Paedophile* painted on his front door. How it had escalated, even though she'd denied it. Denied everything. But the day the police had caught her at his house with a knife, well. Jessica had laughed, softly, sadly. Not much she could do to deny that. Although Sophie had tried to, tried to tell anyone who'd listen that it wasn't her, had nothing to do with her.

'But she was there?'

'She was there. And they found a knife.' Jessica had turned to Fortune, put a hand on his arm. 'Listen, I liked Sophie. I liked her a lot, and respected her more. But ...' She paused, sighed. 'She wasn't right. She was ... troubled. Out of control.'

Psycho Bitch, Fortune had thought. Oh Sophie. My Sophie.

His mobile rang and brought him back to his hotel room, where light from the day outside was finding a way through the heavy curtains. He raised himself onto an elbow and reached for his phone on the bedside table.

'Hello? Yes?'

'Fortune.' It was Owen. It was all Fortune could do not to hang up, call back later and blame it on bad reception.

'Owen. How are you?'

'I'm not too fucking good, is how I am. No, not fucking good at all.'

'Right.' Fortune couldn't think of much else to add, so he kept quiet.

'That money? The ninety million? We haven't fucking found it.'

'No,' said Fortune. 'I spoke to Alex. He told me.'

'Yeah? He tell you that not only have we not found the missing ninety million, we've also just lost, Fortune, are you fucking listening, we've just lost another seventy million.'

'Oh Jesus.'

'Yeah, I've already asked him for help. Nothing fucking doing. So my question is, when are you going to get your arse back to Dubai and sort this shit out?'

'I don't know,' Fortune said.

'Sorry? Tell me you didn't just say "I don't know".'

'It's complicated.'

'No,' said Owen, 'it's perfectly fucking simple. You get yourself on a plane today, or you're finished.'

'My daughter's missing. She's still missing.'

'This I know,' said Owen. 'This I'm aware of. But I need you here. Now.'

'I'll try my best. See what I can do.'

'You'll do more than your best,' said Owen. He paused. Fortune imagined him behind his desk, the absurd skyline of Dubai behind him, ostentatious and shameless. 'I'll give you two days. Two days to sort yourself out. If you're not back, you're over. Done. Are we clear?'

'We're clear,' said Fortune.

'Fucking hundred and sixty million, gone. You're going to need to tell me how this happened.'

'I'll do everything I can,' Fortune said again. 'I have to go.'

'Two days,' said Owen. 'I'll see you.'

'Yeah.'

Fortune hung up, collapsed his elbow, sank onto his back on the bed. He looked at the ceiling and swore quietly to himself for what felt like a long time.

In his prime, Fortune had been able to hit a golf ball over two hundred yards, turn par fours into birdies – or at least he would have been able to except that his short game was a joke. He'd get on the green in one, take five putts to hole the bloody ball, which became so embarrassing he stopped playing, even though one thing Dubai wasn't short of was golf courses.

He'd called Marsh, but once again the policeman hadn't been available and Fortune had left a message, wondered what he could do to stop himself from losing his mind, stuck in London with nothing to do, nobody to visit. He'd asked the hotel if there was a driving range nearby and they'd called him a taxi, and now here he was, launching golf balls into the cold empty air. He was the only person at the range, a raised platform overlooking a field with lines painted across it to give the golfers some idea of how far they were hitting. He should be stroking the ball, knew that distance was all in the timing, not the power. But he wasn't here for finesse; he was here to hit something as hard as he could, take all his frustrations and regrets out on innocent golf balls. Thwack. The ball flew through the air, made over a hundred yards. Barely. He was breathless after ten minutes and thought he was going to vomit. He had to stop as a coughing jag took hold of him. Cancer, he decided, didn't do much to improve your game.

He stopped coughing, reached down for a ball and placed it on the tee. He took a couple of practice swings, but before he could commit, his mobile rang.

'Hello?'

'Mr Fortune? It's Marsh.'

'Oh, Marsh, right. Good. Need to speak to you. See you.'

'Are you okay? You sound out of breath.'

'Yeah, fine. Listen, I need to see you. There's something we have to talk about.'

'Yes?'

'It'd be better face to face.'

'I'm very busy, Mr Fortune.'

'It's about my daughter.'

'Yes, I imagine it would be.'

'Have you heard of somebody called Charlie Jackson?' Marsh didn't answer and Fortune stood, holding his phone, looking over the driving range, his balls lying in the short grass.

'You know about that?' said Marsh eventually.

'You knew too?'

'Of course. We did investigate your daughter.'

'So, have you questioned him? He's got a motive, right? Might have meant her harm.'

Marsh sighed. 'All right. You'd better come in. I'll be here till six.'

He hung up and Fortune put his phone away, picked up his club and took a few more swings. He felt a tightness across his chest on the back lift, like it was strapped up, constricting. He dropped the club, kicked the ball off its tee and fought back a cough. His golf days, he figured, were behind him.

They were back in the same room, though Marsh looked tired, looked like hell; looked like Fortune felt. His suit was creased and his skin was grey under the strip lighting, and there was a smell coming off him, coffee and sweat and staleness. He was drinking a coffee, a coffee that he looked like he needed, as though without it he'd fall asleep where he was sitting.

'Are you all right?' asked Fortune.

Marsh nodded without much conviction. 'There's been a murder. First couple of days, they're the worst. Can't stop, can't sleep, just got to hammer it.' He drank coffee. 'Takes it out of you.'

Fortune smiled. 'I thought banks worked you hard.'

Marsh didn't smile back. 'So. You want to talk about Charlie Jackson.'

'Yes. Yes, I do. I heard about what happened. With my daughter. Why didn't you tell me?'

Marsh shrugged. 'Didn't think it was relevant. Didn't think you needed to know. Would want to know.' He lifted his coffee cup again, then put it back down. Empty. 'Trying to protect you. I've got a daughter myself.'

'Do you see much of her?'

'Not as much as I should.'

Join the club, thought Fortune. 'My problem is, I heard that this Charlie Jackson, whatever he said, actually did sleep with that girl. The underage kid.'

Marsh nodded. 'You're probably right. He's a piece of crap. I spoke to him, interviewed him. Bastard smiled at me the whole time.'

'So ...'

'So what would you have me do? I was investigating your daughter's disappearance, not whether Charlie Jackson had got it on with a fourteen-year-old.'

'Fifteen.'

'Whatever. I can't investigate everything, and anyway, his lawyer would have slaughtered me.'

'So you just let him go?'

'I had no reason to hold him.' Marsh sighed. 'I checked him out, asked him for his movements. Didn't find anything.'

'How hard did you look?'

'Hard enough.'

'She was being harassed. My daughter. Someone online. A troll.'

Marsh rubbed at the corner of an eye. 'The shoes.'

'He knew what colour they were.'

'He took a guess. Some kid somewhere, alone in a bedroom. Reads her blog, takes a guess.' Marsh shrugged. 'The IP address, we traced it. Can't be specific, only get a general location, but it was nowhere near Jackson's home. We did investigate.'

Fortune shook his head in a way that let Marsh know that he didn't believe him, didn't have any faith in his word. Marsh frowned, sighed, irritated.

'Christ's sake. All right. You want to know the problem? The problem was, nobody believed your daughter. She wasn't believable. She had issues, problems, she was out of control. I can't imagine I'm the only one to tell you.'

Marsh had him there, Fortune thought. He said, lamely, 'It doesn't sound like her.'

'No? Read this.'

He laid a piece of A4 paper in front of Fortune. On it incidents were listed. *Noise complaint. Officer sent to investigate. Reports of dealing from property. Officer sent to investigate. Noise complaint. Noise complaint. Complaint of harassment. Malicious email sent. Reports of dealing from property. Antisocial behaviour. Online abuse. Noise complaint. Physical harassment.* The dates weren't far apart. She'd been visited by the police weekly, more.

'She was troubled. Incoherent, a lot of the time. I think she had mental health issues. I know there was talk of referring her, even sectioning her.'

'No,' said Fortune. 'She had a job. She was successful.'

Marsh took a tape from his pocket and put it into the machine between them on the desk. 'Listen to this. Maybe this'll convince you.'

He pressed play, sat back and looked at the ceiling. He didn't seem happy about what he was doing. Fortune watched the machine.

Why won't you listen to me?

Miss Fortune ...

You, you, why won't you? Why won't you? Why why why why?

Please, Miss—

I can't I can't I can't. I can't. I can't.

At first Fortune didn't recognize his daughter's voice. Hysteria had made it ragged at the edges, a tearing shriek that sounded more like an animal in pain before he realized that it was saying words, was trying to communicate. He listened with horror, felt his scalp tighten and tingle.

Miss Fortune, you need to calm down ...

Won't listen won't listen won't listen. There. Is. Somebody. Doing. This to me.

You were carrying a knife.

It's not my knife. It's not my knife.

It had your fingerprints on it.

Why won't you believe me?

I want to, I do, but Miss Fortune—

Sophie let out a howl, a bereft, pained sound like a mother who had been told her child was dead. It was awful, heart-breaking, the sound of a woman in utter desperation. He'd been in Dubai. When this was happening, he'd been in Dubai, working for a bank.

Marsh pressed stop and the awful noise cut out, replaced by silence. Fortune's breathing was fast and laboured.

'I'm sorry,' Marsh said. Fortune didn't reply, couldn't reply. Couldn't think of anything to say, didn't trust himself to speak. 'Your daughter was due in court,' Marsh said. 'Jackson had taken out a restraining order on her. She was due in court the day before she disappeared.' He paused. 'I'm sorry,' he said again.

'I understand,' Fortune said. 'I see.' He stood up, and Marsh stood as well, crossed to the door and opened it. Fortune walked through, told Marsh that he could find his own way out, didn't look at him as he said the words. As if he was ashamed of his own daughter's hysteria, her carrying-on.

Marsh watched Fortune walk slowly away and hoped that, one day, Fortune would accept that his troubled and out-of-control daughter was dead. That she was dead, that she had probably brought it on herself, and that she was never coming back.

nineteen

THERE WAS NO WAY OF KNOWING HOW LONG HIS DAUGHTER'S things had been there, she told him. She said that it was an old hut, probably for fishermen, when the river had been public land and full of trout. In fact it was incredible that anybody at all had found it, but then kids get everywhere, don't they? And, actually, even more incredible that they hadn't just made off with the computer, since it looked like it was worth a fair bit and in good condition. Turns out you can still trust people, that people are still honest, even kids.

She told him that Sophie's clothes had been neatly folded, placed carefully on top of the computer, which was on a table in the fisherman's shack. That was why, she told him, the computer was still undamaged. Fortune imagined the shack, rotten boards and an asphalt roof, weeds and grass growing around it, through it. He imagined the river, brown and swollen with the recent rains, running fast, eddies on the surface and currents below, deep and indifferent. Imagined his daughter's body tumbling and scraping over rocks beneath the river's surface, catching on the branches of willows that touched the water. Her hair fanned, waving in the current, her eyes open, unseeing.

They knew it was his daughter, she told him, because there was a credit card in her name in her wallet, a driving licence. She told him that when they opened the computer, her name was on the welcome screen, above the rectangular box for the password. She said that, even though they had not recovered a body, they had no doubt about what had happened. His daughter had taken her own life. She had taken off her clothes and folded them carefully, which was common, surprisingly common in the case of suicides. Nobody really knew why. Guilt maybe, not wanting to leave a mess behind them. The folded clothes were a kind of subconscious expression of that. Maybe.

Fortune listened to the voice on the phone without speaking. The woman sounded kind, although he suspected that she was talking more than she normally would, was talking too much because of nerves. Did he really need to know why his daughter had folded her clothes?

Anyway, she told him, Sophie's effects had been sent to the police station, and if he wanted them, all he had to do was ask at the desk, with two forms of identification, one of which had to be photographic. Was that okay? She said that Marsh had said it would be easier for him than his wife. That he was nearer. Fortune told her that yes, that was okay and yes, he wanted his daughter's effects. She told him that she was very sorry to have called with such bad news and that, if he needed to speak to somebody, she had a number for a counsellor who was very good and specialized in this kind of thing. By this kind of thing, Fortune imagined, she meant something less specific than drowned daughters, but he told her no anyway, that he didn't need to speak to anybody. He thanked her and she told him that she was sorry again and hung up, leaving

Fortune alone in his hotel room, more alone than he had ever felt before.

At the police station, Fortune had to wait while a woman argued with the uniform behind the desk about a seagull she had found. She had it in a cardboard box. She was telling the policeman that it had a broken wing and that it would die if it didn't receive treatment, while he was patiently explaining to her that this wasn't a veterinary surgery and that there was nothing he could do, that injured seagulls weren't a police matter. The seagull sat quietly in its box as this was going on, regarding its surroundings stiffly through its yellow eye. Eventually she agreed to leave, holding her box in front of her with as much offended dignity as she could muster.

'Help you?'

'My name's Fortune. You have the belongings of my daughter, Sophie Fortune.'

The policeman nodded. 'She lost them?'

'She ...' Fortune stopped, couldn't bring himself to say the words. *She killed herself.* 'She died.'

'Oh. I'm sorry. Right. Wait here, please.' He left, leaving Fortune alone in the station's quiet waiting room. There were seats lining two walls, facing each other, and posters above them warning people about car theft and child abuse and the dangers of living without smoke alarms.

'Mr Fortune?'

Fortune turned. The policeman was holding a box, another box, this one taped closed. He placed it on the counter gently, almost reverentially. Fortune was grateful for this gesture, even if his daughter's final possessions had only been taped up in a brown cardboard box.

'I'll need to see some identification. Sorry.'

Fortune showed the policeman his passport, put it back in his pocket and picked up the box. It wasn't heavy.

'Thank you,' he said.

'Not a problem,' the policeman said. 'I'm sorry for your loss.'

Fortune nodded and walked out of the station carrying his daughter's things. He walked down the steps, put the box down on a bench, took out his mobile and called his wife. She would have been told, he guessed, but he had to call. He listened to the phone ring, dreading the conversation and feeling relief when it went through to voicemail. He didn't leave a message. What could he say? Instead, he lit a cigarette. As the smoke hit his lungs, he coughed, coughed and coughed and coughed, couldn't stop.

'Christ. That doesn't sound good.'

Fortune turned to see Marsh, who had followed him down the steps. 'No,' he managed.

'My father died of lung cancer,' Marsh said. 'That what you've got?'

Fortune nodded, trying to swallow a cough, keep it behind his teeth. It turned into an undignified splutter. 'Apparently.'

'Serious?'

'Might be. Haven't seen my doctor. He's in Dubai.'

'Oh.' Marsh looked at Fortune. 'Listen, I'm sure it's no consolation, but I am sorry.'

Fortune nodded again. 'Thanks.'

'I wanted to catch you before you left. I don't suppose we'll see each other again.'

'No?' Fortune frowned.

'We're closing the investigation. Officially.'

'What? No. It's still ... You haven't found her.'

'We might never find her,' Marsh said. 'It's a big river. I'm sorry, but I'm certain that she's in it. There's no other scenario.'

'Of course there is,' said Fortune, though he couldn't think of one.

He sat down on the bench, next to the box of Sophie's things. He put his forearms on his legs and looked at the ground.

'What'll you do?'

'I don't know,' he said to the ground. 'Go back to Dubai.'

'I'm sorry,' Marsh said again. Fortune nodded, still not looking up. He felt Marsh walk away, his footsteps. He sat on the bench for some minutes before getting up, picking up the box and heading off to find a taxi.

The box contained jeans, trainers, an AC/DC T-shirt, hooded top, Puffa jacket, underwear. Her wallet, too. If you didn't know better, Fortune thought, the possessions could have belonged to a man. Except for the bra. He looked through the wallet. Credit cards, driving licence, business cards: a photographer, a freelance journalist. Couple of restaurants, a bar. Environmental Health, somebody's name; must have been one of the officers who'd come to her house about the noise, the partying. He put it all to one side and opened her computer.

It was password-protected and Fortune tried the usual suspects: her birthday, 1234, 'password'. None of them worked, although he hadn't expected them to. He sat in front of the screen, wondering whether he should even be looking. It felt as if he was in her room, hunting for her diary, poking around in places he had no right to be. He had, once. Not looked for her diary, but gone through her drawers, found a packet of cigarettes. He remembered her face when he had confronted her about it. No remorse, just anger that he had dared to disregard her right to privacy. A huge argument, refereed by his wife, who had, ultimately, taken Sophie's side. Perhaps she'd been right. Probably she'd been right.

He scrolled through his phone and called Alex in Dubai. It was late over there, gone midnight. Oh well.

'Fortune?'

'Am I waking you up?'

'No. Yes. Yes, of course you are, it's late, you know?'

'I need your help with something.'

'Yeah?'

'Do you know how to hack into a computer? A Mac?'

'What? Fortune …'

'Do you know how?'

'Um …' Fortune imagined Alex sitting up in bed, rubbing his face, trying to wake up. 'Hack into a Mac? Why?'

'They found my daughter's things. Next to a river.'

'They … Christ, Fortune, I'm sorry.'

'Thanks. The thing is, I can't get into her machine.'

'Okay. Okay.' Alex was silent, thinking. 'You in front of it?'

'Yes.'

'Okay.' Alex sighed, thought some more. Said, 'Do exactly what I tell you.'

Five minutes later, Fortune was in, looking at the screen of his daughter's laptop, a door into her life. He thanked Alex, told him he appreciated it.

'No problem. Fortune?'

'Yeah?'

'Are you coming back now?'

Fortune thought of Marsh, the investigation, which would soon be closed, if it hadn't been already. 'Soon. Very soon.'

'It's terrible here, you know? That money, it's still missing.'

'I know. I'll be back soon. Promise.'

'Okay. Please don't call me again today.'

'I won't. Thanks, Alex.'

Fortune hung up, put his fingers on the keyboard of the computer. He wondered what he would find. Wondered whether, whatever it might be, he even wanted to find it. He put the cursor over File, chose New Finder Window, and started looking.

twenty

21/2

It gets worse. It just gets worse and worse and worse.

Today the police came, again. This time it was the drug squad. They told me that there'd been reports of dealing from my flat, people coming and going, the smell of drugs, and loud music. They told me that they took any allegations of drug dealing seriously, and could they come in? It turned out I didn't have a choice as they just pushed right past me and started looking around. I asked them if they had a warrant and they said they didn't need one. A male officer said it with a smile, as if to say, what are you going to do about it?

They didn't find anything, because there's nothing to find except sleeping pills. A lot of sleeping pills. Enough, if you know what I mean. More than enough.

Charlie Jackson's taking me to court.

Oh, and Larry fired me.

I can't write any more. I need to go to sleep.

Josh, please come soon. Come very soon. Before it's too late.

Fortune had found it on her desktop, dated just weeks ago. His daughter's filing system was a mess, her desktop crowded, chaotic, folders within folders, photos, documents. He hadn't known where to begin. He pushed the computer away, across the glass-topped table in his hotel room. The room was gloomy, the screen of the computer bright. He tried to process what he had just read. What had been going on in his daughter's life? Could she have become so delusional that she didn't believe it was her creating these problems? He had read of schizophrenia, heard it mentioned by doctors during the worst of Sophie's episodes, the times she was lowest and most irrational. Had she been that ill?

The other alternative was that she was right, and she was blameless. That all this, all the incidents, the complaints, the investigations, had been caused by somebody else. But he thought of his daughter outside Charlie Jackson's home, carrying a knife. That had happened. That had definitely happened. He scratched at his head, rubbed it hard. My Sophie, he thought. What happened to you?

Finally, there was Josh. Who was Josh? He'd never heard of him; Jean hadn't mentioned him, or Jessica. He must be a boyfriend, a boyfriend who worked away, like Fortune worked away. He hoped that was all he and Josh had in common. Sophie deserved better.

He opened a browser and typed *Charlie Jackson* into the search bar. He hit Images and looked at shot after shot of the man his daughter had become obsessed with. He was good-looking, around thirty, blue eyes. Very blue, the kind of blue that seems unreal, that you can't help looking at. Dirty-blond hair, never clean-shaven in any shot. He had a kind of Hollywood action-hero look, the blue eyes undercutting that, giving him an innocence, an open vulnerability behind the square jaw, the regular features. Confident, but sensitive. Fortune shook his head at the screen. Jesus. What did he sound like? Jackson was pictured in headshots, on red carpets, holding awards, arm around glamorous women. He looked like he had an okay life. Nothing to complain about. He looked the kind of man who would have it easy as long as he lived.

Fortune picked up his phone and called the number Jessica had given him. She'd told him to call any time, not to hesitate.

'Hello?'

'Jessica? It's Fortune.'

There was a brief pause as she went through her mental Rolodex. 'Hi.'

'I wondered if I could ask a favour.'

'Sure. I'll try.'

'First, did my daughter, did Sophie … did she mention a boyfriend?'

Another pause as Jessica thought. Fortune heard laughter in the background, faint music. 'Am I interrupting?'

'Mmm? No, no, I'm on a boat. Heading up the Thames, some release party for a …' She dropped her voice. 'For an awful record made by an even more awful reality TV personality. It's horrendous. She's pissed already, wearing stilettos on a boat, can hardly stand up. If she doesn't puke before we get there, I'll eat my metaphorical hat.'

'Sounds like fun.'

'Like stubbing a toe,' Jessica said. 'Boyfriend, did you say?' She thought again. 'I think she was seeing somebody, but I never met him. We didn't socialize much, outside work.'

'His name's Josh.'

'Doesn't ring a bell. Oh, there she goes. She's down.' Jessica laughed. 'Christ's sake.'

'I want to talk to Charlie Jackson.'

'Hang on.' Jessica spoke to somebody her end. 'Can someone pick her up, please? And stop her drinking any more? She'll be on the six o'clock at this rate.' She came back to Fortune. 'Sorry. Don't know why I care anyway. The drunker she gets, the better the story. Anyway, Charlie Jackson. Why do you want to talk to him?'

'Just ...' Fortune wondered. 'I just want to find out what happened.'

'She stalked him, Fortune. She became obsessed, wouldn't let go.'

'I need to hear it from him.'

Jessica sighed. 'I can't.'

'Just tell me how I can contact him.'

'I don't have his number.'

'You can get it.'

'Probably,' said Jessica. 'But I won't. It gets out, I'm finished.' She was silent for a moment. 'I can tell you where he lives. That kind of information, anyone can get hold of. I can do that.'

'Thanks.'

'No problem. But Fortune? You don't think you should leave it? I don't think you'll like what you find out.'

'Maybe,' said Fortune. 'But I wasn't there for her before. I need to do this.'

'Okay. Okay, fine. Listen, I've got to go. Things are getting interesting this end. I'll text you.' Fortune heard shouting, something smashing.

'Thanks.'

'Delete the text.'

'Will do.'

'Bye.'

Jessica hung up. Fortune imagined her prising the champagne glass out of the reality lady's garishly painted fingertips. What a world his daughter had fallen into.

Fortune spent half an hour looking through files, folders, photos. Chaos, just like his daughter's life had become. He found scraps of information, numbers of people he'd never heard of, ideas for features, interview notes, video clips. Unfinished articles and pages of random thoughts. Her boss – what had his name been? Larry. Larry had told him that Sophie had been good, had talent. Looking through the random clutter of her files, Fortune couldn't find much evidence of that. Just the same Sophie he'd always known, careless, unfocused, infuriating.

He gave up and closed the computer. He'd look again when he had the energy. Right now, he felt tired, his chest tight. He realized he hadn't eaten since lunchtime the day before, but he didn't feel hungry. He lay down on the bed and waited for Jessica to text him Jackson's address. He wondered what he'd do when he met him.

twenty-one

FORTUNE HAD NO PROBLEM WITH CONFRONTATION. YOU couldn't run a company's global operations without getting into people's faces now and then. You couldn't deal with ridiculous, unreasonable targets handed down from above without sometimes being unreasonable to the people below you. Piling on the pressure, handing out ultimatums, that was his job. Maximizing efficiency.

Still, he wasn't feeling exactly comfortable. Charlie Jackson's house was on one of those exclusive London squares with a private garden in the middle, the gates locked, keys only held by the wealthy residents. It had its own tennis court, and benches, which Fortune could be sitting on. Instead he was standing on the pavement opposite Jackson's house, smoking and, he couldn't help but think, looking plenty suspicious. What kind of person stands on a pavement for over two hours, doing nothing? It was cold, and it was windy. At least it wasn't raining. As Fortune thought this, a fat drop of rain landed on the burning ember of his cigarette with a weak fizz. He looked down at it in exasperation. Why hadn't he brought an umbrella?

Jessica had come through with the address and Fortune had arrived at ten, rung the buzzer and waited for an answer. Nobody home. So he'd waited. And waited. Even having a dog would help. People walk dogs. Middle-aged men walk dogs. Middle-aged men don't loiter on pavements for hours. Unless they're homeless, and Fortune didn't look homeless. He didn't look that healthy, he was willing to admit. But he was still presentable. No, what he needed was a workman's tent, like in the films. That or a plumber's van, something he could park up for hours. That was what he needed.

At least there weren't many people about, nobody giving him suspicious looks. The only activity was at the other end of the square, where there was some kind of building project going on, looked like work on a basement. Fortune had read about the super-rich in London excavating their basements, digging two, three floors down. The opposite of Dubai, where everything was about building upwards. Fortune suspected it was all to do with penis envy, the Arab man's inferiority complex. My skyscraper's taller than yours. What did that say about Russian oligarchs who dug down? Something to do with guilt, burying their millions rather than flaunting them. Maybe. Who knew? Fortune sighed. He was bored, so bored.

The rain got harder and Fortune looked up bleakly at the leafless tree he was standing under. Not a lot of protection there. He checked his watch. Past midday. Enough. He'd come back another time. He started to walk away, waiting for a black cab to pass before he crossed the road. It stopped further up the street and Charlie Jackson stepped out and handed money through the driver's window. Fortune hurried up the street. Jackson was walking up the steps to his door, key in his hand.

'Mr Jackson?'

Jackson turned and looked down at Fortune. His eyes really were that blue. He seemed preoccupied, busy. 'Yes?'

'I wondered if I could talk to you.'

'About what?' said Jackson. 'Actually, you know what, no, I haven't got the time.' He had a London accent, a kind of refined cockney that Fortune couldn't decide was authentic or not.

'It's important,' he said.

'So is me getting in and taking a piss,' said Jackson. 'Fact, that's more important. So see ya.' He turned to the door, put his key in.

'It's about my daughter.'

Jackson stiffened; Fortune saw it in his back, his shoulders. 'Oh?' He probably lived in fear of angry fathers demanding to know what he'd done with their daughters. What he'd done *to* them.

'Sophie Fortune.'

Jackson turned. 'You're kidding. Her? You're the dad?'

'I'm her father.'

'Well, my son, that's some daughter you've got there. One in a million.'

'I want to speak to you about her.'

'Listen, I'm gasping for a leak, and anyway, I've got nothing to say.' Jackson paused. 'You know, you shouldn't be talking to me anyway. There's a court case, you know that, right?'

'I know.'

'All right, cool, cool. Very cool.' Jackson smiled. 'So, here's a suggestion. Why don't you piss off and leave me alone?'

Fortune watched Jackson. There was a half-smile on the younger man's face, the beginnings of a contemptuous smirk, an easy confidence. Fortune didn't take to it one bit. He walked to the bottom of the steps, climbed up.

'You know she's missing?'

'I heard.'

'They found her computer. I took a look at it.'

'Oh?'

'Yes. And I found something, something about you. Something I don't think anybody else has seen.' He paused. 'Yet.'

'Bullshit. Utter bullshit.'

'Photos.' Fortune had no idea where he was going with this. He'd found nothing. But at least Jackson was no longer smiling. 'Like I said, nobody has seen it yet.'

Jackson glanced up and down the street, as if to check the press weren't already circling. He looked down at Fortune and sighed. 'All right. You'd better come in.'

Who, thought Fortune, put an aquarium in, actually *in*, a wall? The inside of Charlie Jackson's house looked like one of those places he'd occasionally seen on MTV, the kind of place a rock star would design. Actually, scratch that. It looked like the kind of place a sheikh would design, if he had taste. Which didn't mean that Jackson had taste, he just had more than your average Arab plutocrat. There were cream leather sofas in the living room, a glass coffee table, a chandelier that looked like it had been stolen from Versailles. Jackson stood on the cream rug, facing Fortune defiantly. He was short, a small man. He was probably carrying around a lot of resentment, Fortune thought, a long-held inferiority complex.

'I won't offer you coffee,' he said.

Fortune nodded. 'I just want to know what happened. With my daughter.'

'What happened?' Jackson looked about, at his sofas, made a decision. 'Might as well sit down,' he said reluctantly.

Fortune sat. Jackson sat opposite him, the glass coffee table between them.

'What happened was, she tried to set me up with some underage tart. When that didn't work out, she turned full-on bunny boiler. Like, psychotic.'

Psycho Bitch, thought Fortune. 'How so?' he asked.

Jackson frowned, looked at Fortune in puzzlement. 'You don't know?'

'Not really.'

'Emails, bombarded me. Wouldn't leave me alone. Threats. Christ, you know she was completely deranged, right? Up her tree.'

'No.'

'Come on. You were her father.'

'Why do you say "were"?' asked Fortune. 'Do you know something I don't?'

That stopped Jackson for a moment. Then he shook his head, smiled. 'So you're as crazy as she is. Like father like mental daughter. Oh dear.'

'What else?' said Fortune, trying to ignore Jackson's smirking contempt.

'What else? You want to know?'

Fortune nodded. 'I would.'

'Really? You sure? All right. Wait there.'

Jackson stood and left the room. Fortune looked around while he waited. There were black-and-white photos of nudes on the walls, framed. They looked like the kind of thing you'd see in a Pirelli calendar, prurient yet tasteful. Well, kind of.

'Here.' Jackson came back into the room and carelessly threw an A4 envelope onto the coffee table. 'Take a look. Take a good look.'

Fortune sat forward and reached for the envelope. It was already open. He upended it and shook out what was inside. He saw a photo, a naked form but not like the ones on the walls.

This was young, very young, and frightened and contorted and in pain. He looked away, picked up the envelope and covered the photo with it.

'Jesus.'

'From your daughter. She sent it to me. Sent a whole lot. Nice, huh?'

'I …' Fortune struggled for words. 'I don't know what to say.'

'The police knew what to say. They told her that it was an offence to possess these kinds of images, told her she was sick. They took them away, thank God. Only got this one because it arrived later. You get a good look?'

Fortune didn't answer.

'She denied everything, that's what the police told me. Told me she lost it with them. Mental bitch.'

Fortune put his head in his hands and closed his eyes. The image he had seen, the photo, reappeared in his mind, as unwelcome as the words *Psycho Bitch*. Like the body he'd seen in the morgue, there were some things you couldn't unsee.

'And turning up here, shouting, screaming. I wouldn't let her in. My neighbours, coming out of their houses, Jesus Christ. I called the Old Bill, they arrive, van full of them, find a knife. A big kitchen knife.'

'I was told,' said Fortune. 'The police told me.'

Jackson nodded. 'So come on,' he said. 'Let's have it. What do you think you've found?'

Fortune looked up. 'What?'

'On her computer. What is it?'

Fortune prided himself on his honesty. He wasn't, he knew, good at lying. 'Photos,' he said again, hearing how lame he sounded.

Jackson raised his eyebrows. 'Oh? Of what? Me romping with some schoolgirl? High on drugs in some hotel room?'

'Maybe.'

Jackson looked closely at Fortune, his blue eyes narrowed. 'You're talking crap, aren't you? There's nothing.'

'How do you know?' said Fortune. Jesus, he sounded like a schoolboy, clumsily bluffing, pathetically transparent.

'All right,' said Jackson, standing up. 'Out. Get out of my house. Trust me, I will call the police. Thanks to your daughter, I've got the wankers on speed dial.'

Fortune stood and looked at Jackson, who was smiling, an expression of arrogance mixed with pity.

'But you did it, didn't you?' he said. 'Slept with that underage girl. Then got to her. That happened, right?'

Jackson shook his head. 'You sad little boy scout. Just get out.'

'My daughter was right,' Fortune said. 'Whatever happened, she was right about you.'

'Out.'

'I'll see you again.'

'Sure. Sure you will.'

Fortune turned and walked out of the room, down Jackson's hall to his front door. As he opened it, Jackson spoke from behind him.

'You know, whatever happened to her? To your daughter? She had it coming. Believe me, the mad bitch had it coming.'

Fortune paused, considered turning around, defending Sophie's memory. But if he was honest, he didn't know what the truth was. Didn't know his daughter, had no idea what she'd become. He walked slowly down the steps, back into the drizzle. He badly needed a cigarette.

Smoking and walking, Fortune thought back on what Jackson had told him, while trying not to think about the picture he had been shown. It existed in his mind as something ghastly, monstrous, hardly seen and impossible to understand. That people could do those things. To children. And what was his daughter doing, looking at such photos and sending them to Jackson? He didn't want to believe she had done it, had sent the picture, but he couldn't ignore the evidence. She had brought a knife with her to his house. Why? he thought. Sophie, my Sophie. Why?

His phone rang and he picked up. 'Hello?'

'Ah, yes, Mr, ah, Fortune.'

Dr Aziz. Fortune dropped his cigarette, put it out guiltily. 'Yes?'

'You, ah, are still in … You are not in Dubai?'

'Still in London.'

'You, ah, you really need to return. You need treatment.'

'Yeah.' Fortune looked about him with the phone to his ear, at a pair of acrobatic starlings, a double-decker advertising a beach holiday. 'I know.'

'So, you are, ah … you are coming back?'

Fortune did not answer for some moments, then he sighed. 'Yes,' he said. 'Yes, I'm coming back.'

twenty-two

ONE OF THE PERKS OF BUSINESS TRAVEL WAS ACCESS TO THE lounge. No screaming children, no package holidays. No groups of teenage holidaymakers, getting into the spirit before their plane left. Fortune looked around the lounge at the other privileged few, mostly men, past middle age, wearing suits. Comfortable, complacent. Just like him. Unremarkable. Unlovable.

A voice broke the calm, an announcement. A delayed flight, QR4584 to Dubai. Fortune's plane, which apparently had some technical issue. He looked about the lounge for expressions of petulance, the snap of a newspaper, angry jabbing at a phone's keyboard. There were one or two, men like him who had places to go, business to attend to, and couldn't afford to wait. He sat for some moments, then reached into his hand luggage and took out his daughter's computer. He didn't know why he'd taken it with him, perhaps to keep up the pretence that he wasn't really abandoning his investigation, if you could call it that. To maintain the fiction that he hadn't given up on her, accepted her suicide.

The clutter and confusion of Sophie's desktop was about as far from the efficient, smooth, organized environment of Fortune's airport lounge as it was possible to be. How did she ever find anything? How *had* she ever found anything? he corrected himself. Past tense. Get used to it, he thought, she's gone, though he still didn't believe it, not really. He clicked on a folder titled 'Junk', looked at the sub-files inside. 'Personal', 'More junk', 'Musings', 'Weird junk'. He smiled despite himself, clicked on 'Weird junk'. Inside were Word files, all with different titles. 'Way home', 'Boys', 'Things I don't dare say'. He opened up the last one and read what Sophie had written:

I have no idea what 'good' wine tastes like
I can't do long division, haven't got a clue
I don't like children, or ever want them (I don't think)
Giving people a tip makes me stupidly anxious
Sometimes the only thing that makes me happy is gin
I can't contemplate the future
I don't like myself
Other people's bad news sometimes makes me feel better
I wish I had the nerve to be ruder to people

Fortune could identify with one or two of them. Gin, certainly. He approved of that. And not liking himself. Plus, he was fairly sure he'd have been able to help Sophie with the last one. The thought made him smile briefly, before a picture of the river where they had found his daughter's belongings, the water swollen and swirling, came into his mind, imagined but still all too real. Again, he felt a strange guilt at breaching her privacy. He thought about closing the computer, leaving her secrets undisturbed. What right did he have, after all? It wasn't like he had earned Sophie's trust, had done anything to deserve this intimacy.

He closed the document, went back and opened up 'Personal'. There were many documents, and Fortune had looked at most of them. Mostly admin stuff, rental agreements, old payslips. There was a folder called 'Forget it', which he hadn't looked in yet. He opened it. There was only one document inside, titled 'To Dad'.

Fortune gazed at it for some time. *To Dad*. The business lounge was hushed and the screen, the title of the document, seemed as loaded with power and quiet menace as a bomb. *To Dad*. What had she written to him? He could not imagine that it would be good, that it would be an affectionate note to a loving father. He hadn't been a loving father. He had been a poor father, a neglectful and distant father. He knew this. Did he need to read about it, to have it confirmed to him by his dead daughter? He looked at the screen with a feeling of dread. Because he couldn't not read it. But he so wished he didn't have to.

He looked up, saw that his plane would not be boarding for an hour. What else was there to do? He took a breath, considered going for a cigarette, decided against it. After. After he had read this.

Dear Dad,

It's been a long time since we properly spoke. It's been years, so many years, and I feel bad about that. I wish we could talk. I wish we could erase all this time that we've been strangers to each other, and start back like we used to be. When I'd hold your hand and you'd swing me up onto your shoulders, and you were Dad, and I didn't want anything else but you.

I know that it's my fault, or at least, a lot of it is. I know that I was difficult and you didn't know what to do with me, what to say to me. The thing is that I didn't know what to do with myself either, and I needed you to tell me that it would be okay, that I was worth something. That you loved me. I always wanted you to tell me that you loved me, but the worse I got, the less you did. Until I realized that you didn't love me any more, that I'd ruined it all and it was too late.

Perhaps this is just something that happens, something inevitable, when two people can't understand each other. I do still love you so much, and I don't want to think that you left me, walked away because you had had enough. But I have to say this to you. I wish you hadn't. I wish you had been able to make some effort to understand me and to help me. Just a little effort. Who knows? It might have helped. It really might have.

Do you remember when I was little, and we got separated on the Tube? And I was all alone and I had to wait, and then you came and found me? I wonder if you remember. I said to you that I knew you'd come, that I never doubted it. I knew you'd be there for me, because you're my dad.

I can't say that any more, and just the thought of it makes me want to cry. I don't blame you. I've been so difficult, and for that I apologize, from the bottom of my heart. And I know that it's too late for us, and that I will never send this letter. I don't even have your address. But I want to say sorry, and that I wish so so much that I could still say that you'll be there for me, just like you were once.

Love,

Your daughter, Sophie xxx

Fortune didn't know how long he stared at that screen, at the document that, with a generosity and kindness he would never have the chance to reciprocate, had laid bare all the faults in their relationship. Sophie, he thought. It's me who's sorry. I've been sorry for years, but never had the courage or humility to tell you. And now it's too late, and you've left me this letter, and it will haunt me for the rest of my life.

'Sir?'

Fortune looked up, saw a woman standing above him. She was looking at him with concern and Fortune realized that he had been crying, that his cheeks were wet with tears.

'Are you okay?'

'Yes,' Fortune said. 'Yes, fine.'

'Could I get you anything?'

'No thanks.' The woman turned, but before she left, Fortune said, 'Actually, yes. Could I have a gin and tonic?'

'Of course. You're sure you're okay?'

'I'm okay,' said Fortune. 'Just a gin.' He paused. 'Thank you.'

The woman came back with his drink and Fortune drank it in one hit, feeling his heart expand and warm as it hit him. Christ, he needed a cigarette. He put his daughter's computer away, picked up his bag and headed for the exit, walking through Departures to the smoking area. He lit up in the cold air and took a lungful, breathed it in deeply and tried to hold it, to stifle a cough. A young woman was smoking too and she nodded to him, the secret fraternity of the unfashionable. Fortune nodded back and heard his phone ring.

'Fortune?'

'It's Alex. Just checking you're on your way.'

'Yes. My flight's been delayed, but I'm at the airport.'

'Okay. Cool.' Alex sounded relieved.

'Is there any news?' asked Fortune. 'What's the situation?'

'The situation is the money's still missing. Sadler's working on a new angle, something about the specific amount.'

'The amount?'

'Yes. He thinks it's significant. Like, why not just steal a nice round number? Why steal just under ninety million? Just over seventy? He's got some hang-up about it.'

'Maybe it's down to exchange rates,' said Fortune.

'What I said. But he doesn't agree. Says that's irrelevant. Says there must be something to it.'

'All right,' said Fortune. 'I guess that's why we're paying him. Well, I'll give you a call when I land.'

'Do that.'

Fortune hung up, put out his cigarette and headed back to the lounge, all the way telling himself that, whatever the letter from his daughter had said, he definitely wasn't abandoning her this time. There was just nothing left for him to do.

Business travellers boarded before the rest of the passengers and Fortune was one of the first onto the plane, seated by the window near the front. He could barely touch the seat in front with his feet. While he waited for the other passengers to fight their way into Economy, he scrolled through emails on his phone, looking for one from Alex. He couldn't remember when he'd sent it, must have been four, five days ago. Maybe six.

'Welcome on board, sir,' said a stewardess. 'If you need anything, just call with the button above you. Anything at all.'

'Thanks,' said Fortune. Business class. You could almost believe that they genuinely cared. Almost. He scrolled down, opened up an email from Alex. Not that one. Closed it, scrolled further down, found another. This was the one. With the amount stolen, the first amount. $89,917,042. A lot of money, a huge sum. But Sadler was right, it was a strange sum. Why not just take a hundred?

'Could you put your seat belt on, please, sir?' the same stewardess asked him. She was English, long dark hair, very red nails. Pretty. Fortune fastened his belt. 'Sure.'

He looked back at his phone. There was something about the number. It seemed to hold some kind of significance, but he didn't know what. Some meaning greater than just the sheer amount of money it represented. He looked at it, shook his head. Maybe it was because of the letter he had read, the letter from his daughter. He just wasn't thinking straight. That was probably it.

His daughter. He felt a stillness in his chest, a sudden arrest of movement. His daughter.

'Excuse me,' he called to the stewardess. She was walking away from him, rows away, but turned and walked back. 'Yes, sir?'

'Do you have a pen and paper?'

'A pen, yes.' She took it out of her skirt pocket. 'No paper. Sorry.'

'Doesn't matter,' said Fortune. He pulled out the in-flight magazine in front of him. 'You don't mind?'

'It's yours,' said the stewardess.

Fortune opened it, found a perfume advert with a lot of white space, wrote the number down. 89,917,042. Underneath, he wrote the same number backwards, carefully, making sure he got it right. That it *was* right, even though it couldn't be, couldn't possibly be; even though it was wrong, wrong, wrong.

240,719,98.

24.07.1998.

The day his daughter had been born. The twenty-fourth of July 1998.

He unbuckled his seat belt, stood and reached into the overhead bin for his hand luggage. He pulled it down and walked the short distance to the exit. The same stewardess was standing next to it. It was closed.

'Sir?'

'I need to get off this plane.'

'But, sir, the doors are closed. We're about to leave.'

'I need to get out.'

'But ...'

'Now. Now. I need to get out right now. Do you understand?'

'I ... Wait, please.'

She walked quickly down the aisle, found a colleague, an older man, and spoke to him. The man approached Fortune.

'I'm afraid it's too late to leave the plane, sir,' he said. 'We've completed boarding.'

'I need to get off,' said Fortune. 'Right now.'

'I'm sorry, sir,' the man said. The stewardess was watching in concern. 'It's just not possible.'

Fortune looked at the door. There was a large lever on it, with a curved arrow pointing to the left and the word 'OPEN'. It looked possible to him. He reached for the lever, pulled it and felt the door give.

'Sir!' the steward shouted. Somewhere behind him he heard a woman scream, a passenger. Fortune didn't care. There was no way this plane was taking off with him on it. No way in the world.

twenty-three

SOMEBODY IS DOING THIS TO ME, SOMEBODY WHO KNOWS FAR too much about me. It might be Charlie Jackson, it could be him. I don't know. But somebody is trying to destroy my life by taking it apart bit by bit. And you know what? I'm not going to let it happen. I will not let it happen.

Yesterday, Sam the World's Worst Landlord™ called to tell me that I was being evicted. For some reason, and I don't know why, I can't say why, this pissed me off even more than getting the sack, even more than all the crap about stalking Jackson, even more than when they found my knife at his place. Kicking me out of my own flat, making me homeless, it's just ... it's not on. It's not fair.

I knocked on the door of every apartment, house and shop within shouting distance of my flat, and I asked everyone who answered, 'Have you had any reason to complain about noise recently?' And you know what? They all said no, that they hadn't heard anything unusual, and that it was pretty quiet, really, for a street in Hackney. We should count ourselves lucky.

Yeah, right.

I had an interview with a solicitor, who has been given my case, the one Charlie Jackson has brought against me. He was young and didn't seem to rate my chances of getting off too highly. It was in his office, which was small and sandwiched between a betting shop and an off-licence called Bargain Booze. I sat down and he spent a few minutes leafing through my file before looking up at me across his desk and saying:

'Do you have a record of mental illness?'

No preamble, straight in there. No guessing what angle he was looking to take.

'Yes,' I said.

'Have you ever been accused of harassment before?'

'No,' I said. 'Because I've never harassed anyone in my life.'

He ignored this declaration of innocence and instead said, 'Have you ever attempted suicide?'

'Yes.'

'How often?'

Do you know what? I had to think. I really did. 'Four times,' I said, eventually. One of them wasn't even half-serious, but I guess all attempts count, particularly if you end up in hospital having your stomach pumped.

'Are you on medication?'

'No.'

'Have you been?'

'Yes.'

'What kind?'

'Prozac,' I said. 'Lithium. Some anti-psychotic I can't remember the name of. Chlor something.'

'Why did you stop taking them?' he said.

Because they made me shake, I didn't say. Because they made me sweat through the night and lose interest in everything, robbed me of any emotional stake in this world. Because what

I needed was purpose and independence and somebody to love and to love me, and I'd never get that sleepwalking through every day. What I actually said was:

'Because I got better.'

'We'll need to do a psychological evaluation,' he said. 'See what comes out.'

'You think I did it,' I said. 'Don't you?'

'It doesn't matter what I think,' he said. 'Does it?'

So here I am. No job, nowhere to live, unless I get sent to prison, which according to my useless solicitor is looking pretty likely. How the hell has somebody managed to do this to me? The coward. The petty, malicious, sneaky, odious coward.

Josh says I need to get away. He says that by staying where I am, I'm just inviting more trouble. He's flying to Paris in a couple of days and he's given me the name of a restaurant and a time to meet. He's going to be there to meet me, in another country, far from all of this. It's the first thing I've looked forward to for weeks. For a day or two, all this will be gone, distant. Who knows? Maybe I won't come back. How would that be? Start a new life in some faraway country where nobody can get to me. I'll see what Josh says. Maybe he'll come with me. Imagine. Just imagine that.

twenty-four

IN THE POST-9/11 WORLD OF GLOBAL JIHAD AND SHOE bombers, people opening the doors of moving aeroplanes were treated with hostility bordering on the abusive. Fortune's hands had been cuffed behind him with plastic ties and a security guard had hustled him through Departures, holding his hands high behind his back so that his shoulders burned and his own momentum caused him to almost run. Three more guards had hurried alongside them, passing aghast passengers waiting to board other planes, mouths open in shock that it, that *terror*, was happening again, here, *now*. One of the guards had run ahead and unlocked a nondescript door in a carpeted corridor, the guard holding his arms pushing him through.

They had placed him in a windowless room with two chairs and a table. He had been made to stand with his legs apart and hands resting on the wall as they took away his passport, wallet, phone, asked him to take his shoes off. It was hot and bright and very, very quiet in the room and Fortune had not been able to avoid thinking of extraordinary rendition, wondering whether Afghans or Syrians had also been held here before unmarked planes flew them to underground facilities in Poland, Ukraine, Jordan. The walls were a pastel green and there was nothing to drink and nowhere to go to the lavatory, and one of the fluorescent tubes flickered with an angry buzz. They had left him without telling him when they might be back or what might happen to him. He accepted that jihadists came in all manner of guises, but still. Surely they didn't come in slightly-overweight-ex-pat-fifty-four-year-old guise. Or perhaps they did, hence his treatment. Whatever, he was stuck where he was, with nothing to do but think about what he had just discovered.

That the amount of money stolen had corresponded with his daughter's birthday was clear. The question was, could it be a coincidence? Fortune had left school at sixteen and maths wasn't his strongest subject, but he imagined the odds were heavily stacked against it. In which case, what did it mean? Did it mean that Sophie had been right, and there had been somebody tormenting her, playing with her, setting her up? And what kind of person was capable of stealing a hundred and sixty million dollars from one of the most secure banks in the Middle East? He couldn't get a handle on it, couldn't find any way of making it add up. It sounded crazy. Hell, it *was* crazy, all of this. He was locked in the depths of Heathrow, in the hands of rent-a-cops who had most likely sent innocent men to be tortured in faraway lands. Crazy didn't begin to cover it.

The door opened and a man and a woman came in, both young, in their early thirties, both wearing suits. The man had rimless glasses and was clean-shaven. The woman was petite and had South Asian colouring, maybe Indian. They closed the door behind them. The man was wearing a gun at his belt, a rare enough thing in the UK to surprise Fortune, even though every cop in Dubai carried a weapon. Fortune stood up from the chair he had been sitting in.

'Mr Fortune?' the woman said.

'Yes.'

'Sit down, please,' she said. Fortune remained standing and the man said, 'Sit down. Now.'

Fortune sat, and the woman sat opposite him, the man staying at the door.

'Date of birth?' asked the woman.

'Thirteen oh-eight nineteen sixty-three,' Fortune said.

'Address?'

Fortune thought for a moment. 'In Dubai or England?'

'England.'

Fortune gave his wife's address, confirmed his mobile number, the name of his employer, his monthly salary, the date he had entered the UK, the names of his wife and daughter and the school he had attended, the grades he had achieved, five recent transactions he had made with his credit card, an insurance write-off claim from ten years ago, the make and model of car involved. He was amazed at the information they had managed to collect, so fast. His whole life in minutes.

'Who are you?' he asked.

'Doesn't matter,' said the woman. 'Not right now. You need to answer our questions.'

'I want to know who you are. Who you're with.'

'With?' said the woman. 'We're with the British government. Now, if you don't mind, stop asking questions and let me do my job.'

'Okay,' said Fortune. 'All right. Ask away.'

'Why did you open the door to the plane?'

'I wanted to get out.'

'Why?'

Why? Fortune thought about his story, how crazy it sounded. He looked at the woman. He had never seen anybody so humourless. What would she make of his explanation? Not a lot, he suspected. 'I had a panic attack.'

'Really.' She didn't seem impressed by that answer.

'I've been under a lot of stress,' he said.

'Your daughter.'

Christ, they knew that too? 'Yes.'

'Right. Took her own life?'

Fortune nodded. 'I'm not myself.'

'No.' The woman gazed at him and Fortune tried not to look away. She had brown eyes and was quite pretty, in a hard, take-no-prisoners way. 'You know that plane's still on the tarmac? We had to go through the hold, find your luggage.'

'Oh. Right.' Fortune hadn't thought of that.

'Never mind half the plane panicking. You understand that?'

'I guess,' said Fortune. He sounded like an errant schoolboy and was disgusted with himself for it. This woman was young enough to be his daughter.

'So, again. Why did you open the door?'

'I just, I needed to get out. I had this insane idea that my daughter was still alive, and that I couldn't leave her. I couldn't just, I couldn't … I couldn't abandon her.' Halfway through his explanation, Fortune realized that it was the truth. That was exactly what had happened. He just didn't mention the money. Don't mention the money, he thought. They'll think you're crazy.

'Christ's sake,' said the man at the door, but the woman held up a hand, her back to him, and he stopped talking. No question about who was in charge here, thought Fortune. He'd employ her in a second. She was his kind of manager. Tough as they came.

'All right,' she said. 'Here's what's going to happen. I'm going to keep your passport. Okay?'

'Why?'

'Why? Because I want to do some more checking, and I don't want you getting on any more planes and losing it. Fair?'

Fortune nodded. 'Fair.' Jesus, this woman commanded respect.

'Okay. Here.' She pushed a card across the table. It had her name on it, Sunita Gandham, and a number. Nothing else.

'Mysterious,' said Fortune.

'You have any problems, want to talk, you call me,' she said, ignoring him. 'If I don't answer, you leave a message. Understand?'

'Yes.'

'Where will you be staying?'

Fortune hadn't thought. Didn't know. Back to the same hotel, he guessed. At least he knew the barman. He told her the name of the hotel and the man behind her looked it up, asked him what street it was on. Asked him to describe the lobby. Fortune imagined there was a photo of it on the hotel's website and that the man was looking at it. He described it, making it sound like every other hotel lobby in the whole world, but it seemed to satisfy the man because he nodded to the woman, a quick jerk of the head.

'Okay,' she said.

'Okay?'

'Okay, you're free to go. Okay, I think you're a dickhead but I think there are extenuating circumstances. Okay, there's a decent chance I won't have to arrest you. Yes?'

Fortune nodded. 'Thank you.'

'Don't thank me. Fab? Get his things?'

The man nodded and left, and Fortune and the woman sat in

silence. After a couple of minutes, she said, 'Sounds like you've had a time of it.'

'You could say.'

'Your daughter. That's tough.'

Fortune nodded. 'Yes.'

The man called Fab came back in with Fortune's luggage, phone, wallet and shoes. Fortune stood up and took it all from him, then knelt to put his shoes back on. He tied them, feeling the burn of both sets of eyes on his neck. He stood up and waited awkwardly, not knowing what to do.

'Well?' said the woman, Sunita. 'Go on. Piss off.'

As Fortune waited for a taxi, he called Owen. It wasn't a call he wanted to make. He lit a cigarette, watched the smoke plume into the dark, cold night air as he listened to the ringing tone.

'Yes?'

'Owen? It's Fortune.'

'Fortune. You're back in Dubai?'

'No. No, I'm still in London.'

'I didn't hear that.'

'It's true. I need to stay.'

Owen was silent for a moment. 'Remember what I said?'

'I remember.'

'So that's it. You're done. Finished.'

'I need to be here.'

'And I need you here, yes, because some bastard's stolen a hundred and sixty million dollars from my bank, and my fucking head of operations, which is you, by the way, has spent the last weeks fucking about in London looking for his daughter, who, just to be clear, isn't fucking coming back.'

Fortune felt a tug in his heart, an increase in his pulse, felt his chest flood with adrenalin. To hell with it, he thought.

'You there?' said Owen.

'I'm here. I'm here, and I'm going to find my daughter, and you, you can find some other poor sap to do my job. I quit, I'm out. Good luck.'

'You fucking can't—'

'Yes I can,' interrupted Fortune, and hung up. He breathed out, found his cigarettes, lit one. As he inhaled, he had to admit that, actually, that call had felt a lot better than he had imagined.

This was the third time in five days Fortune had made the journey from the airport to his hotel, and he knew the choke points, where the traffic would be. But it was late by this time and it took under an hour, Fortune paying the extortionate fare with even more reluctance than the last two times. He checked back in, the woman behind the reception desk raising her eyebrows in enquiry, then lowering them again when she saw his face. Fortune took his key and shook his head at the porter, figured he'd parted with enough money in tips. He knew what the room looked like, how the TV worked. He'd been here twice before.

In his room, he called Alex. He owed him that. Besides, he had another question for him.

'Fortune?'

'Have you heard?'

'Owen told us. You're not coming back?'

'No. No, I'm not. I'm sorry.'

Alex sighed. 'Hell, I can't do this myself.'

'You've got Sadler. Owen will find someone to replace me.'

'Yeah. Some other big swinging dick.' Alex stopped. 'Sorry. I didn't mean ...'

'Don't worry about it.' Fortune almost laughed. 'I've got a question.'

'Yeah?'

'The second amount that was taken. How much was it exactly? I know it was around seventy million.'

'$71,023,032,' said Alex, immediately. He knows it by heart, thought Fortune, feeling a pang of guilt as he wrote the number down. He was abandoning Alex, an employee he liked and held in high regard.

'I'm sorry,' he said again.

'Yeah,' said Alex. 'Whatever. See you around.'

'I hope so.' Fortune hung up and looked at the figure he had written down. Wrote it again, starting with the last number and working backwards.

230,320,17.

23.03.2017.

The twenty-third of March. This year. Fortune looked at his watch. Ten days away. Ten days from now. The first number, the first amount stolen, had been the day his daughter had been born. This second one, what did it mean? Did it mean nothing? Or did it tell Fortune the day his daughter was destined to die?

twenty-five

'THERE ARE THINGS CALLED SOLID LEADS, AND THEN THERE'S speculation.'

Fortune was sitting opposite Marsh once more in a too-hot interview room on a cold morning, and Marsh wasn't making any of the right noises. None at all. He leant forward, presumably the better for Fortune to understand the significance of his next words.

'This? This is speculation. And the police are funded by the British taxpayer, who doesn't expect us to run around the country chasing shadows based on speculation.'

'You can't believe it's coincidence.'

'It's coincidence until something appears to make me think differently. Right now I have a missing young woman, presumed suicide, and a father who's turned up with a story that I struggle to believe.'

'So how did the money disappear?' said Fortune.

Marsh shrugged. 'Did it disappear? If it did, were you the person to steal it, to make me, us, the police, keep the investigation open? To find out the answer to that, I'll need men, bodies.' He pushed himself back into his chair, hands on the edge of the table. 'I haven't got those resources. If I asked for them, I'd be laughed at. *If* I asked for them. Which I won't, because I don't believe a word of what you say.' He sighed. 'The more I see of you, the more I see your daughter.'

'What do you mean by that?'

'I mean that you're irrational, and very difficult to deal with. Though I understand you're unwell.'

'Irrational?' said Fortune, ignoring Marsh's attempt to patronize him. 'These are numbers I'm giving you. Figures. They're verifiable. Irrational? No. Sorry, I can't accept that.' He was aware that he was raising his voice and stopped, tried to bring himself under control.

'And aggressive,' said Marsh. 'Your daughter, she gave me all that too.'

'I'm sorry,' said Fortune. 'It's just that this is new information. You have to understand that.'

Marsh didn't react, as if Fortune hadn't just spoken. Instead he said, 'What were you doing at Charlie Jackson's house?'

'What?'

'Come on. What were you doing there?'

'I just wanted to talk to him,' said Fortune. 'Get a feeling for him.'

'Uh-huh.' Marsh nodded to himself, as if what Fortune had told him made sense, which it didn't. 'He told me you were hostile, that you lied to him, tried to blackmail him. That true?'

'No,' said Fortune, although he had to concede that Jackson had a point. 'Anyway, I don't understand why you're taking his side in this. He's clearly a nasty piece of work.'

'Maybe. But he's in the public eye. He's got a reputation, people looking out for him. Lawyers. Plus, he's done nothing wrong.'

'Except for maybe kidnapping and holding my daughter.'

Marsh raised his eyebrows. 'Okay,' he said. He started to stand. 'I think we're done.'

'No,' said Fortune, trying to keep the desperation out of his voice. How many times had he pleaded with this man? 'Come on, just hear me out.'

'There's more?'

'No, just ... You need to look into this.'

But Marsh just leant forward, hands on the table. 'Mr Fortune, we're done here.'

'No we're not,' said Fortune, an attempt at bravado.

'We are,' said Marsh. 'I'm leaving, I'm going to send a uniform in, and he's going to escort you out. And next time I see your number on my phone, I'll reject the call. Clear?'

For a brief moment Fortune believed that he understood how his daughter had felt, faced with such unreasonable, uncaring authority. He realized that he was holding his shoulders hunched and tight and he relaxed them, sat slumped.

'Get some help,' said Marsh. 'Do yourself a favour.' He walked to the door and opened it and left without looking back. After a while, Fortune stood and followed him out of the room, and made his way to the entrance of the police station, a journey he'd made too many times now.

Jackson didn't look surprised so much as weary when he opened his door to see Fortune standing at the top of his steps.

'No,' he said. 'No, whatever it is, piss off.'

But Fortune had anticipated a reception along those lines and didn't say a word, just pushed past Jackson with all the strength he had left. In the entrance hall, he turned, and Jackson, still standing at his front door, holding it open, said, 'What the hell do you think you're doing?'

'Just tell me,' Fortune said. 'Just tell me the truth. I need to know.' There was supplication in his voice and he hated himself for it, hated himself for having to beg to this man, this lazy, assured, entitled bastard. But it was for his daughter, for Sophie. He needed answers.

'I'm calling the cops,' said Jackson, taking out his mobile. Fortune reached forward and pulled it out of his hand, throwing it down the steps, into the street, where it burst apart with a pleasing noise. He closed the door, turned to see Jackson looking at him in disbelief.

'Look,' said Fortune, 'I just ...' He blinked, blinked again and kept his eyes closed. He couldn't get breath into his lungs and he could feel his legs beginning to go. He lowered himself onto the first step of the staircase in Jackson's hallway. The floor was tiled, a Victorian pattern. His chest hurt; it felt like it was strapped up and somebody was pulling it tighter and tighter. He took a breath, took another, tried to control his breathing. He felt transported, as if he was having some kind of out-of-body experience, weightless, fuelled by the fury he felt. What had this man done to Sophie?

'Get out of my house,' said Jackson.

Fortune tried to control his breathing, regain control. He felt like he'd been underwater for too long, his chest straining with the lack of oxygen, burning. At last he looked up. 'I want to know where my daughter is.'

'Listen,' said Jackson. He bent down and took hold of one of the lapels of Fortune's coat. 'I. Don't. Know. Understand? I don't know what happened to that psycho bitch daughter of yours, and I don't give a damn.' He let go, stood up straight. 'Do you get it?' He raised his voice, almost a scream. 'I don't give a damn.'

'What was it?' said Fortune. 'She was going after you, so you thought you'd take it to her? Leaving those comments on her blog. Telling the police lies about how she was harassing you. Is that it?'

Jackson put his hands to his head, rubbed the sides of his face, hard. 'I don't know what you're talking about.'

'How did you get the money out?'

'What money?'

'The money.' Fortune put a hand on the banister, pulled himself to his feet. Jackson was looking at him in disbelief, like Fortune was a chimpanzee who'd somehow found its way into his house. 'What was it, a message? Because it worked. I'm here.'

'You're as crazy as she was,' said Jackson. 'Out of your mind.'

That was the second time that day Fortune had been compared to his daughter. He had no problem with that. She was his daughter, and he loved her. And he was going to find her.

'I'm not leaving,' he said, 'until—'

'Charlie?' Fortune was interrupted by a voice, a female voice. He turned to see a girl at the top of the stairs, a very young girl. She was holding a sheet around her and looked scared, her mouth open. 'Charlie? Charlie, what's happening?'

'Nothing,' said Jackson. 'Go back upstairs.'

'How old are you?' said Fortune. He turned to Jackson. 'How old is she?'

'Old enough,' said Jackson. 'Now will you please leave?'

Fortune took out his phone, held it up and took a photo of the girl. 'She doesn't look old enough.'

'Charlie? Who is he?'

'I know people who worked with my daughter,' said Fortune. 'On the magazine.' He took a step back from the stairs, two, and caught Jackson and the girl in the same shot. 'If you don't tell me what I want to know, they'll be getting this.'

'Charlie?' said the girl, panic in her voice. 'I don't want my dad to know.'

'Shut up,' said Jackson. 'Shut up, shut up. Shut up.'

'Don't worry,' Fortune said to the girl. 'I'm not here to hurt you.'

'Who are you?'

'It doesn't matter. Has he done anything to you?'

'Who?' she said, looking confused. She was young, couldn't be older than sixteen. Fifteen. 'Charlie? No.'

'Is he keeping you here?'

'What?' She frowned. 'What do you mean?'

'Against your will,' said Fortune, trying to be patient. 'Is he keeping you here against your will?'

'No. Who, Charlie? No.'

'How old are you?'

'None of your business,' the girl said, guilt in her voice along with defiance. 'Charlie? *Charlie*?'

Jackson looked up at the girl, then at Fortune. 'What do you want?' he said.

'My daughter.'

'I told you. I don't know where she is. The police already asked me. I wasn't even in the country when she went missing.'

'No?'

'No. No, no, no. I was in the Caribbean.'

'What?'

'Between the time she was last seen and when they ... when she was reported missing, I wasn't in the country. I wasn't here. Understand? I don't know what happened to her. I. Don't. Know.'

Fortune had a sense of things falling around him, as if he was standing beneath a disintegrating tower block, the ground giving way beneath him. Like nothing would ever be the same again, a point of no return.

'Is that true?'

'Yes, it's true. It's true. That, what's his name, Marsh? Kept me in overnight. Kept asking, asking and asking and asking. I wasn't here. I wasn't in the country.'

'If I call him? I've got his number.'

'He'll tell you. He'll tell you, because he knows. I don't know anything about your daughter.' Jackson held both hands in front of him, fingers open like he was clutching an imaginary football, trying to crush it. 'I wasn't here.'

Fortune thought, thought hard and quickly, worked out what he could do. He'd broken into a man's home, a man who was a household name. He had no right to be here, no grounds. Jackson hadn't been in the country. Fortune believed that. He couldn't lie himself, but he knew when people were lying to him; it was part of the job. Part of management. What now?

'How old is she?' he asked, putting his phone away.

'What's it to you?' said Jackson.

'How old are you?' said Fortune, looking at the girl, who looked back at him with the baffled innocence of a child.

'Charlie?' she said.

'This didn't happen. Okay?' said Fortune. 'You say nothing, I say nothing.'

Jackson shrugged.

'I'm going to leave you alone now. We're done.'

'Whatever,' said Jackson. 'Just get out.'

Fortune walked past Jackson, opened the front door and walked back out into the day. At the bottom of the steps he passed the wreckage of Jackson's phone. At least, he thought, he'd accomplished something.

twenty-six

4/3

I have to get this down, need to get it down properly while it still makes some sense, no, not sense, but while I can still remember what happened, and in the right order. It doesn't make sense. It doesn't make sense at all and I think I'm mad, I think I'm completely mad like everybody says and that everything I think is real isn't, and somewhere, in some other reality, my life, my real life, is going terribly wrong. I don't know what's real any more, or what's true. I can't trust myself.

So yesterday I packed my bag, went to St Pancras and caught the Eurostar. There was a piano at the station, just put there for anyone to play, and this Chinese girl, I think she was a tourist, sat down and played some amazing piece of music. People were just stopping and watching, and pretty soon there was a huge crowd, transfixed by this little girl's playing. Did that happen? I'm sure it happened, really happened. It seemed real. And the check-in, putting my bag though the X-ray machine and walking through the metal detector. Then sitting in my seat, a window seat, watching the countryside blur by, and then into the tunnel and my ears popping from, I don't know what, change of pressure? And then coming out the other side, into France, which at first didn't seem different except the roofs of the houses aren't the same, and then coming into Paris where the architecture's so different, tall, thin houses, slate roofs, so ornate, and the sides facing the tracks covered in graffiti, all in French. I didn't imagine that either. How could I imagine something so detailed, when I'd never even been to Paris before?

Josh told me where to meet him. He said he'd reserved a table at one o'clock. It was in a brasserie opposite the Gare du Nord, called Terminus. It was this amazing place, just like it would have been back in the thirties, brass and chandeliers and deco detailing, just spellbinding. Beautiful, so beautiful, and the people who were eating, so stylish. It was just perfect. The maître d' took my luggage and showed me to my seat. Next to me a waitress was setting fire to a pancake, flambé, I think that's what it's called. I guess they'd call it a crêpe too, not a pancake. Anyway, she set it on fire and then served it to the table behind me, and I sat there looking around me and all the stuff from the last few months seemed so very, very far away, and so unreal. I could breathe. I remember thinking, I can breathe. Like the air was lighter that side of the Channel.

I'd arrived at about ten to one, so I wasn't surprised that Josh wasn't there. I had that first-date nervous feeling, but good, more like anticipation, a lovely warm feeling. And I waited, and looked around at the beautiful people, and then it was one o'clock. Then it was ten past. Then it was twenty past, and I tried Josh's number but there was no reply. Then it was half past one and the maître d' kept looking at me and

*I tried not to meet his eye, and then I started to cry because
of course Josh wasn't coming. I tried not to let anyone see
that I was crying but the maître d' came over and asked me
if I had any news, and I said no, I didn't know anything,
and he was very kind and said that perhaps I would like to
order anyway? But I didn't, and I said I was sorry, and he
told me it was okay, that there was nothing to worry about.
And I couldn't stop crying and he brought me my luggage
and I didn't know what to do, where to go. It started to rain
and I was in Paris and I could have done anything, but I just
walked back to the Gare du Nord and waited for a train,
because I couldn't think of anything else. I kept trying Josh,
but there was no answer, and everything had felt so fine but
now it just felt bad again, bad and wrong. I remember that. I
remember sitting in the Gare du Nord, looking at the depar-
ture board, and everything feeling bad and wrong. Wrong,
wrong, wrong.*

*So I found a train and I went through passport control
and when I was through I put my bag into the X-ray
machine and walked through the metal-detector arch, just
like when I'd come. And then I walked to Departures but a
man stopped me and asked me to follow him, and he opened
a door in the wall and inside was another man and a metal
table. They were wearing blue shirts with insignia on them
but they weren't police. They were both English and they
asked me to put my bag on the table and to step away and
put my back against the wall. They unzipped my case and
on top was a metal box, like a tin, that I'd never seen before.
They opened it and pulled out a parcel wrapped in clear
plastic and asked me what it was and I told them that I'd*

*never seen it before, that it hadn't been in my case when I
left London and that somebody must have put it there, they
must have, must have must have must have. And they looked
at me like everybody else does, like Sam does when I tell him
I didn't make any noise, like the police do when I tell them I
didn't take the knife, like Larry at work does when I tell him
I've done nothing wrong. They looked at me like I was mad,
and now I think they must be right. Because it was in my
case and they told me it was drugs and I don't know how it
got there, I don't. And they questioned me and took my saliva
and escorted me to the train, and one of them sat with me,
and when I got to London more people were waiting for me
on the platform and they told me I'll go to prison, I'm going
to go to prison for a long time.*

    *And now I'm at home and I don't know what to do. I think
I'm mad and I have nowhere to live and no job and nobody
who loves me. And Josh, Josh has gone. Josh has disappeared,
like he never existed. I thought I loved him. I thought he loved
me. Maybe he just decided I was mad, too. I don't know. God,
I just don't know.*

By the time Fortune had finished reading the document he had
found buried on his daughter's computer's desktop, he knew,
knew with a certainty he'd never had before concerning her, that
she hadn't been mad. That she hadn't been mad at all, which
was almost miraculous, given what had happened to her, what
had been done to her. She hadn't taken those drugs, they'd been
planted on her. Somebody had done it, maybe at the restaurant.
Somebody who'd known where she'd be, and when. It was beyond
obvious. Now, he thought, now we're getting somewhere.

He was in his hotel room, the remains of an unsatisfactory coq au vin on the desk-stroke-table, a half-empty bottle of Bordeaux on the bedside table next to him. He reached for his phone, found Jessica's number. He didn't have anyone else to call. She was the only person he knew who'd known his daughter in London, who might have some idea of what to do. There were nine days left. Nine days until the date of the stolen money. Nine days to save his daughter.

He listened to it ring, wondered whether Jessica was out again at some media event, putting up with some other wannabe starlet's disgraceful behaviour.

'Yes? Hello?'

'Jessica? It's Fortune, I'm sorry to bother you.'

'Fortune?' She sounded suspicious, and Fortune had the shameful thought that she might think he was hitting on her.

'I need your help,' he said.

'Again?'

'Just, it'll only take a minute. I was just wondering, her boyfriend. Josh.'

'What about him?'

'Do you know his surname?'

'No. Didn't even know his name until you told me. Sorry.'

'Are you sure? Please, think. Are you sure she didn't mention it?'

'Fortune, we weren't that close. I don't know.'

'Okay,' said Fortune. 'Never mind.'

'I'm sorry,' she said. There was silence on her end. Maybe she wasn't out. Maybe she was at home, looking at the remains of her own unsatisfactory dinner. Probably not. She wasn't like him.

'Did she say anything at all?' he asked. 'Anything about him? Where he worked, where they met, anything like that?'

'No,' said Jessica. 'Sorry. I think they met online. I think. He must have a profile, they must have been connected. Have you looked?'

'No,' said Fortune. 'But I will. Okay. Thanks.'

'No problem.' She paused. 'Hey. Did you go and see Jackson?'

'Yes.' He paused, added, 'I think I upset him.'

Jessica laughed, a low chuckle. 'Did you now? Well, I imagine he deserved it.'

'Oh, he deserved it. I don't quite know what for, but he deserved it.'

Jessica laughed again. 'Look after yourself,' she said.

'I'll try,' said Fortune. 'Thanks.'

He hung up and went to the desk, where his daughter's computer was open. Social networks, why hadn't he thought of it? He wasn't on any of those, never had been. Who was he going to share the minutiae of his life with? He opened up a browser window and headed to Facebook. Sophie's name was in the top corner, still logged in. It was so easy to access her life, everything she did, everyone she knew. You idiot, he thought. Why didn't you do this before?

From what colleagues had told him, Fortune imagined that social media was created so that people with frivolous and inconsequential lives had a platform to air them, because, understandably, traditional media didn't care what you'd just eaten for dinner or if your rabbit had had a leg amputated; nor was it in a hurry to publish it. Looking at the posts on his daughter's page, he thought they were probably right. Photos of nights out, links to articles about weight loss and celebrity scuttlebutt, invitations to parties and openings, videos of animals doing apparently cute things. He scrolled down through them impatiently until he realized he wasn't going to find anything of interest there. Instead he moved to the top of the page, found Friends, opened it up. There were a lot of them, all young, all pictured, it seemed, in nightclubs with their mouths wide open, grinning, laughing, having fun. Fun. That was something he hadn't contributed to Sophie's life. What a waste, what a terrible, miserable, inexcusable waste.

He stopped at a shot of a man, the Statue of Liberty behind him. Josh MacDonald. Born 23 May 1987. Went to school in Bournemouth. University of London, UCL. Works as a DOP – Fortune had to check that one: director of photography. There were photos of him on set, behind a camera, on a beach, in a club, a bar, arms around friends, smiling, raising a drink. He had long blond hair and was good-looking. Josh MacDonald. This was the man his daughter believed she loved? Well. He felt a ludicrous jealousy, some atavistic stirring, that she should have been besotted with a man so unlike him, with qualities so different. No, not different: better. Outgoing, creative, adventurous, generous, gregarious. Everything Fortune wasn't. He sighed as he gazed at the shots of his daughter's lover. What had gone wrong?

This was the man who had invited her to Paris, then stood her up. And on the way home, she'd been stopped by Customs with drugs in her luggage, planted there. He'd invited her. He'd known where she would be. What did he do, ghost into the restaurant, find her case, plant the drugs, then walk away, leaving her sitting alone, watching the clock, wondering what was wrong with her, why her life was coming apart at the seams?

And what then? Had he come to her house, taken her by force, held her, sent Fortune a message, that he had her and that

Fortune only had days to find her? He didn't know, but he'd work it out. He'd got to Jackson, he'd get to this man. He didn't know how, but he had nine days left. He'd find him.

twenty-seven

THERE WAS A MAN AT OXFORD CIRCUS WEARING A SANDWICH board that read 'Repent of your sins and turn to God'. He was holding a microphone and telling anybody who would listen, which wasn't many, about the surest way to heaven. He caught Fortune's eye as he walked past, but Fortune was wearing his sternest senior-management-shit-to-do look and the man decided against trying to convert him to the true way. In any case, Fortune suspected it was too late. Way too late.

The streets were busy with shoppers carrying bags of clothing from Selfridges, Gap, Browns; a crowd of kids outside Niketown. Fortune pushed his way through, took a left onto Great Portland Street, leaving the crowds behind so suddenly that it felt as if he'd stepped through some portal into an empty post-apocalyptic future. He walked up the quiet street, keeping an eye on doorways, gratings, wondering whether the man would still be here or whether he'd be gone, moved on or given refuge somewhere else, somewhere warm. It was cold, and a light rain was falling from a white sky, grey clouds scudding maliciously across it.

He had nearly walked past the man before he noticed him, tucked into a doorway and wrapped in a dirty grey blanket. He was young and thin and there was an upturned baseball cap in front of him with some coins in it, not very many. Fortune looked down at him. It had to be the man from his daughter's blog. The man who had come to her aid. *Last Night a GI Saved My Life.*

'Jake?'

The man blinked, surprised. 'Yeah?'

'My name's Fortune.'

'You Old Bill?'

'No.'

"Cause I've got nothing on me. I don't inject, none of that. I'm clean.'

'It's not that,' said Fortune. 'I think you knew my daughter. Sophie.'

'Who?' The man frowned, coughed. 'Sophie?'

'You helped her. She was attacked.'

'Oh.' He thought. 'You're her dad? How is she?'

'She's gone missing,' said Fortune. 'She's been gone for weeks.'

The man, Jake, made an effort to get up, stood and looked at Fortune. 'No. You're joking. Really?'

'Yes. I just wanted to talk to you. About what happened.'

'Yeah, sure, no problem.' Jake pulled his blanket tight around his shoulders and looked up at the sky. It was starting to rain harder.

'Pint?' Fortune said.

'Well,' said Jake. 'Since you ask. Lead the way.'

That morning he had put a call through to Marsh without expecting him to pick up, not after their last meeting. What had Marsh said to him? Get some help, that was it. He listened to the ringtone, was surprised when Marsh answered.

'What now?' Marsh said.

'Did you know that my daughter had been arrested for drug trafficking?'

Marsh sighed. 'I was aware, yes.'

'But you didn't think to tell me?'

'No. Got nothing to do with me. I'm not Customs and Excise.'

'But you knew about it?'

'I knew, yes. Might explain a few things, don't you think?'

'What kind of things?' said Fortune.

'Like the dealing at her flat. The parties, her behaviour.'

'There was no dealing,' said Fortune. 'Or parties. That, all that, it never happened.'

'Really?' said Marsh. 'How'd you come to that conclusion?'

'If you'd done your job,' said Fortune, 'you would have reached it too. Only you didn't think my daughter was important enough to put the work in.'

'I'm going to hang up now,' said Marsh.

'My daughter did nothing,' said Fortune. 'Nothing. You've got it wrong, all wrong.'

'Goodbye,' said Marsh, leaving Fortune with a silent phone to his ear. Perhaps he shouldn't have accused the policeman of not doing his job properly, though he couldn't say he regretted it. There wasn't anything more Marsh could do for him, or for his daughter. No. Not for the first time in his life, Fortune decided that if you wanted something done properly, you were better off doing it yourself.

'What'll you have?' he asked Jake.

'Lager,' said Jake. He paused, scanned the optics. 'Or ...'

'Would you like a Scotch with it?' asked Fortune.

'Now you're talking.'

The barman was watching them warily. Jake still had his blanket around him and his nails were filthy, his hair matted. Fortune couldn't help but notice that he didn't smell great either. Still, this was the man who had saved his daughter. He caught the barman's eye and said, 'Is there a problem?'

'No problem,' the barman said. 'No problem at all.'

He got their drinks and Fortune handed him a twenty. They took the glasses and headed for a table, Jake walking with the apologetic hunch of the chronically disenfranchised. They sat.

'How long have you been on the streets?' said Fortune.

'Six months, bit more,' said Jake.

'You were in the army?'

Jake nodded. 'Afghanistan.' He picked up the Scotch, took a sip, downed it. He closed his eyes as he felt it warm his chest and exhaled in pleasure.

'Sophie said you found it hard, coming back.'

'Could say.' Jake didn't continue, instead picked up his beer.

'I guess it must be difficult.'

'Yeah. She was nice, your daughter,' Jake said, changing the subject.

'I know,' said Fortune.

'Really ... how can I put it? Open. Friendly. She had this kindness, like, dunno. Generous.'

She didn't get it from me, thought Fortune. He said, 'So. What happened?'

'She didn't tell you?' said Jake.

'No. I just read about it. So I thought, you know, you might be able to tell me more.' And help reassure me that my daughter wasn't mad, thought Fortune, though he didn't say it. Make sure that what she wrote about actually happened, that she was attacked, and that you did save her. That she wasn't completely delusional. Even thinking it made Fortune feel guilty, but still. He had to be sure.

'She gave me a tenner,' Jake said. 'Doesn't happen often. Then later I see her again, and this guy grabs her, and that's enough for me, I'm up and over there and I pull him off her.' He shrugged, drank. 'Not much more to say.'

'Thank you,' said Fortune.

'Whatever,' said Jake. 'Anyone'd do the same.'

'No they wouldn't,' said Fortune. 'They really wouldn't.'

'So what's the score?' said Jake. 'You said she'd disappeared.'

'I don't know,' said Fortune. 'The police think she took her own life.'

'No,' said Jake, certainty in his voice. 'No way. Not her, not Sophie. Wasn't the type.'

'You don't think so?'

'Listen,' said Jake, 'I've seen it happen. Seen people do themselves. They've given up, run out of options. Sophie, she was happy, interested. Wanted to know about me. No.' He shook his head into his pint. 'She wasn't the type.'

'Maybe,' said Fortune, thinking of her suicide attempts in the past. But perhaps she'd changed. Jean had thought she'd changed. 'Thanks.'

They sat in silence for some moments. Fortune watched Jake. He was young, couldn't be over twenty-five, and had an open face, thin but gentle.

'So how about you?' he said. 'What's your story?'

Jake sighed, turned his pint with one hand, the condensation mixing with the dirt on his fingers, making sooty streaks of moisture on the glass. 'You wouldn't understand.'

'Probably not,' said Fortune.

'Not just you. Anybody. That's the problem. I had a girlfriend, lived with her. But when I came back ...' He took a drink. 'It wasn't the same. Not like it was. Nothing was.'

'Because of what happened in Afghanistan?'

Jake closed his eyes, nodded, opened them again. 'My mate, next to me, stepped on a mine. There was just this noise and earth and blood, I could see it through the sun, like a mist. Of him. Turned into this mist, and some bigger pieces. And then Stacey, that's my girlfriend, when I'm back she says to me, can't you put your cup in the dishwasher? And I thought about my mate, and why the hell does putting a cup in the dishwasher matter, what's so important about that when other things, terrible things, are going on, but I knew she wouldn't understand and I just lost it. And that was it. End of.'

'She threw you out?'

'I was happy to go. Couldn't stand it any more. Prefer it on the street.'

They sat in silence again, before Fortune realized that they'd both be happier alone. He took out an envelope and put it on the table between them.

'What's this?' said Jake.

'Money. For helping my daughter.'

'I didn't do it for the money.'

'I know,' said Fortune. 'I know that. All the more reason, right?'

Jake picked up the envelope, opened it and looked inside. He looked back at Fortune. 'There's a lot here.'

'A thousand. If you need more, just let me know. Have you got a phone?'

'Yeah.'

'Give me the number.'

Fortune put Jake's number into his mobile and called it to check he'd got it properly.

'Got no battery,' said Jake. 'Need to get it charged.'

Fortune stood up. 'You take care. If you need anything, call me.'

'Why are you doing this?' said Jake.

'I told you,' said Fortune. But it was a good question. Why *was* he doing it? Because he thought that it would atone in some way for the lack of attention he'd given Sophie? He was making up for that failure by giving a man who had helped her a pile of cash? No. No, that was as paltry a get-out as the member of his staff who had missed all his targets but tried to persuade Fortune to keep him on because he'd taken a decent catch at the company cricket match. Too little. Too little, and much too late. Still, Fortune thought, it made him feel marginally better about himself. Which was something, at least.

'Well,' he said to Jake. 'Can't take it with you, right?'

Jake frowned, looked at Fortune closely. 'You okay?'

'Yes. Why?'

'Seen that look before. You're not well, are you? Not well at all.'

'No.'

'I hope you find your daughter,' said Jake. 'She was one of the good guys.'

'I hope so too,' said Fortune. He got up and left the pub, leaving Jake to drink away his memories of war.

Fortune still had the card the official at the airport, Sunita Gandham, had given him. He didn't know what agency she worked for, but it had to be something to do with borders and control. She'd said to call any time if he wanted to talk. And he wanted to talk. Needed to talk. And, he figured, she was now the only person he knew who could help.

'Hello?'

'Ms Gandham? My name's Fortune. We ...' How to put it? 'We met at the airport a couple of days ago.'

'We met,' said Sunita. 'Right. I remember. What do you want?'

No pleasantries. He remembered her uncompromising demeanour, her hard eyes. Why did he think she'd do anything for him? 'I was wondering if you could help me.'

'Oh?'

'My daughter. You know she disappeared.'

'I know.'

'You probably know she was stopped recently, too. Coming into the country.'

'Hold on.'

Fortune listened to footsteps, the sound of people talking, a door opening and closing, then silence. 'You there?'

'Yes,' said Fortune.

'Okay. Now listen. I shouldn't be talking to you. This is an ongoing investigation, and more importantly, it's not *my* investigation. Understand?'

'Yes.'

'So this is between the two of us. Right?'

'Okay.'

'All right. So what did you want to ask me?'

Fortune took a deep breath. 'I think my daughter was set up. There were things going on in her life ... things that don't make sense.'

'Uh-huh,' said Sunita. 'And this is my concern how?'

'It isn't,' said Fortune. 'But I have a name. The person who I believe set her up. She was invited to Paris, but the person who invited her never showed.'

'So she said. I've read the transcript of the interview.'

'The name's Josh. Josh MacDonald.'

Sunita sighed. 'I know the name. I know all about him, date of birth, education. Your daughter gave it all to us.'

'So he's being investigated?'

'He was being investigated,' said Sunita. 'Was. Listen, I don't know what was going on in your daughter's life. Frankly, it's not our concern. We work the borders, not domestic crime, so whatever was happening, it's somebody else's problem.'

'Nice,' said Fortune. 'How does that square with your conscience?'

'Nothing to do with my conscience,' she said. 'Just the way things are.'

'So that's it?' said Fortune.

'Not quite,' said Sunita. 'I can tell you one thing. Josh MacDonald? He doesn't exist. He never existed. There is no such person. So, you tell me. How does a figment of somebody's imagination plant drugs in their luggage?'

twenty-eight

JOSH HAS BEEN IN TOUCH. JUST LIKE THAT, OUT OF THE COLD. He told me that it wasn't his fault, that it had nothing to do with him and that somebody was messing with him. He told me that he was being set up, and that there had been allegations made about him, false allegations. He said he'd been accused of breaching his NDA, and of telling the competition about the new ad campaign he'd been working on. He told me that money had gone missing from his bank account and that malicious messages had been sent from his email account, only he hadn't written them. He said it's happening to him now too, just like it's been happening to me.

He told me that he had never sent an email about meeting in Paris. He said he'd flown straight to London; why would he fly to Paris? It didn't make any sense. And it's right, it doesn't. Why didn't I think of that?

We're meeting tonight but Josh doesn't want us to be seen together, he thinks it's dangerous. Somebody's out there, somebody who means us harm, though he doesn't know why and neither do I. He said it's better to stay under the radar and meet somewhere secret. Why? Because he's got a plan. He's got a way to get us out of this, at least that's what he says. Is it true? Can this be true? Have I actually got an ally?

We're meeting tonight and it feels like the last roll of the dice. I'm not even thinking about it. I'll go, and see what happens. What else can I do?

twenty-nine

FORTUNE WOKE AND HIS FIRST THOUGHT WAS: EIGHT DAYS. Eight days left. Eight days in this strange fantasy land he now occupied, where reality was twisted, misunderstood, upside down. Where the only people who knew what was really happening were him and his daughter. His daughter, who wasn't dead, who was alive, captured, waiting, hoping. His daughter, who had stopped believing in him years ago. In his artificial hotel limbo, where every evening his room was reset, cleaned and tidied and washed and restocked so that it appeared the same as the first day he'd opened the door, it could be hard to make sense of time passing. But not any more. Eight days. He had eight days, and he didn't have the first idea where to go, what to look for, or who to talk to. He had nothing. And in eight days, and he did believe this, his daughter would die.

He lay in bed and tried to ignore the pain in his chest, the tight constriction that in his dreams often manifested as a snake, winding around and around, squeezing and pressing, black and putrid as he imagined his cancer to be, a vile interloper consisting of nothing but dank, dark rot. He lay in bed and breathed and tried to think, and plan, and tried not to cough. The mornings were the worst, tens of minutes spent barking and hacking into the sink, great globs emerging, weirdly coloured alien entities ejected onto the white porcelain. The mirror above the sink reflecting his face, pale, sagging, racked. Every morning he wondered, how did I become this? Exactly what the hell happened?

There was a knock at the door and Fortune sat up. Who could that be? Who knew he was here?

'Hello?' No answer. 'Hello?' Louder this time.

The door opened wide and he had a brief moment of panic before he heard a rattling and a maid walked in pushing a trolley. Fortune remembered that he hadn't hung the *Do Not Disturb* sign, but then what time was it? He looked at his watch and saw it was gone eleven. When had he ever slept past eight?

'No, thank you. Thank you. I'm good.'

'Good?'

'Yes, I'm good. I mean, sorry, I mean come back later.'

'Ah,' said the maid. 'Okay. Okay, I come back later.' She backed out of the door, pulling her trolley with her, cleaning materials clanking. Fortune lay back in his bed, again trying not to cough, holding it all in like an explosive he wouldn't let go off. God, but he was tired, so tired, the inside of his head dizzy, seasick. He closed his eyes and tried to think. Eight days. He had eight days.

So, a stocktaking. Where was he? What was the situation? He counted it up on his fingers, his hands invisible under the sheet, pressing a thumb to each finger to keep track. One. His daughter had been tormented by an online troll, who had known details about her that he shouldn't have. Two. She was missing, presumed dead, though he didn't believe that. Three. She'd had false allegations made against her, partying, drugs, stalking, antisocial behaviour. Four. She'd been attacked, threatened with acid. Five ... He ran out of fingers, transferred to his other hand. Five, a hundred and sixty million dollars had been stolen from the bank he worked at, in two attempts, each matching a significant date: his daughter's birth, and a date eight days from today. Six. His daughter's boyfriend had recently proved to be non-existent, a fabrication.

Was that it? He lay in bed with his eyes closed and wondered if he had forgotten anything. Probably. It was hard to keep track. He touched another finger to thumb. Seven. Her father had practically disowned her from the age of, what, thirteen? Disowned her, dismissed her, disapproved of her, deserted her. Behaved disgracefully. Disgustingly. Yes, that wove throughout the stocktaking. Fortune's absence, his culpability, his inadequacy as a father and husband. Now, this morning, lying in bed, he could think of no way of making up for it. No more avenues to pursue, save for walking into the police station and holding Marsh hostage, demanding that he do something, that he listen, that he act. As if.

How long had it been since he'd eaten? He couldn't remember. At least a day. He got up with difficulty and dressed himself like an old man would, pulling his trousers on in slow motion, one leg in, then the other, sitting on the edge of the bed. He was breathing like he was summiting Everest. He stood up, put a hand to the wall on the way out of his room, and felt his way down the corridor. It rolled and wallowed like a ship's gangway in a storm, Fortune again putting out a hand, trying to keep his balance. He got to the lift and pressed the down button, seeing two arrows as if he was drunk. He was sweating now, his chest so tight it was as if someone was turning the screw on a monstrous vice, and he was trapped in it like some laboratory rodent. He tried to breathe and heard the muffled *ting* of the lift arriving. How could it be muffled? He was standing right next to it. The doors opened and he walked in, stumbled, and fell to his knees. He put a hand on the brass balustrade and caught a glimpse of himself in the mirrored wall. In the lift's gloom, under the bright lights, his face shadowed, he looked like some creature from a horror film, dreadful and barely human. He must eat. He must eat, look after himself, keep going for just a few more days.

He pulled himself up with difficulty and was only barely upright when the lift doors opened. He composed himself and walked out, into the lobby, then headed for the breakfast room, concentrating on walking steadily as if he was a drunk in a pub trying to find his inebriated way to the loo. Look after yourself, he thought, furiously. Sophie needs you. You're all she's got. You, you fool, you weak, contemptible man. Think you've got what it takes, huh? Think you've got what it takes to save your daughter? Sitting down with relief, ordering coffee, Fortune wasn't sure. But he knew that he'd try, give it his everything. That he promised.

thirty

A CATFISH. A CATFISH, AND I FELL FOR IT, HOOK, LINE AND sinker. Like some teenager, wet behind the ears. Pathetic. Sad. No, tragic. That's it. Sophie, you idiot. You silly hysterical desperate needy tragic idiot. You almost deserve it. Except I don't want to die. No, I don't deserve that, I'm sure I don't. But I think it might happen, I really do.

Josh didn't exist, and he never existed. There was never any such person, just a catfish, an online profile and nothing more. What did we have, the two of us? An email exchange, a couple of phone calls. And I thought I loved him. Based on that, just that, I thought I loved him. Well, maybe not loved. But I wanted to love him and thought that I could, that it might be possible. And I told him everything about my life, about my fears, my friends and family, my frailties. All because I liked his photo and I thought his job was cool and his emails made me smile. Really? Really, Sophie? Seriously?

Everything that happened, *he* did. Not Josh; Josh doesn't exist. The other one. The one who's keeping me here, in this room. In this cell. The one who pretended to be Josh, who set me up, who made complaints about my non-existent parties, who hacked my account and sent emails to Jackson, who stole a knife from my kitchen, who planted drugs in my luggage, made me lose my job, tried to spray acid in my face. Who ruined my life, robbed me of everything I have, and almost made me lose my mind. The troll. He did all this.

So Josh wrote to Sophie. I'll refer to her as Sophie for now, because I'm too horrendously ashamed to acknowledge that it was me who fell for it. Sophie, she reads this email. And the email tells her that somebody's out to get the two of them, and that nowhere is safe. Oh, thinks Sophie. It's happening to you, too. Well, that makes me feel a whole ton better, because a problem shared, etc., right?

You know the London Fields Brewery? he asks.

Yes, says Sophie. Let's not forget, Sophie is an idiot.

There's a builder's yard next to it, he replies. I'll be there. I've got a mate, he's lent me his van.

Of course, at this point, Sophie smells the proverbial rat and tells Josh that she's not, what, not *comfortable* with this plan. Right?

Wrong. Oh, so, so wrong.

No, Sophie eagerly sends her reply.

Okay, she says. What time?

What time!

She almost deserves it, to be frank.

Anyway, Sophie arrives at the appointed time. And sure enough, there's a builder's yard. And there's a van parked in it. And something else. A groaning sound. Words, faint, weak. *Help. Help me, somebody. Please.*

So Sophie rushes over to the van, because Sophie is simple, she doesn't have a scintilla of sense, not an ounce of nous, not a milligram of moxie. She rushes over, and somebody's there, only they don't look injured, no, they look … well, she doesn't actually know, because at precisely this point, Sophie the Simpleton has been hit by something and is unconscious and is being, let's call it what it is, *kidnapped*.

My cell isn't big. I don't know where it is; it could be anywhere. It could be in the middle of a city, or the middle of Syria. I'm sitting against the back wall, watching the door. There's nothing else to look at, and it's the only thing I'm frightened of. Of it opening. It's a couple of metres away, green and made of metal. It can't be kicked open because I've tried, tried and tried. The floor is concrete and the walls are brick and there's nothing in the cell except a bed and a bucket. The bed has sheets on it. It's basically your average bargain hotel, only the concierge is a lunatic. There's a window right above my head, but there's no electric light, so when it's dark it really is pitch black. I pray for it not to get dark, as if I can influence the laws of physics or something. When it's dark, there's just me and my breathing and almost nothing else. In London, there's always noise, always something to listen to. In here, there's nothing, nothing at all. It's like I don't exist any more, just like Josh never existed; like I've been vanished from the world, disappeared. But. Ah, yes, but. And here's the big but. At least I know that, whatever happens, I'm not mad. I'm not mad, and I never was. And I guess that's got to be something.

Josh doesn't exist, so he's not going to rescue me. The police never believed me anyway. My dad's in Dubai, working, working, always working. There's nobody to save me, nobody coming to my rescue. I'm in the hands of a sadist, a wacko, a total psycho, and nobody in the whole world cares. I am scared. Oh, I am so, so scared.

thirty-one

FORTUNE FINISHED EATING. HE HAD TO ADMIT THAT, TERMI-
nal cancer or not, a plate of bacon, eggs and mushrooms made a
hell of a difference, once you managed to actually ingest it. Plus
coffee, a whole lot of coffee. And nipping outside for a restor-
ative cigarette. He sat back down and looked out of the window
of the hotel's breakfast room, into the world outside: a wet road,
taxis, cyclists, a cement mixer grudgingly stopping for a zebra
crossing. As well as he'd eaten, he was still, essentially, dead in
the water. What should he do next? All he knew was that his
daughter was out there somewhere, alive and frightened. At
least for the next seven days. He felt his heart beat as his anxiety
dumped another load of adrenalin into his system. What the
hell was he going to do?

His mobile ringing interrupted his thoughts and he took it
out of his pocket, recognized the number.

'Alex?'

'Jesus, Fortune, thank Christ. All right. Okay.' He paused, took
a breath. 'Fortune, what ... what the hell did you do?'

'What?'

'I wanted to talk to you first. I know I shouldn't, but ... Jesus,
Fortune, how could you do it?'

Fortune turned, phone to his ear, looked out over the hotel's lobby, where an elderly couple were towing their luggage from the lift, backs bent. 'Do what?'

'Please. How long did we work together?'

'Alex,' said Fortune, 'what the hell's going on?'

'That's what I want to know,' said Alex. Fortune pictured him in Dubai, shirtsleeves, tie loose, his oh-crap-what-now face on. 'That's exactly what I want to know.'

'You need to give me something to go on here,' said Fortune.

'Okay,' said Alex.

'Okay, fine.' He sounded angry, frustrated. 'Recognize these numbers?' He read off a string of numbers. Fortune lost track halfway through, thought they rang a bell.

'Again?'

Alex read them off again.

'Sounds like a bank account.'

'Know whose?' said Alex.

'Could be mine,' said Fortune. 'I think it's mine. Savings.'

'How much have you got in it?'

'Around a hundred thousand,' said Fortune. 'Why?'

'Wrong,' said Alex. 'Way off. There's a little over a hundred and thirty million sterling in it. That's just over a hundred and sixty million dollars. Sound familiar, those numbers?'

Fortune leant back in his chair, felt sweat break out on his forehead. 'Yes.'

'You know I have to release this information.'

'I know.'

'I just wanted …' Alex paused, tried to control his emotions. 'I just wanted to know why. Why you did it?'

'I didn't,' said Fortune.

'Come on, Fortune,' said Alex. 'It's me. I need to know. You owe me that.'

'I didn't steal it,' said Fortune. 'It wasn't me.'

'I'm going to see Owen in, like, five minutes.'

Fortune closed his eyes, felt himself sinking into the chair, losing any certainty he'd had, which wasn't a lot. 'I understand.'

'But I don't. I don't, Fortune. Why?'

'Alex, I didn't do it. It's complicated. Tell Owen, tell whoever you have to. But I didn't do it. I promise you that.'

'Right,' said Alex, his voice suddenly flat. 'Whatever. I'll see you, Fortune.'

'Alex—' began Fortune, but he'd hung up, leaving Fortune with a dead phone pressed to his ear, held too tightly. He put it down on the table in front of him, leant forward and rested his forehead on the table, its cool surface soothing against his hot skin. Okay, he thought to himself. All right. Now it's happening to you. But that's okay. If Sophie could cope with it, keep her head, or almost, then so can you. Keep calm. Don't panic. You can do this.

Fortune didn't bother to go to his room, just walked out of the hotel and called a cab, asked the driver if he knew the nearest branch of HSBC and told him to get him there quickly. He didn't know much, didn't know who had transferred the money, didn't know how they'd done it. But what he did know, as the taxi passed commuters walking to work under umbrellas beneath a spiteful rain, was that very, very soon, alarms would be going off. He'd worked in banking long enough to know how it went, had fielded enough suspicious payments himself, investigated them, traced them back to their source to find a 'warm body' who could guarantee their provenance.

If what Alex had told him was true, somebody would be looking at Fortune's account, wondering why well over a hundred million pounds had just landed in it. Was it money laundering? Was it connected to terrorist funding, or an international sanctions breach, the funds sitting in his account before heading off to Cuba or North Korea? If the money was in his account, then he needed to know more about how it had got there. He couldn't do that online; he'd have to speak to somebody real. But, he figured as he pulled up outside the bank, it might be a good idea to ask the taxi to wait, just in case. You never knew.

He was kept waiting at the customer service desk due to the fact that he had insisted on speaking to the manager, because it was very important and very, very sensitive, and no, he realized the woman at the desk was probably very well trained, but still. The manager. Now, please, right bloody now.

The manager was an overweight thirty-year-old, the kind of figure Fortune mistrusted on sight because if you can't iron your shirt then it's very unlikely that you'll be meticulous in your day-to-day dealings. In fact, he thought unkindly, the manager looked like the kind of man who'd grow into somebody like Marsh, a sedentary incompetent promoted above his abilities. But he smiled and shook the hand that was offered, and the manager told him his name was Michael and asked what, exactly, could he do to help?

'I'd rather not do this out here,' Fortune said.

'Then in my office?' said Michael.

'If you don't mind.'

Fortune followed Michael, whose white shirt was badly tucked into the back of his trousers. He was the kind of man, Fortune thought, remembering some old joke, who'd look scruffy in a wetsuit. Michael opened a door with a code and waited for Fortune to walk through, then passed him and opened another door into his office. He walked around the desk, put out a hand to the chair opposite. He sat; Fortune sat.

'So, Mr Fortune. How can I help you?'

'I need to look at my accounts.'

'Of course. But you can do that anywhere.'

'I think there might have been some ... irregular activity.'

'Oh?' Michael smiled, a complacent smile, the kind that a man well used to the irrational financial fears of the public wore. The kind that said, *Oh, okay, you're paranoid. I see. I get it.*

'I think somebody might have put a hundred and thirty million pounds into it.'

This statement from Fortune froze that smile. Michael twitched his head, frowned a little. 'I'm sorry?'

'A hundred and thirty million. Right now, I believe it's sitting in my account. What I want to know is, how did it get there? Which is why I want to talk to you. So,' and Fortune took a breath, in business mode but willing himself to stay patient, 'how about you get my accounts up, and we take a look?'

He gave Michael his account number, sort code, went through the security questions, his date of birth, mother's maiden name – Hemmings – and the first two numbers of his PIN.

'So let's have a look, shall we?' said Michael, his composure slightly restored by the questions, a small re-establishment of power and control. 'Let's see.' He looked at the screen, moved the mouse, looked some more, then blinked very slowly, staring at the screen as if it was playing out a lurid murder scene. Fortune studied Michael's desk. There was a picture on it, him with a woman and child. The woman was pretty, very pretty, and Fortune idly wondered if Michael would make a better job of family life than he himself had managed. Eventually Michael turned away from his screen and looked at Fortune.

'A little over a hundred and thirty million,' he said, unsteadily. He cleared his throat, tried again. 'A little over a hundred and thirty million pounds was deposited in your account twelve hours ago.'

'By?'

'I couldn't say.'

'Can you find out?'

'We'll certainly try,' said the manager. 'I've got a few notes on your account. From our financial crime compliance people. They'd like to speak to you.'

'I'm sure they would,' said Fortune. So they could put two and two together and make several million. The money goes missing from his ex-employer's accounts, turns up in his. The shortest investigation in FCC history. 'Look, I need to know, right now, where that money came from. What can you tell me?'

'Nothing. An account number I don't recognize. Starts with three zeros, which is always a sign. Could be from anywhere, Geneva, Caymans. But, Mr Fortune, I can't tell you anything about it anyway. I'm not allowed.'

'Listen,' said Fortune. He sighed, sat forward, realized he'd left it a little late for a charm offensive, but what the hell. 'I really, really need to find out where that money came from. Because if I don't, somebody's life is in danger. Clear, real danger. Do you understand?'

Michael swallowed. He hadn't been on any course to prepare him for this. 'Not really, no,' he managed.

'Give me the account number.'

'I can't. It's illegal. It's under investigation.'

'I'll come around and find it myself.'

'No,' said Michael. He fished underneath the desk and looked at Fortune, this time with defiance. 'I can't tell you.'

'What did you just do?' said Fortune. 'What did you just press? An alarm?'

'You should stay here,' said Michael, 'right where you are. We'll work out what's going on.'

But Fortune was already up and opening the door to Michael's office, pressing a button to open the second door, then out into the main bank floor, trying not to run or look suspicious, pushing open the door to the bank and walking out into the rain. His taxi was still waiting and he opened the door, got in, told the driver to take him back to the hotel. As they pulled away, he looked out of the back window in time to see Michael run out and look around, the rain soaking his white shirt so that Fortune could see the pink of his lazy, generous flesh beginning to show through.

thirty-two

FORTUNE COULDN'T REMEMBER PUTTING THE *DO NOT DISTURB* sign on his hotel door. He couldn't have done it when he left, because it had been all he could do to stand up, walk down the corridor, call a lift. Must have been on before; he must have hung it the night before. That must have been it.

He inserted his key card, heard the click and saw the small light on the lock turn from red to green. He opened the door. The lights were off and the curtains were drawn, what little light there was outside not making it inside the room. The door swung closed behind him before he could turn on the light switch, and for a moment he couldn't find it, couldn't remember where it was, though he'd been staying in this room for what felt like weeks. At last he found it, turned it on, and caught sight of himself in the mirror. He looked terrible, a man he could barely call overweight any more, who probably wasn't. The cancer diet. Everyone should try it.

There was a short entryway before the room opened up. In front of Fortune was a table. On the right was the main part of the room, where the bed was. It was still in darkness, but he could see right away that somebody was on the bed, and that whoever it was, they weren't moving. He turned on the main light and saw that it was Charlie Jackson. He was lying on his back, his head towards Fortune, bent back over the edge of the bed so that from Fortune's standing position, Jackson's eyes looked right into his.

'Are you all right?' said Fortune, but he didn't expect an answer. The last dead body he had seen, apart from that poor girl in the morgue, had been his father's twenty years ago, but he recognized the look. Eyes open but without sight, all comprehension gone, all hope, laughter, disdain, hate. He walked towards Jackson's corpse, walked slowly before reminding himself that Jackson was dead and it was unlikely he'd wake up. He got closer, closer still, and bent to see that Jackson had a wound in the side of his head, like a broken floorboard but red, light and dark, a mess of dry blood, a wide stain on the white sheet beneath his head. Fortune wondered who could have done such a thing and then backed away from the body, stood up straight. He realized with a twist in his heart and a drop in his stomach that this was his hotel room and that he was the prime suspect, given that he'd been to see Jackson a couple of days before and that his daughter had been involved with him and that Fortune had recently stolen millions and was clearly unhinged. He was the only likely suspect and he was in deep, deep trouble.

He walked backwards, bumped up against the table, felt with his hands behind him and skirted it, found a chair and sat down. He looked at Jackson for some time, then stood and turned off the light and sat back down, watching the indistinct shape of Jackson's corpse in the gloom. Like it might magically come alive, back to life, and all of this might go away. Like it might never have happened, Jackson, the money, his daughter, everything. Jackson didn't move but Fortune knew that he had to, that he had to get out of there. He needed to put a lot of distance between himself and where he was right now. Because he was now wanted for embezzlement on a massive scale, and very soon would be for murder as well.

How had this happened? Who was doing this to him? And who – and at this thought he grunted in the darkness, almost in appalled admiration – would believe him? He'd been set up, manipulated, toyed with from the off. Only now could he truly empathize with what his daughter had been put through. The gradual, unanswerable deconstruction of her life. Now, it seemed, it was his turn. But why? All this effort. Why?

He stood up and found clothes, luggage, started packing in the near darkness. He never wanted to look at Jackson's face again, never wanted to see those dreadful eyes. He needed passport, cash. His passport he'd given to the customs official, Sunita Gandham. Cash, he had less than a hundred on him, and his accounts would have been frozen. It had been decades since Fortune had been short of cash. Right now, he didn't have any. No passport, no cash. Great start.

He heard a noise, a buzz. He stopped packing, looked around and saw a light next to the bed. The screen of a mobile phone, illuminated in the room's artificial twilight. It wasn't his, wasn't his phone; that was still in his pocket. He walked towards the phone like it was a suspect device, bent down to get a better look. It was just a phone. A phone with a message notification on it. From Starry Ubado. *Starry Ubado*. His daughter's troll, the man who had left her such vile comments, left such hatred. He picked the phone up and tapped the screen. The message opened:

How are you enjoying it?

He looked at the message, gazed at it, but after a few seconds it disappeared, again like it might never have happened. *How are you enjoying it?* The question was beyond cruel, was gleeful in its malice. Starry Ubado. The person who had abused his daughter, dismantled her life piece by piece, taken her. And who was now taking a wrecking ball to Fortune's life. Who the hell was he? Fortune felt a deep anger, an impotent fury. Involuntarily his hands made fists and he felt his heart racing, anger, heat on his skin.

He pressed reply and a blank message appeared. *Who are you?* he typed, and hit send. He watched the screen for some time, for minutes, but nothing happened, nothing came through. Starry Ubado, whoever you are, I'll find you, he thought. I don't care what it takes, what it costs me. I'll find you. It's all I have left to live for.

The phone had the time displayed on its screen and Fortune realized that he had been in his hotel room for nearly an hour. Time to move. He put the phone into his pocket, put his daughter's computer in his case, and looked around. What had he forgotten? For a brief moment he considered wiping the place for prints, before remembering that he had been living here, that everybody knew him by sight and that, basically, he was screwed and there was no point, none at all. He put on his coat, pulled out the handle of his case, and wheeled it to the door. Again he caught a glimpse of himself in the mirror. He looked like a typical jet-lagged approaching-retirement-age corporate trouble-shooter, predictable, boring, the kind of man who, he was sure people would say, was the last person you'd expect to leave behind a corpse, its head broken open, on their hotel bed. He checked that the *Do Not Disturb* sign was still in place and wondered just how long it would stay there, how long he'd got.

Fortune had a credit card and he used it to pay his hotel bill. He walked to the nearest cashpoint, used the same card to withdraw five hundred pounds, the most it would allow. He didn't expect the card to work for long, imagined it would be cancelled soon enough, once one bank department managed to talk to another and tell them what he'd done. Which, actually, he hadn't done. He didn't know how far five hundred pounds, six hundred including the money he already had, would get him in London. He didn't know the price of milk, or bread, or the Tube. Why would he? But, he suspected, it wasn't going to go very far. Not very far at all.

There was one thing, however, that had got Fortune through thirty years of high-pressure corporate life. He was, he knew, excellent in a crisis. Impossible to fluster, cool-headed, the kind of person who could make quick decisions in stressful situations that, when the dust had settled, usually proved to be excellent. Cold-blooded was another way of putting it, he supposed. Although it remained to be seen how well these skills transferred from the corporate world to life on the run.

The first thing he needed was to lose his mobile phone. He opened it, took out the battery and SIM, dropped all the pieces in different bins. Next, somewhere to sleep. Somewhere cheap, somewhere with Wi-Fi, and somewhere discreet. He knew plenty of discreet places, but that kind of discretion always came at a price, one he couldn't afford. He bought a ticket for the Tube, a day's travel: £12. He blinked at the machine. Jesus. How did people live in this city? He rode the escalator down to the platform and took the Central Line eastbound to Oxford

Circus. If you wanted advice on living below the radar, off grid, there was one place he knew to go.

Jake was in the same doorway as the last time Fortune had seen him, two days ago. He was asleep, curled up underneath his blanket in the foetal position, and he looked very young and very vulnerable. Fortune hesitated, didn't want to wake him, but Jake opened his eyes and said, 'Back again?'

'I wondered if you'd still be here. Wasn't the money enough?'

'I prefer it out here. I put it in the bank.'

Fortune nodded, not understanding but willing to accept Jake's choice. 'I need your help.'

'Yeah?' Jake blinked his eyes open properly, sat up, yawned, shivered. 'What kind of help?'

'Do you mind?' Fortune said, nodding at the space next to Jake.

'What? Yeah, sure, whatever, man.'

Fortune laid his case down in the doorway and sat on it. Jake watched him curiously. 'You joining me?'

'I might do,' said Fortune. He took out cigarettes and offered one to Jake, who took it. Fortune lit their cigarettes and they sat there, watching people pass by, smoking quietly. It was dry, but there was a cold wind and Fortune soon felt it, wondered how anybody could live out here 24/7.

'What kind of help?' Jake said again, exhaling smoke as he spoke that was immediately stolen away by the wind.

'I'm in trouble,' said Fortune. 'Sophie, too.'

'What kind of trouble?' said Jake. 'I know about trouble.'

'She's been kidnapped by somebody who plans to kill her in seven days,' Fortune said. 'And very soon I'll be wanted for murder.'

'Yeah?' said Jake. He took a last drag of his cigarette, right down to the filter, flicked it away. 'Never met that kind of trouble.'

'I haven't got much money, and I need somewhere to stay. Cheap. I need internet connection. No questions. Know anywhere?'

'Want your own room?'

Fortune looked at Jake, frowned as if he'd asked Fortune whether the earth was round. 'Of course I want my own room.'

Jake laughed. 'Course you do. Ever hear the phrase "beggars can't be choosers"?'

'I'm not there yet.'

'Doesn't take long. Believe me. You want your money back?'

'No.'

'Sure? It's no problem.'

Fortune wondered how many other people were like Jake, open and honest and generous. He hadn't met many, working in finance. Not over the past couple of decades.

'I'm sure,' he said. 'So. You know anywhere I can stay?'

'Know plenty of places,' said Jake, getting to his feet and looking down at Fortune. 'But first you're going to need to ditch that coat.'

The place Jake showed Fortune was a Victorian town house in west London, which they walked to because Jake couldn't afford the Tube. It took an hour and Fortune felt the toll of it, felt old, his hands shaking when they stopped, his breathing short and ragged. Plus, his new coat was nowhere near as warm as the camel hair. It was green and came from a vintage clothing store and could have done with a wash.

'You all right?' said Jake.

'No,' said Fortune. He sat on a low wall, hands on his knees, head bowed. 'I've got lung cancer. Probably terminal.'

'Wow,' said Jake. 'Anything else?' He laughed. 'You know, you're good for me. Nice to know someone worse off.'

'Charming,' said Fortune.

'You ready?'

Fortune stood. 'Yes. This is it, right?' The house had unpainted window frames, dirty net curtains behind the glass, debris piled beneath, in the basement level.

'This is it. Hey, you said you wanted cheap.'

'Let's go.'

They walked up the steps. Jake rang the bell, which made a whirring sound like an engine that refused to turn over. They waited, listening to sounds within. A man opened the door. He was wearing a leather jacket and had dark hair, dark skin, stubble. Fortune, a man accustomed to five-star hotels and obsequious staff, felt his spirits die a little.

'Yeah?'

'My friend here's looking for a room.'

'Twenty a night,' the man said.

'Have you got Wi-Fi?' Fortune said.

'Yeah, I got Wi-Fi.' Fortune couldn't place his accent, thought perhaps it was Turkish. Or Bulgarian, Romanian, Albanian. Or Kosovar. Could be from anywhere. 'You want Wi-Fi, it's twenty-five a night.'

'Single room?'

The man shrugged. 'Yeah. Single room.'

'Can I have a look?'

'Never seen a room before? You want it, give me the money.' He had an agitated air, the man, his hands bunching and unbunching, like he really needed to be doing something else, couldn't wait to get back to it. Dismantling stolen cars, thought Fortune. Or worse.

'What's your name?' Fortune said.

The man shrugged. 'Why you want to know? Georgi.'

'Georgi. All right, Georgi, is there water? A shower?'

'Think this is?' Georgi said. 'Yeah, I got that. You want the room?'

Jake laughed to himself, a soft chuckle. 'I guess, if you don't like it, you can always find somewhere else tomorrow.'

'Shit,' said Fortune, a rare profanity. 'Okay,' he told Georgi. He took out money, handed it to him. 'Here. Are you going to carry my bag?' But Georgi had already turned away, gone back inside. Fortune turned to Jake. 'Would you like a bed too? I'll pay.'

'Nah,' said Jake. 'You're all right.'

'Too good for it?'

'Something like that. You need me, you know where to find me.'

'Thanks,' said Fortune.

'No problem,' Jake said and skipped down the steps. He looked back at Fortune and laughed again. 'Sweet dreams,' he called up.

Fortune nodded, picked up his case and headed inside, to a different kind of life entirely.

thirty-three

HE PLAYS GAMES. HE LIKES TO PLAY GAMES, IT'S WHAT HE does. Everything's a game. Everything. But there's only going to be one winner, isn't there? It's not a fair contest. He calls the shots, he pulls the strings, he manipulates and plays with people. With me. It's all a game for him, but it's not for me because I don't know all the rules. I know this one though: at the end, I die. That's the aim of the game. I lose. I die. But it's no fun for him if it's not a game. It has to be a game.

So here's what's new: the troll is at least, like, a hundred times more evil than I thought he was, and about as crazy, too, in a very, very scary way.

This morning he knocked on the door and said, you need to turn and face the far wall. Why? I said. He didn't answer immediately, but then he said, because I told you to. And if you don't, I will leave you with a life-changing injury.

Like on the news. I always wondered what that meant, a life-changing injury. Losing an arm? An eye? Whatever, I didn't actually want to find out, not right then, so I turned and faced the wall and told him that I'd done it. I heard the door open and close and I thought he was in the room, and my whole back felt like it was covered in static electricity, I was shaking all over. But then I heard his voice from through the door, and he said I could turn around. So I turned around and there was a black sack on the floor, or it might have been a pillowcase. He said, put it on your head. Right over your head so you can't see. So I picked it up and I put it over my head, feeling scared and ridiculous all at the same time, but at least it was clean, it had been washed, it was made of cotton and I could smell the fabric conditioner. It's on, I told him. And I heard the door open and he took my arm and said, follow me.

He's got this weird way of talking, precise and with this kind of ... certainty. Like he's some kind of religious convert, and he doesn't need to question what he does because he *knows* that it's right. Listening to him talk, you just know that there's no negotiation to be had. It's going to be this way. End of. Honestly, he terrifies me.

Where are we going? I asked him, and he said, we're going to the Games Room. What's that? I said. And he was silent for a while, and then he said, the Games Room is a magical place, full of surprises and unexpected happenings. He didn't say anything else, and after a while I said, what? But he didn't answer, just led me along.

Then he opened a door and pulled me through, holding onto my arm. He told me to stand still and not to move, so I didn't, I just stood there. And then I heard the door close and he spoke through it, telling me that I could take my hood off. For some reason I really didn't want to, I really really didn't want to, but what else was I going to do? So I took it off, and took a look around the Games Room.

It was quite small, kind of suburban-living-room size, with brick walls painted black. There was this totally incongruous standard lamp in the corner with a red shade and red tassels hanging all round it, and its bulb must have been very weak because it hardly gave any light. There was nothing else in the room except for two iron rings set into the wall, and a hook in the middle of the ceiling. And a pile of paper in the middle of the floor. That's it. Maybe, I thought, it won't be so bad. How bad can it be?

So, the game, the troll said through the door. Are you ready? He didn't wait for a reply. You have got exactly ten minutes, he said. I would like you to arrange the papers in the correct order. If you get the order correct, you eat. If you don't, then you don't eat for two days. Do you understand the rules?

You're nuts, I said.

He didn't laugh at this and he was silent, and I regretted telling him he was nuts. But then he said, ten minutes. If you want to eat, I suggest that you concentrate.

And off he went, leaving me alone in the Games Room, staring at a pile of paper. I was so confused, so bewildered and baffled that I almost laughed, although I didn't.

There were six sheets of paper. I spread them out on the floor. On each sheet were two letters.

AK.

TF.

SS.

OM.

GA.

FL.

You? No, me neither. I stared at those sheets of paper for, well, for ages. It felt like ages. It's amazing how slowly ten minutes can pass. States, that was my first thought. AK. Arkansas? GA was definitely Georgia. FL was Florida. OM ... Omaha? Was that a state? Or Oklahoma, but I thought that was OK, though it could be OM. TF? It wasn't Tennessee, and I couldn't think of any other states beginning in T, but then, I wasn't an expert. SS? No, nothing. And anyway, what kind of order would you put them in? South to north? Alphabetically? Size, smallest to biggest? Not a clue.

Next, chemical symbols. FL could be fluoride, or fluorine, or fluorescent, or ... who was I kidding? I knew as much about chemistry as I did about how aeroplanes work.

Next, countries. GA could be Gambia, AK could be Afghanistan, if Afghanistan had a K in it, which of course it didn't. Oh Christ, I thought, oh God, it must have been ten minutes already and I had no idea what these letters meant. None at all. My mind was turning fast, but turning nothing, just this churning vacuum of cluelessness. I felt like I used to in maths when I was asked a question on quadrilateral equations and all I wanted to do was run away. That feeling of time passing and my mind a blank. I shuffled the papers on the floor, put them in different combinations, hoped something would leap out. Hoped that some obvious connection would reveal itself and I'd go, oh yes, of course. Duh. But it didn't.

And of course the troll came back and through the door and he said, well?

Well, I haven't got a clue, I said.

Oh. He sounded surprised, and disappointed. Really? You didn't work it out?

Nope.

He sighed. Then I'm afraid there will be no supper.

He didn't say anything else, and I had nothing to say in response. What was there to say? So after a while he gave up and said, put the sack over your head. And I did, and the door opened, and he led me back to my cell and locked the door and I took the sack off and tried not to think about food.

And guess what? I didn't get any supper. Or breakfast. I didn't get diddly. And the next day it was the same thing, and by this time I was starving and really, really wanted to eat. I was fantasizing about Big Macs and kebabs and Indian takeaways; I'd kill for one lousy prawn cracker. And yes, I was thinking about those letters, and what they could mean. Thinking and thinking and thinking. And maybe it's because I was hungry and slightly delirious, but I got it. I got it, even though it seemed impossible, crazy, unreal.

AK. Anthony Knight. Banker, boring, drove a Ferrari, acted like that conferred some special status on him, gave him carte blanche to act like a dickhead. What was I thinking?

TF. Ted Fulbrook. Not the brightest. Or the best, come to think of it.

SS. Steve Smith. Seemed nice at first, but he had these awful tattoos, and it turns out he used to be a football hooligan. Nice.

OM. Ollie Matthews. About the loveliest guy you could ever meet, but just when it was getting serious, he tells me he's going round the world for a year. Didn't invite me. I cried for days.

GA. Gary Allen. Tosser, basically.

FL. Frannie Livings. Nice guy, ended amicably because we had, as far as we could tell, and we did discuss it, absolutely zero in common.

That's right, the troll took the six people I've slept with (except for two he doesn't know about, nobody knows about, and I'd rather forget about) and asked me to put them in order. How did he find out? Is there anything he doesn't know about me?

The last thing he said to me was that he hoped I'd get better at it, get better at his games. He said I still had six days to go, so there was plenty of time.

Oh God. Six days. What's he going to do to me? What has this sick bastard got planned?

thirty-four

ONE THING, FORTUNE THOUGHT GRUDGINGLY, ONE SMALL redeeming feature, was that he could smoke in the house, due principally to the fact that Georgi obviously couldn't care less about what went on inside it. His bedroom was half a room, small to begin with and now boarded in the middle to make two narrow spaces with a single bed in each, nothing else, open at the end to a communal door. He could hear his neighbour snoring on the other side of the intersecting wall as clearly as if he was in the same room. Which, Fortune realized, he technically was.

After he'd been shown his room, which was on the second floor, up uncarpeted stairs covered with paint stains from previous owners, he'd dropped his bag and gone downstairs to the communal kitchen. It had been full of men, smoking and drinking and cooking, large men who looked tired and spoke to each other in languages Fortune did not recognize. They had watched him with suspicion when he had said hello, had stopped talking amongst themselves, and Fortune had left the house and found a McDonald's. At least that was something. He had eaten. When he got back, he washed in tepid water in a bath with a rust stain beneath the taps. The light in the bathroom didn't work, so he'd made do with the light from the corridor, shining weakly through the glass above the bathroom door. No radiators worked. The house was gloomy and cold and strange, filled with so many nationalities, and Fortune felt as if he had stepped into a different world, a dark, dismal, Soviet version of Britain.

Now, lying in bed, he tried to get some sleep and ignore the sounds from his neighbour, the voices outside the door, the feet on the stairs, constant, up and down, doors opening and closing. He was used to hush, muted sounds, warmth and comfort. He wouldn't find it here.

The next morning, he was woken by the sun through his curtain-less window, the cold starting a coughing jag he couldn't seem to stop. His neighbour knocked on the partition between them and said something that Fortune didn't understand. Fortune sat up, rubbed his head and looked through his luggage. His daughter's computer was gone. And the phone, the phone that had been left in his hotel room, the phone he'd received a message on. Gone.

He put on his shoes and took a moment to collect himself. Then he walked around the partition. The man in the bed was half asleep. He had dark hair, and he wasn't either small or especially big. Fortune bent down and got his face right next to his. The man wasn't expecting it, and his eyes opened wide, scared.

'Where is it?' Fortune said.

'What?' said the man. 'What?'

'Computer. Understand? Computer. Phone. Where are they?'

'Don't know, don't know,' the man said.

Fortune frowned, shook his head. 'Yes you do.'

'I don't know,' the man said again. Fortune watched him for a moment, then stood up and looked around the man's side of the room. There was nothing but a bag, the strong kind you use for shopping. He picked it up and emptied it. There were clothes, a bottle of shower gel, a book in a foreign language. Nothing else. Fortune pulled away the man's sheet. He was wearing all his clothes, even shoes.

'Get up,' Fortune said.

The man stood and pushed himself back against the wall, trying to get as far from Fortune as possible. Fortune lifted the mattress and looked underneath. Nothing there.

'Arms up,' he said. The man looked confused and didn't move, so Fortune patted him down, moved the man's arms out of the way, felt his body, worked his way down each leg. The man had a phone in his jacket pocket but it wasn't the one Fortune had found in his hotel room.

'Police?' said the man, and Fortune realized that he had no idea who Fortune was, didn't realize that he'd been the man sleeping next to him all night, waking him with his coughing.

'No,' said Fortune. 'Yes. Doesn't matter. Go back to bed.' The man blinked, moved towards the bed and stopped, looking at Fortune for permission. Fortune stepped away. 'Yes. Bed. Go back to bed.'

He went back next door and sat down on his bed. He put his head in his hands. Think. Your only lifeline to your daughter's been stolen. The phone, you need to get the phone back. Think. Somebody in this house took it. You can't intimidate them all. You're a fifty-four-year-old man with cancer. You need to find someone who can help, make them help. The landlord. Georgi. Put the pressure on him, he'll put the pressure on the rest. You need to find Georgi and force him to help.

How? Bribe or bullshit, thought Fortune. Bribe or bullshit. What did he have? Just over five hundred pounds, and he needed that. Plus, five hundred, even for a slum landlord, wasn't that much money. No, bribery was out of the question, wasn't going to work. He clenched his fists against the sides of his head. Think. Every second you sit here, the harder it'll be, the further away that phone, that computer, will get. You need to move.

He looked through his luggage and found his daughter's wallet, put it in his pocket. He left his room and took the stairs, one flight, two, down to the kitchen. There were men in it, but fewer than the night before.

'Has anybody seen Georgi?' Fortune said.

They looked at him and didn't answer. There were three of them, all standing. Two were drinking coffee and one was drinking a can of lager, a brand he didn't recognize. They were dressed for work, building work, boots and overalls. They were all smoking, so Fortune took out a cigarette and lit it, reckoning it might establish a bond, warm them to him. He inhaled, exhaled, smiled at them. They didn't smile back.

'I need to speak to Georgi. You know? Georgi? Need to speak to him.'

They still didn't answer, and Fortune reverted to Plan A. Bribe. He took out a twenty. 'Come on. Where is he?' They looked at the twenty but didn't react. 'Come on,' Fortune said again.

The man drinking lager finished it, put the can down and walked to Fortune. One of the other men spoke to him, what sounded like a warning, but he just laughed and took the twenty out of Fortune's hand. He walked out of the kitchen and stopped at the door, lifting his chin for Fortune to follow him. He walked down the stairs to the basement, stopping halfway down and gesturing Fortune past. At the bottom was a large room with a leather sofa and a wide-screen TV. There was a huge aquarium along one wall, full of tropical fish. Fortune thought of Jackson, the aquarium he'd had in his wall. He might as well have wandered into a different house, this room was so luxurious, a nouveau riche Eastern European gangster imagining of a sophisticated bachelor pad. It was lit by recessed spotlights and Georgi was watching TV, his back to Fortune. On the TV a cowboy was riding a bull at a rodeo, trying to stay on as the bull bucked and leapt, one hand flailing in the air, the other clamped to the animal's neck.

'Georgi?'

Georgi leapt up, a sudden movement, frightened, or just the reaction of a man used to unpleasant surprises. He looked at Fortune and frowned. 'What you want?'

Fortune walked forward purposefully, with as much authority as he could manage. He took out his daughter's wallet and pulled out the card she'd been given by Environmental Health. He handed it to Georgi, who took it, looked at it, then back at Fortune.

'Sit down,' said Fortune. Give orders. Establish control. Don't give him time to think. Georgi sat and Fortune walked around the sofa, looking down at him. 'Turn it off,' he said, nodding behind him at the TV. Georgi picked up a remote control and clicked it. 'Right,' said Fortune. 'Do you know who I am?'

Georgi nodded. He didn't look happy.

'Good. So, here's what's going to happen. I'm working undercover, inspecting ... hotels.' He said the word with as much acid contempt as he could manage. 'Yours, frankly, is a disgrace. I could have you closed down in forty-eight hours. Less. You're breaking every regulation in the book: fire, immigration, hygiene, you name it. Understand me?'

Georgi looked up at Fortune. He'd recovered a little, recaptured some of his belligerence. 'Yeah?'

Fortune took a moment to look around the basement, to let the tension build. 'You want me to make the call now? I'll make the call now.'

'What you want?' Georgi said. He caught on quickly, was probably used to corrupt officials from wherever he was from. Knew the game, and how to play it. Knew Fortune wanted something and that, maybe, he had a get-out-of-jail card.

'I've had a computer stolen. From this house. A computer and a phone. On the computer are ...' Fortune pretended to weigh his words, to show that this, right here, was a delicate situation. 'Are personal items. Material that I need to get back.'

'Stolen? Here?'

'While I was asleep. And I need it back. Now.'

'What kind of computer?'

'A Mac. This big.' He held his hands apart. 'And a phone. The two were stolen together, and I need them both.'

Georgi shrugged. 'Don't know, man.'

'Then you'd better find out,' said Fortune. 'I'll give you ...' He pulled back his sleeve and checked his watch. 'Five minutes. Five minutes, and if you're not back with my computer and phone, I'll make that call. You understand me?'

Georgi thought for a moment, then stood up. 'You wait here.'

'That's the idea,' said Fortune. 'Five minutes. Yes? Five minutes, and I make the call. Computer. Phone. Five minutes.'

'I get it,' said Georgi. 'You wait.'

He left, walking quickly up the stairs, and Fortune sat down on the leather sofa, sank back into it. His heart was beating quickly, his stomach churning with nerves. The only way to his daughter was through that phone. Jesus. Please, please, let me get that phone back. I need it I need it I need it. He cursed himself for being so naïve, for allowing it to be stolen in the first place. Ridiculous. He put his head back on the sofa, closed his eyes and willed himself to stay calm, not to panic. It'll be okay. It probably won't be okay. It has to be okay. Sophie, I'm coming for you. I'll find you, I promise.

thirty-five

IN THE END IT HAD TAKEN GEORGI SEVEN MINUTES TO FIND
Fortune's phone and computer, but given that Fortune had
nobody to call anyway, no way to back up his threat to close the
place down, it didn't much matter. Five minutes, seven, fifteen,
what difference did it make? Georgi had clattered down the
stairs, breathing hard, Fortune's stolen items in his hands. That
it had only taken seven minutes told Fortune one of two things:
either Georgi had organized the robbery himself, or he knew
exactly who had. That didn't matter much either. Fortune had
what he needed, and that was good enough.

He had taken the phone and computer without speaking to
Georgi, not a word. He'd gone back to his room and sat down
on the bed. There was a message, another message from Starry
Ubado. He tapped the screen and watched the message appear.

Are you ready to play?

Fortune tried to breathe regularly, evenly, tried to keep his
thinking clear and purposeful and forget what was at stake. Just like
last time, the message disappeared after a few seconds. He replied:

What do you want?

He waited. He could hear his neighbour, hear his heavy
breathing as he slept. There was the sound of a siren outside,

receding, further and further, until he could no longer hear it, then the creak of a floorboard, feet on stairs, descending.

A new message:

It's complicated.

What kind of answer was that? Don't be passive, thought Fortune. Don't be meek, a pushover.

Who are you?

Another wait. Fortune stood and looked out of the window. A crow was pecking at something, what had once been a creature, maybe a fox, flattened by a car. Maybe a squirrel. Maybe …

New message:

That's a good question. You've got six days.

Six days. So it was true. He'd got it right. The date, the code in the stolen money. He had six days. Ready to play? Fortune had already been playing this monster's games for days, weeks.

How do I know you've got her? That she's alive?

He hit send and waited, unaware that he was holding his breath. This was it, this was the moment. The moment he found out whether his daughter was alive, that she hadn't taken her own life, that she hadn't been mad.

Ask me a question.

Fortune thought. He didn't have to think for long.

'I knew you would come and find me.' When did she say that?

This time the wait was long and he paced the tiny room like a tiger in a zoo that had long since lost its mind. He sat down. Got up again. Paced. Looked out of the window. Paced some more. Sat down. Stood up. Waited and paced and paced and waited. The mobile was on the bed. Don't look at it, he thought. You know what they say about watched pots. Don't look. He didn't look. He looked. New message:

She got lost. On the Tube. That's when she said it.

Fortune read it again, and again. He took a deep breath, feeling the closest to joy that he could remember. His daughter was alive. Her soft hand in his, the weight of her on his shoulders. *I knew you would come and find me.* His daughter was alive. He blinked away tears and wiped his eyes with the back of his hand. He typed:

What do you want?

First things first. Who am I?

I don't know.

You disappoint me. But no matter. That, then, is your first task. Find out who I am. Then the game really begins.

Fortune gazed at the message, wishing he had pen and paper, some way to write it down, to keep a record. But it disappeared, like all the other messages. Then another appeared in its place:

Six days. You'd better work fast.

Fortune was on a train, in a window seat, the seat next to him empty. He watched fields blur by, catatonic cows, a lake, grey under the huge slate sky, leafless trees, the flat Essex landscape bleak and hopeless. He had nowhere to go except his house. His wife's house. He needed money and a car. Shelter, and somewhere to think.

Who am I? You're Starry Ubado, you're a mystery, you're an evil bastard, a manipulator, a puppet master. I don't know who you are, Fortune thought. He hadn't spoken to his daughter for months, knew nothing about her life. Jackson, her non-existent boyfriend. They were the only people he knew of. And Jessica. It wasn't any of them. But then, who?

The train slowed and a female voice announced that they were approaching New Street. People stood and took down luggage, awkwardly pulling on coats with bent arms. On the platform, Fortune saw police, a lot of them, uniformed officers, some of them with dogs. He wondered how they had found him. He'd dumped his phone, so it couldn't be that. CCTV? Facial recognition? Maybe they'd expected this, expected him to head home, back to his wife, and they'd just been waiting for him to make his move. The train stopped and he looked around, up and down the carriage, thick with people. Where could he go? He was trapped, nowhere to run. This was the end.

An announcement came over the train's speakers, telling passengers that they mustn't leave, that they must stay in their carriages, repeat, stay in your carriages, do not leave the train. Do not leave the train. There was a ripple of complaint, sighs and tuts and shaking heads, as people stood and considered and eventually sat down. The police were talking, standing, waiting. For what? Fortune watched them, his hand against his forehead, hiding his face as if he was blocking sunshine. Another train arrived, on the other side of the platform. The police stood to attention and turned to face it, forming a solid line. The train stopped and the doors opened and men stormed out, pouring out of the doors like soldiers going over the top, wearing blue shirts, full of purpose and energy. The police held their line and the men funnelled up the platform, singing, chanting, shouting abuse. Football fans. Chelsea, FA Cup, fourth round. Fortune breathed deeply, concentrating on his heart, trying to keep it steady. Relax. They're not here for you. The supporter's chants became fainter as they passed through the station's entrance. The passengers stood again and Fortune with them. He couldn't wait to get off the train. Christ, he needed a cigarette.

Fortune didn't have much choice but to take a taxi and hope he wouldn't be recognized, that his picture wasn't all over the news. Embezzler. Murderer. He knew that he must be wanted, but at the same time he couldn't make it feel real, couldn't really believe it. It didn't seem possible. He paid the taxi at the bottom of the drive and once again walked up the gravel, past a car he didn't recognize, and rang the doorbell of the home that was no longer his. He hadn't called, didn't even have the number, had never learned it. It was stored on his discarded mobile. He didn't even know the number of his own home.

A man opened the door. He was around Fortune's age, tanned and lean. He looked in far better shape than Fortune, not that that was much to boast about. Like saying he was more sprightly than a corpse. Fortune wanted to cough but tried to stifle it, keep it behind his lips, willing himself not to show any weakness. Not to this man who was in his home.

'Yes?' the man said.

'I'm looking for Jean,' said Fortune.

'Who are you?'

'I'm her husband,' Fortune said. He left a pause, then said, 'Who are you?'

The man's eyes widened briefly. 'You're her husband?'

'Yes. And this is my house.' At least for the moment, Fortune thought.

'Do you know the police are after you? They were here earlier.' The man was slightly shorter than Fortune, wearing a red sweater that looked like cashmere, looked expensive. He had the bronzed skin and steel-grey hair Fortune associated with eighties American soap operas, *Dynasty*, *Dallas*. Well-fed, wholesome and healthy. Hale, that was the word. Fortune had never disliked anybody so immediately in his life.

'Is Jean here?' he said.

'What do you want?'

'I want to talk to her,' said Fortune. 'Obviously.'

The man shook his head. 'No.'

'No?'

'You're wanted for murder. No, you can't see Jean. You're a danger. Now, leave or I'll call the police.'

'Spare me,' said Fortune. 'You'll call the police anyway. Let me talk to Jean. Now.'

'I've told you already,' said the man. Fortune had to admit that he was no weakling, no pushover. Confronted by a sixteen-stone wanted murderer whose wife he was sleeping with didn't seem to be fazing him too much. Fortune considered pushing past him, forcing his way in, but was saved by Jean, appearing behind the man.

'What are you doing here?'

'I need help. Somewhere to stay, and money. And I need a car.'

Jean frowned. 'I can't help you. The police were here, they told us what you've done.'

'I didn't do it. Any of it.'

'The victim was in your hotel room. You'd already attacked him, the police told us. That's right, isn't it?'

'Yes, but ...' The man was watching Fortune carefully, as if prepared to step in if necessary. Standing in the doorway of the home that Fortune had paid for. Irritating wasn't the word. 'I didn't do it,' Fortune said.

'And the money? You didn't steal the money?'

'No. No, it wasn't me. None of it was.'

'Please,' said Jean. 'Just go.'

'I need money,' said Fortune. 'They've frozen my accounts.'

The man said, 'Wait there,' put a hand on Jean's arm and went back into the house. Fortune looked at his wife. She stared back, unflinching. Fortune wondered whether he should tell her about their daughter, about Sophie, about how she was still alive. Would she believe him? Probably not. Anyway, what was the point in getting her hopes up? He had six days to save her, and the police weren't going to help. Money. Car. That was all he needed.

'Please, Jean. I really need your help. Money and a car, and I'll go, I'll leave you alone.'

The man came back carrying a hammer. Fortune recognized it. He was being threatened with his own hammer. How had things come to this?

'You need to go,' said the man. 'Now.'

'Please,' said Fortune to his wife, ignoring the man. 'Help me out. You can say I took it by force, I don't care. I need a car.'

'I've called the police,' said the man. 'They're on their way.'

'You idiot,' said Fortune. 'You ...' He stopped, didn't have the time. 'Jean, please, please believe me.'

'Why?' said Jean. 'Why would I believe anything you say?' She turned to the man. 'You see? You see what he's like?'

The man nodded. 'Now, are you going to leave?'

'You realize this is my house,' said Fortune, 'and Jean's my wife?'

Jean laughed. 'Don't go there,' she said. 'Don't you dare go there.'

'Jean, come on ...'

'No. No, no, no. How many years were you sleeping with that woman?'

'Can we not—'

'Four years? Five? Practically had another family. You don't get to lecture me. You don't.'

'Look,' said Fortune, then stopped. He was suddenly exhausted and needed to sit. He looked around and walked to the car on the drive, rested up against it. He took out a cigarette and lit it unsteadily, inhaled, coughed. He had to put his cigarette on the ground while he coughed, both hands on his knees, wishing he could stop but unable.

'Oh for Christ's sake,' said Jean. Fortune heard her footsteps on the gravel, felt her hand on his shoulder. 'You're not well, are you?'

He shook his head, stood upright. 'No. Not really.'

'Is it serious?'

'Serious as it gets.'

'Oh Fortune.' She looked at him with concern, and sadness. A real sadness, as if he was already dead, as if he was a visitation, a melancholy ghost come to remind her of what had been. But then, wasn't that what he'd been during their marriage? A ghost, an occasional visitor, only half there? Yes. Yes, that was exactly what he'd been. 'What have you done?'

'Please,' he said. 'Any money you've got. And a car. I need a car. Please.'

She blinked, wiped away a tear, then called to the man. 'Jeff, how much cash have you got?'

Jeff. He should have known, thought Fortune. The man was a hundred per cent Jeff, Jeff through and through.

'Jean ...'

'Just do it. Please.' She turned to Fortune. 'Wait there.'

She walked to the house and went inside. Fortune picked up his cigarette and stood smoking, listening for sirens. How long would they take? Five minutes? Ten? He had no idea. Jean came back out of the house, carrying notes in one hand, keys in the other.

'Just over eight hundred. And you can take the car. But if anyone asks, I didn't have a choice. Right?'

'Right. Course. Thanks, Jean.' He took the money, a thick wad of notes, and the keys.

'Now you need to go.'

'Yes.'

'Look after yourself,' said Jean.

'I'll try.'

He looked at the key and pressed the button with the open door icon, hearing the central locking engage. He picked up his bag, opened the back door and put it in. He got in the driver's side and felt under the seat for the lever to rack it back. He started the engine and found first gear, wondering how long it had been since he'd driven a car. A long time. Never mind, it was like riding a bike. He felt the clutch bite and headed down the drive, catching sight of his wife in the rear-view mirror, holding herself against the cold until Jeff, wholesome, handsome Jeff, appeared and put his arm around her shoulders, keeping her safe and happy. What the hell, thought Fortune, looking away and concentrating on the road ahead. He'd do a better job of it than Fortune ever could.

thirty-six

WHEN DID YOU SAY, 'I KNEW YOU WOULD COME AND FIND ME?' That's what the troll just asked me. Why did he ask it? Why did he want to know? It was with Dad, when I got lost on the Tube, that's when I said it. But only Dad knows what happened, we never told anyone else. And he's not the troll, Dad's not the troll, he can't be. So what does it mean? Does it mean that Dad's out there, and he's looking for me?

No, don't be silly. You haven't spoken to him in months, he's over in Dubai, doing what he does. Telling people what to do, working them to death, squeezing them dry. But then why? Why the question? I can't work the troll out. Can't get a handle on him. He likes to play games, that much I know. But what kind of game is he playing now?

Yesterday he asked me if I needed anything. I said yes, I need to get out of this shithole and away from you, as far away as possible. He laughed at this, or made a sound that might have been a laugh. Who knows? He said that it was a shame, because he liked me and he wished that he had had a sister like me. He said that it would have been fun, that we could have made up stories together, played together, blah blah blah. I told him that he was crazy and that I'd rather have my toes cut off one by one.

He didn't laugh at that one. No, instead he told me to put my hood back on. Why? I said. Because, he said, we're going back to the Games Room.

I still don't know what he looks like, but he's young, I'm pretty sure of that. I didn't see his face when he took me and he makes me wear the hood when I leave my cell, so he could be black or white, he could have one eye or two heads as far as I know. I wonder why he doesn't show his face, and can't help hoping, though I'm probably clutching at straws, that he doesn't want me to see it because he's going to let me go. In a few days, he's going to say right, well, that was fun but the game's over, so off you go.

Yeah, right.

This time, there was no paper, but on the wall was a number, written in chalk. Just a number, and a dollar sign:

$89,917,042.

That was it. And the troll said to me through the door, if you can tell me who that money belongs to, then you can eat. You have exactly ten minutes. Do you understand the rules? I didn't answer, just looked at the number, and he said again, do you understand the rules? I was starving, I was so hungry I felt weak and my legs were trembling and I had these shooting pains in my stomach that made me double up in pain. Yes, I said. Yes, I understand. The troll went away, I could hear his footsteps, and I sat down on the floor. Come on, Sophie, I thought. Concentrate. Ignore the hunger, you've got this one. You can do it. Come on.

What did he mean, who does the money belong to? It belongs to the USA, because it's in dollars. It belongs to somebody who's seriously loaded. Maybe it belongs to a lottery winner. No. Too easy, too vague. He plays games, games that need working out.

All right. Think. The last time it was your boyfriends. It was like he was showing off, demonstrating his power, his knowledge of you. Making sure you knew that he was in control, there was nothing he didn't know, nothing he couldn't do. Okay. So maybe this game is about you too.

So I sat on the floor, which was concrete and stained with rust-coloured marks I didn't want to think about, and I tried to ignore the rings in the walls and the hook in the ceiling and the freaky standard lamp with the red lightshade that looked like it was stolen from a semi in Croydon, and I looked at the number. Stared at it. And pretty soon I read it backwards, because it seemed like a good idea, and I got it straight away. Well, okay, not straight away, but well inside the ten minutes. It belonged to me, because it was my birthday. The day I was born. Easy and not that impressive, I thought to myself. Anybody could find that out.

I banged on the door and yelled, telling the troll that I'd got it, that I'd worked out his stupid game. The money belonged to me. I almost said, so where the hell is it? but I was scared he'd change his mind and keep me starving, so I didn't.

Did you solve it? he said.

Yep.

Did you find it difficult? he said.

Not particularly.

Good, he said. He sounded relieved, like he'd been worried that he'd made it too difficult. Maybe he didn't want me to starve to death. Maybe things aren't going to be so bad after all. Maybe it was all a big joke, just a game, nothing more. Maybe. Then again, maybe I should get real.

I ate pizza and drank orange juice, and there was a packet of biscuits, and it all tasted so good, so, so good, I never knew pepperoni could taste so damn good. And after that I lay in bed and tried to sleep, which wasn't hard, because I've got this new technique. What I do is, I imagine the troll coming into my cell and I jump on him and subdue him and hit him and hit him, and after I've finished hitting him, I hit him some more until he's crying and whimpering and telling me how sorry he is. And then, guess what? Yep, I hit him some more.

Why did the troll ask me about what I said to Dad? I wish he was on his way to save me. I wish that he'd turn up and rescue me from the troll, just like he rescued me when we were on the Tube. But it won't happen. He's not that kind of person. He's not really a dad, just somebody who used to pretend to be, until it got too difficult. Five days left. That's what the troll told me, when he gave me my food. Five days until he does whatever he's going to do. I'm so scared. I am so, so scared.

thirty-seven

HE LIKES TO PLAY GAMES, THOUGHT FORTUNE. IT'S WHAT HE does, whoever he is. Fortune had driven north, away from London, towards the coast and into Suffolk, keeping off main roads and away from CCTV cameras. He'd stopped at a caravan park, hadn't been sure if it was open, but when he'd banged on the door of reception, a teenage boy had appeared and told him that yeah, it was open, if he didn't mind being cold. The boy had called him 'bruv', which hadn't impressed Fortune much, but he figured that if you were on the run, it was unrealistic to expect five-star treatment. He paid the boy a hundred pounds for a week, off-season rates, though judging by the state of the caravans, its on-season wasn't a lot to write home about.

He'd bought tinned food and a bottle of Scotch at a roadside store. He'd nearly finished his four hundred duty-free cigarettes and asked the man behind the counter for forty Marlboro. No way, he'd said, no chance, they couldn't cost that much. Could they? Really? That much? He'd been staggered. If they'd been that expensive back when he was young, he'd never have started smoking. He'd bought a paper, too, and looked for a mention of him, or of Charlie Jackson, but there was nothing. It was probably too early. He'd probably be on the front page the next day.

Now he was sitting in the caravan, the sky dark outside, smoking and drinking and searching through his daughter's computer, trying to see if he'd missed anything within the chaos of her filing system. He likes to play games, he thought. Starry Ubado. The troll. *Who am I?* He must have left a clue, left Fortune some way of guessing. He tried to remember the messages on the phone, tried to remember the exact wording in case there was any hidden meaning. But he couldn't remember, and anyway, the messages had been short and to the point. There'd been nothing ambiguous there.

He looked back at his daughter's blog, at the comments the troll had left. Again, nothing. No ambiguities, no hidden messages. *Bitch. Hope the driver rapes you. Hope you get Aids.* Unpleasant, horrendous, but straightforward. Nothing to see here. Move along.

The name. Starry Ubado. What did that tell him? That the troll was African, of African origin? Only he didn't believe that. It was an invention, it wouldn't be his real name. So why had he chosen it? Starry. Fortune poured himself more Scotch and tapped his cigarette into a mug because there was no ashtray, which was no surprise as there were signs all over the caravan warning the occupants not to smoke, no smoking, it is forbidden to smoke. He was wanted for greater crimes, Fortune figured, and almost smiled. Starry. Starry night, star signs, stars as in celebrities. Was that it? A celebrity, somebody in Sophie's past, somebody she'd written about? But no, he'd already been down that road with Charlie Jackson. Whoever had killed Jackson, Fortune couldn't believe it was another celebrity. Celebrities killing celebrities, some kind of internecine showbiz conflict. Christ. He rubbed his face. Come on, he thought. Think. Who are you?

He wrote the name down on the margin of his paper and looked at it. Just a name. Just a weird name. There was a crossword on the back of the paper. Fortune used to do them, used to enjoy them when he was younger. Anagrams, that was what they were full of. He'd been good at working them out. He looked back at the name. Starry Ubado. He wrote each letter again, placing them randomly. He plays games, he thought. He started making words from the letters. Board. Darts. Dartboard? No. Only one D. Bay. Bat. Bury. Boat. Bar, bard, barb. Bastard. He stopped. Bastard. Leaving the letters r, o, y, u. He felt a big emptiness in his chest, felt his heart within it, like it was dropping, falling. R, o, y, u. Your. Your bastard.

He picked up the phone that had been left in his hotel room. He wrote a message, his fingers trembling, and hit send. Five words:

I know who you are.

He poured more Scotch and lit another cigarette while he waited for a reply. He didn't have to wait long.

Who am I?

You're my son.

Your bastard. Yes.

What do you want?

Fortune drank and smoked and watched the screen, waited for it to light up. Again, he didn't wait long.

You found my name. Now you just need to find me. Five days.

Fortune knew that at one point he and Jean had been happy, had had hopes for the future, plans that involved each other. Had it been some fundamental incompatibility that had made them drift apart? Or had it been the fact that Fortune had never really wanted a family but had known it was the thing to do, find a wife and start a family, only once he had all that, he'd hated it, dreaded his time at home, realized that he preferred work. Much preferred it. Valued it more, prized it more highly. Found more meaning in it. So the more he worked, the better he felt and the less time he had to devote to a family he didn't want or understand. Was that it? He poured more Scotch. He didn't know. It had stopped feeling right, him being at home. He and Jean had stopped talking, started passing each other in the kitchen, withdrawing.

And then he'd met Claudia. At work. Where else? Claudia. A secretary, obviously. Young, beautiful and twenty-two. Exciting, enthralling, dazzling. A to-hell-with-it shake of her black hair, before diving into something illicit, dangerous. Leaving her underwear in his pigeonhole. Booking a hotel for a lunchtime liaison. Following him to his car after work, one dark night, getting in with him and ... Fortune swept away by the attention, the mystery, the exoticism of it all. She was so young yet so ... in control. Confident. And he became infatuated, addicted to the danger and thrill of it all, his lack of choice in Claudia's mad whims, her scary excesses. The antithesis of his home life, of the squabbles and the silences and Sophie, always Sophie, screaming and demanding, and Jean shattered ... And of course the more time he spent with Claudia, the less time he spent at home, even less time, leaving Jean alone with Sophie, holding the baby. She could only have been, what? A year? Eighteen months?

Fortune heard the sound of a car engine outside the caravan, getting closer, headlight beams sweeping across the interior. He stood and looked out but couldn't tell what kind of car it was, or whether it was the police. Why would anybody be out here at this time? He stood, motionless, listening as the car came nearer, nearer, then stopped. He heard the sound of a door opening, then closing. He looked at the bottle of Scotch, wondering whether he could use it as a weapon. He realized he was holding his breath and let it out quietly. He heard footsteps just before the knock on the caravan door.

'Yes?'

No answer. He walked to the door and opened it. The teenage boy from reception was standing there, swaying slightly. Drunk.

'Hello?'

'Yeah, bruv, just … just checking,' he said. He sounded slow, confused. Drunk and stoned. The hope of our nation, thought Fortune, right here. 'So … everything cool?' the boy asked.

'Yes.'

The boy looked at the cigarette in Fortune's hand, his hand against the frame of the caravan door. 'Not supposed to smoke.'

'Oh. Sorry.'

'Well.' The boy paused again, ruminated. 'Maybe, like, don't?'

'Okay,' said Fortune, though he didn't put out his cigarette and the boy didn't seem too concerned. He was skinny, with a shaved head and some kind of tattoo on his neck, and he looked like he could use some vitamins. 'Anything else?'

'No,' said the boy. 'Just that.'

'All right,' said Fortune. 'Good night.' He closed the caravan door and poured more Scotch, wondering why he wasn't drunker. He should be drunk by now. He listened to the car leave, heard it accelerate. The boy didn't look old enough to drive. He listened to the engine, revving too high, in the wrong gear, then heard a heavy sound, some kind of collision. He stood motionless but didn't hear anything else for some time, until he thought he heard the distant sound of a car door closing. He opened the caravan door and looked out into the darkness, but he couldn't see anything, and there were no other sounds. He closed the door and sat back down, in the dark and silence of the caravan.

A memory surfaced in his mind, another occasion when he had been sitting in darkness, this time at his office desk, alone, long after everybody had left for the day. He'd been finding things to do, making sure that he was too late for dinner, too late to help with Sophie. His phone had rung, and he'd picked up.

'Yes? Fortune.'

'Come to the lobby.' It had been Claudia. Her voice only half remembered now, but husky, that much he hadn't forgotten.

'Why?'

'Just come. Come to the lobby, do not leave.' She'd giggled. 'Just wait.'

He'd got up and walked past the rows of empty desks, down the corridor to reception. It had been dark there, too, and empty. He'd waited, how long? Minutes. Growing impatient. Then the lift had pinged, the arrow above lit up. The doors had opened and there had been Claudia, a fur coat shrugged off her shoulders, rucked around her waist, the tops of her arms bare. Everything bare. Wearing heels and a smile. That had been Claudia.

How long had it been? How long had he juggled work and family and Claudia, trying to keep all the balls in the air? Two years? No longer, whatever Jean thought. He thought of their relationship, him and Claudia, like a star, a star that burned and burned but could not sustain, that was always heading for some dreadful and explosive end. He'd tried to finish it, tried many times, but she was more dangerous at arm's length than she was up close, her passion turned into white-hot rage, uncontrollable, powerful and without reason. She'd threatened him: she'd tell his wife, tell the police, make up allegations, take him to a tribunal. Ruin him, destroy his life, his family. Until at last she had told him that, anyway, it was irrelevant because she was pregnant, the child was his and now he had to leave his wife and make a new life with her. And he had said no, no way, she was on her own and it was over. They were through and he no longer cared what she did, he'd had it, done.

But it wasn't done. *She* wasn't done. She'd gone to his house, spoken to his wife. Had told her everything they had done, the details, the full extent of the deception and betrayal. Jean had reacted with cold disinterest, their meeting, Fortune imagined, like the forces of light and dark, the ultimate clash of opposites, fire and ice. Claudia had left, left Fortune, left her job, disappeared. But Fortune had never forgotten her, and Jean had never forgiven him, and their marriage had never recovered. They'd made some perfunctory attempts, some dinners out, a couple of holidays, but it was too late. They had stayed together for Sophie, for her school, the golf club, Fortune's work functions. It was easier that way, appearances maintained. But trust had gone, and love with it.

And, what, four years later? Four years later he had heard that Claudia had killed herself. Hanged herself. Some ex-colleague of hers who had thought that Fortune 'ought to know', though he suspected she just wanted to see his reaction, feel the vicarious thrill of delivering bad, salacious, shocking news.

You, thought Fortune, pouring the last of the Scotch and lighting another cigarette. You are a weak and selfish and contemptible man, and it's only now, when it's far, far too late, that you realize it. He wished that he could go back twenty,

twenty-five years, and try again. Do it better, make an effort, contribute some love. Try to understand his wife and daughter, two good people who had once believed in him. He laughed at himself, softly, contemptuously. He'd never had time for people who traded in if onlys.

thirty-eight

WHO AM I? FORTUNE KNEW THE ANSWER TO THAT NOW. HE wasn't just a troll. He was his son. *Your bastard*. But it was only a partial answer, not a solution. He had no name, no address, no idea who he really was, where he lived, what he did for a living. Nothing. He was a ghost, a person he hadn't even known existed, had never wanted to exist. Fortune sat back at the table, the same table he had drunk at the night before. He took two aspirin, added another. Two for the headache, one for the cancer, he thought. He didn't imagine they'd cure either.

Think. He put his head in his hands and closed his eyes. *Think.* You need to find out where he is. But first, you need to find out *who* he is, who he really is. His name. You need his name. Start there.

Okay. What was Claudia's surname? Emmerson. Claudia Emmerson. From ... where was she from? She'd been twenty-four when they, what, when they split up? Whatever, she'd been twenty-four, and twenty-four-year-olds, when they have their hearts broken, go home. They go back to their mother. Who lived ... Hell. Where did she live? Where did Claudia come from? He knew, he knew, he had known, once, twenty years ago he had known. Somewhere down south, near the coast. Brighton? No. Hastings. That was it. She was from Hastings, had moved up to

London for work and rented a room. Hastings. All right. It was a start, he had a start.

He packed his bag, locked the caravan behind him, got into his car and drove back to the entrance. There was a car parked sideways outside reception, but as Fortune drew closer, he saw that it wasn't parked, it had crashed, the side of it badly dented, one tyre in a ditch. The natural consequence of putting a drunk teenager behind the wheel, he thought. He drove past, but before he reached the entrance, the teenage boy ran out and waved his hands. Fortune stopped, dropped his window.

'Did you do that?'

The boy nodded. 'Last night.'

'You'd been drinking?'

'A bit.'

A bit. Right. 'Is it your car?'

The boy shook his head. 'My mum's.' He chewed his lip for a moment, then said, 'Help me get it sorted out?'

'Sorry,' said Fortune. 'I've got to be somewhere.'

'Please?' said the boy. 'My mum's going to kill me.'

'Where is she?'

'Holiday. With her boyfriend.'

'I see.' Fortune paused and watched his exhaust make thick clouds in the rear-view mirror. 'Are you supposed to be renting out caravans?'

'Needed the money,' the boy said. It wasn't an answer, but it was close enough.

'When's she back?'

The boy shrugged. 'Few days.'

Fortune looked at the boy, wondering how old he was. He looked fifteen, but he also looked malnourished, so he could be older. One thing was certain, he wasn't too bright. Fortune sensed an opportunity. It was a long shot, and it wasn't something he wanted to do. It wasn't a good thing. But it was an opportunity, and he had to take what he could. For Sophie's sake.

'Listen,' he said, 'I'd like to, but I really can't. I do need to be somewhere.'

'Please, bruv, come on. Please?'

Fortune sighed and killed the engine. He caught a glimpse of himself in the rear-view and had to do a double-take. He looked tired and ill and he had the beginnings of a beard. He'd never had a beard before. People like him, they just didn't.

'Look, I've got a friend who works with cars. He could help. I can give you his address.'

'No, but I can't, man. I can't drive, don't have a licence.'

'Right.' Fortune nodded. 'Well, I'm sorry.' He started his car and put it into gear, but he didn't drive away. The thing was, he needed transport. Okay, so he had a car, but the police would be looking for it. Fortune knew about automatic number-plate readers. He'd be on the road a long time and there was no way he'd get away with it. His plan had been to ditch the car somewhere and hitch the rest of the way. But now he had a better plan. He waited and revved the engine. Here he was, playing brinkmanship with an underage hung-over pothead. What had he become?

The boy put his hand on the ledge of Fortune's open window.

'Can't *you* do it?'

Bingo, thought Fortune, without much pleasure. He cut the engine a second time, and looked around slowly at the boy, leaving a long pause. 'What?' he said, eventually.

'Take it. I'll …' The boy thought for a couple of seconds. 'You can stay here for nothing. Long as you want. Well, until my mum comes back. If you help.'

'What about my car?' said Fortune. Ask him a question. Empower him. Bring him in, get him involved.

'Leave it here.'

Fortune smiled. 'So you can crash mine too?' Use of humour. Textbook.

'No, I swear. Swear I won't.'

'So ...' Fortune closed his eyes, pretended to think. 'I take your car, get it fixed up, bring it back and I can stay here for nothing?'

'Yeah.'

'Who'll pay for the repair?'

The boy put his hand in his pocket and took out the money Fortune had given him. 'I've got this.'

Fortune grimaced. 'You'll need more than that.'

'All I got. Come on, please? Bruv?'

Fortune sighed again, deeply. 'What's your name?'

'Lee.' *Lee.* He was as much a Lee as Jeff was a Jeff.

'I'll be away at least a night,' said Fortune.

'Nah, that's fine. That's sweet.'

'Christ.' Fortune shook his head, opened his car door and climbed out. Just that exertion made him cough, left him light-headed. 'I must be crazy. All right, give me the keys.'

Lee's mother's car was a ten-year-old Golf that had done over 100,000 miles, most of which, Fortune suspected, had been driven in the wrong gear. He was worried about the tyres, doubted they'd pass a roadside inspection, and kept his speed a steady seventy, good motorway practice, treating each lane as an overtaking lane. He'd used Lee's mother's computer to search for Emmersons who lived in Hastings, and come up with three. At least it was unlikely he'd be recognized. He looked three stone lighter and ten years older than any recent photo, plus about three social classes lower, thanks to the coat Jake had made him buy.

He listened to the radio on the way and heard his name mentioned on the news as a man wanted for questioning in connection with the death of Charlie Jackson. He watched cars pass him and realized that the people in them, going to work or to visit friends or to buy groceries, whatever, were now ineffably and entirely different to him. They were free, could do anything they wanted, had no constraints. He had to con children into lending him cars, had to pay in cash, economize, sleep in caravans, keep off the radar. A different life, a life he had never imagined. He remembered the stories of escaped prisoners of war he had read as a child, British soldiers at large in Germany, always on the move, with forged documents and constant fear. That was him, now, in a society built for surveillance, cameras everywhere, a near-police-state infrastructure. And he couldn't let himself be found, because his daughter needed him. At least, he thought, Lee didn't look the kind who followed the news.

He came off the M25 and headed south, turning the radio off and trying not to think about the dangers he was surrounded by, the near impossibility of staying undiscovered. Twenty miles outside Hastings he heard sirens and saw a police car behind him, headlights alternating. He wondered whether it was worth trying to outrun it, but no, not in Lee's mother's wreck of a car, so he indicated, pulled over and watched the police car blow past, the officers inside not even giving him a glance. He stopped at a service station and bought a map of Hastings and a phone charger for the mobile the troll had left him. That his son had left him. Don't think about it. Keep moving. It's Sophie that matters. Four days. Find her. Find him, find her.

The first Emmerson, whose name began with P but whose gender was a mystery, lived in an apartment in a tall Victorian town house overlooking the sea. Fortune rang the buzzer and waited, unsure if it had sounded or not. The house had been painted white, although it was now a kind of dirty grey, the colour of the scummy foam that washed over the beach's pebbles.

'Yes?' The voice was distorted by the intercom system, tinny and distant, hard to hear over the wind blowing in off the sea, although he could tell it was a woman.

'Mrs Emmerson?'

'Miss Emmerson, yes,' said the voice. 'I don't want to buy anything.'

'I just wanted to speak with you,' he said. 'I'm doing some research into the Emmerson family.'

'Family?' said the voice. 'I don't have any family.' The voice was thin, and even through the intercom Fortune could tell that it belonged to an elderly person.

'You never knew a Claudia Emmerson?'

'Claudia Emmerson?'

'Yes.' Fortune waited, waited for some moments.

'There is no Claudia Emmerson,' the voice said.

'I know,' said Fortune. 'But did you know her once? Years ago?'

'I have told you,' said the voice, wobbling with geriatric indignation. 'I do not know anybody of that name.'

'Are you sure?' said Fortune. She sounded senile, he thought. She probably wasn't sure about anything.

'Will you please go away?' said the voice, a high-pitched quaver. 'I'm missing my radio programme.'

'Yes, of course, Mrs, sorry, Miss Emmerson. Thank you for your time.' Fortune released the intercom button. Scratch Miss P. Emmerson off the list, he thought. Next.

thirty-nine

TODAY I WENT BACK TO THE GAMES ROOM. BUT TODAY WAS different. Today, the troll told me to put the hood on, and take everything else off.

What? I said.

Everything. Your clothes. All of them.

Why?

Because it's part of the game, he said. Don't worry, I won't touch you.

No, I said. No, I won't.

Yes, he said. You will. Because if you don't, I will cut your toes off. He said it with that conviction he has, that implacable certainty. He will cut my toes off. I don't doubt it, not for a second.

So I did it. I took off everything, folded my clothes and put them on the bed, then put the hood over my head. It was cold, standing there with nothing on, but that wasn't the only reason I was trembling. This was, what do you call it? An escalation. This was worse than anything he'd asked me to do before, worse than anything he'd threatened. I told him that I'd done it and stood there with the hood over my head, feeling like a captured Iraqi soldier about to have a dog set on him. And the troll led me to the Games Room, and locked me in.

Ten minutes. Ten minutes to work it out, he said, or you won't get your clothes back. Do you understand the rules?

Yes, I said.

And he went.

On the wall were six words:

Intoxication.

Immodesty.

Adultery.

Gluttony.

Wrath.

Murder.

And underneath them:

What should come next?

Okay. Here we are again, I thought. Here we are again, and you are going to get your clothes back. You won't let him humiliate you. This is about power, about him showing you he can do anything he wants to you. Don't let him. Think.

The thing is, the troll might know everything about me, but I'm starting to get a handle on him too. He thinks that knowledge equals power, and that's the key to the puzzle. Knowledge is his weapon, which means that these games rely on knowledge about me. The solution to this game involves something I've done, or something I am. It's just a question of working it out.

My first thought was: it's the seven deadly sins. Only I was pretty sure intoxication wasn't in there. I knew sloth was, because when I was a kid I used to wonder what an animal was doing in the list. And envy, envy was definitely in there. So it wasn't the deadly sins. Dismiss it. Move on.

Was it something I'd done myself? Intoxication? Tick. Immodesty? Tick. Adultery? No, I couldn't say that I'd committed that, unless one of the men I'd slept with was married, which I didn't think they were, and anyway, it was a bit of a stretch. Gluttony? Certainly. Wrath? Yep. Murder? I could definitely rule that one out. I was sure I'd have noticed.

So. What else? I knew that time was ticking, but I would not panic. I would not. I would think and concentrate and work it out.

Intoxication.

Immodesty.

Adultery.

Gluttony.

Wrath.

Murder.

What should come next?

That's the key to it, I thought. What should come next. Not 'what comes next', but 'what *should* come next'. Meaning that it didn't, but it should.

Gotcha. It hit me, from where I don't know, but I saw adultery and gluttony, and the thought came into my head and I looked at the other categories, and yes, I thought, it must be. It must be.

Intoxication. J.P., a well-known and usually squeaky-clean member of a boy band, falls out of a nightclub, hammered, seriously off his head on booze and powder. He climbs into a taxi and the driver's having none of it, so J.P. swings at him, in front of the cameras of half a dozen paparazzi.

Immodesty. C.C., a TV presenter in the mix for hosting a prime-time Saturday-night family show, has shots of her naked self leaked all over the internet. Goodbye lucrative TV contract, hello D-list personal appearances in Essex nightclubs.

Adultery. Cabinet minister has it off with his secretary. Yawn.

Gluttony. H.T.D., rapper and all-round bad boy, piles on the pounds to the point that all he can now wear are tracksuits and hats.

Wrath. H.T.D., portly rapper, beats up his girlfriend.

Murder. R.L., model, has abortion. Tastefully reported, with a moral angle about a woman's right to choose. But, basically, a scandal piece. Not my finest hour.

Those were the last six stories I wrote for the magazine, the last six stories that carried my byline. Oh, I'm an expert in sin, a student of it. And what should come next? That cradle-snatching bastard Charlie Jackson, that's what, only he got away with it. Got completely away with it.

What should come next? Paedophilia? It didn't sound right. Perversion? No. It had to sound biblical, like in the Commandments or something. Lust. It was lust. Lust should come next. I knocked on the door, banged on it. Lust, I shouted. It's lust. It's Charlie Jackson and it's lust. And the troll came back, and he sounded disappointed, and he said, yes, that's right. He told me to put the hood on and he opened the door and tossed in my clothes, and he dragged me back to my cell and threw me into it, like I'd ruined his day, like he despised me.

Like he despised me. Sophie, grow up. He's destroyed your life, kidnapped you, starved and humiliated you, and he's going to kill you. Of course he fucking despises you.

forty

NEXT ON THE LIST WAS A MS S. EMMERSON. SHE LIVED DOWN A
rutted lane between two terraces, in a house that looked as if it
had started life as a shed and had had other buildings attached
to it over time, a confusing jumble of lean-tos and corrugated
iron and painted brick walls, a gravel and weed apron in front
of it where a convertible VW Beetle was parked, looking like it
wouldn't be going anywhere soon. Fortune knocked on what he
guessed was the front door and waited. A cat squeezed fluidly
out of a hole in the Beetle's roof and mewed at him, looking at
Fortune as if he held some kind of answer, which he didn't. The
door was opened by a woman with short silver hair, wearing a
paint-covered T-shirt.

'Help you?'

'Hello. Yes, I'm doing some research into the Emmerson
family.'

'Oh?' The woman had half-moon glasses on a chain around
her neck and she put them on. 'Is that so?'

'I was wondering if I could ask you a couple of questions.'

The woman leant against her door frame and looked Fortune
up and down. 'What kind of questions?'

'Just about your descendants, people in your family.'

'Genealogy,' said the woman.

'That's right,' said Fortune, smiling, trying a laugh. 'Some people don't understand the word, that's why I don't use it.'

'I'm with you,' said the woman, though she didn't smile back, instead watched Fortune with a level gaze. 'So what would you like to know?'

'Do you have a daughter, or a niece, or any relation really, called Claudia?'

'Claudia?'

'Yes. She's, well, she's kind of the starting point of my research.'

'What kind of research?'

Fortune searched for a plausible answer, though he knew as much about genealogy as he did parenting. The woman pushed herself upright and said, again, 'What kind of research?'

'Like I said.' Fortune paused, then added, 'Just general genealogy.' He almost winced as he said it, aware of how lame it sounded.

The woman cocked her head, one way, then the other, like a small bird sizing up a worm. 'Who are you?' she said.

Fortune backed up a couple of steps, but he needed to know, needed an answer from this woman. 'Claudia, that's the name. Do you—'

'Are you that man?' she asked him. 'From the news?'

Fortune didn't answer, just turned around and walked back down the rutted lane, as quickly as he could without looking as if he was running away, which he was. From behind him he heard the woman call, 'You are, aren't you? You're that man,' but by this time he'd turned the corner into the street where his car was parked. He still had one name left to try, and if Ms S. Emmerson was going to the police, he'd better work fast.

The last name on Fortune's list was a T. Emmerson. He had the address but, he now realized, not a good enough story. He thought back to the woman, and how inadequate his explanation had been, how flimsy. His off-the-shelf genealogy cover wasn't doing it, wasn't cutting it. He needed something that closed down questions instead of encouraging them. *Why do you want to know about Claudia?* Because I'm doing research into the Emmerson name. *Why?* That was what anybody who knew her would ask him, and right now he didn't have an answer. He sat in his car and thought. Money. That was it. Claudia still owed money of some kind, and Fortune was out to get it. A bailiff, he was a bailiff. A debt collector. He imagined that he would have made a pretty good debt collector, though that wasn't a lot to brag about. Cold, businesslike, incapable of empathy. Not a person anybody could like. So okay. He's a debt collector and he's after some money, a twenty-year-old debt, the kind of thing people don't want to know too much about. The kind of thing people prefer just to disappear. He'd spout some legal mumbo-jumbo about unpaid estate, lasting legacy, compound interest. That'd do it. Claudia had died owing money and the debt had caught up. Cynical? Yes, very. But it would probably work.

T. Emmerson lived in a fifties house, the kind built by the government in haste, the kind nobody imagined would still be there in seventy years' time. It still had an unfinished look, as if it was waiting for somebody to come and render it, apply an extra coat of paint. The front garden had a gate, curled metal painted green, and there was a motorbike that looked almost as unloved as the lawn did. It was exactly the kind of place that Fortune had worked his entire life to distance himself from, to rise above. He pushed the gate open, walked up the cracked path and knocked on the door. He waited, then knocked again. He stepped back and looked up at the windows of the first floor, but as he did so, the door opened and a man said, 'What?'

'Mr Emmerson?'

'Last time I checked,' the man said. He was wearing a vest and had thick-lensed glasses and stubble and doughy white arms. He looked old and unwell. Hell, he probably looked like Fortune did. Those in glass houses, et cetera.

'My name's ...' Christ, he hadn't considered that one. 'Thomas.' First or second name? Who knew? 'I work for a debt recovery firm.'

The man had one hand on the frame of his door and he leant his forehead against the back of it, lifted his head, butted his hand. 'Not again.'

'It concerns a ...' Fortune pulled out the phone, pretended to read something from it. 'Claudia Emmerson.'

The man turned his head at this and stood up properly. 'Claudia?'

'You know her?'

'I did. She was my sister.'

'I need to speak with her.'

'You know she's been dead for, I don't know ...' He closed his eyes, did a mental calculation, took his time over it, which led Fortune to suspect that maths hadn't been his thing at school. 'Twenty years. More.'

'Oh. Really? That's information I wasn't aware of.' Fortune jabbed at his phone in a ludicrous parody of an official in possession of an important device that did complex things. 'Then I'll need to know the next of kin.'

'Why?'

'Because the debt needs paying, and if Claudia Emmerson really is dead ...' Fortune paused at this point, to suggest that he was by no means convinced by this claim, 'then the debt will naturally revert to the next of kin.' Which, he was well aware, was nonsense. But by the looks of Mr T. Emmerson, he had no idea of how the law worked, or didn't.

'Shit. Serious? Shit. I mean, I don't know. What does that mean, the next of kin?'

'Normally a husband.'

'Didn't have one.'

'Parents?'

'Dead.'

'Siblings?'

'Do what?'

Fortune sighed. 'Brothers or sisters?'

The man paused. 'Well, there's me.'

'Anyone else?'

'No.'

'Right,' said Fortune. 'I see.' He stopped, laughed. 'Of course, there's children, too. I got it in the wrong order. Children first, then brothers and sisters. So if she had a child—'

'She did,' the man said, quickly.

'Oh? I don't have any record of that.'

'No, well, she ... It wasn't like ... he wasn't exactly normal.'

'Not normal?'

'Well, by that I mean he seemed okay, but see, it wasn't like she and the dad, they weren't together. And course, then she dies, doesn't she, kills herself, and then the kid, I mean what's going to happen to him, my parents are old, and me, me? I, no, it ain't going to happen. So off he goes, doesn't he?'

'Does he?' Fortune took a step back, jabbed again at his phone.

'Yeah.'

'Where?' said Fortune, still looking at his phone, not daring to look at the man, show the hope and need in his eyes.

'Don't know. Off he goes. You know?'

'You didn't ask?' Now he looked up at the man, who seemed uneasy.

'Well, I mean. What am I going to do?'

'Got a name for him?' said Fortune, aware that this was it, this was the moment. Win or lose. Heads or tails.

'The kid? Yeah, he was called ... wait.' The man took his glasses off and rubbed his eyes, thought. 'No, weren't that. He was called ... like, a weird name. That much I remember.'

'Please think.'

'Yeah, am doing. Thing is, he weren't here, I didn't really know him. And Claudia, she weren't exactly what you'd call mum of the year either. Still, used to scream at him. What was it? Bloody shut up, bloody ... Hector. That was it. Kid was called Hector. What about that?'

'And you don't know where he is?'

'Not a clue.'

'Because if I can't find him, then that debt? It reverts to you.'

The man put his glasses back on and said, 'Listen, if I did, seriously, I'd tell you.'

Fortune didn't doubt it. 'All right. So all you can tell me is that your sister, Claudia Emmerson, had a child named Hector Emmerson, and that you have no idea where he is.'

'Erm,' said the man, trying to process what Fortune had just said. 'Yeah. No. Don't know where he is. Right?'

'Thank you,' said Fortune. 'I might be back. If I can't find him.' He turned and walked back down the path to the gate, but when he was halfway, the man called out.

'How much? How much, if you need it paid?'

Fortune turned, looked at the man, the shabby home, thought of the lack of effort and care he had shown to his sister, his sister's son.

'Just shy of a hundred and sixty million dollars,' he said. 'Have you got that kind of money?' He turned without waiting to see the man's reaction, opened the gate, closed it, and walked back to his car. He had a name. It was something. It was infinitely more than he'd had a day ago. But there were only four days left. There was so much work to do, so much. He wondered whether he could do it; not whether he could out-think the troll, but whether, if he kept on going like this, he would still be alive. He wanted to sleep. He couldn't drive back to the caravan park. He needed to sleep, now. So badly.

forty-one

UNLESS THE HECTOR EMMERSON THAT HE WAS LOOKING FOR was a dairy farmer living in Iowa, then Fortune believed that he'd found his son. His son, whom he had neglected even more completely than he had his daughter. What kind of legacy was he leaving? The most shameful kind. The most ignominious, worthless, wretched kind. *Enough*, he told himself. Don't think about it. Act, don't think. It's Sophie that matters. Everything else is just noise, incoherence, madness. Sophie, concentrate on Sophie. You've got three days. You haven't got time to feel sorry for yourself.

He'd woken up five hours earlier in the front seat of Lee's mother's car, in a lay-by off an A road, parked between an HGV out of Poland and a fast-food van selling deep-fried heart attacks. He'd bought a bacon sandwich from the unhealthy-looking woman behind the counter, bacon sandwiches, it turned out, being one thing he could still manage, apparently cancer-proof. He'd eaten sitting in the front seat of the car, the door open, blankly watching trucks and vans and cars hiss past on the wet road. Cars passing, time passing. Three days left. He needed to move. And to do that, he'd need to keep the car. He dialled Lee's number. He had to buy some time.

'Lee?'

'Yeah.' His voice thick and slow, from drink, drugs, maybe both. 'Where you at, man?'

'I'm sorry. The car's taking longer than I thought.'

'Oh.' There was a long pause as Lee tried to think of a response. 'How come?'

'Because when you crashed it, you also fried the central locking. Totally. It needs replacing.'

'Oh no, man. No, I ain't got money for that.'

'It doesn't matter. Like I said, this car guy, he's a friend of mine. I'll get it sorted, but it's going to take time.'

'How long?'

'A couple of days.'

'My mum's back in, like, three days, man. I need that car.'

'Trust me. You'll get it.' Fortune needed to handle Lee's anxiety, and decided that attack was the best strategy. It made him feel guilty as hell, but what choice did he have? He needed the car, needed it to find Sophie. 'I'm doing you a favour here. If you want me to bring it back now, I'll do it. And leave the explaining to you.'

'No, man, no.' Lee couldn't get the words out fast enough. Fortune imagined Lee's mother. She must be a formidable woman, to instil this much fear in young Lee. 'Just bring it back before she gets here, yeah?'

'No problem. I'll call you.' Fortune paused, imagined Lee's anxiety. Poor kid. 'And Lee?'

'Yeah?'

'Don't worry. Really. It'll be fine. I promise.'

'Okay.'

Fortune had hung up, driven to a roadside restaurant with Wi-Fi and searched for Hector Emmerson. He only came up with two, one in the States, the other in the UK, a software engineer who worked at a place called AIX Industries. He looked them up and found an address in east London, not so far from where his daughter had been living and working. Could finding his son be this easy?

'Are you okay?'

Fortune glanced up from his seat in the café of the service station at a young woman who was looking down at him with concern. 'Sorry?'

'You ... you've got blood on your shirt.'

He looked down and saw stains, dark on the pale material. He'd only seen himself in his rear-view mirror that day, only his eyes. He excused himself, closed his daughter's computer and walked to the toilets. He stared at himself in the mirror. He was pale and his lips were cracked and bloody, his beard matted below his mouth. He was unrecognisable, which he had to concede wasn't the worst news. Jesus but he looked ill, his eyes dark, deep in their sockets. He smiled at his reflection, a smile that didn't reach his eyes, a smile that made him look like a ghastly wraith come to visit evil on some unfortunate.

He turned on the taps and washed his face, cleaning himself up as well as he could. It would have to do. He had a fresh shirt in the car. He needed to get to east London and find Hector Emmerson. He tried not to think about the time remaining, the fact that he was almost certainly too late already. Three days. It wasn't long enough. There was no way it was long enough. It had to be long enough.

Fortune hadn't known what to expect of AIX Industries, but in his head he had imagined some kind of lab, a clean and brightly lit modern building full of gently humming machines, buzzing fluorescent tubes and quiet efficiency, a plate-glass building on some sterile industrial estate. What he found was an old brick warehouse on the edge of the Olympic Park, on a street that had just missed out on regeneration, sandwiched between a garage advertising cheap MOTs and a Chinese supermarket wholesaler. He parked up the street and walked back down. It was raining gently and there was a smell of petrol and something else in the air, some non-specific odour of urban decay.

There was a buzzer next to the door and Fortune pressed it, but before he got an answer, the door opened and a young man with a large beard backed out of it, carrying a computer tower. He looked at Fortune and said, 'Help you?'

'I'm looking for AIX Industries.'

'You found it.' The man sounded hostile, pissed off. 'Who're you looking for?'

'Hector Emmerson.'

'You're shitting me.'

'Sorry?'

The man hesitated, glancing up and down the street, for what, Fortune couldn't guess. He looked back at Fortune, studied him carefully. 'God,' he said.

'What?'

'You … you look like him.'

'Like Hector Emmerson?'

'What are you, his father?'

'No,' Fortune lied. There was no way he was going to admit to something like that. 'You know him?'

The man smiled, a smile as lacking in humour as Fortune's had been at the service station. 'Oh, yeah. Yeah, I know him.' He paused. 'Kind of.'

'Well?' said Fortune.

'Well, if I ever see him again, I'll tear his head off,' the man said. 'I shit you not.'

'Care to expand on that?' said Fortune.

'Not really,' said the man, then sighed. 'Okay. Okay. You'd better come in. But hear me, you haven't picked the best time. Just a friendly warning. Sure you want to come in?'

'I'm sure,' said Fortune. What choice did he have? The man hesitated, then said, 'Open that door for me,' and when Fortune did, he walked in and Fortune followed, wondering just what the hell AIX Industries was.

Inside, there was a stairwell with stone steps leading up to the first floor, but the man passed them and pushed through another door into a warehouse space. It was large and half empty, trestle tables set up with computers, monitors, wires trailing across the floor. There was a pinball machine in the corner, though it wasn't on. In the centre of the space was a table with people standing around it. There was food on the table, and bottles of wine; it looked like some kind of party. In the far corner of the room was a huge server stack, green and red lights flashing on it, a tangle of wires covering it. However decrepit the building looked from the outside, inside was some serious tech, Fortune could recognize that. A significant amount of processing power. The man put his machine down on a table, turned and said, 'Name's Eddie.'

'Fortune,' said Fortune.

Eddie didn't offer to shake hands and they stood looking at each other awkwardly before a woman holding a glass of white wine called over, 'Ed? Who's the visitor?'

'He's looking for Hector,' said Eddie.

Everybody standing around the table turned at this, staring at Fortune in silence. It seemed that Hector Emmerson had left some kind of mess behind him. The silence was broken by the woman, who walked over to Fortune, still holding her glass. She stopped, slopping some wine onto the concrete floor.

'Nic Strensky,' she said. 'I'm the founder of AIX.' She had an American accent.

'I'm Fortune. I'm looking for Hector Emmerson.'

'Who isn't?' said Nic. 'Hey?' This was directed at the group standing around the table of food, canapés and sausages on sticks. They all nodded in agreement, resigned, and Nic turned back to Fortune. It occurred to him that she was quite drunk. 'Why d'you want to find him?'

'He's ... he's been doing things. To me, to people I know.'

'Hacking.' A statement, not a question. Fortune nodded. 'It's what he does,' Nic said. 'Hacks people's lives. Destroys them. Plays games.'

'He's done it to you?'

Nic nodded. 'What you're looking at right now is the final desperate breaths of AIX Industries before it flatlines for good, which'll be in ...' she looked at her watch, 'a couple of hours, when our equipment is taken away.'

'Because of him? Hector?'

Nic nodded, sighed. 'You got it. All down to him. Goddamn guy, turns out he's pure evil. Pure evil incarnate.'

'What'd he do?'

'Listen, I'd love to talk, but we're kind of in the middle of something here.'

'I see. Sorry. It's just, I do need to find him. It's important.'

'So's this. My co-founder, he's dead. This is his send-off, from what's left of AIX.'

'Please,' said Fortune. 'Just a few minutes of your time.'

Nic sighed, looked at Fortune, then at the group of people. At last she nodded. 'Come back in an hour. I'll talk to you. But I warn you, I doubt it'll help. It turns out I know less than nothing.'

An hour later, Nic Strensky seemed to have sobered up slightly. They were sitting in an office, the walls made up of windows in wooden frames: an old foreman's station, or where they used to do the books for the warehouse. They were opposite each other, on two sides of a desk that was covered in paper, a monitor on it, a computer tower underneath. Nic had made coffee and had offered Fortune a cup, which he'd accepted. She had short hair and a strong face, intelligent eyes, perfect skin. She looked like the kind of person who did yoga while eating pulses. In fact, Fortune thought, she looked about as healthy as he looked sick. Which was very.

'You know him?' said Nic.

'No.'

'You his father?'

Fortune hesitated at this, looked at Nic's open gaze and said, 'Yes.'

'But you don't know him.'

'No. No, I've never met him. I didn't know he existed until a couple of days ago.'

Nic nodded, lifted her cup and smiled at its rim. 'I warn you, I don't think you're going to be a proud father.'

Fortune nodded back. 'I figured.' He paused and looked behind him, at the now-empty office. 'So what happened? What do you do here?'

'Did,' said Nic. 'What did we do.' She paused, drank more coffee. 'We did great things, is what we did. Important things. World-changing things.'

'Here?' said Fortune, his tone surprised, as if to say, what could possibly happen of importance in a place like this? He regretted it immediately, seeing Nic's face harden.

'Here,' she said. 'We were running an AI project. Artificial intelligence. We had investment, like, seriously, we couldn't turn the VCs away. They were throwing money at us; everybody, like, everybody in the tech community was talking about us.'

'What kind of project?'

Nic shrugged. 'You wouldn't understand, but it was around logic, decision-making. It was brilliant. Peter, that's my co-founder, he was this genius and he'd found just this most incredible algorithm, this ...' She paused and leant back in her chair, her coffee cup in both hands. 'This thing of beauty, elegance. It was a masterpiece.'

'Okay,' said Fortune, nodding but none the wiser. 'So what happened?'

'What happened? Hector Emmerson happened. We brought him in, he was good, very good, we needed ...' She stopped. 'Listen, it's technical. You really wouldn't understand.'

'Try me.'

'The problem we had, with AI, is we can do the algorithm but it's about processing, about speed. It's so sophisticated, so many computations simultaneously ... We can get robots to make decisions, incredibly complex decisions involving millions, billions of variables and considerations. Better than a human could, more rational, more sensible. But every decision was taking too long. We're talking seconds, rather than microseconds. It was too slow, it wasn't working.'

'Right,' said Fortune, nodding, half understanding. Decisions. Speed. It sounded plausible.

'Anyway, we needed to make it faster. And Hector, he could speed things up, had this magic way with code. He was getting five, six hundred per cent increases. Decision time was coming down to acceptable tolerances. He wasn't cheap, and he was, like, really *weird*, but he was worth it. At least, we thought he was.' Nic laughed. 'Turns out he wasn't. He really wasn't.'

She spotted something over Fortune's shoulder, stopped talking and stood up. As she passed Fortune on her way out of the office she said, 'Wait there. Time to administer the *coup de grâce*.'

Fortune turned to see her talking to a man holding a clipboard. He said something to her and she rubbed her hand in her hair, ground the heel of her hand into an eye, then took a pen and scribbled something on the clipboard. Two more men appeared and started unplugging machines, carrying them out of the office, taking everything that AIX Industries had, all they had left, while Nic stood and watched them, looking as bereft as anyone Fortune had ever seen.

forty-two

I AM SURROUNDED BY GHOSTS AND THEY ARE TRYING TO TELL me things, terrible things. Things that I don't want to hear, that I don't want to think about, because what happened to them is going to happen to me, I'm now sure of it. Whatever they went through is waiting for me in two days' time, some horror that I don't want to imagine, that I *can't* imagine. There's a history here in this cell, I can feel it breathing, feel it watching me, waiting.

The walls talk to me. They talk to me all the time and I can no longer ignore them. At first I could, I could pretend that it didn't mean anything and that it was okay, just normal kids, writing graffiti like they always have. But there's so much pain and suffering and horror living behind those words. I can't pretend any more. This place is full of evil and it's waiting for me too, grinning and licking its lips.

I haven't lost my mind. I'm not mad (she says, again). I'm not I'm not I'm not. But still. I know all the voices. I've even given them names. I hear them talk to me, hear them suffer and plead and beg for me to help, but I'm too late, years, decades too late. And anyway, what can I do? It's not like I'm in a better position than they were. The poor things. I think they were children. I think they were children and I think they were killed here, in the Games Room. I don't know why I think that; perhaps they steal in when I'm asleep, small shadows whispering their fates into my ear. Okay, maybe I have lost my mind.

There's Matthew. I call him Matthew. He thinks he deserves it, what's happening to him. *I am a bad person.* It's written on the wall above where I sleep, scratched into the brick. *I am a bad person.* And below that, *I think bad thoughts.* And underneath, *I can't help it.* I hope that it was enough, his repentance, enough to get him out of here. But I worry for Matthew. I don't think it *was* enough.

Frank's different. Whatever happened to him, he would have faced it with indifference, with a *fuck you* look. I think this chiefly because everything he wrote on the wall involved the word *fuck*, pretty much. *Fuck St Basil's. Burridge go fuck yourself. Never break me.* Okay, that last one doesn't have a fuck in it. But hey, it's a total *fuck you* anyway. I like Frank. Frank's my kind of guy. God only knows what they did to him.

Then there's Hugo. Hugo is small and frail and very, very scared. He has none of Frank's defiance. He doesn't understand what's happening to him or why. *I'm sorry.* That's what he writes. He writes it again and again and again. *I'm sorry. I'm sorry. I'm sorry.* He never says what he is sorry for, because he doesn't know. He just knows that he is being punished. I imagine his tears, alone in the dark. Trying to stop but unable, helpless. All he can do is say that he is sorry. How long was he down here for? He has scratched out *I'm sorry* ninety-five times, at least that I can find. It might be more. Please, come on. Come on, show some pity for the poor child. Hasn't he apologized enough?

Evil happened here and evil is still happening. The Games Room has rings bolted to the walls and a hook in the ceiling and blood on the floor. The world doesn't know, and the world doesn't care. It's just me and the troll, and soon I'll be gone, just like Matthew and Frank and Hugo and God knows how many other poor souls. I'll be with you all soon, I tell them at night, before I sleep and they come to me to whisper their ghastly secrets. I'll be with you soon, and I promise you all, I'll do my best to give you the comfort you needed when you were alive.

Two days. Two days left. I wish I was like Frank, full of *fuck you* courage. But I feel more like Hugo. Small, scared and helpless. If you're out there, Frank, would you mind giving me a bit of what you had? I could really use it right now.

forty-three

'HE KILLED HIMSELF,' NIC TOLD FORTUNE AS SHE SAT BACK down, the men behind him taking the last of AIX Industries away, the warehouse space all but empty.

'Who did?' asked Fortune, thinking of Claudia, hanged, and of his daughter's belongings found in a hut next to a river.

'Peter,' said Nic. 'My co-founder. This was kind of like a goodbye to him. A wake, I guess.'

'I'm sorry,' Fortune said. 'I intruded.'

'Yeah, well …' She trailed off, ran out of things to say.

'You knew him well?' said Fortune.

'Yes,' said Nic. 'Yes, I knew him well. We were a team, a good, no, a great team. I was the business head, he was the genius. What we had …' She zoned out again, lost in the what-might-have-beens, the glittering future that AIX Industries had once looked forward to. 'We were going to change the face of artificial intelligence. We're talking about genuinely intelligent machines. Driving cars, operating on patients, totally autonomous. Making better decisions than people could.'

'So what happened?' asked Fortune. If the investors had been pouring that much money into AIX Industries, it must have been dramatic.

'Like I said, Hector Emmerson happened. He came in and he was strange but effective, his work was excellent, brilliant. But there was something about him … He wasn't quite right.' She laughed, a hollow sound. 'Course, the company was full of geeks. Software engineers, the good ones, they're all on the spectrum. But Hector, he was … unnerving. The way he'd look at you. Like he was evaluating, calculating. Like you were a problem, a challenge.'

Fortune nodded. 'He likes playing games with people,' he said. 'You're right about that.'

'He hit on someone who worked here. A girl, woman, whatever. Asked her out to dinner and she said yes, don't ask me why. Desperation, maybe. So he picks her up and they park outside a building and she says, this isn't a restaurant, and he says, no, it's my flat. Smiling, like he was being all smooth, like this was how it was done, this was the way to seduce somebody. And this girl, she says, uh-uh, no way, and she tries to get out but she can't open the door, and he gets angry, asks her what's wrong. She's pulling at the door and he's screaming, asking her what did I do wrong, what's the matter, like he just doesn't get it, doesn't get it at all.'

'Did he let her out?'

Nic nodded. 'In the end. She told me about it, and I had him in here the next day, told him that he was lucky we weren't pressing charges. He stood there with this smile on his face, like I was being ridiculous – no, like I didn't get it, didn't understand. This supercilious smile. I had to get Peter, get him to explain to Hector that he was out of here, there was no more work for him, he was done. He never lost the smile, as if he held some secret knowledge we couldn't even guess at.' She shivered. 'The guy was so creepy.'

'I imagine he didn't take it well,' said Fortune.

'No,' said Nic. 'No, you could say that.' She stood up. 'Listen, that goddamn pinball machine's being picked up in like twenty minutes. Never did find enough time to play on it. You mind?'

'No.'

She paused at the door. 'We can talk while we play,' she said. 'Come on.'

Fortune followed her across the empty warehouse floor, cavernous now that the desks and equipment were gone, Nic's footsteps echoing around the space. He watched her as she bent to turn the machine on at the wall, imagining what it must have been like when the building was full of the youngest and brightest, queuing to play, taking time between coding the future. It was an old Terminator model, the first one, that came out in … Fortune tried to remember. Must have been the eighties. God, but he was old. Back then, he'd had it all in front of him. Don't think about that, he told himself. Don't even go there. You need to find Sophie, not feel sorry for your own serial shortcomings.

'You okay?' Nic was watching him with concern. 'You're not looking so good.'

'I'm okay,' Fortune said. 'All this …' He shook his head. 'You can't imagine.'

Nic looked at him curiously for a moment but couldn't get a read. She turned back to the machine, pulled the handle back and launched a ball. The screen went crazy, lights, sounds, Arnold Schwarzenegger scowling at them through shades. Fortune remembered the film, vaguely. A robot, a motorbike, sunglasses. A ludicrous plot that he had enjoyed despite himself. Nic played the flippers and spoke without looking at him.

'So, next day, after I talk to Hector? We come into the office and everybody, every single employee, our credit history is ruined.' The ball ricocheted off a triangular island, straight between the two flippers. Nic swore and launched another ball while the backboard blinked and bleeped and lit up in contempt. 'We're all blacklisted, nobody will touch us. How about that?'

'He did it?'

'Who else? But that's nothing. That was just, like, what? Like the aperitif. The hors d'oeuvre. Somehow, and to this day I don't know how, nobody knows how, but somehow he found our algorithm, he hacked his way through everything we'd put in place, all the encryption, and he open-sourced it. Published it online. He hit a key and the future of AIX was done. Gone.' Nic missed another ball, a shining bullet straight down the middle, and turned to Fortune. She threw her hands apart, imitating an explosion. 'Nothing left to invest in, the IP all over the net.'

'Oh,' said Fortune. He couldn't think of anything else to say.

Nic turned and launched the final ball, playing the flippers hard, bitterly, like it was them, not Hector Emmerson, who was the cause of all this.

'A week later, Peter threw himself off a motorway bridge. Ten years' work, gone. Worthless. All his employees, his investors, betrayed. He couldn't deal with it. Who could have?'

'You did.'

Nic's final ball bounced up, hit a metal skull, shot down a hole in the machine's playfield and back out again, the backboard lighting up like a Vegas casino, her score rocketing and old-school digital numbers flickering, struggling to keep up.

'Like I said, I was the business head. Couldn't understand the half of it, tell you the truth. And I've got a doctorate in cognitive neuroscience.'

'I'm sorry,' said Fortune.

'Yeah,' said Nic, then, 'Goddamn it,' as she lost her final ball. 'Excuse me,' she said, then straightened up, looked at the backboard and laughed.

'What?'

'Nowhere near. The high score. It was Peter, see? Never knew that he had it. Just like he had it all. Talent, genius, I guess. He was funny, he was cool, he was kind.' She spoke without looking at Fortune, softly, to herself. 'We, all of us, we were just kids. Just kids with a really brilliant idea. How could it have come to this?'

Fortune waited for her to turn around; when she didn't, he said, 'Did you go to the police?'

'With what?' said Nic. She leant back against the machine, her palms on its glass surface. 'We didn't have any proof. Hector hid his tracks, we couldn't pin anything on him. Besides ...' She stopped, closed her eyes briefly.

'Besides what?'

She opened her eyes and there was a look there, of fear, fear and shame. 'Besides, we didn't know what else he could do. We were ... okay, okay, we were scared of him. We didn't know how he did what he did, didn't know how far he'd go. He was like totally untouchable, pulling strings, manipulating. He'd massacred our credit history but it felt like, I don't know, like something a petulant child would do. He could do far worse, we were sure of that.'

Fortune thought of Charlie Jackson, dead in his hotel room. Of his daughter, held somewhere, terrified. Yes, he agreed silently, he's capable of a hell of a lot worse than that.

'Do you have a photo of him?'

'Nope.'

'Do you know where he lives?'

Nic looked away from Fortune, avoiding his gaze. 'No.'

'Come on.'

'I don't. The man's a ghost.'

'Yes you do. You don't run a ... what was this business worth? Fifty million?'

'More,' said Nic. 'Last valuation was four hundred, and that was the VCs. It was worth a lot more, it was worth ...' She lifted her hands towards the ceiling, then dropped them in a gesture of despair, of complete desolation. 'It was worth more than money.'

Fortune sighed, suddenly tired, and sorry, very sorry for this ambitious and broken young woman. Broken by his son. He bowed his head and shook it. 'I'm sorry, I really am. This is, I can't imagine. I've never built something for myself, always worked for others. Been a cog.' He snorted, in self-disgust, then looked back up. 'But Nic, you do know where he lived. In a business like this, you must know where your contractors come from. You must check them out. If you don't, then somebody else will, the amount of money the investors had sunk in this. They get vetted, and that'll include an address.' He regretted pressing her, regretted bringing it back to the here and now. But he needed to find his son. He had no choice.

Nic frowned at him, this bearded, creased, sick-looking approximation of a man, and re-evaluated her opinion. 'You're his father, I know that. But ... who are you?'

'It doesn't matter, it really doesn't. Please, Nic. Where does he live? I need to know.'

'I don't know.'

'Please.'

'We …' Nic hesitated, closed her eyes and took a deep breath. 'The police didn't want to know. So we broke in. We … we kicked the door down.'

Like it was an offence punishable by death. These kids, Fortune thought. Living in their unreal world of AI, virtual reality, where kicking a door open is a crime beyond imagining, a transgression of enormous moment. As he thought this, he realized how far he'd come, how far he'd drifted from the respectable, ordered world of his previous life.

'Good on you,' he said. 'I'd have done the same. Listen, just tell me where it is. Tell me where it is and I promise you, everything he's done? He'll be held to account.'

'I don't believe that.' Nic said it flatly, like the enemy was so powerful, so resourceful and omniscient that no mortal could possibly prevail against him.

'Believe it,' said Fortune. 'Look at me. Do I look like I have anything to lose?'

'No,' said Nic. 'But you don't know him.'

'He's only human,' said Fortune.

Nic laughed. 'You think? You ask me, he isn't even close.'

forty-four

HECTOR EMMERSON, THE MAN FORTUNE WOULD NOT, COULD not think of as his son, lived in a sixties brutalist apartment building five minutes from Old Street station, a forlorn sink estate hidden behind the hipster cafés and gastro pubs that lined the main streets. Fortune rang every number on the entrance phone, then did it again, waiting in the dusky gloom until someone inside got bored of the disturbance and buzzed him in.

The door that the people of AIX Industries had broken down was closed, but it only took a shoulder to push it open, just an old pizza takeaway box wedged underneath to keep it shut. The apartment consisted of a kitchen, living room, bedroom and bathroom, every room small, high-rise battery housing for the post-war generation. It was also empty, completely empty, except for furniture: a sofa and two armchairs in the living room, and a made-up bed in the bedroom. Fortune walked into the kitchen and opened the fridge, which was clean but had nothing in it. He opened drawers and found cutlery, plates, but no food, nothing to indicate anyone actually lived there. He went back into the living room and looked out of the window. The apartment was on the eighth floor and night was falling outside, lights illuminating a chain-link playground where a group of kids were playing basketball, a dog chasing the ball, what looked like a pit bull, an angry bundle of muscle.

He closed the curtains, opened his case and found his remaining clean clothes. He didn't have a towel, but he didn't care; he went to the bathroom and took a shower anyway, drying himself with his old shirt. He had been on the move since he woke up in the lay-by and he was tired, very tired, his thoughts erratic and unfocused, a black sense of despair closing in, his vision tunnelling. He had to sleep; if he wanted to continue, he needed to sleep. He turned off the lights, dragged one of the armchairs against the front door and got into the bed, the sheets clean and crisp, the mattress soft. He closed his eyes, and before he could wonder just why the bed should be so welcoming and warm, he fell immediately asleep, a deep submersion into the cocoon of this strange bed in this empty apartment in this bizarre and confusing world he could not escape.

It was still dark when he woke, aware of a nagging irritation in his back, a sensation that had found its way into his dreams, manifesting as an insistent prodding from an unknown presence. He sat up and felt beneath the sheet, pulling out a folded piece of paper. He opened it and spread it out on the bed. It was a photocopy of a newspaper article. The room was dark, and Fortune stood and turned on the light, then went back to the sheet of paper. At the top was a date, 11 February 2002. He sat down on the bed, lit a cigarette, and read:

ORPHANAGE CLOSES AMID SCANDAL

An orphanage part-funded by the Church of England has been closed down amid claims of child abuse and a regime of violence. The institution, St Basil's, which was established in the late sixties, had been under investigation following the death of a fifteen-year-old boy. It is understood that the boy was a charge of the orphanage, and that his body was found in woodland thirty miles from the orphanage, bearing evidence of beatings and torture. According to DCI Paul Spencer, 'These marks were not only recent, but suggested a historic catalogue of abuse. On investigation, disturbing discoveries were made within the grounds of the orphanage and this, coupled with testimony from current wards, led us to the conclusion that St Basil's posed a very real threat to children.' No charges have so far been brought, but it is understood that the warder, Oliver James Burridge, is under caution. More to come.

In this empty apartment, Fortune immediately understood that this was a clue, that it had been deliberately left for him. He had been meant to find it. He was suddenly aware of a dark intelligence around him, so much like a real presence that he shivered as if somebody was standing behind him. A malign presence, pulling strings, dictating Fortune's every move.

He packed his belongings and left the apartment, taking the paper with him. He could not get out fast enough, something about the antiseptic cleanliness of it all unnerving him, the deliberateness, as if it had been prepared especially for him. He felt old and tired and stupid, a relic of another age, incapable of matching this new intelligence, this dark design. He had to keep going, but he didn't know if he could.

*

The neighbourhood was scattered with trendy coffee shops offering exotic blends, all served up with Wi-Fi, naturally. Fortune ordered an Americano and a pastry and sat in front of his daughter's computer, searching for St Basil's. There were plenty of news reports, even a Wikipedia entry. He quickly built a picture of an institution where beatings, confinement and psychological and sexual abuse were the norm, where children lived in perpetual fear of the men who were paid to protect them. In many ways it was a familiar story, but that did not minimize its specific horror, the fact that this had happened in today's society, under the eyes of people whose job it was to prevent exactly this kind of suffering and abuse.

But as ever, a child's word against that of an adult carried little weight, particularly given that the warder, Oliver James Burridge, had connections in high places. His brother was a Conservative MP who later sat in the House of Lords, and nothing ever stuck. Many ex-wards came forward to testify against the regime at St Basil's. Grown men whose lives had been blighted by what had been done to them, emotionally damaged men who were condemned forever to live on the fringes, terrified of society. Torture was mentioned, again and again. But back in the days when corporal punishment was a legitimate form of discipline, where was the line that tipped it into abuse?

The killer of the boy dumped in the woodland was never found. Nor were at least sixteen other boys, runaways who had been reported missing over the years. The orphanage was closed, the wards dispersed, scattered about the country, their secrets with them. A report a decade later observed a disproportionate incidence of suicide among children, now adults, who had attended St Basil's over the previous decades. But by now it was of academic interest, a statistical artefact. Data. What was done was done. Society moved on, learnt lessons, put more checks and balances in place, and the victims were left to cope with the aftermath in any way they could.

Fortune stopped reading. He knew a cover-up when he saw one, could read between the lines. He left the coffee shop, lit a cigarette and walked to where he had parked his car. He tried to fight his sense of guilt but could not, could no longer push it away. If he had let his daughter down, then what he had done to his son was an order of magnitude worse. You didn't know about him, he told himself. You didn't know he existed. You didn't know that he'd been born, disowned by his family and sent to St Basil's. What could you have done? But this rang hollow, just like the investigation into St Basil's rang hollow. You could have kept in contact with Claudia. Made sure that she was okay, that she was coping. And when you learnt that she had taken her life, what did you do? Nothing. Tried to forget. Sins of omission, the haughty disregard of the comfortable white male, disconnected from the less fortunate. He thought of Dubai, of the foreign workers, the maids, the labourers, the exploited underclass with no recourse to any kind of justice. It wasn't so different here. Somebody, somewhere, was scared and helpless and ignored by the rest of society. And people like Fortune simply pretended it wasn't going on. Everything that was happening, he was prepared to concede, he deserved. But not Sophie. Sophie had done nothing. Sophie was as much a victim as the boys of St Basil's. At least he could still save one soul.

forty-five

A MAN I HAVE NEVER MET BEFORE IS GOING TO KILL ME IN TWO days' time.

A man I have never met before is going to kill me in two days' time.

A man I have never met before is going to kill me in two days' time.

If I say it to myself enough, maybe it will seem real. Even normal. People are killed all the time. History is full of them, mostly forgotten. Killed for no good reason, here, then gone. Because they stole some bread, or believed in the wrong god, or just looked so strange they were denounced as a witch. They didn't deserve it. I don't deserve it either. Do I? I don't believe I do. I hope I don't.

Yesterday I asked the troll if he was going to kill me and he didn't say anything, and then he said, 'Probably,' like I'd asked him if it was going to rain. Probably. I said, 'How are you going to do it?' This was through the door, me one side, him the other. He was quiet for a long time, and then he said, matter-of-factly, like a dentist reassuring a patient, 'Don't worry. It won't be so bad.' *It won't be so bad.* So I started hammering on the door and kicking it, kicking it, screaming at him, calling him every name I could think of. Bastard, evil bastard, shit, coward, bastard

bastard bastard. And when I stopped, there was silence, a long, long silence, and I thought he'd gone but then he said, 'It's not your fault.' And then he went away and I called after him again, but this time I was telling him that I was sorry, sorry, so so sorry, I didn't mean it, please, come back, come back and talk, can't we talk? But he didn't come back and I can't stop thinking about what he said. *It won't be so bad.* What does that even mean? How do you kill someone without it being bad? Of course it's bad, it's terrible, oh Jesus, I can't do this any more, I'll kill myself before I let him do anything to me. I will. I will.

Do I deserve this? Maybe I do. I've done some bad things, I've hurt people, manipulated them, used them. I'm not a good person and I've never thought I was. My own father doesn't want anything to do with me. Can I blame him? After all the grief and trouble I gave him? All right, Sophie, okay. You've got nothing better to do, so let's conduct an audit. Let's see. See if you deserve it.

Let's start with the good stuff. It shouldn't take long. I've never killed anyone. I've got a job. Well, actually I got sacked, but that doesn't count since it wasn't my fault. Okay, job. Tick. Friends? Kind of. Not many. Not enough. But some, so, yeah, okay. Job, friends. What else? I did okay at school and went to university. That's more than a lot of people. I achieved something. And I mean well. I really do, I mean well. It doesn't always work out, but I try my best, most of the time. I try to do the right thing. I'm not evil. Yeah, right, high fives all round. I mean, seriously, is that the best I can do? Here lies Sophie Fortune. She kind of had a job, a couple of friends and three mediocre A levels, oh, and she definitely wasn't evil, we know that because she never killed anyone. What an epitaph.

I'm gabbling. Slow down. Calm. Okay. Let's talk about the less good stuff, or, if you will, the bad stuff. I was, I am ashamed to say, terrible to my parents, by which I mean BAD. Any time I didn't get my own way, I lost it, threatening, screaming, threatening some more. And pretty soon, I'd threatened to kill myself so often, it seemed like it was an actual thing. Somehow in my head I'd managed to normalize it. Go on, kill yourself, why not? It's the only way out, the only way to control your life and get your own way. It's taking selfishness to a whole new dimension. Or was I, in actual fact, mad? I really don't remember. But what I do know is that I was an insufferable, self-centred, manipulative, toxic young woman. Taking an overdose and then calling my mum, thinking it was normal, that it would serve her right, teach her a lesson, she deserved it, she'd made me do this. Who thinks like that? Seriously?

I don't know. I worked on it. I tried to become a better person. I thought I was getting somewhere, making acceptable progress. But maybe it was too late, like the people who give up smoking but not in time because the cancer's already there and the damage is done. Maybe I do deserve all this.

Oh God. I just thought of what he said. How it won't be so bad. What he's going to do to me, it won't be so bad. What does that mean?

I hope it means he's not going to stab me. I don't want to be stabbed. I don't want to be crying, screaming, watching him do it. Please don't. *Stab.* Please, not again. *Stab.* Please, you're going to kill me. *Stab.* The feeling, the metal inside me, watching my own blood leak out as I beg. Anything but that. If it's something different, if it's quick, if it doesn't hurt, if he's telling the truth, then maybe it really won't be so bad.

Sophie, what are you saying?

forty-six

FORTUNE CHECKED HIS DWINDLING CASH RESERVES AS HE walked towards Old Street roundabout, on his way back to the car. He heard footsteps and had begun to turn when a skinny kid in a hooded top pulled his wallet out of his hand and took off down the pavement. Fortune didn't chase him, didn't have the energy; anyway, most of his money was in his pocket, and it wasn't like he could still use his credit cards. It could be worse. No big deal.

But then he heard a police siren wail into life and looked behind him at blue lights flashing through the front grille of an unmarked BMW, two male plain-clothes officers in the front seat. The kid stopped, looked around and saw the lights and started running again, now fifty yards away, heading for the roundabout. The traffic was heavy on the street approaching the roundabout, the street Fortune was on, and the BMW struggled through it, cars parting slowly, too much traffic. The kid ran across the roundabout, across three lanes of traffic, Fortune watching as a flatbed truck carrying scaffolding hit him and he fell, the front wheel of the truck rolling over his midriff.

There was a moment of stillness, of shock, then the BMW pulled up next to the kid and the police officers jumped out, knelt down next to him. They got on the radio and called the medics, even though anybody could see that it was too late. One of the policemen looked for the wallet, Fortune's wallet, the one they'd seen being stolen, to make sure they were covered. That they'd had legitimate grounds to be chasing him. The driver of the truck climbed down and saw the kid and put his head in his hands, turned around in a slow circle, looking up at the sky.

Fortune watched it all happen, standing perfectly still on the pavement, the action hyper-real, the police in sharp focus as if he had suddenly been gifted twenty-twenty vision. One of the officers was still kneeling next to the kid, but the other was looking through the wallet. He stopped, holding something in his hand. Probably Fortune's credit card, or his driving licence. He glanced up and looked straight at Fortune, a hundred yards away, then pressed something near his neck and spoke, must be to HQ, calling it in. *I'm looking at him now*, he'd be saying. *Send backup. Send a lot, and send it now.*

Fortune turned and walked away, in the opposite direction. He was aware of the sound of horns, angry drivers wondering what the hold-up was, not knowing that some kid had just been killed. The street was busy and he pushed past pedestrians, walking fast, looking around him, searching for options. He turned and couldn't see the officer following him, but then a woman went into a shop and Fortune saw him, running towards him, no more than fifty yards away. Fortune was walking next to a building site, green-painted wooden boards hiding it from the street. There was a gap in the boards for site traffic and he walked through. On an expanse of muddy ground was a building, huge, only the concrete structure finished so that it looked more like a multistorey car park than the office block it would become. People were working inside, sparks flying from an angle grinder cutting through steel. Fortune hurried across the mud and walked into the structure, past a man with some device on a tripod, looking through a viewfinder. It was gloomy, and he passed from one dark room into another, through doorless openings.

'Help you?' asked a man in a hard hat, looking up from where he was squatting, laying blue plastic piping on the floor. Fortune didn't answer, kept on towards the rear of the building. Keep walking, he thought. Don't look back. He heard a man's voice shout, *'Police!'* from behind him, a long way behind him, and he took a left into another room, all the rooms big, the concrete floors wet from recent rain, no windows installed yet. He couldn't outrun the police. He was old and terminally ill and he hadn't eaten properly for he didn't know how long, and his lungs felt like tiny hard balloons, thick rubber incapable of inflating.

He reached the back of the building and looked up at a greasy ochre slope of wet mud criss-crossed with the tracks of diggers and trucks, pooled with dirty water. He started up and slipped, his businessman's shoes giving him no grip, made for boardrooms, not building sites. He dug his toes in, knowing that he was too slow, too slow, the police on to him, behind him, closing, closing.

He kept going, climbing up the slope and listening to sirens in the distance, the whop-whop-whop of a helicopter that he couldn't yet see. At the top of the slope was a yellow JCB with its scoop lifted, facing downwards. Fortune put a foot on its gridded metal step and pushed himself up. He opened the door to the cab, reached over to the handbrake and released it. He climbed back down and waited. Nothing. At the bottom of the slope he saw the plain-clothes officer run out of the building and look up at him, unable to believe that this man, this fugitive, had fallen into his lap. Thinking of the promotion. The ceremony, the cameras. The JCB's wheels moved, an inch, a foot, gathering speed through the resistant mud, which was unable to stop the tons of steel. It might give the officer something else to worry about, thought Fortune. Maybe.

He didn't wait, but walked forward, through another site entrance and into a small side street, the street silent and empty, silent until he heard the sound of an impact, a muted thud.

Sirens and noise, helicopters. They had thermal imaging, Fortune had nothing. He leant against the brick wall of a building on the other side of the street and assessed. He was breathing heavily, finding it hard to get enough oxygen in. And he hadn't even started running yet. He was in one of the world's biggest and most policed cities and he had to get away. If he didn't, his daughter was dead. Think. He slumped down into a crouch and put his hands over his ears. Think. Think think *think*. You can do this. You need to do this. What was it a previous boss of his had said, used it as a catchphrase? *Failure is not an option.* The sirens were getting closer and he had no plan. No plan at all. But failure was not an option. It didn't matter what it took.

A street cleaner passed, a stooped man who looked way past retirement age, thin and unshaven and pushing a cart. Fortune stood back up and crossed the street to him.

'Give me your coat,' he said.

'Do what?'

'Give me your coat. Here.' He dug in his pocket and pulled out a handful of money. 'I'll pay. If you don't give it to me, I'll take it from you.'

The cleaner looked at Fortune and must have seen something unhinged in his eyes, because he took the money and shrugged himself out of his hi-vis jacket. Fortune took it and put it on. It was too small and he could feel its tightness across his shoulders. Okay. He looked like the street cleaner, could easily pass as a down-at-heel minimum-wage council drone, particularly given that he looked like hell, malnourished and exhausted and beaten.

He walked quickly, keeping his head down, going for the perennially subservient look of the bottom-rung worker. He got to the end of the street and took a quick glance behind. A police car pulled up at the far end and he turned right, kept going, looking around, knowing that this was a temporary measure. What he needed to do was get back to his untraceable car, Lee's mother's car, the best escape he had. The only thing was, having walked through the building, up the street and taken a right, he had no idea where he was. He'd turned too many corners and lost his bearings. *Shit.* What was the name of the street he'd parked in? White Horse Street. It didn't matter, he didn't know where it was or how to get there. Now he was on a wide street full of people, but not the same street he'd left. And the police were right behind him. How long would it take for the cleaner to talk to them? Look for the man in the hi-vis jacket. That's your man. All he was doing was postponing his capture, nothing more. He needed to gain some kind of advantage. Turn the tables. Right. Against the combined forces of the Metropolitan Police, men and cars and helicopters. Of course. Easy.

He passed a hotel, upmarket, stone stairs up to a set of revolving doors, a glass canopy over them to protect the doormen. Fortune didn't understand a lot about modern life, but there were a few things he was fluent in, and hotels were one of them. He stopped and thought. He looked down at his shoes in dismay, caked in building-site mud. He'd need a story if he was going to be let in to the hotel. He didn't look like their kind of clientele. He turned back and walked up the steps.

'Yes?' said one of the doormen, long coat and gloves, suspicious expression.

'Gas,' said Fortune. 'I've come from the building site. I need to speak to your manager.' The story didn't make a lot of sense, but Fortune figured gas was one of those things you didn't question.

'Go to the front desk,' said the doorman, looking down at Fortune's shoes doubtfully. 'They'll help you.'

'Thanks,' said Fortune, and pushed through the revolving doors, checking behind him, but the doorman was looking out into the street, his back to him. A man ran past the front of the hotel. Fortune recognized him as the plain-clothes officer who had chased him through the building site. A marked car passed immediately after, a kinetic blur of sirens and lights. He'd need to work fast. Very fast.

forty-seven

FORTUNE STOOD AT THE FRONT DESK AND WATCHED A COUPLE drop their key card, number 316. He crossed to the other side of the lobby, where there was a seating area, armchairs around a low table with newspapers on it. There was a phone on the table and he picked up the receiver and hit the button marked Front Desk. He heard it ring and watched across the lobby as a woman behind the counter picked it up.

'Front desk,' said the woman. Fortune turned his back, shielding himself from view, and spoke in a whisper.

'There's a man in my room,' he said. 'You've got to help me.'

'Sir?' The woman sounded confused. 'Would you mind—'

'In my room,' Fortune hissed, sounding close to panic. 'I'm in the bathroom. I've locked myself in, with the phone.'

'Sir, what number is your room?'

'Three-one-six. You need to help me. It's him, the one who killed that TV guy.'

'Sir, stay where you are. I'm calling the police.'

'He's out there,' said Fortune. 'I ...' He clamped a hand over the mouthpiece and knocked the receiver on the table, three, four times. 'He's trying to get in.'

'Don't panic,' said the woman. 'Just stay there.'

'Oh Jesus,' said Fortune. 'He's found the phone line, he's ...'
He put a finger on the hook to cut the connection, then placed
the receiver back down, stood up and turned. The woman on
reception was speaking into the phone, looking flustered, scared.
Why did this have to happen on her watch?

Fortune walked away from the hotel's entrance, looking for a
back way out, picking up a card as he passed the front desk. He
pushed through double doors into a dining area with a bar at
one end, then through another set of double doors into a kitchen
area, busy, a waitress standing at the pass as a chef placed plates
underneath the hot lamps. Apparently Fortune's hi-vis jacket
conferred some kind of status, because nobody challenged him
and he walked through the kitchen, past chefs juggling flaming
dishes, hot faces, towels over every shoulder.

'Way out?' he asked a young man deftly placing scallops in
a frying pan, who looked up and jerked his chin, indicating
behind him. Fortune found a door, a fire exit, and pushed on
the metal bar. The door opened and he walked through, onto
an iron stairway that led into a car park, huge bins underneath
him through the latticed metalwork. He could still hear sirens
and he rattled down the stairs, taking off the hi-vis and lifting
the cover of one of the bins to push it in. He walked through
the car park and pulled out his phone, looked at the card he had
taken and dialled the number. He was breathing heavily and he
stopped walking, waiting for somebody to pick up.

'Borders Hotel.' It was the same woman, speaking quickly,
tense.

'He's still here,' Fortune said. 'He's crazy, he's a madman.'

'Sir, the police are on their way.'

'He says he's got a hand grenade. He says he'll set it off if anyone comes in.' If you're going to tell a lie, Fortune had always heard, it's better to make it a huge one.

'What does he want?' said the woman.

'I don't know,' Fortune said, summoning up as much panicked fear as he could. He was no actor, this he knew. 'He's off his head.'

'Sir, the police are here.'

'Tell them to stay away. He's got a grenade.'

'I will tell them,' said the woman. 'Please try to stay calm.'

'I—' said Fortune, then killed the call. He reckoned that, with the addition of the hand grenade, he'd created enough noise and confusion to keep the police guessing for a while, maybe an hour, more than long enough. He turned out of the car park and headed for the Tube, taking the steps into the busy sanctity of the ticket hall. He bought a single and passed through the barrier, down the escalator to the platform, keeping his head down, away from CCTV cameras. He took the first train that arrived and rode it two stops, two short, jarring, crowded and blissful stops to safety.

Back at the car, Fortune called Lee. His mother would be back any time, and Fortune was miles away. He'd only just got away from the police. He couldn't have them knowing what he was driving, or he wouldn't last a day. Which meant that he needed to keep Lee onside.

'Yeah?'

'Lee?'

'Oh man, where are you? My mum's coming back like any minute.'

'She's back today?'

'Today, tomorrow, I don't know. What I know is, her car ain't here.'

'I'm on my way. It's fixed, all sorted. I'll be with you tonight.'

'What if she's back?'

Fortune imagined Lee at the caravan park, glumly surveying the chaos he'd created, the unwashed dishes and empty bottles and cans, the burn marks from the joints he'd been incessantly smoking. All this, and some guy had taken off with his mum's car, the car he'd crashed when he was blasted off his mind. Fortune couldn't help but feel sorry for him. But he still needed the car.

'I'm on my way. If your mother comes back, tell her I needed to use it in an emergency. I'll be there soon.'

'Oh man. Wish I'd never let you take it.'

'Yeah? You'd prefer to explain where the dents came from?'

'No. Yeah. I dunno. She's gonna kill me.'

'It'll be okay. Stop worrying. Look, I've got to go. I'll be with you soon.'

'Better be, man.'

Fortune cut the call. Poor Lee. He couldn't imagine the boy had a bright and shining future waiting for him, and he, Fortune, certainly wasn't helping. Next he sent a message to the troll, to his son, not expecting an answer and not receiving one. He'd been off grid for days now, waiting for Fortune to show up, he supposed. There wasn't much need for communication. Find me or don't, that was all there was to it. And Fortune had two days left. It wasn't enough time, wasn't nearly enough. He started the car, and headed for the orphanage, St Basil's. If his son wasn't there, then Fortune was out of ideas. Out completely.

forty-eight

TODAY THE TROLL TOOK ME TO THE GAMES ROOM AND IT WAS the worst thing that has ever happened, worse than I could ever imagine. I'd prefer to be dead, right now, just not be here any more, not alive. I've had enough, it's too terrible, too frightening, and I think the troll is mad, utterly mad. He is the worst person I have ever met. What did I do? What did I do to him that he does this to me?

He must have put something in my food because I woke up in the Games Room but I can't remember how I got there. So he must have drugged me and waited and come in and carried me in there. Because when I woke up, one of my wrists had a plastic cuff around it, those ones the police use. There was another plastic cuff connected to it, and that was attached to a bike lock, a plastic-wrapped cable that was looped through one of the bolts in the wall. It was a combination lock. I was sitting with my back against the wall and my cuffed hand was raised and attached to one of the bolts and I couldn't move, not far.

So I sat there. It wasn't dark because the lamp was on so it was only gloomy, the corners of the room in darkness. I sat, and I waited. I didn't know what he was going to do. Wasn't there still a day left? Didn't I still have a day? He couldn't kill me now, it wasn't time. He couldn't come, he couldn't come with a knife and attack me and keep cutting and stabbing as I kicked and lashed out until I got too tired and couldn't fight any more and he found the right place, the right spot and I died. He couldn't.

Then the door opened and I started to scream, I couldn't help it, but the troll didn't come in. He stayed outside where I couldn't see him and he threw in a net, like a fishing net with a long handle, and he said:

Work out the combination and you'll be able to reach that. There are no rules. No time limit.

What? I said.

You heard. He started to pull the door closed, then said: One more thing. A question. Are you ready? You need to listen.

I was sitting on a concrete floor stained with the blood of what I think were children, chained to a ring in the wall. Was I ready? No, I said. Of course I'm not.

But he didn't care. He just said: Do you believe in fortune?

Believe in what?

Do you believe in fortune?

And he closed the door.

And I just sat there, looking at the net, wondering what the hell was going on. Thinking about what just happened, and what he'd asked. And my arm was getting tired, and I didn't know what the net was for, and I would have loved, loved, loved-loved-loved to have got my hands on the troll. I closed my eyes, imagining that same old fantasy of beating him up, and when I opened my eyes I saw it, saw it immediately. It was moving, coming out of the shadows in the corner of the room, moving, stopping, moving. So quick, so unpredictable. Here. There. Move, change. A spider, but huge, out of some jungle nightmare, how had it come through the wall, how had it got here, in this room? It was scuttling, busy, planting a leg, planting another, then a blur, so fast. Slow, slow, slow, quick. And silent. No sound, all movement. I got my knees up and tucked them under my chin, then pulled my legs in and tried to get all of me as far away as I could from the spider. It was as big as my hand, bigger. Much, much bigger. So big, and so fast.

It's not like it was hard to find out that I've got a fear of spiders. I went on about it all the time, it was in my blog, it was on my profile. It was me, part of me, and it always had been. Oh God, I thought, I told him, I told Josh. I told him all about it, only he never existed because he was the troll and Josh *never actually existed*. And this spider was so big and it was coming towards me and I couldn't move, my arm was locked to the wall and I was screaming, screaming, I'd never been so scared, and I was crying and screaming and the spider was just there, there in front of me, a couple of metres away. Just looking. It could get to me in seconds, two seconds, that's all it would take. My wrist was bleeding and blood was running down my arm from where I'd cut through my skin with the plastic cuff, but I couldn't feel any pain.

The spider didn't move and I remembered, I'd been panicking so much I forgot, I remembered what the troll said. About the combination. If I could work it out, I could get away. What had he said? Do you believe in fortune? The lock had six dials, which meant it needed six numbers. He'd said work it out. Like it was something I should know, something I'd got the clues for. And then the spider, that huge spider, scuttled towards me and I screamed and it ran close to me, it was so quick, and it climbed up the wall, climbed up the bricks, and it was above me, next to me and above me, just there, just looking down at me, and I didn't dare move but I needed to try combinations and I was just crying, crying like a child, crying and crying and right then, there, that was the first time ever in my whole life I think I had really, truly, honestly wished that I was dead.

forty-nine

ST BASIL'S WAS A BIG VICTORIAN BUILDING THAT HAD BEEN unsympathetically added to with red-brick extensions, looking like parasites clinging to their host, ugly and unwelcome. It was at the end of an uneven drive that had probably once been smooth but had long since lost the battle against the weeds, the tarmac cracked and crumbling. The drive was lined with trees, and Fortune could imagine them in summer growing over the lane, creating a leafy tunnel. But right now they just looked skeletal and grasping, uncut branches brushing the top of Lee's mother's car, reaching for the windows.

The orphanage was in the heart of Essex, a couple of miles outside a Hollywood producer's wet dream of an idyllic English village. It even had a duck pond in the centre, with actual, real-life ducks gloomily swimming in it. At the bottom of the drive Fortune had passed a sign that looked like it had been there a long time, telling him that St Basil's was for sale via Seymour Estates, call this number. Beneath that sign was another that read *Private Property*, but it didn't say to keep out, and Fortune wouldn't have done so in any case. He passed the ruins of a red-brick building, the roof sagging, the chimney broken. Halfway up the drive, he emptied the car's ashtray out of the window, leaving a cloud of ash in the air behind him.

He exited the tunnel of trees and drove up through overgrown green grounds to the grand facade of St Basil's. Up close he could only think of school, parents dropping off tearful kids for another term of miserable boarding. Only the kids here hadn't had parents. Well, he corrected himself. One of them had.

He had bought a heavy-duty torch at a hardware store, something that could equally light things up and knock people down. He also had a pair of bolt-cutters and a sledgehammer, which he hoped would get him through most obstacles, the first of which was a chain securing the handles of the double doors leading into the orphanage. He cut it, the crack of the metal snapping loud in the empty landscape. There were no other cars, no signs of life, not even birds, as if the entire estate had been quarantined and abandoned, its secrets too grim for the real world to accept. Fortune wasn't a superstitious man, but still, he wasn't relishing looking inside.

The doors were locked as well as chained, so he swung at the lock with the sledgehammer and they opened reluctantly, stiff with age and lack of use. He half expected a storm of bats to fly out, a cadaverous seven-foot butler not far behind, silver platter in hand. It was dark inside, the only dim light coming in through too-small diamond-paned windows. The entrance hall was paved with huge stone flagstones and was empty except for a dust-covered piano and, for some reason he couldn't fathom, a stripped-down moped. Fortune recognized it, a Honda Cub 90. He called out, 'Hello,' and waited as his voice echoed up the staircase in the centre of the hall, down corridors, into rooms. Nothing. Nobody came out, there was no distant maniacal laughter or organ music. Still, he couldn't help but think that if any place was likely to be haunted, it was here. The walls felt as if they were holding their breath, deciding what to do, how to deal with this undesirable interloper. If the troll was here, he didn't want to be found.

He searched the downstairs rooms, which were large and mostly empty and looked like they might have been classrooms, one room with a desk, another with a stack of chairs in one corner. Everything was covered in dust, and it was cold, very cold. He found a corridor that led past toilets to a kitchen, where two vast old butler's sinks were set into a heavy oak counter, a great Aga squatting sullenly opposite, a massive and heavily scored oak table between them. There was no evidence that anybody had been there recently.

Fortune walked back to the entrance hall and climbed the stairs to the first floor, walking down corridors lined with doors, these rooms full of bunk beds that, stripped of blankets and in this light and cold, made Fortune think of the Gulag. He probed with his torch into the dark corners, half expecting to discover a pale face, covering its eyes in terror. Further along there were bathrooms, showers on one side, rows of toilets without barriers opposite, so that the boys would have had to empty their bowels while their peers watched and washed. Fortune didn't know why, but it was this detail, more than anything else he had so far seen, that disturbed him the most. He thought of the restrooms in his office in Dubai, their hush and discretion and comfort. Sometimes the differences between one human's condition and another's seemed so extreme, the gulf between them so wide, that they might as well be different species. Yet his son had sat on these toilets, had suffered these indignities. Probably at the same time as Fortune had been enjoying the most generous comforts the Western world could provide. The thought seemed so enormous that he couldn't quite comprehend it, didn't have the emotions to fully appreciate or process it. How many tears had been shed in this place? A shower, a river, a sea of them. A grief beyond imagining.

He found nothing on the first floor, so he climbed to the top floor, his chest beginning to feel tight, not finding enough air to satisfy his heart or lungs. He started coughing and had to sit on the stairs until the fit passed. The place was full of dust. It was probably that, the reason his coughing was getting worse. It must be that.

Walking along the murky corridor, he noticed for the first time that the dust was so thick on the floor that his shoes left marks, like they would in a sprinkling of snow. There was another set of marks next to his. Somebody else had been here, recently. The troll. He turned off his torch, holding it like a club, and called out again, 'Hello?' Again there was no answer. He followed the marks, slowly, edging along as if he was approaching the edge of a crumbling cliff. They led to a door at the end of the corridor, a wooden door, panelled like all the others. It was closed. He called out again, through the door, and waited. Still no answer. He knocked on the door with the torch, a loud sound in the silent corridor, then looked behind him fearfully, fighting a feeling that some ogre was creeping down the corridor, stealing up on him. But there was nothing there.

He tried the handle, round, brass, and it turned. He pushed the door open wide, still standing outside in the corridor. The room was dark and he couldn't make out what was inside, but there was something, something hanging and twisting in the disturbed air from the opening door, deeper in the room. Not one thing, many things, indistinct and faintly moving. He took a step back, aware that his heart was beating loudly, pushing hard and painfully against his chest. He turned the torch on and shone it into the room, playing its beam all around.

His daughter was hanging, head lowered, arms dangling by her sides. She was pale, very pale, and there were so many of her, ten, fifteen Sophies, all turning and twisting forlornly in the dark room, suspended from the ceiling on rope. The figures were full length, and black and white. Fortune walked into the room, among the hanging effigies, as if he was walking between lines of forgotten washing. All the figures were the same, her form neatly cut out from life-size photographs. She looked as if she was sleeping. Fortune gazed at her, at his daughter, at how serene and beautiful she was, this young woman he barely knew. He felt a deep rage, an impotent fury that someone could do this, to him, to her, play with them so maliciously, be so precisely cruel.

He pulled every figure down, laying the stiff paper forms on the floor. He did not think his daughter was dead. If she was, then what was the purpose of this? But he did think it was a message, about what was going to happen to her. Revenge, for the death of the troll's mother. For her suicide, and all that had happened to him after. He understood. He got it. He spoke the words into the empty room. 'All right. All right, okay. I get it.'

He walked back downstairs, down to the hall, picked up the sledgehammer and bolt-cutters and stepped out of the main door, into the light. He walked back to his car and returned the tools to the boot. There was a bench underneath one of the building's front windows, and Fortune sat on it and lit a cigarette. He exhaled a thick cloud of smoke into the cold air, watching it slowly disperse, not a breath of wind. The troll wasn't here.

Something was, some malicious vestige of what had happened, unquiet remnants of the misery and pain and fear that had occupied this place. But no troll. He had two days left to find him and his daughter, and he was out of ideas.

A distant sound disturbed the quiet, a car engine, getting closer and closer, which meant that it must be on the drive, must be coming towards him. He stood up and dropped his cigarette as a four-by-four appeared, a white one. It stopped face-on to him, ten metres away, and he could see a man behind the wheel, wearing a cap, his face hidden. The man cut the engine but stayed in the car, watching Fortune, face dark under his cap. At last he opened his door and climbed down.

'Help you?' he said.

'Who are you?' said Fortune.

'No,' said the man, walking towards Fortune. He was big, the man, in his twenties, wearing some kind of uniform, rent-a-cop style, blue shirt, combat trousers, boots. He stopped, four feet away. 'No, you don't ask the questions. What are you doing here?'

'Nothing.'

'Says *Private Property*,' said the man, lifting his chin and nodding behind him. 'Didn't see the sign?'

'I saw it.'

'Ignored it.'

'I suppose I must have done.'

'So, you shouldn't be here.' The man looked around. 'You here alone?'

'Yes.'

'Got a name?'

Fortune nodded. 'Most people do.'

The man smiled, not amused. His face was pocked with acne

scarring and Fortune suspected that he had been bullied at school, taken his frustration out in the gym. Going by the size of his arms, there'd been a lot of frustration to vent. 'Want to tell me it?' he said.

'No.'

The man sighed. 'I could arrest you.'

'No you couldn't,' said Fortune, evenly. 'We both know you don't have that kind of authority.'

The man looked past Fortune's shoulder. 'Did you cut those chains?'

'No.'

The man smiled again. 'I'm going to call the police.'

'I'm leaving anyway.'

'Criminal damage,' said the man. 'Trespass.'

Fortune didn't have time for this. 'How did you know I was here?' he said.

'Motion camera,' said the man. 'Your car tripped it, got a nice clear shot of you parked up.' He said it proudly, as if he had invented the technology himself, something that, judging by his vacant smile, Fortune doubted. But he sensed an opportunity.

'Clever,' he said. 'I didn't see it.'

'Weren't meant to,' the man said, triumphant in his camera's hidden cunning.

'Is this place still for sale?'

'Still,' said the man.

'How long's it been on the market?'

'Years,' said the man.

'A place like this?' said Fortune. 'Not been snapped up by some footballer?'

The man smiled again, the kind of look people wear when, for once, they are in possession of knowledge somebody else doesn't have. 'You don't know about it?'

'About what?'

'This place.'

'No.'

The man nodded, paused, a long pause. Fortune willed himself to wait out his absurd portentousness. 'Bad things happened here,' he allowed, eventually.

'What kind of things?'

'Used to be an orphanage. The boys, they ...' He paused again, this time to consider his phrasing. 'They did things to them.'

'Right,' said Fortune, patiently, and said again, 'What kind of things?'

The man shrugged. 'Beatings, torture. Some people say, you know ...'

'No.'

The man shrugged again, shifted his weight uncomfortably. 'Sex things.'

'Oh,' said Fortune, nodding. 'God,' he added, fairly unconvincingly.

'I know,' said the man. 'So people don't want to buy it. Say it's haunted.'

'Is it?'

'Don't know,' said the man. 'Tell you what, though, wouldn't catch me in there.'

'No?'

'Not a chance,' he said. 'Don't mind admitting. And I'm no coward,' he added, quickly.

'Won't catch me in there either,' said Fortune. 'That kind of history's bad for business.'

'What kind of business?' said the man.

'I scout properties. For clients. I have a client, a hedge fund manager, who wants a big place around here. I thought of this, but now you've told me that ...'

'So you haven't been in?'

'No. And I'm not going to now, either. Not worth my while, a place like this.'

The man nodded, considered. 'Still going to need your name,' he said.

'Harry,' said Fortune. 'Harry Marsh. But,' he added quickly, to head off any demands for proof, 'I'd rather you kept this quiet. My job's to be discreet. You understand? If people know who I am, what I do, the asking price ...' He pointed up at the sky. 'It suddenly goes that way.'

He wasn't too sure he understood what he'd just said himself, but the man considered for a moment, then nodded. 'All right, but you need to leave.'

'Like I said,' Fortune replied, 'I was just on my way.'

'I'll wait for you to go,' the man said. 'Just in case.'

'Sure.' Fortune nodded. 'You're doing a fine job.'

He turned and walked to the car. He started it up and turned around, heading towards the drive, giving the man a brief wave as he passed. He might have got away with that, but he still had no plan. He drove back through the tunnel of hopeless, leafless trees, their branches this time seeming to reach out to his car in silent supplication. As if to beg him not to go. As if to tell him that he shouldn't be leaving, that there was still work for him to do here. But the troll wasn't there, not any more. He was someplace else. The only problem was, Fortune had no idea where.

fifty

WHAT WAS IT HE SAID TO ME? WHAT DID THE TROLL SAY, before he left? Just before he left, he said … Think. Think, Sophie, but I couldn't think because there was a spider and it was above me on the wall and it was huge, it was huge and I couldn't think, I couldn't think at all. My arm was greasy with blood and it hurt, it stung, and I could barely see for tears, could barely breathe for all the blubbery snot. I was crying like a child, a mess. I couldn't think. What had he said?

Do you believe in fortune?

That's what he said. Do you believe in fortune?

I looked at the combination. Six numbers. I thought of the, what was it? The second time I was taken to the Games Room? My birthday, backwards, that was the game. Game? Please. Using my left hand, I reached awkwardly across my body, my fingers slipping on the tiny wheels. I couldn't get them to move, I couldn't control them. What was it? Come on, Sophie, your birthday, backwards. Nineteen ninety-eight … 8, 9, 9, 1. July. 7, 0. Shit. No. Too many numbers. Okay, okay, stop. Think. Ninety-eight. Forget the nineteen. 8, 9, 7, 0. Twenty-four, so, oh Jesus, how hard could this be? 4, 2. Done. I pulled at the lock. Nothing. It wouldn't open.

I looked up at the spider. It hadn't moved, like it was waiting. Watching. Watching me cry and sniff and try to remember when I was bloody born. I tried again. This time, the right way round. 2, 4 ... what next? 7? No, come on, Sophie, you need six numbers. So 0, then 7. Then 9, 8. Done. Pull. Nothing. It wouldn't open, it wouldn't open, and I pulled and the plastic cuff bit into my wrist and the blood was running down my arm and I couldn't breathe, couldn't get enough air into me, it was getting darker and darker and darker. I closed my eyes and tried to focus. Calm down. Breathe. Breathe. But I couldn't keep my eyes closed because there was a spider on the wall and it was right above me. Stop. Calm. Breathe. Breathe, breathe, breathe.

Do you believe in fortune?

Okay. Okay, you can do this.

Numbers. Fortune, numbers. Unlucky numbers, the kind that bring bad fortune. Thirteen. What was it, with the Chinese? Four. They didn't have floors in buildings with the number four in. Thirteen, four, fourteen, twenty-four? Too many numbers. Anyway, it wasn't that, it was a stupid idea. Come on, Sophie. Think.

Okay, okay, maybe it was a trick. The troll loved games and this could be a trick. Do you believe in fortune? So, right, so maybe it wasn't about bad luck, maybe it was really just about *luck*. Like, I could put any numbers in, it didn't matter. So I put the first numbers I thought of into the combination. How would that work? It didn't matter, just try it. Whatever. I reached over with my left hand again and fumbled with the dials. 1, 6, 3, 4, no, 7, 1 again, 5. Pulled on the lock. Nothing. No surprise there. Sophie, you cretin, you idiot. You sad excuse, you travesty. Think. Think.

I looked up and the spider wasn't there. It had gone and I could feel it on me, under me, everywhere, I imagined the insidious pressure of its legs all over me, a dreadful subtle touch, panic stopping my breathing again. Where was it? Where had it gone? Not being able to see it was worse, somehow. Like it might drop from the ceiling onto me. Where was it?

You need to get out of this, I thought. You need to find the combination and get out of here. I looked at the net, tried to reach it, strained towards it, the plastic cuff like a knife under my skin. I couldn't get near, not even close.

Do you believe in fortune?

Do you believe in Fortune?

My dad. Everybody called him Fortune, they always had done, like he didn't even have a first name. Did I believe in him? No, course I didn't. But then I thought of the Tube, of losing him and how he had come for me and how I had believed in him once, a lifetime ago. When I had said, *I knew you would come and find me.*

Do you believe in Fortune?

I wanted to. I did so want to. I'd always wanted to.

When was Dad's birthday? I couldn't remember. How old was he, even? No idea. Fifty something. Who was it told me once, that Dad had been born old? Who had said that?

It didn't matter. Think. When was he born?

Summer.

When?

August. Definitely. In the summer holidays. He wasn't there, because he was working. We'd call him up from Spain, Greece, Rome, wherever me and Mum were. Happy birthday, Dad. Yeah, I know you'd love to be here. Yeah, I understand. Yeah. Yeah. Yeah, happy birthday.

All right. Year. Wait. Work it out. He had a fiftieth. Not a party, but he had a fiftieth birthday, he turned fifty, and it was … after university. During my first job. No, second. I remembered thinking, if I'm still doing this when I'm fifty, I might as well end it now. Someone actually kill me? So that made him fifty-four now. Okay. What year? 1963. Yes, '63. Okay. Okay, Sophie, that was good. That wasn't bad.

Day.

Oh well now, there was a thing.

I didn't have a clue.

Okay. Didn't matter. Start at the beginning, and work your way forward.

So I turned the dials, as quickly as I could. 0, 1, 0, 8, 6, 3. Nothing.

I turned the second dial. 2. Nothing. 3. Nothing. I was pulling and pulling and my wrist, it was a mess, I looked like the world's most determined suicide. 4. Nothing. 5. Nothing. I looked up for the spider but it wasn't there, and then I looked down and it was on my leg, on my leg, right there on my ankle, one of its legs raised like it was thinking, planning what next. Oh God. I froze, didn't move at all, stopped breathing, my muscles tensed, locked. It was on my *leg*.

I turned and reached again for the combination. 6. Nothing. 7. Nothing. 8. Nothing. I looked back at the spider and it hadn't moved but I could feel its weight on my leg, light, like a towel, nothing, but it was so big, so so big, and black, and it was the worst thing I'd ever seen. 9. Nothing. My wrist was open, the bloody gash black in the dim light. 10. Nothing. 11. Nothing. The spider darted quickly up my leg, past my knee, and stopped. I made a sound, some noise I'd never made before, small and lost. 12. Nothing. Come on. Please please please come on. 13. I pulled and the lock slid apart. I was free. The spider was there and I thought, come on, Sophie, come on you can do this, and I stood and kicked and the spider fell off and I ran to the net and picked it up and put it over the spider. I ran to the door and hammered on it, hammered and hammered and hammered, and when the troll opened the door I saw his face for the first time, and then I don't remember anything else.

fifty-one

THROUGHOUT FORTUNE'S RESEARCH INTO ST BASIL'S, THE trawling and sifting through the news stories and features, one name had kept cropping up, one byline had appeared more than any others. A local journalist, Essex-based, who had tenaciously kept enquiring, asking questions, speculating. His name was Jack Sumner and his interest in the case, judging by his coverage, hadn't been entirely professional.

Fortune stopped at a roadside diner and ordered coffee. While he waited, he called the paper's news desk and asked to speak to Jack Sumner. The woman asked him what it was concerning.

'St Basil's.'

'Oh.' She seemed surprised, and paused for a moment. 'Could you tell me what your interest in it is?'

'No,' said Fortune. 'Is he there?'

'Not today,' she said, and paused again. 'But if it's concerning St Basil's, he'll want to hear. Do you have a pen?'

'Yes.'

She read him a mobile number and Fortune thanked her and hung up. A waitress brought his coffee to the booth he was sitting in and he thanked her, then dialled the number. It was answered after a couple of rings.

'Hi, Jack here.'

'Hello,' said Fortune. 'I'm calling regarding St Basil's.'

'Yes?'

'I wondered if you could help.'

'With?'

'I'm looking for people who might have worked there.'

'Mind if I ask why?' Sumner's voice was open and friendly, but there was a note of suspicion behind it.

'I need to ...' He paused. Here goes nothing. 'I'm looking for an ex-ward who, well, it turns out he's my son.'

'Your son.'

'I only just found out. I'm looking for him because I think he might be in trouble.'

'Right,' said Sumner, slowly, like he was considering whether or not Fortune was insane. 'I don't quite see ...'

'I think he's disturbed, due to what happened there. He's been making threats. Creating problems in my life.'

'What kind of problems?'

Like kidnapping and threatening to murder my daughter, Fortune thought. He said, 'He's stolen a lot of money. Made false allegations, mounted some kind of campaign. It's complicated.'

'Sounds it.' Jack Sumner was silent for a moment. 'Why do you want to speak to somebody who worked there?'

'To get some background,' Fortune said. 'To find out what happened to him there, what went on.'

Sumner laughed. 'Good luck with that.'

'It's important,' said Fortune.

'Don't need to tell me,' said Sumner. 'How are you planning to get the information?'

'By asking,' said Fortune.

'Yeah, I tried that,' said Sumner. 'Didn't get me far.'

'I'll ask to begin with,' said Fortune. 'If that doesn't work, I've got other strategies.'

'Interesting,' said Sumner. 'Want to share these other strategies?'

'Not if you want to be an accessory after the fact,' said Fortune.

Jack laughed. 'Okay, now you're speaking my language.' He was silent again, this time for so long that Fortune wondered if he was still there. But then he said, 'I only know the whereabouts of one of them. Burridge.'

'Oliver James Burridge? The warder?'

'The top man,' said Sumner.

'Where is he?'

'In a nursing home. Apparently he's had it, suffered some kind of stroke, can't eat without dribbling. Serves the bastard right.'

'Can I ask,' said Fortune, 'why you're so interested in St Basil's?'

'I'm a journalist,' said Sumner. 'It's my job.'

'And?'

Another silence. 'Okay, and my wife's brother was a ward there. Only he didn't come out. Just disappeared, never seen again. How does something like that happen?'

'Seems to have happened a lot.'

'And yet nobody's been brought to justice. Helps when your brother's a peer of the realm.'

'I heard about that.'

'Yeah,' said Sumner, disgust in his voice. 'Come a long way, haven't we? This country.'

Fortune thought of Dubai, of its stratified society, its codified injustice. Home didn't seem so much better. 'Could you tell me where I can find him?'

'Burridge? On one condition.'

'What's that?'

'You don't show the old bastard any mercy.'

'I think I can promise that,' said Fortune.

Sumner told him to hold on, and Fortune waited for a couple of minutes before Sumner came back with the address, a nursing home outside Brentwood. Not far away. Fortune thanked him and promised he'd call him back, give him any information he found. Then he hung up and finished his coffee. It wasn't late. He still had time to see Burridge today. All he needed was a story. Shouldn't be a problem. He couldn't see anybody stopping him.

It turned out that getting in to see Oliver James Burridge at Glades Nursing Home was a formality, mainly due to the fact that, clearly, nobody was much concerned for his welfare. Fortune asked at the reception desk if Burridge was there and the receptionist said, 'Who?'

'Oliver James Burridge.'

'Oh. Yes.' The receptionist had a look on her face as if Fortune had just asked her if she fancied a threesome. 'Did you want to visit him?'

'Please.'

'You're family?'

'No. Just an old friend.'

'You understand that Mr Burridge is very poorly.' Still granting him the title of mister, despite his reputation, the things he was thought to have done.

'I know. I thought, him seeing me, it might do him good.'

The receptionist looked at Fortune with distaste and Fortune had to fight the urge to tell her that no, she had it wrong, he wasn't like that, wasn't like Burridge. 'He doesn't get many visitors.'

'That doesn't surprise me.'

'You know about him?'

'Of course.'

'And you still want to see him.'

'Yes.'

The receptionist nodded, but it wasn't a nod of understanding. Why would anybody want to see such a monster as Oliver James Burridge? Fortune could understand her point of view. 'All right,' she said, no friendliness in her tone, purely professional. 'I'll just go and ask him. What's your name?'

'I thought I could surprise him. He hasn't seen me for a long time.'

The receptionist frowned and was about to refuse, then must have decided that protecting the safety of an evil old man wasn't worth her time or energy. 'Well, you'll need to tell me,' she said. 'To sign in.' She put a pen on an open book filled with columns to write down who you were, who you were there to see, the registration plate of your car, time in and out. Fortune scribbled down *Harry Marsh*, deciding he might as well be consistent.

'If you'd like to follow me, Mr … Marsh,' she said, turning the book to read it. 'I'll show you to his room.'

She came around from her side of the desk and pushed through a door with a wired glass circle cut in it, down a corridor, around a corner, then another, before stopping before a door.

'I'll tell Mr Burridge you're here,' she said. 'I won't say anything else.' She slid into the room, only opening the door slightly, and Fortune waited outside, wondering whether, if Burridge didn't want to see him, he had it in him to overpower the girl. Morally he thought he probably did. Physically he wasn't so sure. But the receptionist reappeared and said, 'Come in.'

Fortune walked into the room, which wasn't large and had a vase of flowers on a table next to a window, a blind shutting out most of the light. Burridge was in a bed that had been adjusted so that he was in a seated position. He looked without much curiosity at Fortune, an old man, frail-looking, with watery eyes. The receptionist watched him without emotion, then said to Fortune, 'You can find your own way out,' and left, closing the door behind her.

There was no window in the door and they were alone, just him and Burridge. Burridge looked at him, didn't say anything. Fortune walked past him to the window and opened the louvred blind slightly, so that dim daylight came into the room.

'Who the hell are you?' Burridge said to Fortune's back. Fortune didn't answer. Throw him off, he thought. Make him start guessing. Don't make it easy. 'I said, who the hell are you?' Burridge's voice was weak, faltering, but still held an authoritarian tone. 'Well? Answer me, man.'

Fortune turned and walked to the bed. There was a red alarm cord hanging next to it, and he reached up and tied it up, shortening it, out of Burridge's reach.

'My name's Fortune,' he said. 'My son was one of your wards.'

Burridge looked up with difficulty at the red cord, then back to Fortune. 'Only took in children without parents,' he said.

'Yes, well. This one slipped through the cracks. Maybe you remember him? His name was Hector. Hector Emmerson.'

'What is it you want?' said Burridge.

'I want to know what you did to him,' said Fortune. 'I want details.'

'Did to him?' Burridge's mouth opened and closed, once, three times, a wet, sloppy sound. He still had a fine head of hair, Fortune had to give him that, iron grey and swept back in stiff waves. But underneath the face was weak, the muscles no longer doing their job, one of his eyes sagging at the corner. 'What do you mean, did to him? I should like you to leave.'

Fortune gave Burridge's ear a sharp tug and Burridge turned and looked at him in surprise. 'I'm sure you would,' Fortune said. 'But that's not going to happen. Not until you tell me what you did to Hector Emmerson.'

'I will not speak to you,' said Burridge. His voice was upper-class, and despite his frailty and position of helplessness, it still held a condescending sneer.

Fortune, less educated and cultivated than the majority of his colleagues, had dealt with condescension all his working life. It tended to piss him off. He walked to the window, took the flowers out of the vase, walked back to the bed and emptied the water on Burridge's head. Burridge spluttered, his mouth once again opening and closing, Fortune thinking of a landed fish, uselessly gasping.

'Now then,' said Fortune. 'I'm going to leave this room with the information I need. Even if I have to kill you for it. Do you understand?'

'How dare you?' said Burridge, his voice a furious whisper, no longer able to raise his voice.

Fortune walked to the other side of the room, where a kettle stood on a table, next to paper cups, tea and sugar. He lifted the kettle. Empty. He opened the door to the en suite and filled the kettle from the bath tap. He went back into Burridge's room, turned the kettle on, and came back to the bed.

'When that kettle has boiled, I'm going to pour it over your head,' he said. 'It will hurt. Looking at the state of you, I imagine you'll probably die.'

'Damn you,' said Burridge. 'Damn your eyes.'

People still said that? thought Fortune. He sighed. 'You need to tell me what happened to Hector Emmerson. You haven't got much time.'

'I have no idea what you're talking about,' said Burridge.

'I think you do. I think you know exactly what happened at St Basil's, and you're going to tell me.'

'I have nothing to say to you,' Burridge said. It was still there, the condescending sneer. He closed his eyes, kept them closed, and Fortune looked down at him in exasperation. He didn't want to pour boiling water over a frail old man's head, regardless of what atrocities he had probably committed in the past. Hell, he wasn't capable of pouring a kettle of boiling water over anybody's head; the thought itself was too horrible for words. The room was silent apart from the quiet hiss of the air conditioner and the gentle roar of the kettle heating up.

'Time's running out,' said Fortune. Burridge didn't answer, kept his eyes closed. Fortune had an urge to pull him out of bed and boot him all the way down the corridor outside, imagining Burridge yelping with each well-aimed kick. If this was what evil looked like, he thought, it was indeed banal. A frail old man acting like a child, pretending he couldn't hear what was being said to him. Life had never seemed a more futile enterprise.

The kettle boiled and clicked off. Fortune walked over to it, picked it up and put it back down again. He closed his eyes and sighed, as long and deeply as his lungs would let him. There was no way he could do this. What would it achieve anyway, apart from killing Burridge? He sighed again and turned, to see Burridge crouched on his bed, unsteady, reaching up for the red emergency cord. It was just out of his reach, and he flailed at it and lost his balance, falling off the edge of the bed, landing on his head and neck, urine leaking through his pyjamas, darkening the blue stripes. He lay still, not moving.

Fortune looked down at him in dismay. Time to go, he thought. He pulled open the door, closed it behind him and hurried back to the reception desk. He hadn't wanted that, it hadn't been part of the plan. Not that there had ever been much of a plan.

'Finished?' the receptionist asked him, looking up at the sound of the door opening.

'Yes,' said Fortune. 'All done.'

'You're really a friend of his?'

'Well,' said Fortune. 'Not exactly a friend.'

'They say he did terrible things.'

'Who do?'

'People.' The receptionist looked away, down at her desk, as if ashamed of what she had said.

'People are right,' said Fortune. 'He's a terrible person.'

'Then why ...?' started the receptionist.

'It doesn't matter,' said Fortune. 'I just needed to ask him something.'

'Did you get an answer?'

'No.'

The receptionist nodded and seemed to consider something, before coming to a decision. 'I shouldn't say this, but ...' She stopped and looked around, making sure that nobody could hear what she was about to say. 'A man came to see him, must have been three, four months ago? He said that if anybody came asking about Mr Burridge, to tell them to call him.'

'Who was he?'

'I don't know. He said he knew Mr Burridge from when he was younger.'

'Did he have a name?'

'Robert something. Hold on.' She opened a drawer, rummaged around and came up with a card. 'Here. He gave me this.'

Fortune took it. A business card, raised black ink on cream stock. Robert Foster. A mobile number and an address. 'He didn't say anything else?'

'No. But I told him I'd do it. Because of … the things he did. Mr Burridge.'

'Thanks,' said Fortune. 'I'll call him. And Mr Burridge? I think my visit took a lot out of him.'

'Okay.' The receptionist nodded.

Fortune turned and walked out of the building, back to his car, feeling a sense of panic. So little time, and Burridge was, if not dead, then certainly a dead end. What the hell was he going to do now?

fifty-two

THE FIRST THING FORTUNE SAW AS HE WALKED INTO ROBERT Foster's front room was a lion, its mouth open in an outraged roar, furious to find itself in a decrepit bungalow in Essex. The lion was being morosely regarded by an owl, wings spread in mid-flight, claws raised in preparation to strike, mounted with its back to the wall. A generously antlered elk's head was next to the owl, again mounted on the wall, as if it had accidentally charged through it and quickly accepted its situation as hopeless.

Fortune had tried calling Foster's number but there had been no answer. He had no time to waste, no time to wait, so he had driven to the address on the card. Foster lived in a brick bungalow in a poor neighbourhood of similarly abject homes, the streets they were built on made of huge pre-fab sheets of concrete, all of it sloppily constructed in the sixties to house the working poor. Judging by Foster's front garden, he spent a lot more time stuffing animals than he did cutting back the tangles of encroaching brambles and holly. Fortune had pushed through the branches and barbs and found the front door open. He'd called out but received no answer so had walked in, past a Victorian case of mouldering birds of paradise, unconvincingly glued to branches. The front room had only contained animals, dead animals, their deaths done no honour by Foster's clumsy craftsmanship.

There was nothing to see there, so Fortune turned and walked along a corridor lined with papers and broken cases and boxes, to the kitchen. It was empty apart from Foster, who was slumped in a striped deckchair, his arms hanging over the sides, snoring loudly. There was an empty bottle of Scotch lying next to the deckchair, although given that there was an amber pool of liquid next to the bottle, it looked like Foster had given out before it had.

Christ, thought Fortune, an ache in his body that seemed to be emanating from his bones, his eyes gritty from lack of sleep, his mouth a dirty oven. Couldn't it ever be simple?

He shook Foster's shoulder but only got a moan in response. He considered giving him the same treatment he had given Burridge and pouring a jug of water over his head, but he needed Foster, needed his help and cooperation, so instead he dug around in the kitchen cupboards and came up with coffee and filters, to go with the antique percolator on the kitchen counter. As he made the coffee and waited for it to brew, he couldn't help but wonder why a man like Robert Foster, a drunk and incompetent taxidermist, had ever bothered outlaying money on such an expensive business card. Marketing was marketing, but it would only ever get you so far.

Foster was overweight and under-shaved, ginger stubble on his face, his too-short black Ramones T-shirt exposing a flaccid white belly. Fortune pinched the man's nostrils and waited, then waited some more until Foster quivered in his chair and shook his head like a bull tossing its horns.

'The hell are you?' he said.

'My name's Fortune. I went to see Burridge.'

This seemed to hit home, Foster's eyes widening, though still unfocused. He struggled to sit up. 'Burridge?'

'And now I'm here.'

'I can see that. Burridge. From St Basil's?'

'Yes.'

'You went to see Burridge.' He said this to himself, then leant forward, his arms around his knees. Fortune felt a passing, yet strong, wave of sympathy for this sad and broken man. Foster looked up, rocked in his deckchair and stood unsteadily. He backed up and put a hand on the counter, taking a sneaky look at the empty bottle of Scotch on the floor. He grimaced in disappointment, and looked at Fortune. 'Why are you in my house?'

'I want to ask you about Burridge.'

'Why?'

'Because he ruined my son's life. And now my son is trying to ruin mine.'

It took Foster some time to absorb this, to sort out the inherent conflicts. 'What, like some kind of revenge?' he said eventually.

Fortune shrugged. 'I suppose so.'

'What's he called? Your son?'

'Emmerson. Hector Emmerson.'

'Hector?' Foster looked around, as if he'd just had a wallet stolen, then said, 'Wait there,' and walked carefully out of the kitchen, putting a hand on the counter to steady himself. Fortune watched him go, then looked around. There wasn't a lot to see. Either Foster lived on takeaways, or he'd found a way to survive without eating.

Foster came back with a large green plastic bottle that claimed to be weedkiller, but given that he was drinking out of it, Fortune suspected that it was part of the man's Plan B. Foster stopped in the doorway and grinned.

'Hector. Prince of Heck?'

Fortune shrugged again. 'Hector Emmerson.'

'The boy genius.' Foster laughed. 'Mentally brilliant. Brilliantly mental.'

'How'd you mean?' said Fortune. He'd have loved to sit down, but there was only the deckchair. 'You mind if we go into the other room? I can't keep standing.'

'Sure. Good idea.' Foster waved his bottle of weedkiller. 'Want a drink?'

'I'm all right. Mind if I smoke?' Fortune could hardly believe he'd even asked.

Foster smiled. 'Sure. Just don't set fire to my lion. Thing's worth four grand.'

Fortune watched Foster tip more of the weedkiller, or whatever the bottle contained, down his throat. They were sitting on armchairs facing each other, and he had the feeling that Foster was only half with him, that he hadn't properly surfaced from his deckchair.

'Hector Emmerson,' he said again. 'Give me something.'

Foster laughed. 'Why'd you want to know?'

'I told you. He's my son.'

He laughed again, this time harder, a genuine reaction of incredulity. 'Your son? Jesus. I hope you don't want to be proud of him.'

'Not particularly,' said Fortune. 'Do you think you can tell me about him?'

'Hector Emmerson,' said Foster, and giggled. 'Your son. He

was the worst person at St Basil's, if you don't count the warders. Just, like, the worst. Serious.' He paused, said quietly, 'Or best.'

'Worst how?' said Fortune.

'Clever.' Foster waved his green bottle. 'Amazing. Like, anything he said he would do, he did. Didn't give a shit. Everyone else, terrified. Him?' He lowered his head, shook it, spoke into his lap. 'Didn't give a shit.'

'Give me an example?'

Foster was quiet for some time, head down, and Fortune worried that he was asleep. But then he raised his head and said, 'Like, he spent a week there. An entire week. And when he came out, he acted like it was nothing. Like he'd been on holiday.'

'Spent a week where?'

Foster smiled, drank, said, 'The Games Room.'

Fortune frowned and wondered whether he was getting any sense at all out of the man. 'The Games Room?'

Foster nodded, then seemed to abruptly lose interest. His chin dropped, and Fortune hoped he hadn't passed out.

'What happened there? In the Games Room?' he said.

Foster put his green bottle carefully down on the carpet, then sat forward on his chair, his head hanging above his knees. He didn't answer, and Fortune waited, then asked again, 'What happened?'

'They found you out,' Foster said. 'Worked you out. They got under your skin.'

'You mean psychologically?' said Fortune.

Foster nodded at the floor, then looked up with a strange smile. 'Or with knives. Whatever worked.'

'What was it? The Games Room?'

'What the hell do you think it was?' said Foster, in drunken irritation. He reached down and knocked his hand against his bottle, nearly toppled it but caught it in time. This seemed to calm him, and he said, softly, 'It was a room where they played their games.'

'What kind of games?'

Foster drank, closed his eyes and leant back in his chair. 'Depended.'

'On what?'

'On what you were most afraid of.' Foster was silent, and Fortune again wondered if he'd passed out, but then he said, 'Me, I was scared of being hurt. Simple really. So that's what they'd do. If you were scared of the dark, they'd lock you in it. One kid was scared of dogs, must have had a bad experience, whatever. They locked him in with the German Shepherds.' He sighed, shook his head. 'That kind of thing.'

'Why?' said Fortune.

'Why? Because they were evil, totally evil, malicious, cruel, capricious, dreadful people. And because it was all part of the game.' He stopped and thought. 'We were. Part of the game. That's what I realized. We were like, their toys. Their playthings.'

Fortune didn't know how to respond to this, lacked the emotional equipment. What could he offer this man, this damaged, ruined man? *Godforsaken* was the word that came into his mind, unannounced, surprising; not a word he would ordinarily think of. But it was right, it was the right word. Godforsaken. Foster was silent, his eyes blank, focused on nothing, nothing except the past and what had happened there, his godforsaken past. At last he said, more to himself than Fortune, 'They'd toss a coin. That was the worst. At the beginning, always at the beginning. Heads, you got off lightly. Tails, you got the full treatment.' He looked up and met Fortune's eye, showing a brief moment of lucidity. 'Whatever they had planned. It was like, and we actually believed this, it was like they were making it fair. Giving us a chance. But we didn't win. We never won. Nobody won.'

Fortune thought of the cruelty of it all, offering children false hope, the choice between bad and terrible. Heads, you lose. Tails, it's worse. What would that do to a child, what effect would it have? He looked at Foster, prematurely old, drinking himself to death. He thought of his son, his twisted and precise anger. That's what it would do.

'What did they do to Hector Emmerson?' he said. 'What was he scared of?'

Foster smiled at this and sat up, waving his bottle in Fortune's direction. 'Ah. Well, that was the thing. They never worked it out. Least that's what we all thought. Turned out he wasn't scared of anything. They beat him, tortured him, did, God, I can't imagine. Never got to him.'

'Did they ...' Fortune paused, in unknown territory, unused to dealing with such profound emotions, needing to show sensitivity. But Foster answered before he had to navigate through his sentence.

'Sex? Yeah, all that. We did what they asked us. What else were we going to do?'

'Who were *they*?'

'The adults. The ones in charge at St Basil's.'

'All of them?'

'No. No, not all of them. But those ones didn't last, usually.'

'How could this go on? Didn't you say anything?'

'Me?' Foster shook his head slowly, dopily. 'No. No chance. Kid called George, he tried it, they said he ran away.' Now he nodded, down at his knees, thinking back. 'Nobody thought he ran away. None of us. They took him to the Games Room, and we never saw him again.' He laughed, a small noise, looking down at his dirty carpet. 'I think he got tails.'

'Did this happen to everybody? Did everybody go to the Games Room?'

'Not everybody. Only the ones they didn't like. Or did like. You know. In that way.' Foster shrugged. 'I don't know. None of it made sense. We were just kids.'

'Why did you go and see Burridge?' said Fortune.

'Why? To tell him he was an evil bastard,' said Foster.

'And?'

'And he looked at me like I was nothing, like I was hardly there. Looked at me and said he should have worked harder on me.'

Fortune nodded, stood up. 'You need coffee.'

'All right with this,' said Foster, hoisting up his bottle of weedkiller like it was a trophy, and the award for best actor goes to …

'Put it down,' said Fortune. 'I'll get coffee.'

In the kitchen, he looked through cupboards until he found a mug. He opened the fridge in search of milk, but there was nothing in it except an open can of beans and a green piece of meat that could have been anything. There was something ineffably miserable about Foster's house, its shabbiness presided over by dead animals, all dignity lost, torn out of them.

Back in the living room, Foster was still drinking. Fortune took the bottle out of his hand and Foster didn't complain, just watched Fortune stupidly. The bottle was almost empty of whatever the hell had been in it. Pretty soon Foster wasn't going to be much use, regardless of how much coffee Fortune managed to get into him.

'Where was the Games Room?' said Fortune. 'Was it in St Basil's?'

Foster belched softly, slumped back in his chair. 'No. Don't know.'

'How'd you mean?'

'Never knew. Put a hood on us. Take us outside, put us in a car. Take us somewhere. Down.' Foster's eyes were closed and he nodded to himself, chin against his chest. 'It was down.' A pause, a long, long pause. Then, like a child muttering in its sleep, woken from a dream, 'We went down stairs.'

'Where?'

'Don't know.'

'Maybe they did it to confuse you? Disorientate you? Drive around, then back to the orphanage?'

Foster nodded, a tiny movement of his head. 'Could have.' He exhaled, long and hard, left another pause and then said, 'Don't know.'

'Anything else? What did it look like? The Games Room? Was it big, small?'

Foster didn't answer and Fortune thought he'd lost him again. He stood up, walked over to his chair. 'Wake up, Robert. Please. You need to help me here. I need something else. Give me something else.' He reached down and shook Foster by the shoulder, then shook him again, hard. 'Please. Who else was there? Who else did these things? Give me a name.' He took Foster's chin and pulled his head around and up so that he was looking at Fortune. Foster's eyes were half closed, vacant. 'A name. You must have another name.'

'Bagsy,' said Foster. 'It was Bagsy. Always Bagsy.'

'Who's Bagsy?' said Fortune.

Foster smiled, didn't answer. He closed his eyes and Fortune gave his chin another tug, hard. 'Who's Bagsy?' he said again.

'Always there,' said Foster, eyes still closed. He started singing, more to himself than anybody he imagined might be in the room with him. 'Bagsy. Bagsy, we all ha-ate Bagsy. Bagsy, Bagsy, we all ha-ate ...' He trailed off and Fortune felt the weight of his chin in his hand, heavy and doughy.

'Who is he?' he asked desperately, but Foster's eyes were closed, and when Fortune let go of his chin, he collapsed back into his armchair, out cold.

Fortune stood and looked around at the dismal animals. He'd have as much chance of getting something out of them as he would of rousing Foster. One day. He had one day left to find his daughter. He wouldn't find her here. Where was the Games Room?

fifty-three

FORTUNE WAS TEN MINUTES AWAY FROM GLADES NURSING Home when his phone rang and he pulled over, killing the motor before answering. He didn't want to be stopped for unsafe driving, not now.

'Hello?'

'Who am I speaking to?'

It was a woman's voice, a voice Fortune didn't recognize. Careful, he thought. 'Who is this?'

'This is the idiot mum of the idiot who gave you my damn car,' the woman said.

'Oh,' said Fortune. Poor Lee. 'Yes. It's true, I did take your car.'

'So I want it back. Now.'

'Did Lee tell you why I've got your car?'

'He gave me some story.'

'Did you hear about Charlie Jackson?'

'Guy who got killed?'

'That's right,' said Fortune. 'I killed him. And I told your son, I told him that I'd kill his mum, that I'd kill you, if he didn't give me your car.'

Lee's mother didn't answer, probably too shocked to speak.

'He didn't want to, he's a brave kid. But he didn't have a choice. He must really love you.'

'You're that man?'

'I'm that man,' said Fortune. 'And I've got your car, and you're not going to get it back.' He paused, and added, 'I'm sorry.'

'I'm going straight to the Old Bill,' the woman said.

'Do that,' said Fortune. 'Just go easy on Lee. You've got a good son there.'

He didn't necessarily believe that last statement, but he thought it was the least he could do, after all the trouble he'd put Lee through. Perhaps this would serve as some kind of lesson, a new start, although he doubted it. Oh well. He hit the red hang-up icon. He'd done his best.

It was dark when Fortune arrived back at the nursing home, eight hours after he'd last been there, the reception a fluorescent-lit oasis in the middle of nowhere. There was a different receptionist than during the day, a bored-looking man who probably wasn't expecting anyone to arrive this late. He glanced up when Fortune walked in out of the night, and put down a copy of the *Racing Post*. He was middle-aged and skinny, with silver stubble. He looked tired, tired and untrustworthy, with a gold hoop earring and a swallow tattoo on his arm. The kind of man who got the night shift, minimum wage, sit there until the sun comes up and don't steal the medications, keep away from the diamorphine. Fortune smiled and prepared his story. He needed to speak to Burridge, there'd been some news, a family tragedy. That should do it. If, that was, Burridge was still alive.

'Yes?' the man said.

'I need to see Oliver Burridge.'

The man blinked, said warily, 'Mr Burridge?'

'Yes.'

'Are you family?'

'Almost,' said Fortune. 'We were close.'

'But not family.'

'No.'

'Why do you want to see him?'

The man seemed suspicious, on edge, and Fortune thought that getting past him wasn't going to be as easy as the woman who'd been there last time he came. 'I've got some news for him. Rather distressing news.'

The man nodded, stood up and walked around the desk, into the reception area. There were chairs lining the walls and he put out an arm, inviting Fortune to sit. Fortune didn't sit.

'He's dead, right?'

The man looked surprised, then nodded to the chairs. 'Perhaps if we ...'

'Is he dead?'

The man closed his eyes briefly, then bowed slightly and said, 'I am sorry.'

'How did he die?'

'He had a fall. It was quick.'

So I killed him, thought Fortune. He didn't feel much at the news, no great remorse. Maybe it would come later. What he felt was dismay, that he couldn't speak to Burridge, find out where the Games Room was. Where his daughter was.

The man was watching him closely, but Fortune didn't care. He didn't know what to do or where to go. He had no plan; he was happy to just stand there and think. But nothing came. He could go back to Foster, wake him up and try to get more out of him, but Foster didn't know anything. Burridge was dead. Bagsy, who the hell was Bagsy? He had the rest of the day, and there wasn't much of it left. Eight o'clock. Eight o'clock, and tomorrow his daughter would be killed. He had to go back to Foster, try to wake him. What was left?

Fortune smiled at the receptionist, night manager, whatever he was, and walked back out to the car park. It had started to rain, proper rain, sheeting down, the kind of rain most people would think, no, stay here, wait for it to stop, it'll drench you in a second. He could see curtains of spiteful water lit up by the nursing home's high outside lights. He pulled up the collar of his green coat, his nasty green coat. He had to move. Think, he thought, as he walked into the downpour. Think think think. But there was nothing. He had less than a day left, and no good plan. No plan at all.

Fortune opened the boot of Lee's mum's never-to-be-seen-again car, looking at his tools in the weak glow of the boot's light. This was all he had, the extent of his planning. A torch, a sledgehammer and some bolt-cutters. Who did he think he was? The rain was falling so hard he could feel the impact of the drops through his clothes. He was still bending down when he heard a voice behind him, a question:

'Who the fuck actually are you?'

Fortune didn't move. It was the receptionist, and the level of fury in his voice, the level of grief-stricken rage, made Fortune's back cold. The rain on the roof of the car was loud, and he could imagine the drops bouncing off the metal, a frenetic dance. He concentrated on breathing, took a moment, then said, head still in the boot of the car, 'I'm sorry?'

'Reckon you're here to give him news? Family news? He ain't

got family, and he don't know you. Definitely don't. So, again. Question. Who are you?'

Fortune felt with his hands around the boot of the car, trying to do it carefully, with no obvious movement. The bolt-cutters were within reach, but they weren't what he wanted. He reached further, trying to hide the motion.

'Weren't here earlier?' said the man.

'No,' said Fortune. His knees were shaking, trembling, against the rear bumper of the car. He couldn't maintain this, couldn't stay bent down much longer. The cancer, in his bones. No sleep, no food. He was near the end, his body knew that much, plus he was now wet and cold. He lifted the handle of the sledgehammer, gently, freeing the torch caught beneath.

'I know you were,' the man said.

'Can't help you there,' said Fortune, surprised at the nonchalance in his voice. But then, he was now holding a blunt instrument.

'No,' said the man. 'No, that ain't going to do it.'

Fortune straightened and spun around with the heavy-duty torch. He connected with the temple of the man behind him, the skinny night guard. There wasn't a lot of speed behind it, but something that heavy didn't need a lot. The man went down on one knee on the car park's tarmac.

'What's your name?' said Fortune.

The man didn't answer, just shook his head slowly at the ground. He spat, then said, 'No chance.'

Fortune tapped him on the head with the torch. 'Come on. You can do better than that.'

The man spat again, then said, 'Paul.'

'Got a surname?'

'Baggot.'

'Paul Baggot?'

'That's right,' he said, looking up at Fortune with a contemptuous sneer. Rain had slicked his hair down and made his face seem thinner than before. A spiteful face, hard done by and cruel. 'You've got it. First name Paul, second name Baggot. Paul Baggot.' He spat again. 'Well fucking done.'

Fortune tightened his grip on the torch, his fingernails digging into the heavy rubber casing.

'You couldn't let him go?' he said. 'Had to stay nearby, keep him close? Is that why you work here?'

'No.' Bagsy tried to stifle a moan, failed. 'What?'

'Like his pet, is that what you were?'

'I don't—'

'People call you Bagsy. Is that right?'

Bagsy looked confused. 'And?'

'And you knew Burridge.'

'I knew him.'

'What was your relationship?' said Fortune.

'Relationship? What's that mean?'

'Like, for example,' Fortune said, 'was he your father?'

'No.'

'So?'

Bagsy didn't answer, closed his eyes tight in pain.

'Only,' said Fortune, shaking his head and squatting down with difficulty next to the man, 'he's gentry. And you ...' He paused, waited some more, then shrugged apologetically. 'You're not.' He stood back up. 'You're a grunt, a lackey. Nobody.'

'I'm his right-hand man,' said Bagsy, looking up at Fortune with hatred, blinking his eyes against the falling rain.

'I doubt that,' said Fortune. 'Anyway, let's get it right. You were his henchman. Were. He's dead, remember?' He took a step back. 'I know, because I killed him.'

Bagsy tried to get up, but Fortune hit him on the top of the head, not hard, just enough to remind him that standing up would be a bad idea.

'You worked for him, right?' he said.

'Yes.'

'What did you do?' Bagsy didn't answer, just glared up at Fortune, as defiant as a wronged child.

'I bet you didn't teach Latin,' said Fortune. 'Or maths. Or, or ...' He stopped, pretended to search for the right subject, came up short. 'No. No, you painted the white lines on the football field. Right?'

'I was the caretaker, yes.' Bagsy took a breath, trying to centre himself, to regain some control. 'But I did more than that. A lot more.' He seemed proud at this, as if he was in possession of a darker caretaking knowledge than anybody had ever given him credit for. Which was probably right, thought Fortune. 'Gave me my own place, my own house. Ran the school, me and Mr Burridge.'

'How many little boys did you kill?' Fortune said.

'What?'

'Forget how many you tortured. Forget how many you sodomized, violated, terrified. I don't care. What I want to know is, how many did you kill?'

'They ran away,' said Bagsy. 'It's true. They ran away.'

Fortune looked down at the man, and the man looked back up at Fortune, and it was dark and for a moment the night and the rain and his tiredness made it all seem unreal, illusory. But he held the man's gaze, and after some time, maybe thirty seconds, the man smiled, a wide to-hell-with-you do-what-you-will grin, and it all came back into focus, cold, clear focus. He needed to find his daughter. He needed to find her at all costs, and he couldn't have Bagsy in the middle of things. He swung the torch again, catching Bagsy in the same place. Not too hard. Just enough to make sure that he'd get a decent start. Fortune got back in the car, hoping he wasn't too late.

fifty-four

THE TROLL HAS JUST LEFT. I KNOW WHAT HE LOOKS LIKE, AND what he wants. Except I don't. I thought I did, and I kind of do, but I'm still not sure. I don't know. I just don't know. Oh please, someone, please. What's going on?

Okay. Okay, what happened? Describe it, try to remember it, as it happened. Okay. First off, the troll is tall, and he's big. And young, he's younger than me. I never thought he'd be younger than me. Who can do the things he does and be younger than me?

What else? He definitely isn't normal. The way he talks, like a calm yet completely deranged minister, explaining some batshit theory to a disciple. He makes me think of those videos of jihadists explaining why the West must be destroyed. Calm, certain. Like, the absolute worst kind of person.

So anyway, he knocks on the door and comes in. I'm sitting on the bed, I can feel the springs through the crappy little thin mattress he's given me. He comes in and stands opposite me, leaning against the wall. He smiles, totally relaxed, as if what's going on between us is fine, unremarkable. I don't say anything, because I think he's going to kill me. I think that I must have got the days wrong and this is it, he's going to do it, he's going to kill me, I don't know how. But then he says:

Are you all right?

I don't say anything and he just looks at me, and then he sighs and says it again, slowly.

Are you all right?

No, I say. And I start to cry, even though I don't want to, not in front of this person, but I do, I can't help it.

All this ... He looks around, shrugs. It isn't your fault. It's just what needs to happen.

What do you mean, needs? I say, trying to stop crying, trying to keep my voice normal.

It's part of the Game.

The way he says *the Game*. Reverentially, like it's a religion or something.

I don't understand, I say

I know, he says. Nobody ever did, when they went to the Games Room. But then that's the point. The absolute essence of it.

Like, does that make any sense to you? No, me neither.

So I ask him, I close my eyes and I ask him, I say:

Are you going to kill me?

And I keep my eyes closed, because I don't want to look at him, don't want to hear what he says, but I have to. I have to know.

Yes, he says. I don't want to, but I will. He's silent and my eyes are closed and I can feel my heart beating, my heart, I don't want it to stop beating, don't want this man to stop it from beating. He doesn't have the right. He does not have the right.

And then he says:

Unless your father is dead. Unless he dies.

I open my eyes and look at him, wondering if I just imagined what he said. Wondering if I heard right, or if I'm losing my mind.

What?

He looks at me for a long time, then says:

But I'm not going to touch him. That's the rule. That's the Game. I can't touch him, but if he doesn't die, you don't live.

I don't understand, I say.

And that's the point, he says.

He talks to me like he's explaining something to a slow child, a disappointing daughter. He says, I thought I already explained. You're not supposed to understand. How could you be scared, how could you know fear, properly know it, if it made sense?

I don't answer. What can I say? Nothing makes sense, nothing. What does he know about my father? Who is this man? An ex-employee with a grudge? What did my father do to him to turn him into this monster?

It's what they taught us, he says.

Who?

But the troll just smiles, and shakes his head.

Who taught you?

They did.

Who's they?

That doesn't matter. I'm better than them. I've become better than them.

Than who?

He doesn't answer; just watches me for some time. Then he sighs, pushes himself off the wall and walks towards me. I shuffle back on the bed until I'm up against the other wall.

Don't worry, he says. You've still got a day left. Most of a day.

Then you kill me?

He rubs his eyes and shakes his head again, like he's disappointed.

Didn't I say? Yes. Yes, I kill you. Unless your father's dead.

I don't—

Understand! He shouts it, the only anger I've seen from him, the first proper emotion. He gets himself under control immediately, just a split second of rage. The tiger out of its cage, then immediately locked back in. I wonder what goes on behind that calm facade. What roils beneath.

I know, he says, more quietly. You've already told me. He rubs his head, his short hair, rubs it hard and for a long time. Then he says:

I'm going now. Just remember, your life, and his, is in his hands.

He stops on his way to the door and turns, rocks his head as if he's evaluating what he's just said.

Or perhaps in his heart, he says.

And then he leaves, and locks the door behind him. Dad? Is this all your fault? I barely know you, but I'm locked in a room, and my jailer is some crazed genius loony who can make reality bend and shift and twist, and he knows you. Did you do this? Did you make this happen, create this monster?

fifty-five

FORTUNE WOKE UP IN LEE'S MOTHER'S CAR, ITS FRONT WHEELS sunk in a shallow verge at the side of an empty country lane. He didn't think he could have been driving fast when he fell asleep and crashed, as although the damage to the car was bad, he wasn't hurt. He looked at the crumpled bonnet, attempting to embrace a stubborn elm tree; it made what Lee had done to the car seem no more than a scratch. Sorry, Fortune thought. I am, honestly.

The rain had stopped and it was early morning, nearly six, the sky lighting up at the edges, the stars still pinpoint bright in the purple darkness above, the waiting day promising to be glorious and crisp and clear. Fortune looked up and down the lane and made out a dim sign. He walked towards it. It pointed the way to a country park, Teywood Forest. He'd passed it on the way to St Basil's, on the same road. He couldn't be far away.

He took a moment to assess, make sure he'd got his bearings. The way he was feeling, he wasn't going to be able to walk for long. His chest felt like it had had something forced into it, a cushion, a sequined cushion that stifled and smothered his breathing and at the same time scratched and grated against his lungs, making every short, sharp breath agony. He was going down, down like a sinking ship, getting to the point where the water pouring inside becomes too much and the ship disappears, fast, here one moment, sunk the next, gone. Only the placid, indifferent sea left, as if the ship had never existed. Which was about right, he thought. Who was going to miss him? At least it would save Jean the funeral, the wake afterwards. Here lies a man. Ashes to ashes. *Next.*

He was tired and everything hurt. He lit a cigarette and looked at the road. Which way? He couldn't be walking for half an hour only to have to walk back. He needed to be sure. That way. He'd passed the sign on his right. Definitely. So it must be that way. He finished his cigarette, regarding the packet with gloomy exasperation. Five left. He owned five cigarettes, all he had left in his life. He'd have to make them count.

This was the day. The last day. Fortune walked along the road; well, staggered, he corrected himself. Lurched. But this was the day and he couldn't stop. He had to keep going. Sophie was waiting for him, and the thought of seeing her, of seeing the daughter he had believed dead, gave him fresh energy. The kind of disbelieving excitement a child experiences on Christmas Eve. Is it true? Can it be true? Will it actually, really, truly happen? No matter how tired he was, he'd get there, and when he got there ... Stop thinking, he told himself. Don't think, just act. Or you will never do what needs to be done.

Fortune couldn't remember the last time he'd eaten, but he didn't feel hungry. At least there was that. The country lane was narrow and the hedges bordering it were high, so tall that all he could see was tarmac, leaves and sky. By now the sky was blue, the kind of morning sky that causes elation in the hearts of the very young and the very old, the ones in between too distracted by jobs and money and family and lack of success, or too much success, to notice it. Such thoughts occupied Fortune's head as he slogged on. There was a bend in the road ahead and he couldn't see past it, but as he neared it he saw, he thought he saw, no, he definitely saw an entrance and a sign that told him that St Basil's was for sale via Seymour Estates, call this number. He was here, and he knew exactly where to go. He didn't have a weapon, he didn't have a plan, he didn't have anything. Didn't even have a fully functioning body. But what he had always had, he reminded himself, was the ability to make the right decision when the pressure was on. So. It would be okay. This will work. You will do it. You just don't know how. Yet.

The house that he had passed on his way in, red-brick and ruined. It had to be that. The caretaker's house at the bottom of the drive. Bagsy's place. *Bagsy, always Bagsy.* The willing accomplice, the indentured henchman. The biddable sadist. This was where he had lived, and this was where the Games Room must be, whatever that was. And whatever it was, Fortune was sure, his daughter was in it. Plus, the way Foster had described it, whatever it was, it was no good. It was no good at all.

He pushed open a gate and walked across a gravel drive that had long ago given up the fight against weeds, now more unruly meadow than car park. The house was in a terrible state, window panes broken, their frames rotten, the bricks needing repointing soon or the whole place was going to go. The roof already had, tiles remaining at both ends but the middle fallen through so that the profile of the house resembled Tower Bridge. There was no sound and no sign of life. No dog to bark his arrival, no light to appear, no questioning face at the front door.

He stood and waited. This was it. This was it, and if nobody came out, then he was in the wrong place. And if he was in the wrong place, if he was mistaken, then his daughter was dead. So it must be the right place. Fortune stood in the cold, bright morning and waited, hoping that this was the right place. It had to be.

'Father.'

He turned. He should have known that the troll would steal up on him, gain the advantage. Approach him from where he least expected it, from behind, where he'd just been. It was obvious.

'Hello.' The troll, his son, smiled. Fortune didn't respond, but inside he died, just a little. Again, he should have known. Of course. So obvious, so ridiculously, stupidly obvious. Tall. Big. Acne scarring. Just like Fortune. Like father, like son. The security guard who had confronted him at St Basil's the last time he'd been here. That had been the first time he'd met his son. They were the same person.

'Hi,' said Fortune. So much contempt, so much loathing in the very first word he spoke to his son. God.

'So. You made it.'

'Yes.'

The troll, his son, Hector, shook his head, just a little. 'But only just. I expected you sooner. Hoped to see you sooner.'

'Really,' said Fortune. Not a question, more an expression of disinterest.

'I'd hoped you'd be here yesterday. Even the day before, although that would have been exceptional. But yesterday would have been acceptable.'

'I'm sorry to have disappointed you,' said Fortune.

His son wagged a finger. 'No. No, you haven't disappointed. Most people wouldn't have been able to find me at all. To do it in the given time is still a feat. You shouldn't feel bad.'

Fortune didn't respond, and Hector said nothing, and after a moment Fortune said, pointlessly, 'Well.'

The troll nodded, as if some profound truth had passed between them. 'Shall we?' he said. The troll. His son. Hector. Fortune had to decide what to call him. Hell, he was his son. He had a name. He was Hector. Why not call him that?

'Okay,' Fortune said. 'Okay, Hector.'

Hector turned at this, his face suddenly drained of confidence, of authority. He looked at Fortune, swallowed and turned away. But when he turned back, he'd recaptured the same untroubled swagger he'd had since Fortune had met him. 'Of course,' he said. 'Of course you know my name. You know many things. But you only know the things that I allowed you to find out.'

He led Fortune into the house. There wasn't a lot to it apart from mould and neglect. There was a door built into the casement of the stairs and Hector opened it, stood aside and put out an arm to welcome Fortune into the staircase within.

'Please,' he said. 'You must be curious. And I can tell you everything you want to know.' He smiled. 'I think you'll find it interesting.'

Fortune nodded, giving his son his due. He was a force, of some kind. He put out a hand and felt his way onto the stairs, held the banister and stepped down the staircase. It was dark, descending into the belly of this wrecked house, and if he fell, he wouldn't be getting up again. His daughter must be down there, she must be. Sophie, you must be there. He'd kept his promise. He was coming to find her.

fifty-six

THE CELLAR OF BAGSY'S HOUSE WAS DARK AND SMELLED OF damp and misery. Not that misery had a smell, Fortune knew, but there it was. Now it did. There was a door to the right of the stairs and another to the left, and Hector opened the door on the right, nodded Fortune past him, then closed the door behind them. They were in a brick-walled corridor, dimly lit. It wasn't long, and it had three doors in it, doors made of metal. Fortune understood that he was in a dungeon, in a place where people, children, were kept and tormented, tortured, broken. The corridor was narrow, oppressive, as if the walls and ceiling were slowly closing in.

Hector opened another door, again waiting for Fortune to pass him. The room was brightly lit and surprisingly big, the walls painted white, the floor carpeted. There was a desk and functional wooden chairs, an Anglepoise lamp on the desk. It looked like a GP's surgery. One wall was covered in paper, sheets of words and arrows, some kind of diagram, large and complex.

'Welcome,' said Hector. 'Please. Sit down.'

'I'll stand.'

'You look like you need to sit down. Please. You don't look well.'

Fortune did not want to sit, did not want to show any weakness. But Hector was right, he wouldn't be able to stand for long. He sighed, sat on one of the chairs and looked at Hector.

'Where's Sophie?'

'Sophie is here. But before you see her, I wanted to talk to you. I wanted to show something to you.'

'I'm not interested.'

'I think you will be.'

Fortune didn't answer and there was a brief silence, then Hector frowned and said, 'You will watch. And you will listen. Understand?'

This was his son, Fortune told himself. You made him. But he didn't feel anything for him except a quiet fury and disgust. No, he had to be honest with himself, underneath that there was a sense of sadness, sadness and regret. That this was happening, that all this had happened. But no love. No love, no admiration, no regard. If that was what his son was hoping for, disappointment wasn't far away.

'So,' Hector said, and smiled. 'How did I do it?'

'Do what?'

'The Game. How did I make it happen?'

The way he said *the Game*. Like it was an entity rather than an activity. As if it possessed some mystical power. His son had the zealotry of a cult member, burning with belief and purpose. Fortune had lived in the Middle East. He knew all about zealotry, and how dangerous it was.

Fortune shrugged. 'No idea. I want to see Sophie. Now.'

'Not until you have listened to me.'

'Now.'

'No. I'm sorry, but that cannot be done. Now. The Game.' He

turned to the wall covered in paper and pointed to the top, a sheet with figures on. $89,917,042. $71,023,032. Next to it, 7 DAYS. He turned back to Fortune. 'First, I stole the money.'

'How?' said Fortune. He was, at least, interested in that.

'I am what people would probably call a hacker,' his son said. 'A very, very good one. You wouldn't understand exactly how I did it. Just know that I did, and that it was too easy. Your bank needs to take a look at their security.'

This wasn't Fortune's problem any more. He watched his son but didn't say anything.

'So first I stole the money, stole it twice. How long did it take you?'

'How long did what take me?'

'To work out the dates. The day she was born, the day she would die.'

'Hector,' Fortune said. 'Please. You're my son, Sophie's my daughter. This ...' His voice faltered, something he despised himself for, but he kept going. 'We don't need to do this. It isn't necessary.'

Hector frowned briefly, as if Fortune had given a particularly stupid answer to a very basic question. 'No, I asked you, how long did it take you? To work out the dates?'

Fortune slumped a little in his chair. 'I saw it straight away,' he said. 'Hector ...'

'I think that's a lie,' said Hector. 'There is no way you could have. I estimated a week, and so that is how long I waited. I think I got it right.'

'Got what right?'

'Setting you up. So that you couldn't go to the police, or you would be arrested.'

'I did go to the police.'

Hector looked surprised, a rare show of emotion. 'You did? Oh.' He was silent a second, standing in front of his wall of paper. He nodded to himself, then looked up and said, 'But they didn't want to know. That's right, isn't it? Too vague, too ... weird. The police don't like weird, it falls outside their purview.'

Fortune didn't answer. But his son was right. Was there anything he didn't know?

'In any case, it's of no matter.' Hector pointed again at the wall of paper, the next sheet. On it were Fortune's account details. 'Then I placed the money in your account, and set off the alarm bells. Yes?'

Again, Fortune didn't answer. He felt like a sullen student being given a lecture. He needed to see his daughter. He needed to get out of here, away from this person. He moved to stand up, but Hector wagged a finger.

'No. No, no, no. I'm not finished.' He took the next piece of paper from the wall and gave it to Fortune. Fortune took it. It was a picture of a girl, young, maybe fourteen.

'Who is that?' said Hector.

'No idea.'

'It's me,' said Hector. He seemed quietly delighted by this. 'That young girl is me. Charlie Jackson thought it was a girl called Rosie, who lived in Balham, who was his biggest fan and would do anything for him. And I do mean anything. You can imagine her excitement, to be meeting her idol, a clandestine liaison in a hotel room. So, so excited.' He made a small noise, perhaps a laugh, some sound at the back of his throat. 'And when Charlie Jackson knocked on the door, imagine his surprise. Imagine his surprise when Rosie was me!'

'How did you kill him?'

'I hit him. I hit him very, very hard with a hammer. Only once.'

Fortune thought of Bagsy and the torch and shook his head. It wasn't the same. He hadn't hit him hard.

'And I left the phone, and sent you a message. And now …' Hector took a step back from the wall. 'Now, the game was on. I gave you your daughter's laptop so you could work out who I was. Your first task. I gave you two days for that. You did well. You see?' He pointed up to a sheet, STARRY UBADO written on it, 3 DAYS next to it. 'I then allotted you one day to find my mother's brother.' An arrow on the sheet he'd pointed at led to a second sheet, UNCLE TREVOR written on it. T. Emmerson, Claudia's useless brother. Was everything Fortune had done, all his actions, been predicted before he'd even thought about it? What was it they said about destiny? That it was all already planned, nothing you could do. He'd been directed, manipulated, controlled as if by some deranged god. By his son, Hector Emmerson.

Next sheet, AIX Industries.

'I'm willing to bet they didn't remember me with affection,' said Hector.

'He killed himself. The guy who came up with the algorithm.'

'I know.' Hector shrugged. 'Honestly? He believed it to be a lot better than it really was. I told him that. I told him it wasn't so special. He was very resistant.'

Next sheet, the story of the orphanage closing down. The article Fortune had found in Hector's apartment, in his bed. How the hell had he known that Fortune would sleep there, discover it? How?

'So then you found Burridge. By the way, how did you do that?'

'Spoke to a journalist.'

'I see.' Hector made a face, an ambiguous grimace. 'I suppose that's one way. And of course, here's where you lost a day, because you didn't get anything out of him, and so you had to visit Foster. The first time there was a need to resort to my Plan B.'

'How'd you know I went to see Foster?'

Hector sighed, smiled. 'The truth is, Foster never went to see Burridge. It was me. I went, and I simply gave reception Foster's details.' He pointed to a sheet with Foster's address and number on it. 'It wasn't like he was going to argue. The man can't remember what he did ten minutes ago. He was drunk, I assume?'

Fortune just looked at his son and tried not to show any emotion.

'You should have done better. You really should have got Burridge to talk.'

Fortune considered telling his son that he had killed Burridge, maybe killed Bagsy too. But no. He didn't know what effect that might have, had no idea how he would react to anything.

'He wasn't a nice person.'

Hector laughed at this, a real laugh. 'Nice. Burridge.' He shook his head, smiled at Fortune. 'You're too much.'

Fortune didn't return the smile. He watched his son like he would watch a big cat, wary, unpredictable.

'Anyway,' Hector said. 'You found out about Bagsy, and here you are. At his house. At the Games Room.'

'Why?' said Fortune. It was the only question he wanted an answer to. 'Why did you do this? To me? To Sophie?'

'Because there was a need to,' said Hector. 'To show them.' He gestured around the room, the brick walls, this subterranean prison. 'To prove to them.'

'Prove what?'

Hector closed his eyes, kept them closed for a long time. It was quiet in the room and Fortune could hear his son's breathing. After maybe a minute had passed, Hector opened his eyes and took a breath.

'The Game is designed to make you feel weak,' he said. 'It changes for everyone, it is a dynamic event. It is intended to make you feel frightened and weak and confused. They were very good at it. They were like gods. So powerful.'

'Who's they?'

'Them. Burridge. Bagsy. All the others, the other players.'

Fortune nodded, but said, 'I still don't understand.'

'But if they are gods, then so am I.'

'You don't want to be like them.'

'No. No, I want to be better.'

'Better?'

'They did what they did here. To children. I can do it out there, in the world.'

'Do what?'

'Play the Game.'

'What you're doing … it isn't a game.'

'Of course it is. It's the best game. And I've hacked it, optimized it, adapted it for playing out there.' He gestured above him, dismissively. 'Finding weaknesses. Exploiting them. Taking away control. I think I've proven myself to be a master.'

Fortune looked at Hector, realized that he was fundamentally flawed, broken, that his morality had been perverted beyond recognition. He wanted to outdo Burridge and Bagsy. Emerge from their shadow, eclipse them. Like a child needing to prove itself better than its father, stronger, greater.

Only his father was Fortune. Didn't that count for anything? No, Fortune thought. No, of course it doesn't. Because you're no kind of father, and never have been.

'But why me?' he said. 'And why Sophie?'

'Because you put me here. I wanted to show you what I learnt. All the things I learnt. What I can do, thanks to you.'

'You don't need my approval.'

Hector laughed. 'Approval? No, no, I don't. But I want you to know how it felt.'

'How what felt?'

'Being in the Games Room.'

'I've never been there.'

'That doesn't matter. The Games Room isn't a place. It's a feeling.'

'What kind of feeling?'

'The one you have now.'

Powerless. Scared. Anxious. Confused. Yes, Fortune thought. I know that feeling. Now I know it.

'Anyway,' said Hector, 'you'll go there now.'

'Where?'

'To the Games Room. That is, if you want to see your daughter. Are you ready?'

Fortune stood up, feeling his legs trembling, wondering for a moment whether they would give up on him.

Hector smiled. 'Let's go visit my sister.'

fifty-seven

SOPHIE WAS STANDING ON A WOODEN CHAIR IN THE DARK
Games Room. She had a noose around her neck, the rope connected to a hook on the ceiling. She looked tired and very, very
scared. Her eyes widened and her jaw dropped when she saw
Fortune. She looked at him and was silent, and then she started
to cry without abandon, her mouth misshapen as the sobs
racked her.

'Sophie. Sweetheart, it's okay. I'm here.'

She looked so tired, but she was still Sophie, still his beautiful
daughter, the little girl whose eyes had sparkled with such
delight in the sun, all those long and wasted years ago. She was
still alive, and could still be that carefree, glorious spirit.

'Dad?'

'Yes.'

'Are you really here?' Sophie's voice broke and she began to
sob again. The rope had little play in it and she needed to stay on
the chair. If she fell, if she lost her balance, she would die.

'Be careful, Sophie,' Fortune said, as gently and calmly as he
could.

'I took care of her,' said the troll, standing behind him. 'She's
quite healthy.'

For the first time, Fortune felt genuine hatred, possessed with an anger that was violent, outraged. The troll dared to do this, to his daughter? He felt his fingers bunch into fists, felt himself tremble with rage. He willed himself to remain calm, keep his voice steady.

'Sophie,' he said. 'Sophie, it'll be okay. I've come to find you.'

'Dad. Dad, be careful. He's ... he's ...' She couldn't find the right words, couldn't think of an adequate way to describe Hector.

'I know,' said Fortune. 'It'll be okay.' He didn't believe it would be okay, not for a second. But that was what fathers did. What they were supposed to do. Reassure their children.

'All right. Shall we begin?' said Hector. He stepped past Fortune to the chair and gave it a slight shake. Sophie screamed and Fortune started towards her, but Hector held up a finger and said, 'No closer, thank you. No closer, or over she goes.'

Fortune stopped, powerless, always powerless. 'What are you going to do?'

'I wonder,' said Hector, 'if you recognize this set-up?'

'Dad?' Sophie, beseeching him. Fortune didn't answer her, instead said to Hector, 'Your mother.'

'My mother. Who killed herself. Hanged herself, when I was young.' He shrugged. 'I don't remember a lot. The only thing I do remember is her saying, "It's your father's fault."'

'Dad?'

Again, Fortune ignored her. 'I'm sorry,' he said. 'I am very sorry.'

'I'm afraid it's a little late for that,' said Hector. He turned to Sophie. 'You see, he's my father. Your father is also my father. He led my mother to hang herself, and after that my life became ...' He stopped, searching for the correct word. 'Hideous.'

Sophie frowned and said, once again, 'Dad?'

'I'm sorry, Sophie,' said Fortune. 'I'm sorry for not being there. I'm sorry for everything.'

'So,' said Hector. 'Would you like to hear the rules?'

'What rules?' said Fortune.

'Of the Game,' said Hector. 'Every game has rules. We can all agree on that, I hope.'

'I guess.'

'And so here are mine. I cannot touch you. I cannot touch you, and I never could. I can kill you, but I'm not allowed to touch you. Those are my rules.'

'Dad, don't listen to him. Don't listen.' Sophie sobbed, said again in desperation, 'Please don't listen to him.'

'Okay,' said Fortune to the troll. 'And?'

'And that's it. There are no other rules. Simplicity is always preferable.'

'Please, Dad. Please. Whatever he says, don't listen.'

'So what now?' said Fortune, trying to tune his daughter out, trying to concentrate on what the troll was saying.

'Now?' said Hector. He put a hand in his pocket and took out a coin. 'Now we play.'

Fortune thought of Foster, and of what he'd said. They'd toss a coin, at the beginning. That was the worst. Heads, you lost. Tails, you lost worse.

'Dad, please, please don't do this. Don't do what he wants. Please.'

'If you play, your daughter might live. She might, she has a chance. If you don't play, then she dies.'

'What's the game?' said Fortune.

'Dad. Dad, no, please.'

'I toss the coin. Heads, Sophie dies. Tails, you take her place.'

Fortune didn't answer, and there was silence except for Sophie's sobs. Then Hector smiled brightly. 'It's brilliant, isn't it?'

'No.'

'From the start, the first comment I posted on your daughter's blog, to here. All planned. And it worked.'

'Let's get on with it,' said Fortune, doing his best to sound underwhelmed, impatient, unimpressed, trying to hide his fear, fight the rising panic.

'Dad.' Sophie had got her voice under control and spoke slowly, carefully, concentrating on the words. 'Dad, do not do what he wants. That way he wins. It's all he wants, to control people, to beat them. Don't do it.'

'To clarify,' said Fortune. 'You toss a coin, and if it's tails, it's me up there?'

'That's right.'

'Okay.'

'Okay?' Hector seemed surprised. 'Like that?'

'Like that,' said Fortune.

'I thought ...' said Hector. 'I'd given you hours. Hours.'

'I don't need hours,' said Fortune. 'Go on. Toss the coin.'

'You're sure?'

'Toss the coin.'

Sophie screamed, a sound of rage and frustration. 'Dad, no, no, don't do this. Don't let him win.'

Fortune looked up at his daughter. 'There's no winning. It's what he doesn't understand. There's only losing. Sophie? Listen to me. Nobody wins. We all lose.'

'Dad.' She said it with a simple grief, the word shaped by love, love she still held for her inadequate father, despite all his failures and omissions.

Fortune swallowed, blinked and said, 'I love you, Sophie.' He turned to Hector. 'Toss the coin.'

Hector flicked the coin with his thumb and let it fall. He bent down to look at it. Fortune bent too. He could hear his daughter crying. The coin had landed on tails. Tails. Fortune prayed, hoped with everything he had, that his son would keep his word. That he would play by the rules.

'Well,' said Hector. 'It looks like it's your lucky day.' He turned to Sophie. 'You live.'

'No no no,' said Sophie, shaking her head, the rope above her swinging wildly. 'Dad, no. No.'

'You'll leave her alone?' Fortune said.

'I promise.' Hector smiled, put his hand on his heart. 'Hope to die.' He walked to Sophie, reached above her and loosened the noose, pulling it back over her head. She stood there for a moment, then quickly stepped down and ran to Fortune, putting her arms around him, her face pressing into the soft space beside his shoulder. He held her, stroked her hair, felt her warmth against him. Why had he never done this before? Why had he never comforted her after a relationship break-up? Told her it didn't matter, that he loved her, would always love her? Why had he never done that simple thing, met her insecurities and doubts and difficulties with love, rather than detachment? And now it was too late, far too late.

He blinked, blinked again and again, trying to pull breath inside his lungs, his chest tight, but this time with emotion, a feeling he understood as heartbreak. He took his daughter's shoulders and pushed her away, holding her at arm's length and looking at her small face.

'You need to go,' he said.

'I won't go.'

'You have to.'

'I won't leave you, Dad.'

'I came to find you,' said Fortune. 'I came to find you for a reason, and this is it. Now, please. You have to go.'

'Dad. Please.'

He looked at his daughter, at her grief and despair. It wouldn't last. Not for ever. It would pass. Eventually, all this would pass and she would smile and laugh and her eyes would sparkle beautifully. He turned to the troll, his son, Hector, and said, 'You need to take her away.'

Hector put an arm around Sophie's shoulders. She tried to fight him off, but he was strong, very strong, and there was nothing she could do. She screamed, but Hector pulled her away towards the door.

'You promise?' said Fortune, above the noise of his daughter's screams.

'I promise,' said Hector. He nodded at Fortune, a nod of understanding, a nod that told Fortune he could count on him, on his son. Then he forced Sophie around and pushed her out of the Games Room, closing the door behind him. Fortune could hear her screams through the door, but they slowly faded, faded away until they were gone, and he couldn't hear her any more. Would never hear her again.

He put a hand on the back of the chair and a foot on the seat and slowly stepped up, one foot, then the other. He reached up and put the noose around his neck and pulled it tight. He looked at the lamp, at its red shade, the incongruous tassels. The rings on the walls, the black-painted bricks. He took a moment to settle himself, to restore his calm and focus. Concentrate on the task at hand. Don't think, act.

He felt the rope rub against his neck. What a waste, he thought. What an appalling, inexcusable, abject failure you have been. Weak and lazy and selfish, so, so selfish. And nobody to blame but yourself. He sighed and shook his head. Oh well. It is what it is. Deal with it.

He took a breath, one more, then took a step forward, off the chair, into the unknown black void. But as he did, feeling the rope tighten against his Adam's apple, he also felt in his heart a warm and unexpected explosion of joy, at his daughter, at her strength and character and the life she still had left to discover. He knew, knew beyond doubt, that she'd make a better job of her life than he ever had of his. That she'd get more out of it, find more enjoyment, more pleasure, more love. And wasn't that what it was all about? Being a father? Fortune felt that at last he understood, really understood, and felt immeasurably richer for this knowledge, however late it had come. Creating and sustaining a life, and helping that life to flourish. Wasn't that what being a father, ultimately, was all about?

fifty-eight

Dear Dad

For such a long time, I haven't known what to say to you. From when I was ten, maybe. Maybe twelve. For years, years and years. So much time, so much time lost and wasted.

Since you did what you did for me, too, I haven't known what to say. Thank you? That isn't enough. Not nearly enough. What you did for me was gigantic, overwhelming, heroic, and I am in awe of you for it.

You told me then that nobody wins, that everybody loses. And I guess in a way you were right. Hector Emmerson was true to his word and let me go. Then he disappeared. And you're gone.

For a long time I didn't know if I would ever be the same again, if I would ever recover. I've had counselling, I've had medication, I've joined groups and spoken to other survivors of kidnappings.

And you know what? It didn't last. Not for ever. It passed, eventually. And you said there could be no winners, but I feel that I have won something. I have won you back, won back my father. Won back that feeling I had, so long ago.

I once wrote you another letter, but I never showed it to you and I am so glad that I didn't. This is the letter I would want you to read. In that letter, I told you about that time when I was young, and I got onto the Tube, and I lost you. And at the very next station I waited, and sure enough, there you were. And I was never scared, because I knew that you would come and find me, and you did.

I never believed you would come and find me again, that you would save me from the troll. But you did. You did, and I won back that feeling, that feeling I had on the platform. That my dad, that you, would always be there for me.

So perhaps I did win. At least a little. It's now been four years since it happened, and now I know what I want to say to you. All I want to say is thank you, Dad. And I love you, so, so much.

Your daughter,

Sophie